BENEATH STILL WATERS

PRAISE FOR LINNY MACK

"Mack skillfully balances **heartbreak** and **healing**, crafting a cast of emotionally resonant characters."

-Kirkus Reviews (Changing Tides)

"Linny Mack's debut novel, *Changing Tides*, is a **captivating tale** that explores the intricate dance between love, loss, and rebirth. With a narrative that will keep you on the **edge of your seat**, and an ending you won't see coming, this **story will break your heart** and piece it back together, one beautiful shard at a time."

–Buck Turner, bestselling author of *The Keeper of Stars*

"Mack's **striking debut shatters your heart** in fourteen different ways before masterfully piecing it all back together by the end. Cape May, Sophie, and Liam, will have a place in my heart forever."

–Lily Parker, author of *The Best Wrong Move*

"A **breathtaking debut**, *Changing Tides* is a masterclass in slow-burn romance, brimming with depth, heart, and hard-won healing. Featuring **beautifully drawn characters** in their 40s, it celebrates love not as a reckless leap but as a **courageous journey**—one where finding each other begins with first finding ourselves.

–Shaylin Gandhi, author of *When We Had Forever*

"This story of two broken people struggling to heal themselves grabbed hold of my heart and refused to let go. **An ode to fate and found families**, *Changing Tides* is a satisfying, slow-burn romance that will make you believe in second chances."

–Lindsay Hameroff, author of *Never Planned on You*

PRAISE FOR LINNY MACK

"Every page of Mack's debut was filled with the warmth and comfort of found family, the **bittersweet nostalgia** of childhood summers, and the yearning excitement of new love. Her characters have found a forever home in my heart!"

-Christy Schillig, author of *Wish You Weren't Here*

BENEATH STILL WATERS

LINNY MACK

Page & Vine
An Imprint of Meredith Wild LLC

Paperback ISBN: 978-1-964264-60-8

For my readers who followed me from
Cape May to Tidehaven.
Thank you for trusting me with new worlds and new characters.
These stories exist because of you.

PROLOGUE REID

SIX MONTHS EARLIER

SLEEP NEVER STAYS for long.

By the time the sky lightens to that thin, gray veil, I'm already up. The cabin is nothing but quiet behind me, with the kind of silence that presses instead of soothes. The trail beyond my back door feels like the only place where my thoughts slow enough to catch my breath.

I walk most mornings like this—early...before the coast wakes and the town stirs. Before questions and conversations and the low hum of other people's lives disrupt my peace. The marsh is still at this hour, the air cool and damp, the world holding its breath.

It's usually the only time of day I feel even.

I'm halfway down the narrow trail that cuts behind Blackbird Cottage when I hear the sirens. They rip through the quiet, close enough that my shoulders jerk and my breath catches. They are loud, which means they must be close. Something isn't right. They don't usually come this far back. My body reacts before my brain does. My pulse kicks up, my muscles coiling tight, like an old reflex I'd learned to ignore.

The lights come into view through the trees—blue and red bleeding into the gray dawn—and I know, with a certainty I don't question, that something is very wrong.

My feet stop for half a second.

Dr. Penelope Young's face flashes in my mind.

Then I'm moving again. The pull is immediate and unmistakable. The way you hurry without realizing you've started, heart already ahead of your body.

The cottage sits far off the road, nestled between the forest and the marsh. Used by Coastal Carolina University to house research faculty, not many people know it's here. I do because just through the short trail beyond it, my cabin sits in peaceful solitude.

As I break through the tree line, the driveway is already crowded. Patrol cars line the dirt road. An ambulance is pulled all the way up to the porch, its red lights reflecting on the cottage's white siding. Unmarked SUVs are parked with casual authority, like they've been here before. The air smells of salt and damp earth, threaded with the tight, contained tension of those standing around, who probably know more than they'll let on.

I slow only when I see my friend Colt.

He's in uniform near the porch, posture locked tight, jaw set the way it gets when he's carrying something heavy and refusing to let it show. When his eyes find mine, the look that crosses his face isn't surprise.

It's warning.

He steps toward me quickly. "Reid. You shouldn't be here."

"What the hell is going on?" I bark, looking past him.

The front door stands open, light spilling across the porch in a harsh wash. I've walked up those steps more times than I can count. Sat at her table and listened while she paced, talking through funding battles and research setbacks and council meetings that went nowhere because certain men preferred things the way they were. We'd had an unlikely friendship, rooted in a shared love of the marsh and the solitude it offered.

"Where's Penny?" I demand.

Colt sighs, raking a hand through his hair. His eyes meet

mine briefly before he looks away, his gaze fixed on the horizon.

"She was due at the university for a meeting last night. She didn't show." Colt drags a hand over his face.

"That's not like her."

"Right. Her supervisor got worried," Colt agrees. "He came over here, banged on her door. When she didn't answer, he called us."

Before he can say more, the EMTs appear in the doorway.

They move carefully, guiding a stretcher between them. The sheet is pulled high, but the shape beneath it is unmistakable. Smaller than the woman I knew. Quieter somehow. Reduced to something that doesn't argue or laugh or demand better.

Something fractures in my chest.

"She's gone," Colt says quietly.

I swallow the tightness in my throat, but my voice comes out like a whisper anyway. "What happened?"

Colt's jaw tightens, just barely. "Apparent suicide."

The words feel wrong the instant he says them. *No.* She was loud, unapologetic, and impossible to intimidate. This feels like a conclusion reached before any questions have been asked.

My gaze drifts back to the cottage.

The last time I saw her, she'd waved off my concern with a crooked smile.

They don't love me working in what they've already claimed, she'd said. *Especially when I keep standing between them and the money.*

She'd said it lightly enough that I could brush it off. If she wasn't concerned, then I wouldn't be either. I'd told myself it was politics. Money. The same small-town power games Tidehaven has always played. I hadn't wanted to believe it was more than that.

Standing here now, with too many lights and too many strangers already claiming the space, that explanation feels thin.

I scan the scene before me and notice the one thing that doesn't fit.

Plain clothed officers walking around my friend's space

with a presence that doesn't need to announce itself. One of them glances my way, his eyes darting between me and Colt, before dismissing me as insignificant.

"Who is that?" I ask Colt, keeping my voice low.

He exhales, slow and deliberate. "Feds." He looks like he wants to say more but doesn't.

Something heavy settles low in my gut. Feds don't show up for an accident or a suicide. They don't show up when everyone agrees on answers.

Before I can push Colt further, one of the agents steps onto the porch, phone pressed to his ear. As he passes, he gives Colt a brief nod. "We'll handle it from here."

Not *we'll assist*. Not *we'll coordinate*.

Handle.

The ambulance doors close with a dull, final thud, and the sound echoes longer than it should. I feel the familiar urge rise—the need to push, to demand, to tear into whatever box someone's just tried to seal shut. That's my *friend* in there. And I want to know what the fuck happened to her.

Experience has taught me what pushing costs though. I've been wrong before. And I've seen what happens when you move too fast. When you act on instinct without proof. When people get hurt because *you* were wrong.

Colt finally looks at me with something in his eyes that mirrors my own restraint, stretched thin by duty and rules.

"You should go," he says quietly. "I'll come by later."

I nod, even though every part of me resists turning away. As I step back toward the trail, Blackbird Cottage looms behind me, silent now, its secrets already being absorbed into something larger and far less visible.

I know, with a certainty that settles deep in my bones, that whatever's happening here didn't begin today.

And that in Tidehaven, the most dangerous things don't announce themselves.

They wait.

CHAPTER ONE

EMERY

"IF I DON'T get this grant, I'm quitting."

I lean back in my desk chair and fix my stare on the closed office door, willing it to open through sheer force of optimism. If I had telekinesis, Dr. Alan Reyes would be walking through it right now with a smile and very good news.

Across from me, Lena, my best friend and colleague, snorts. "You are not."

"I know," I say, letting out a breath. "But Alan knows how much I want this. He's watched me kill myself over this proposal for months."

"We *both* did," she says dryly, taking a long sip of the Dr Pepper she stole from the faculty lounge. "Did he at least write the letter?"

I bite back a smile, shaking my head. "Of course. And he also said he was calling the Program Officer himself. Which feels... promising. I should have an answer by the end of today, I would think." I hold up my crossed fingers.

Lena studies me for a second. "Look at you being all optimistic."

"I'm trying something new," I say. "Blind faith. Positive self-talk. Delusion."

She laughs. "You've earned this, Em. You've been teaching the same two courses for, what—seven years now?"

"Seven," I confirm. "Introduction to Marine Biology and Estuarine Systems. On repeat. Like academic purgatory."

"And you still care," she adds. "That counts."

"I do," I say, softer. "I just...need something different. A reason to feel excited again." For a brief instant, the fear that my sixth grant proposal will be denied creeps back in. If I don't get this, I don't know what's next for me—a thought I've been scared to say out loud. My brow furrows.

Lena nods, then tilts her head. "Okay, but what's with that face you're making? Something else bothering you?"

I glance away. "What face? I don't know what you're talking about."

Lena clocks the lie and raises an eyebrow. "Are you okay?" she asks, concern coating her words. "You seem off—even for you."

"Gee thanks," I mutter, frowning at her.

"Well..." Lena's mouth turns up at the corner, her eyebrows lifting.

I rub my eyes, smearing iridescent nude eyeshadow all over my fingers and look back at her with a relenting sigh. "I guess I *feel* off lately. Stifled maybe. But I'm trying to combat that with lots of positive self-talk and optimism. Remember?"

She gives me a look that says she knows I'm full of shit. "Come on, Em. What's really bugging you? Is this about Jason?"

I sigh. "It's about *everything.* Work, Jason...the creeping suspicion that I'm thirty-five and somehow managed to design a life that feels like I just missed the mark."

"That's dramatic," she says gently. "But also fair."

"There's been zero ring talk," I add quickly, before she can ask. "Not that I'm pushing anymore. Honestly, it might be for the best. I don't even know what I want right now."

For a while, I was pushing hard for engagement. I told Jason I couldn't move in with him without an engagement ring. But I couldn't afford our place on my own, and he *said* he loved me. He promised it would come. That was over a year ago, when I first got tenure. I was so happy, I thought for sure we were headed toward our happily ever after.

It seems we've stalled at happy-for-now.

Except now I'm not—happy, I mean.

Lena leans back in her chair, studying me over the rim of her soda. "Do you still love him?"

The question lands heavier than I expect.

"I think I'll always love him," I say slowly. "I'm just not sure I'm still *in* love with him. I'm biding my time until I figure that out, I guess."

She nods, like this confirms something she's suspected for a while. "You know you're not stuck, right?"

It's a conversation we've had before—my discontent with my life choices—but I'm sure she's run out of things to say to make me feel better.

If you want to make any money in marine biology, you've got to enter academia or work for a government agency. But I'm starting to think I chose the wrong path. Lena, on the other hand, loves academia. "Never liked touching slimy things," she'd said, scrunching up her nose, the day I met her.

I give her a look. "I hate when you say that."

"I know," she says, smiling. "But you're not. You're smart. You're accomplished. And you're one grant approval away from shaking up your entire life."

I straighten in my chair and point at her. "See? That's the energy I'm going with today."

A knock sounds at my door.

Lena's smile widens. "Speak of the devil."

Dr. Alan Reyes, my department head, pokes his head in. "Emery? Mind if I come in?"

"Hey, Alan," Lena grins, standing. "I was just going." She shoots me a hopeful look, crossing her fingers behind her back as she leaves.

Lena slips past him and pulls the door closed behind her with a soft click. Alan follows her with his eyes, watching as she leaves.

His brow furrows as he takes the seat Lena just vacated. "Did she have a Dr Pepper?"

I grin, trying to decide if I should throw her under the bus. "I think she did."

"That was *mine.*" Alan folds his arms, but he's smiling.

Then a silence falls over us and the air shifts.

Butterflies swarm my stomach, but from the expression on Alan's face, I already know what he's going to say. I brace for it.

"Hey, Em." Alan rubs the back of his neck before speaking. "I got final word from NSF this morning."

I let out a deep exhale, causing tufts of blond hair to fall in my eyes. "Let me guess, another almost, but no."

Alan hesitates, then nods. "Another final review. Exceptional science. But they got a strong proposal from microbiology and shifted the funding at the last minute. I'm sorry."

I don't speak, only stare past him at the ocean maps and research posters cluttering my wall.

"You've done everything right," Alan says carefully, trying to soften the blow. "Five rejections don't mean failure."

"Well, that's a relief," I mutter, rolling my eyes.

Alan gives me a pointed look. "It *means* you're swinging at the big ones." He pauses, scratching his jaw. "But I can see you're tired—getting burnt out, Em. Everyone can see it, if I'm being honest."

Anxiety builds in my chest, and my eyes burn. I blink hard. "Are you trying to get rid of me?"

Alan barks out a laugh. "Get rid of you? No. Don't be ridiculous. You're tenured. But I do think you could use a break."

"You think I need a break?" My voice comes out brittle.

"I think you *deserve* a break," Alan says, pointing at me. "There's a difference."

"Okay..."

"Hear me out. We've got department funds for research sabbaticals. I'd like to offer you one. Six months. No teaching load. Full pay." Alan studies my face, waiting.

"That's...generous." I lift my eyes in surprise. "What's the catch?"

Alan chuckles, pushing his glasses back up on his nose. "This just came across my desk this morning." He reaches inside a folder on his lap that I hadn't realized he'd come in with. "The timing seems serendipitous."

Alan hands me a printout of an email.

"Temporary director of a research center? South Carolina?" I ask, scanning the email. "Why?"

Alan swallows. "The former director in Tidehaven passed away suddenly a couple of months ago. They've been looking for someone to run the place since."

I lick my lips. "What would I do there?"

Alan considers my question, his mouth curving slightly. "Well, the previous director was studying the population decline of terrapin turtles. I'm sure you could pick up where she left off. Or you could enjoy the quiet coastal town, estuarine access, and salt air and figure out what's next. Maybe write a paper."

"Turtles, huh?" I fight the twitch of my lips.

"I seem to remember you telling me you love turtles, oh, about seven years ago," Alan teases.

"I really *do* love turtles." I'm grinning now.

"Think about it? It might help. This seven-year itch is common, you know." Alan rises, making for the door.

"I'll give it some thought."

"Let me know." Alan nods, tapping my door on his way out.

Tidehaven. It *does* have a nice ring to it.

I THINK ABOUT Tidehaven, South Carolina, the whole drive back to the townhouse Jason and I share, but I am still disappointed by the grant rejection. Picking up and leaving New Jersey wasn't in my plan at all. But if I'm honest with myself, I haven't been happy. My job is monotonous; my relationship is mundane. I can't help but feel as if I'm searching for something, but I don't know what. And I'd be going from one coast to another. How different could it be?

Despite all that, I love my job at Cape Atlantic University. The campus is large and sits on Lake Fred. Even though we're only about fifteen minutes from the coast, the university sits nestled on acres of pine barrens and wetlands. It's alive with the sights and sounds of nature and wildlife. It's peaceful. Our student population is around ten thousand, so it feels small, but the culture is a mix of laid-back beach vibes and quiet academic ambition. You can walk through campus and see kayaks leaning against dorms or students hiking the trails. I love it here. It's a big decision to pick up and leave it for six months no matter how tempting a decrease in workload is.

I hadn't heard back from Jason when I texted to let him know I didn't get the grant. Now, the deep thrum of bass hits me before I even open my front door, and I force myself to swallow my irritation. When I push the door open, early 2000s rap—something from the *Get Rich or Die Tryin'* era—blasts from the living room. I step into the foyer, and I don't know why I'm surprised. Jason isn't neat by any means, but the place is a mess and smells like takeout. I nearly trip over his loafers in the entry way, and it doesn't take me long to realize his buddies are here too. Anger floods my cheeks, but I do my best to push it aside. It's Friday, after all. He's probably just blowing off steam. Something I could stand to do.

When I walk into the living room, Jason and three of his friends are crowded around the sectional, yelling at each other over the music, stuffing their faces with wings and pizza. Beer bottles and take-out containers litter the coffee table. Jason is at the center of it all, tie loosened, sleeves rolled up and beer in his hand, laughing at something his buddy Chris said. Video games are paused on the flat screen, and Jason's headset hangs around his neck like the incessant over-grown gamer he is. If I wanted to unwind with my boyfriend and lament over yet another rejection, I came to the wrong house.

I drop my bag with a thud, hoping he'll hear it. No one turns. I walk over to the Bluetooth speaker and turn it off. That gets their attention.

"Whoa," Jason says, whirling. "Hey, babe."

I frown, the frustration in me rising quicker than the tide. "Seriously?"

"You're back early," Jason stands, moving to kiss me.

I cheek him.

"It's after seven." I set my hands on my hips, anger bubbling just beneath the surface.

"Whoops." He lets out an awkward chuckle, turning back to his friends. "We ordered from Pat's. There's probably some left."

I stare blankly at him. "I texted you three hours ago." *Right after I got my rejection.*

"Must've missed it." He shrugs. "It's Friday—we cut out early."

"I got the NSF decision today." My voice comes out sharp.

"Let me guess, another no?" Jason doesn't even pretend to be empathetic.

"That's your response?" My voice catches, and I don't bother to force my anger back down now.

"What do you want me to say, babe? You're smart, yeah, but maybe they just don't want what you're pitching." Jason looks at his friends and chuckles like some kind of hot shot.

Something inside me snaps.

"I spent the last six months teaching a full course load and writing that proposal in all my downtime. I've barely slept. And all I was looking for was a little sympathy from my *partner*." The word tastes bitter. "But I walk in here to this? My thirty-five-year-old *boyfriend* and his friends, drinking and playing video games."

Jason holds up his hands defensively. "Relax. It's just the guys. Why are you always so wound up?"

"I'm wound up because I do everything around here. You crack open a beer and coast. And you didn't even *ask* if I was okay." My throat tightens, and my wavering voice threatens to betray me, but I hold strong.

Jason smirks, his eyes rolling upward. "You seem okay enough to yell at me in front of my friends."

I glance at Chris, Vinny, and Evan—all wearing shiny

wedding rings and avoiding my gaze.

I shake my head. "God, grow up, Jason. I can't believe it's taken me this long to realize what this is." I say, my voice ice.

That gets his attention.

Jason straightens, eyeing me carefully. "What's that supposed to mean?"

I swallow hard, my pulse loud in my ears. I know that once I speak, there's no pulling the words back. And yet rather than be stunned by what I'm about to say, I'm more surprised that I don't stop myself.

"I'm taking a research sabbatical. Six months. South Carolina. And we"—I gesture between us—"are done."

The second the words leave my mouth, something unhooks inside me. A mix of relief and adrenaline. Not the devastation I expected. Instead, I feel lightheaded and terrifyingly clear, like I've just stepped off a ledge and discovered I can breathe on the way down.

Silence hangs in the air until Pete or Vinny, one of them, starts picking up the takeout containers. Another grabs his jacket, walking behind the couch and patting Jason on the shoulder.

"We should probably bounce," he calls behind him. "Sorry, Em."

Jason looks stunned, as if our problems the past year just snuck up on him. "Are you really doing this right now?"

I nod, my voice calm. "Yeah. I am."

The front door clicks closed, and Jason lets out a defeated sigh, ripping the headset off his neck.

I brace for a fight, but it doesn't come.

I inhale a shaky breath and turn away. I'm already halfway to the bedroom, when I hear his muffled apology. I roll my eyes, reaching in my back pocket for my phone.

Opening a text to Alan, I tap it out quickly before I chicken out and tell Jason I overreacted.

I'm in for Tidehaven.

CHAPTER TWO
REID

THE FOG THAT rolls in this morning is so thick I can barely make out the boats in the harbor as I trek down the rocking, weathered dock. It's the kind of dense fog that is easy to get tangled in. I would know, having spent ten years as a Navy SEAL—years I've worked hard to leave behind me.

I cast my eyes on the empty slip beside me where *The Maybird* should have docked an hour ago. I hate when boats are late, not because I care about the schedule, but because late means one of two things—engine trouble, or something worse. I try not to think about the something worse. I came here to leave my pain and guilt in the past. To mind my own business and keep my head down. I don't need to be tangled up in anything. I know that, but it's in my nature to look beneath the surface. I can't always pretend I don't wonder what's really coming in and out of this quiet marina.

I lift my coffee to my lips. It's lukewarm and bitter, but I take a long, slow sip anyway. The dock creaks under my boots with the retreating tide. A skiff to my left bobs lightly, the hull groaning like it has something to say. But it's otherwise quiet and calm, no sound but the water licking the pilings and the rustle of marsh grass behind me. It *should* be peaceful but instead, it feels...off.

Across the inlet, the gulls are restless, circling above the shallows like they've been summoned by something. I crush the paper coffee cup in my fist and scan the area. Not a soul in sight, save for the few crabbers, always out before dawn, their skiffs gliding through the channel like ghosts.

I lift a hand in greeting to one of the commercial captains I have seen countless times. I don't know his name, but I know his boat: *The Salty Lady.* He and some others rent slips and sell their haul to the buyers two towns north of here. They keep to themselves.

"Reid." A voice startles me.

I turn to find my childhood best friend, Tate Maddox, approaching.

"It was supposed to be my turn to open." He stops beside me.

I shrug. "What else have I got to do? I don't sleep much these days." I thrive on routine, a creature of habit.

Tate shoots me a look that tells me he knows this. He's the brother I never had. By the time we were ten, we could read the tides like clockwork. We knew which creeks ran dry by noon and which ones hid redfish under the reeds. We baited crabs with slices of white bread we'd stolen from our parents' kitchens. We caught minnows in mason jars and knew how to cut an engine and drift or speed through the marshes. Sometimes we fished, and sometimes we floated. We could always tell a storm was coming by the way the herons flew. We were barefoot and mud-slicked, but the marsh taught us patience. The water taught us respect.

After high school, I joined the SEALS and Tate took over his dad's marina. When I finally left my post behind, Tidehaven was the only place I wanted to come back to. I grew up here, raised by a single mama and the rest of the neighborhood after my dad took off. But she left when I left, and we don't have much of a relationship these days.

I run a hand over the dock railing, checking for loose bolts. I shouldn't care this much—I only own thirty percent of this place—but it feels more mine than anything else in my life lately. Tate and I built half of these improvements together. Hell, the reason I bought into Driftwood the month I left the military is because I needed something solid to stand on again.

"*The Maybird* is late," I tell him, jerking my head in the direction of the empty boat slip.

"Johnny called me. Engine trouble. He was waiting for a Coast Guard tow," Tate reassures me. "I know what you're thinking, but I don't suspect it's anything more than that."

I let out a growl, raking my hand down my face. I've been out of the SEALs for two years now, but my senses are always heightened. My mind maps exits and worst-case scenarios before I can stop it. I came back here to reset. I've connected with some veterans groups, and I'm doing the work, but it's not easy walking around with all this anger inside me. The safest thing I know how to do is keep to myself.

"You know I can't stop my mind from wandering," I say, turning away, my eyes scanning the horizon.

"You need to." Tate's voice is clipped. He slaps me on the back. "Gonna go open the bait shop."

He starts back up the dock, leaving me to slowly walk slip to slip, checking the lines. I finish my rounds, checking each one off on my clipboard, noting that *The Maybird* still hasn't returned. I tuck my pencil behind my ear and look up. Beau Rigsby, a gruff Alaskan commercial fisherman I've known for years, is already out on his boat, *Miss Tidehaven*, hauling up his first crab pots. Even on weeks off, he's still out on the water on his own boat. You'd think he'd be sick of it. He gives me a nod from the wheelhouse, one hand on the throttle, the other around a thermos of God knows what.

By seven, Tate's got the bait shop lights flickering on behind our no-frills, open-air tiki bar, The Drift Net. By eight, I have fixed a busted hose nozzle and restocked the fuel dock bins. Then there's nothing left to do but putter around the bait shop and The Drift Net. By two, my phone is ringing. I pull it out of my pocket. *Tidehaven Research Center.*

"Reid," I say, forgoing hello.

"Reid, it's Kayla." A young girl's voice comes through the line. "I need your help."

Kayla Cruz is a high school senior. She lives in Tidehaven, but since it's so small, she attends high school in a neighboring town. Kayla loves marine biology, and Penny let her use the labs for her own experiments. After Penny died, the university needed someone local to keep things from falling apart until a new director showed up. I didn't ask for the job, but I don't mind it. It keeps the place open—for Kayla, if nothing else. Who knows? She may be running it herself one day.

"What's up, Kayla?" I ask, raking a hand through my beard.

"It's the skiff at the research center. I can't get it started again, and I only have a couple of hours to get these samples." The urgency in her voice makes my lips twitch.

"I'll be right over." I hang up without saying goodbye, but Kayla is used to that.

When I get there, she is leaning against the dock post, eating a granola bar and wearing a Tidehaven Research Center baseball cap that's seen better days. She grins at me.

"You ever take a day off?" she asks, watching as I step into the boat and get right to work on the lines.

"I'm off now," I mutter.

"That's a lie." Kayla squints at me.

"You want this boat to float or not?" I shoot her a look.

Kayla grins but doesn't press me further. I get the motor open, and my hands move on instinct. The place has been too quiet since Penny died, but Kayla's kept coming anyway. Says it helps her feel close to Penny and the work they were doing. I don't pretend to understand marine biology, but I understand wanting to be somewhere that still makes sense. "I heard the new director is getting in tomorrow," Kayla says carefully.

I look up from where I'm tinkering with the motor. "Who told you that?"

"Tate. Do you think she'll be...nice?"

I loop the last line and sit back on the boat's tiny bench, letting out a sigh. I never like anyone the first time I meet them. "I'm sure she's fine."

Kayla winces then says, "Do you think she'll let me keep using the lab?"

I frown at her. "How should I know?"

"Well, you're in charge right now. Maybe you could tell her. I don't need much. Just a corner. I'll help with whatever project she's working on. Data entry. Fieldwork. Coffee runs. I'm very useful."

Kayla's face is so earnest it forces a smile out of me.

"Why don't you tell her yourself?" I give Kayla a pointed look and start the skiff. The engine sputters, then roars to life.

She smiles so wide her eyes crinkle. "Yay! Thank you!" She's hopping on her toes and moves to hug me when I climb out of the boat.

I hold up a hand, preventing it, and start back up the dock. "Don't mention it."

"It wouldn't kill you to say you're welcome, you know!" Kayla calls after me. "You grumpy oaf."

I turn around and give her a nod, but I can't stop the corner of my mouth from quirking upward. "You're welcome. Lock up when you're done."

Her smile is blinding.

I head for home and an ice-cold beer, already knowing I'll be right back here tomorrow if she needs me.

I MAKE THE short trek back to my cabin, the place I've come to call home. When I was growing up, my mom and I lived in the same neighborhood as Tate. A typical rural coastal neighborhood of modest ranchers built in the sixties, long before the invention of Wi-Fi. I can still picture it—colorful houses with sun-warped siding, crab traps leaning against the side of the house. The occasional pair of waders left out to dry. Everyone had mismatched porch furniture and faded American flags, but they knew each other's dogs. Curtains rustled when a stranger pulled in, and grief moved through houses like tropical storms.

I grew up at the dead end of the street in a sky-blue rancher. My dad's jon boat sat up on cinderblocks under a tarp in the driveway long after he left us. But the neighbors looked out for each other—looked out for me. I could have gone anywhere when I got out, but I came back here. I like knowing people care. I just don't need them watching my every move anymore. I trek through the path to the clearing where my modest log cabin sits in all its glory. When I came back, I slept on Tate's couch for a year while I built this place. It gave me something to do to channel all the pent-up anger and regret I carry around inside me for things I can't undo. Now that it's done, I need to find another outlet.

I march up the steps and unlock the door, moving inside only to grab a cold Miller Lite before coming back to the porch. I sit in a rocking chair and kick off my boots, letting my bare feet rest on the white cedar planks. It's modest, but it's mine.

I take a long swig of beer just as my phone buzzes in my pocket. I pull it out, not knowing what to expect. Not many people text me.

Tate

Yo. The new director arrives tomorrow. I told the University you'll meet her at noon at The Drift Net.

I frown at my phone. Me? What the fuck. I hammer out a reply.

Why aren't you meeting her?

Tate

Because you're in charge of the research center.

Dude.

Tate

DUDE.

I guess I'll see her at noon.

CHAPTER THREE

EMERY

By the time I cross over the two-lane causeway into Tidehaven, I'm panicking that I've made a terrible mistake. There is rural, and then there is *rural.* I'm afraid Tidehaven is the latter. I'm surrounded by marsh on either side of me and signs that warn of tidal flooding on the roadway. I pass crumbling docks and large live oak trees dripping with Spanish moss. It's beautiful, no doubt, but there isn't a Target—or hell, even a Walmart—for miles around.

But I'm here now, and I promised myself I'd give this a real shot. I've had lots of time to reflect the past couple of weeks. The semester ended with me working late every day, grading labs and final papers. Jason tried to make up with me at first, but we'd only end up talking in circles, finding ourselves at yet another impasse. Eventually, we stopped trying. Yesterday's goodbye wasn't dramatic, but it was final.

As soon as I cross the last tiny bridge on the causeway, I'm greeted by a large sun-beaten sign that reads *Welcome to Tidehaven: Home of the Blue Claw. Population 2,200.* Smaller than Cape Atlantic University's student population.

I'm nauseous. For a second, the thought that I've made a catastrophic mistake presses hard against my ribs. Then I tighten my grip on the wheel and keep driving. I didn't come all this way to turn around now.

I swallow hard and press on.

Driving down the narrow main street, I'm relieved to see some semblance of life. I roll down my windows and huff in a breath of salty air. It instantly lifts my spirits. Mama T's General Store greets me as soon as I cross through the first streetlight. There's a physician's office, a dentist, a diner with a weather-beaten red and yellow sign reading *The Salty Spoon.* I pass a darkened bar called The Rusty Anchor that looks like it has seen better days, but when I turn the corner, there's a nice deck with outdoor seating. People are enjoying meals under umbrella-covered tables, and sounds of southern rock fill my car through the open windows.

I roll my shoulders back and ease up on the gas. Maybe this won't be so bad.

Finally, I come up on the Tidehaven Research Center and, just about a block over, The Driftwood Marina. Both fill me with optimism as the sun beats down on the still water surrounding them. There are boats of all sizes at the marina, fisherman gathered on the docks and around a small bar with a sign reading The Drift Net, where I'm supposed to meet my contact in a couple of hours.

I drive slowly, taking it all in and catching the attention of a few of the men sitting at the bar. Not a woman in sight. I offer a small smile through the window of my Toyota Prius and keep it moving, deciding it might be best if I drive right to the cottage I'm staying at. I glance at my GPS. I'm a half mile from Blackbird Cottage, which is owned by Coastal Carolina University for the purpose of housing the director of the Tidehaven Research Center. Aside from a few photos of the outside, I know nothing about the residence. There's no telling what shape it's in.

By the time I pull up the crushed sea-shell driveway to the small white cottage, I've convinced myself that everything will be okay. I'll be here for six months. It's quiet and peaceful, and I'll be free to do whatever research I want without the burden of teaching a full course load.

I put my car in park and step out, taking in the tiny house. The siding is white and weather-beaten, but there's a screened porch, perfect for sitting after a long day. I move to my trunk, pull out my two large suitcases, and drag them up the crunchy path.

I swing open the door to the screened porch and immediately see the only piece of furniture is a broken rocking chair. So much for that.

"I wonder if Amazon comes out here," I murmur to myself, propping my suitcases and digging through my purse for the lock box code.

It takes me a couple of tries to get the combo right but finally the box opens, revealing a gold key on a seashell chain. I push the door open with my hip, its hinges letting out a long, reluctant creak. The smell of musty cedar hits me, the air damp in that coastal lived-in way. Warped wood paneling lines the walls, giving the cottage a log cabin feel to it. An air conditioner sits in the window to my right. I walk over, the floor creaking with every step, and switch it on. It lets out a loud hum of white noise in an otherwise eerily silent house.

To my left is an old couch with sagging cushions and a quilt draped over the back of it, the kind someone's grandmother probably made decades ago. There's a mismatched chair and an end table covered with field guides and tide charts. Those will be helpful. An old brick fireplace centered on the side wall has a small TV hanging above it. That's a relief.

Above the archway into the kitchen is a sign that reads: *Blackbird Cottage: Good Luck for Lost Souls.* I lift my eyebrows. I'd be lying if I said I didn't feel like a lost soul these days. Maybe being here will bring me luck. I walk through the opening, relieved to see a Nespresso machine and a basket of pods.

"So, the last person living here was at least in the twenty-first century," I mutter to myself. I open the old refrigerator, and a burst of cold air hits me. It's empty, of course. My stomach growls angrily, and I realize I'll need to hit up that general store soon. In the far corner sits a stackable washer and dryer that looks older than me. Open shelves hold mismatched mugs, plates, and bowls. The faucet drips once, and I move to the sink to turn it off. The window above the sink looks out to the marsh and my own private dock, a small skiff boat tied to it. A rush of excitement fills me at the thought of exploring out there. Getting my hands dirty again.

I walk down the small hallway and there are only two doors, one to a bathroom with a rust stained clawfoot tub and a small sink. Moving to the tiny bedroom, I'm relieved to see a queen-sized bed on a wrought iron frame, but also thankful I brought my own linens. I walk over to the second window unit air conditioner and flick it on, turning to take in the rest of the room. There's a small end table with a bedside lamp and a single dresser. I pull open the top drawer. It sticks.

I run my fingers through my blond waves, already damp with sweat from the South Carolina humidity. This will take some getting used to but so does every other kind of change. And I'm here now. I'm going to make the best of it.

My phone buzzes in my pocket. I pull it out and glance at the screen. Jason. He's texted me at least ten times since I left yesterday.

Jason

Please let me know that you made it okay. I'm sorry.

Sorry. A familiar word and yet somehow still not enough. I type back, pausing briefly to wonder if what I'm writing is too harsh. I type, then think better of it, tapping delete until the words disappear.

Finally, I settle on a message that is firm but not unkind.

I'm here. I'm safe. This doesn't change anything. We're over, and I need you to respect that.

The three dots appear, then vanish.

I set my phone face down, relief washing through me as I settle into the quiet.

"Welcome home, Em," I say to myself, looking around. "Welcome home."

I HAVE AN hour before I'm supposed to meet my contact, so I decide to take a walk up the road to the Tidehaven Research Center I'd passed on my way in and check things out. It'll be good for me to get the lay of the land. I tuck my phone in the pocket of my jean shorts, grab my cross-body purse and the keys to the cottage, and I'm off.

It's a short walk out of the woodsy marsh to the main road. I'm surprised how fast I get there, but I'm already sweating. I veer off the sidewalk and cross a gravel drive to the research center which sits on pilings and is surrounded by docks. There's a sign that reads *Coastal Carolina's Tidehaven Research Center* and below it a weather-worn banner: *Protect Our Shore. Protect Our Future.* Something pulls at my chest as I take in the white building. It looks more like an old crab shack pieced together with decades of repairs and add-ons than a university building. I peer into a screened porch cluttered with boots and life vests and a couple of folding chairs. A handwritten note that's seen better days hangs on the inside door.

Tidehaven CRC – Field First, Office Later.

A steel navy-blue door leads inside from the dock, and I try the handle. Why not? I'm the director after all. Surprisingly, it opens and I hesitate before walking inside.

I'm not sure why I thought it would be shiny and grant-funded with a university logo and a large welcome desk. No, it's not that. It smells of coastal breeze and wet neoprene. Open windows let the salty breeze blow through. The walls are lined with cork boards covered in tide charts, annotated maps, and photos of smiling researchers holding up fish. Lab desks with steel tops sit shiny and waiting, and I wonder the last time someone sat at one. Counters along the opposite wall hold empty glass tanks.

I set my bag down and look around. I'm told no one has been here in some time, but one thing is for sure. This place doesn't care about credentials or publications. It's not here to impress anyone. And neither am I.

A throat clears behind me. "May I help you?"

The voice is deep and jagged. I whirl around and find myself face to face with a tall, broad-shouldered man, who looks like he belongs to the coast. His dark crew cut and trimmed beard frame sharp green eyes that study me carefully. I forget how to breathe for a moment before I find my voice. "Y-yes. Hi. I'm Emery." I swallow before remembering who I am. "Dr. Emery Caldwell. I'm the new director."

CHAPTER FOUR

REID

I'M NOT SURE what I was expecting when I saw the cute, petite blonde sneaking into the research center, but it wasn't this. I'd planned to meet her at The Drift Net in less than an hour, and it hadn't occurred to me that she'd look like someone capable of knocking my focus sideways. Outsiders are pretty easy to spot in Tidehaven, and Dr. Emery Caldwell has outsider written all over her.

It takes a minute for me to find my voice as I take her in. She's a tiny thing. I've easily got a foot on her small frame. She has blond hair so light it's almost white hanging down her back in waves, sweat dampening her hairline. Big blue eyes stare expectantly at me through round wire-rimmed glasses.

"And you are?" she asks, raising her eyebrows at me.

I slowly rake my gaze up her body and meet her eyes, stifling a cough.

"I'm Reid—Reid Morgan. We were supposed to meet in half an hour." I keep my voice level, trying to push down the sound of irritation. I'm not sure if I'm irritated by her impatience to get inside the building or by my visceral reaction to her attractiveness. I wasn't expecting her to be hot.

"Oh, right." Emery shoots me with an awkward smile then winces. "I was just...trying to get the lay of the land before going to meet you." She shifts uncomfortably. "The door was open so..."

She lets her voice trail off with a meek shrug.

"I am in and out between here and the marina. I don't always lock up during the day." I step around the table separating us. "I'd appreciate it if you didn't break in though." I fish a key ring out of my pocket, twisting a shiny gold key off it and handing it to her. "This is the place. This is your key. Got any questions?"

Emery pushes her tongue in the side of her mouth and squints, examining me. "Yeah. What's *your* job?"

I let out a low chuckle. It's a fair question but one I don't really know how to answer. "I'm part owner of the marina, and I do a little bit of everything. But here? You can call me the maintenance guy."

"Oookay." Emery turns from me, her attention already elsewhere. She walks the perimeter of the room, trailing her hands along the wall before pausing to skim the tide maps on the corkboards.

I will my brain to stop checking her out. It has been a while, but I don't date and *definitely* not the woman in town to run this research center. That has bad idea written all over it. Still, she is clear-eyed and purposeful as she acquaints herself with the lab. I can already tell she's the kind of woman whose intelligence shows up in the confident way she carries herself. And damn if I'm not drawn to her like a magnet, despite every warning I've given myself. Emery stops walking and catches my gaze. "Do you happen to know if the former director left anything behind?"

"Left anything behind?" I repeat. "She uh... She died." I catch the melancholy in my own voice.

Emery shifts awkwardly. "I heard that... I just, I heard *before* she died, she was studying turtles, and I love terrapins. I thought I'd try to pick up where she left off."

I gesture behind me to a short hallway. "Her office was back there. I guess it's your office now, so anything you find in there, I would imagine is up for grabs." I scratch my jaw, casting my gaze down the dimly lit hall.

Emery nods, letting out a breath. "Got it."

I'm just about to ask if she needs anything else, if we need to bother with The Drift Net when the door to the screened porch swings open.

"Reid?" Kayla's voice echoes. "Are you here? Is she here?"

I roll my eyes but call back, "In here, Kayla."

Emery turns just as Kayla walks in the room. Her khaki shorts are stained—probably with marsh muck, her Hollow Creek High T-shirt is cut off at the sleeves, and her curly dark hair is piled high on the top of her head. Her wader boots leave wet, muddy footprints all over the dark floor.

"Jesus, Kayla," I say when I see the mess. I gesture in the direction of the porch. "Go take those off. I just mopped these floors."

Kayla grimaces. "Sorry." Then she looks at Emery. "I'll be right back."

She slips out as fast as she came in, and I busy myself wiping the sludge off the black tile floor. "That's Kayla," I say as I work. "She's been very excited to meet you." That one sentence is more words than I've uttered to anyone in weeks.

Kayla dashes back into the room, wearing a pair of flip flops this time. She marches right up to Emery and holds out her hand. "My name is Kayla Cruz. I love marine biology, and I've been using this lab for two years now. I would love if you'd continue to allow me to use it, and I'd be happy to help you with any projects you're working on."

Kayla speaks so quickly I'm not sure she takes a breath.

"Smooth, kid," I mutter, tossing the dirty paper towels in the trash.

Emery grins, taking Kayla's outstretched hand into both of hers. "Hi Kayla, it's so nice to meet you."

"So, can I stay?" Kayla is doing that bouncing on her toes thing again.

"Of course you can use the lab. And I'll let you know if I have anything you can help with." Emery reaches in a black purse and pulls out a business card. "My phone number is on here. Call me any time."

"Thank you, thank you, thank you!" Kayla squeals.

Emery lets out a small laugh and glances my way. "Does... anyone else use the lab?"

"Currently, no. It's been me and Kayla for the past six months while the university looked for a replacement." I hold up my hands. "We're a quiet pair."

The three of us stand in a brief uncomfortable silence that is broken by the sound of a loud stomach growling. Emery's cheeks flush pink. She swallows, and I find my eyes drawn to her throat, her clavicle, the gentle curve to her shoulder.

"Sorry," she mutters, raking a hand through her hair. "It's been a while since I've eaten. Know anywhere good?"

"Oooh!" Kayla interjects before I can. "I'll take you to The Salty Spoon."

I give her a tight smile, quirking my eyebrows upward. "There you go."

"Salty Spoon it is." Emery picks up her bag and follows Kayla toward the screened porch. "Thanks, Reid," she says over her shoulder.

"See you around, Doc."

I'm on my porch in my favorite place, sipping my favorite beer, when my phone dings. It's got to be Tate because he hasn't checked in yet and I'm sure he's itching for details.

Tate

Dude, I didn't see you at the Net. Did you forget to meet the director lady?

I shove my phone back in my pocket. Tate knows me better than that. I'm nothing if not reliable. I'm not even going to dignify that with a response.

I take a long pull of my beer and look out over the marshes. The mid-afternoon sun is hiding behind a cloud, herons are diving for fish. The call of a gull in the distance puts me at ease. This right here is why I chose to build my cabin just beyond the marsh. Nature is peaceful. I close my eyes, resting my head on the back of the rocking chair.

My cabin isn't far from the Blackbird Cottage that I know *Doctor* Emery Caldwell is staying in, but I didn't let on to her that we're neighbors. That's not my style. I'm a quiet observer. Still, she doesn't look like the type to live in an area that is this remote. She doesn't seem soft exactly, but maybe unused to being this far from a lot of people. And yet she moved through the lab like she's already decided she belongs here, nerves and all. That contradiction kept my attention.

I'm going to be seeing a lot of her, and I can't help wondering what would bring a woman like her to the lowcountry—or what she's running away from.

The beeping of a horn startles me as Tate's white Dodge Ram crunches up my gravel drive. I rise and grab him a beer from my cooler as he kills the engine.

"I texted you," he says, climbing out of his truck.

"I know," I grumble, handing him the sweating bottle.

"Well, did you meet the director?" Tate cracks the bottle open on my deck railing.

"Yeah." I sit back down in my chair.

Tate drops into the one beside me. "And?" He tips his beer toward me, eyebrows raising.

"She doesn't look like a doctor."

"What does she look like?" He leans back, squinting at me before taking a long pull from his bottle.

I roll the cold glass between my palms, my lips twitching. "A naughty professor."

Tate barks out a laugh. "Stop it, dude. She hot?"

I don't answer right away, instead fixing my eyes on the marsh. "Unfortunately, yes."

"Well, good thing you forgot how to talk to people." He rocks backward in his chair, draining his beer in one last long gulp.

"Jesus," I mutter.

"Well, how'd it go?" Tate asks, presumably tired of waiting for me to volunteer information.

"Was fine." I shrug. "She broke into the research center before I could even meet her at the Net." I shake my head. "She's curious. Asked questions I don't have the answers to. Seemed thrilled with Kayla."

Tate lets out a breath and stands, leaving the empty beer bottle on the arm of his chair. "Good. She'll be fine."

I frown, pressing my lips together. "I know. Why wouldn't she be?"

"No reason." Tate shrugs before jogging back down my steps. "See you tomorrow," he calls over his shoulder.

"Bright and early."

CHAPTER FIVE

EMERY

Kayla leads me on the short walk to The Salty Spoon, across the main street and down a block from the marina. While we walk, she jabbers about the research center, her love for marine biology, and Tidehaven itself. She's a wealth of information and while she talks, I take in the sights around me. There are a decent number of people milling about the streets, popping in and out of shops and offices. People stare at us with curiosity as we meander down the block, and I can't help but wonder if I look like an outsider to them.

Kayla swings open the door to The Salty Spoon, and the bell above us rings. The smell of bacon grease and coffee hits me in the face. A few patrons glance up from their plates before going back to their meals. Blue vinyl booths, ripped and duct-taped no doubt from years of loyal customers, line the perimeter of the restaurant. Large windows let the sunshine through. Across the aisle runs a long bar top for counter service. A chalkboard hangs on the wall that reads: *Daily Special: Shrimp Platter. Market Price.*

"Hi, Tess!" Kayla calls, heading straight for a stool at the counter.

"Hey, Kayla," a curvy woman with dark graying hair piled on her head says, heading over to us. "Who's your friend?"

"This is Dr. Emery Caldwell, the new research center director." Kayla grins, gesturing in my direction.

Tess tilts her head, studying me for half a second too long before smiling, as if she can sense that I'm not from these parts. "Ah, well, welcome to Tidehaven." Her thick southern drawl catches me off guard.

I smile back, trying to remain impassive. "Thank you," I say, picking up the menu in front of me. "I'm starving. What's good here?"

"Can't go wrong with a cheeseburger or fish and chips, right, Tess?" Kayla says, spinning on her stool.

"Fish and chips sound good." I close the menu. "And a Coke, please."

Tess gives me a tight-lipped smile and a nod and then directs her attention to Kayla.

"Me too. Same." Kayla grins. Her enthusiasm is infectious, and I push aside my nerves about being the newcomer in town.

Tess brings two sodas and sets them down in front of us, leaning on the counter. "So, Doc," she starts.

I let out a chuckle, waving my hand. "Please, just call me Emery."

"Emery," Tess repeats. "Why'd you want to move to Tidehaven?"

I inhale deeply, letting it out slowly. "I just needed a change of scenery. Reevaluate my path a bit, I suppose. This is a six month sabbatical so hopefully I find some clarity." I try to give her an answer that will suffice without giving too much away.

"Well, Tidehaven will do that for ya," Tess says, wiping her hands on a dish cloth. "Just keep in mind, it's a small town. Everybody knows everybody's business." Her tone sounds like a warning.

Tess walks away to help another customer, and I take a long, slow sip of my Coke as I scan the room. I don't need anyone to tell me—I stick out like a sore thumb. Most of the men are broad-shouldered and windburned, wearing dirty work boots and faded hoodies. There are only two women in here besides Kayla and me, and they're both wearing faded cut-offs with sleeveless tees, their hair in messy knots on the tops of their heads. These people wear the water like a second skin. I, on the other hand, look like I stepped out of an office, pale skin and hands better suited to lab notes than lines and nets. I've studied places like this for a living for the better part of a decade, but standing here, it's clear I haven't lived in one.

Until now.

"So," Kayla says. "What are you going to be working on while you're here?"

I furrow my brow. "Estuarine systems mostly. I want to see what's changing and why. Specifically, species decline. My department chair said something about Dr. Young studying turtles. Do you know anything about that?"

At the mention of Dr. Young, Tess looks in our direction, her gaze stony, but she doesn't say anything.

Kayla looks at Tess and then back at me. "She was," she confirms, her voice low. "But...not everyone liked it."

Now I'm really confused. "Not everyone liked it? What does that mean?"

Kayla stifles a cough. "Just that they're endangered is all." She looks uncomfortable, a stark contrast to the sharp, bubbly girl I walked in here with.

A moment later, Tess delivers our meals with nothing more than a polite nod.

Kayla and I eat in silence for a moment before she says, "Maybe you should study something different."

I clear my throat and sip my Coke thoughtfully. "I think I'll look at her reports and see where she left off," I say carefully.

Kayla looks beside her to see who else might be nearby and listening and then she whispers, "All of her reports are in the filing cabinet under her desk in her office. The key is under the plant pot on the windowsill. But don't say I didn't warn you."

"Oookay," I say, lifting an eyebrow.

"Whoa, look at the time! I have to get home." She hops off her stool. "Tess, can I have a box and my check?"

Tess reappears quickly with the two items. Kayla throws a twenty on the counter and dumps her food into the to-go container.

"I'll see you tomorrow!" Kayla calls to me as she heads for the door.

"Bye, Kayla," I say, but she's already gone.

Tess watches her go, before clearing her throat. "Just be careful where you go pokin', Dr. Caldwell. The marsh keeps better secrets than most folks in this town." She pauses, eyeing me, assessing my reaction. "And it doesn't like to be disturbed."

I swallow. "I appreciate the heads up," I say, careful my tone doesn't betray the unease crawling up my spine.

My expression must give me away because Tess's face softens, and she offers me a smile that doesn't reach her eyes. "Word travels quick around here. Especially when a new person starts asking questions." She drops my check on the counter and walks in the other direction before I can respond, leaving me to wonder what in the world researching turtles has to do with this sleepy little town.

I FINISH EATING and walk up the street to the general store, a small corner market with a light-up sign in the window that reads: *Deli*. Relieved that I'll be able to get some grocery items here, I grab a small shopping cart and start slowly up the aisles, grabbing the basics so I don't starve.

"Hello," I say to the cashier, an elderly woman with wire rimmed glasses and gray curly hair.

She smiles at me. "Hello, dear. I don't believe I know you." She starts scanning my items, placing them carefully in reusable tote bags.

"I'm Emery." I return her smile. "I'm the new director of the Tidehaven Research Center."

The woman stops scanning, clasping her hands together in delight. "Wonderful! I'm Rosie. It's so nice to meet you."

Rosie is offering me the warmest welcome yet, and it makes something settle in my chest. Perhaps it's hope? Relief that coming here wasn't a complete mistake? Either way, I know I'll be visiting her store again.

"That will be sixty-three ninety-five," Rosie says as I dig for my wallet.

I swipe my credit card, and she hands me my bags.

"Thank you," I say shifting one of them to my shoulder.

"Come again." She smiles.

"I definitely will."

As I start my walk toward home, I realize I didn't think this through. I'm easily three quarters of a mile from my cottage. It's ninety degrees and humid, and my grocery bags are much heavier than I thought. It doesn't take long before the sweat is dripping down the center of my spine. It doesn't matter that it's mid-May. I'm not in Jersey anymore.

To make matters worse, I'm wearing my glasses instead of my contact lenses, and the late afternoon sun is still so bright. When I reach the corner before the marina, I pause, setting my bags down, and wiping the burning sweat out of my eyes. I look up when I hear the rumbling of a navy-blue pick-up truck pulling over to the shoulder.

"Need a lift?" a husky voice asks.

Reid. The man I met earlier. The ridiculously good-looking man.

"Oh, uh..." I hesitate, shifting my weight and the bags.

"I'm going your way." He nods in the direction of my cottage.

"How do you know?" I frown at him.

"Because I know where the university puts its people. Blackbird Cottage." Reid cocks his head in the direction I'm walking.

When I don't move, he sticks a hand out the window and meets my gaze. "You coming?"

I shake my head, a smile pulling at my lips. "I don't even know you."

Reid waves a hand. "I don't know if you Yankees know this, but Southerners are known for their hospitality."

I hesitate a second longer before he turns back to the road.

"Okay, suit yourself."

"Wait!" I hold up a hand. "Okay."

"Okay?" He quirks his eyebrows, clearly amused by me.

"Yes." I suck in a breath. "I'd like a ride. My milk is going to spoil in this heat." I start to walk around the front of his truck when he hops out of the driver's side, taking my bags from me.

"We wouldn't want that, would we?" he asks, pulling open my door. He sets the bags on the floor and offers me a hand to climb the rig before closing the door.

I suck in a breath and buckle my seat belt while Reid walks around to his side. He might be the best-looking guy I've ever seen. But I'll be working with him, so I need to wipe those thoughts from my mind.

He climbs in and glances at me. "Ready?"

"Yep." My voice is quiet. Something about his large presence makes it retreat.

"Parking down here isn't usually a problem. Next time you need groceries, you should drive." He keeps his eyes on the road.

"Noted." Just the nearness of our elbows on his center console is sending an electric current up my arm, giving me goosebumps and making the little blond hairs stand tall. I wonder if he even took a second look at me. I glance at his face for the briefest of seconds before forcing myself to face the road. Getting tangled up with someone down here when I just broke up with Jason is *so* not something I need.

"Did you have a nice time with Kayla?" Reid asks, reaching over to turn up the air conditioner. Maybe he *is* feeling the heat. Strangely enough, that would be a relief—to know I'm not alone in my attraction.

"I did. Thank you." I pause, debating whether to ask him about the turtles. I want to know though, so I swallow my nerves and say, "She got a little weird though."

Reid looks my way for half a second before returning his eyes to the road. "Weird?"

"When I asked about the turtles Dr. Young was studying."

"Turtles?" Reid's expression is unreadable.

"Yes, they live in the estuaries I will be studying. I figured she might know something about it if she'd been working with her, but her reaction was strange." I shake my head, bewildered.

"I know where they live," he says, flicking on his blinker as he turns down the narrow gravel road toward my cottage.

"It's just... She left in such a hurry after that. And then Tess told me not to go poking around the marsh...which essentially is my job so..." I trail off waiting for any kind of response from Reid. "Is there something I should know about this place?"

He pulls up to the cottage, putting his truck in park and he turns to me, licking his lips. "Maybe she just means you shouldn't go poking around the marsh alone, as a newcomer." His suggestion is mildly insulting.

I shake my head. "I'm not worried about that."

"Tomorrow, I'll take you on a marsh tour. My cabin is just through those woods. Walk through and when you reach the clearing, take the left side of the fork. I'll show you the estuaries."

He says it to be helpful, like it's no big deal. And maybe that's all it is. But his suggestion sends a rush of heat up the back of my neck. I already know how to read a tide chart. I know how to handle a skiff. I don't need a tour with a guide who smells like salt water and pine, all hard lines and quiet strength. Spending time with him would be dangerous in a way I can't explain. But I know one thing, Jason never made my pulse do what Reid's voice just did.

"I'll be good." I push open the door and collect the bags at my feet. "Thanks for the ride."

"Doc," he calls after me, perhaps trying to change my mind.

I turn and give him a wave before disappearing inside.

CHAPTER SIX

REID

EMERY WALKS INSIDE the cottage, the curve of her waist down to her perfect ass making my jeans tight. I can't take my eyes off her.

"No." I hit the top of my steering wheel. "Bad idea, Reid."

Giving myself reminders about why I chose a life of solitude isn't usually necessary. I know what I need—to mind my own business and get my head right. But then again, I haven't been around a woman that looks like Emery in a long fucking time. Or one who unsettles me like this.

I let out a growl and back out of her drive. My original plan to go home is squashed by my need for a drink. I turn off the drive and head back toward town.

I pull into the parking lot just outside the marina, in between Tate's truck and a Tidehaven Police Department Cruiser. Instantly I know I'll find Tate and our buddy Deputy Chief Colt Riggs sitting at The Drift Net bar.

I walk down the weathered dock and duck my head inside the open-air restaurant. Sure enough, they're sitting at the far corner of the bar, each with a frosty beer in front of them, talking in hushed tones. I stride over, pulling out the stool next to Tate.

"Gentleman," I say, taking a seat.

"I thought you'd left for the day," Tate frowns.

"Morgan." Colt nods.

"Needed a cold one after dropping the new doctor off at her

cottage." I glance away, then back at him, my mouth twitching with dry amusement. I pick up the beer that Willie set on the bar as soon as he saw me coming. I'm nothing if not predictable.

"Let me get this straight. You were home after meeting her and you came back down here to...what?" Tate quirks a brow at me.

"I never locked up the research center. I saw her carrying bags of groceries, and I offered her a ride." I shrug, taking another long gulp.

"Hold on." Colt holds up his hands. "New doctor? Where is Doc Michaels?"

"Not a *doctor* doctor," Tate mutters, swatting Colt's arm. "The new director of the research center."

"Yeah. She's a PhD," I clarify.

"She hot?" Colt asks.

"Christ," I mutter, shaking my head.

Tate barks out a laugh. "Reid says she is. I haven't seen her."

I roll my eyes. "She's hot, all right. And nosy. Tess already told her not to go poking around the marsh."

"Tess isn't wrong," Colt growls, his eyes piercing mine, and I wonder if we're both thinking about Penny. "The last thing we need is a newcomer in here thinking she sees something she doesn't."

"You seen anything shady lately?" I ask, looking back and forth between the two.

"The same shit we see every day. Nothing we can do about it but stay out of the way and stay accommodating." Tate says, his voice so low I almost miss what he says.

"The people that run this town will see to it that that's the case," Colt agrees, taking a final swig of his beer and pushing out of his stool. "Got to get back to work."

My gaze falls to the gun holstered at his hip. He's in street clothes, not uniform.

"Thought you were off." I frown.

"The deputy never sleeps." He throws some cash on the bar and pats both of us on the back before leaving.

A moment later, Beau Rigsby marches angrily up to the two of us.

"I've got a bone to pick with you two," he grumbles, pulling out the stool between us.

Tate's mouth quirks up in amusement. "What's going on, Beau?"

"Someone's been on my boat." He looks back and forth between us, and he's so close to me I feel the need to shift my stool over.

I catch Tate's gaze over Beau's shoulder. "What makes you say that?"

"A man can just tell. Someone is using it when I'm away for work." Beau narrows his eyes. He's back and forth between Tidehaven and Alaska multiple times a month.

"That's...ridiculous," Tate says slowly. "The *Miss Tidehaven* has remained in her slip whenever you are gone. I assure you."

"Then how come my bait knives were in the wrong spot?" Beau looks to me this time.

"Don't look at me, Beau. I'm just the fuel guy." I hold up my hands.

Tate shoots me a glare.

"That's another thing—my tank was three quarters full when I left on my last trip. Now it's over full. Who filled it?"

The hair on the back of my neck prickles. I sigh. "Okay. I'll bite. You find anything else?"

"My engine hours are off by fourteen. Fourteen, Reid." He holds up both hands, fingers spread wide. "I logged everything before I flew out. Came back to that."

"What else?" I ask.

"Two of my crab pots were halfway up the inlet." He looks between us. Tate first—long and deliberate—then me. "I never set pots there. Ever."

My stomach tightens. That area is too close to the boatyard's side channel for coincidence.

"What about the storage compartments?" I ask quietly.

Beau's eyes lock onto mine. Bingo.

"Scuff marks," he says. "Fresh. Someone opened the forward hatch so many times the paint's worn." His nostrils flare. "And—this one takes the cake—the ropes were coiled backward. *Backward*, Tate."

Tate cuts in, holding up his hand. "Beau, listen—"

"No," Beau snaps. "You listen. I know my boat. I know every inch of her. Someone used her while I was gone, and they knew what they were doing. But I know better."

My pulse quickens. Tate's shoulders are tight, his hands too still. Silence hangs in the air.

"You wanna tell me why you look like you swallowed a fishhook?" Beau growls.

Tate pushes his lips together, shaking his head. "Just thinking. Trying to figure it out."

Beau leans in close, his voice a threatening whisper. "Tell me something, boy. Did your daddy let people run boats out of here without permission too?"

Tate rises, towering over Beau. "Leave my father out of this."

I step between the two men. One of them doesn't stand a chance against the other. "Beau, Tate and I will look into it. I promise."

Beau fixes his eyes on me, his jaw tight. "You damn well better. Because I leave again tomorrow, and if I find out someone is using *my* boat to do God knows what, I will sink your whole damn operation myself." He turns and storms out of the Net.

When he's gone, Tate turns to me. "Griff's been keeping an eye out. Making notes. For now, that's all we can do."

Griff Monroe is the retired harbormaster of Tidehaven. He and Mr. Maddox were best friends. Griff lives alone now, and Tate has stepped into the role of surrogate son. I suspect the two of them do a lot of speculating after hours.

I push my lips together. "Dale Langford been sniffing around at all?"

Tate nods. "He pops in and out. Making sure we see him. He

never says much, but he's around."

"Jesus," I mutter, draining the rest of my beer. "I came here because it's quiet, but you know it's hard for me to turn it off. Now Beau is raising questions." What I don't say is I don't know how long I can force down my suspicions about the people who run this town. Penny's image flashes in my mind again.

"Reid." Tate's voice has a warning tone. "I'll handle Beau. You have to leave it alone."

I cough, clearing my throat. "I'll try."

I GET HOME just as the sky is turning to dusk, but I don't go inside. Instead, I hike through the trail, past the clearing until I find myself in front of Emery's cottage. Why can't I let the new girl be? I guess talking to Tate and Colt has spiked my awareness again. I'd been content with the monotony of everyday life, tried to put what happened to Penny out of my mind. But now with someone new here wanting to do some digging in the name of marine research, I'm back on alert.

I walk up the side of the cottage and before I can even open the door to the screened porch, I spot her. She's sitting in the little skiff tied to the rotting wood dock that has seen better days, tinkering with the engine. She must hear me approach because she startles, letting out a gasp.

"Are you stalking me?" Her voice is breathy, sending a chill up my spine.

"Just out for a walk," I say, holding my hands up in defense. I move toward her slowly, the way I'd want to be approached by a stranger. "Thought I'd see if you got settled. If you have everything you need."

Emery looks up, wiping sweat from her brow. Her blond hair is piled into a messy knot on her head, and gone are those sexy little glasses she had on earlier. "You only dropped me off an hour and a half ago."

Shit. She's right.

I ignore her comment. "You trying to get that thing started? It's probably been a while."

At this, Emery softens. "I'll get it." She gives me a confident nod that further piques my interest in her. She's determined not to be helped.

"I told you I'd take you on a tour tomorrow. Don't go out there alone before then," I warn.

"And just who do you think you are telling me what to do?" Emery scowls at me.

I walk further down the dock, the boards groaning. I should replace these for her. I don't need her slipping through one and getting hurt. A briny breeze blows through, rustling the loose hairs from the bun on the top of her head.

I stand back and watch, half-expecting her to fumble. She flips the throttle, primes the engine, and gives the cord a pull. Nothing. She looks at me, her expression unreadable, and tries again. This time the motor sputters before growling to life, smooth and steady. Emery offers me a satisfied smile.

"Not my first time in the marsh." She meets my gaze, heat flickering, calling me out for doubting her.

My jaw ticks. "Didn't say it was."

"No," Emery replies, hand gripping the throttle, "but you were thinking it."

"Don't go far until you know the lay of the land." My voice is sharper than I intend it to be. "Watch the eel grass. Marsh gets shallow near the point. And bring some oars in case you get stuck. No one will know you're out there."

"Aye aye, captain." Emery's voice drips with sarcasm.

The skiff eases from the dock, the motor humming beneath her. She glances back once and our eyes meet, something passing between us. Challenge. Recognition. Something more I don't want to name. Then she disappears into the reeds, the engine thrumming behind her like the beat of my heart.

Too confident. Too curious. Too damn much.

"This one's gonna be trouble," I murmur. And then I head for home.

CHAPTER SEVEN
EMERY

THE CONFIDENCE I had as I steered the skiff away from my dock and Reid fades quickly. Maybe I should have agreed to let him show me the marsh. I'd never admit that to him though. He didn't so much as smile at me all day. Still, I can't shake feeling that I want to know him, despite the easy sparring we've fallen into.

I turn the skiff around once I've given him enough time to leave and head back to the cottage. I kill the engine and reach over to tie the boat up. I trek inside, and despite the air conditioners, the cottage is sticky. I strip right there in my living room, head for the clawfoot tub, and fill it with cool water.

It's been an eventful first day. It feels like a lifetime since I arrived here early this morning, having driven through the night from New Jersey. I close my eyes, resting my head against the cool porcelain of the tub. I don't bother to wash—I haven't unpacked a thing. The purpose of this bath is to bring my body temperature down. Between the South Carolina humidity, the weak air conditioning, and Reid Morgan, I'm downright feverish.

I climb out and towel off, finding a pair of boy shorts and an oversized T-shirt at the top of my suitcase before making myself a bowl of Cheerios and plopping on the couch. It's been a while since I've checked my phone, and there are numerous messages.

Lena
I hope you got there safely and are settling in. Send pics!

Mom
Hi honey, just checking in. Let us know when you get settled.

Mom
So glad you shared your location with me or I'd be way more worried!

Jason
Em, I've made a lot of mistakes in my life but letting you go to South Carolina for six months without me tops the list. I'm sorry I screwed up.

My mom and Lena are the only ones I bother writing a response to. I let them both know I'm in and settled and exhausted. I don't text Jason back. The truth is that the relationship has long run its course. We should never have moved in together. Jason is just feeling bad now because he doesn't know what to do without me. I did everything for him. I probably enabled his man-child behavior.

But I think being here in Tidehaven is good for me. The quiet helps more than I expected. Knowing I have a job to return to in six months also helps me relax. I'm just going to take this for what it is—an amazing opportunity to learn and grow.

I finish my cereal and wash the bowl by hand, since there is no dishwasher here. Then I rummage through my second suitcase and find the bedding I'd packed. I pull it out and inhale deeply. The scent of freesia laundry detergent sends a wave of homesickness through me. I strip the bed quickly and replace the bedding with my own before climbing in. It's not the Four Seasons, but it'll do. The mattress creaks slightly as I shift to get comfortable but then, sleep finds me quickly.

THE MORNING LIGHT gleams through my new bedroom window bright and early. I slept like a rock and feel more rested than I have in some time. Perhaps it's the salt air. I head for the bathroom and then the Nespresso machine. It's only six thirty a.m., so I take my time. I unpack my suitcases, tucking them away in the back of the closet. Then I make myself another bowl of cereal, eating it slowly while I examine the latest tide charts and marsh maps. While I get ready, I consider my plan of attack, but first thing's first, getting to the research center so I can see what's what.

Feeling energized, I hop in my car and head for the narrow strip of downtown Tidehaven. It's quiet on Main Street this morning, only a few people milling in and out of the coffee shop across from the marina. I pull into a diagonal parking spot and climb out, pausing to huff the sea air, the scent of salt and damp wood clinging to it. I unlock the door to the research center, making a mental note to replace the tattered banner hanging on the side of the building.

I push the door open and it creaks, greeting me like an old friend. There's no one here but me, and for the first time since I arrived yesterday, I feel a little hopeful. I set my travel mug down on one of the stainless countertops and pull out my phone, queuing up a playlist of early 2000s hits. The pop sounds of NSYNC bounce off the exposed beams and weathered cabinets. My hips sway, and I roll my shoulders back as my eyes land on the two cabinets bookending the large window that overlooks the marina. I walk to the closest one, swinging the door open and wincing at the chaos inside. I push up my sleeves.

Half an hour later, I've got everything pulled out of the cabinet, and I'm alphabetizing supplies. A pile of expired chemicals and broken equipment sits near the trash can. My music is so loud, I don't hear Reid come in until he shuts it off.

"Hey!" I scowl, whirling around to find him holding my phone. "I like that song."

"What the hell happened in here?" Reid asks, leaning his hip against the table crowded with supplies. He places my phone back on the table and gives me a slow once-over.

"Good morning to you too," I say, dusting off my hands on my frayed denim shorts.

Reid steps closer, examining my handy work. "I leave you alone for half a day and you change everything?"

"It was a mess," I say slowly. "I like things organized."

"It was fine the way it was."

I cross my arms, frowning at him. "It's not your lab." My voice is terse. Who does this guy think he is?

He watches me so intently for a minute that my skin prickles. Then he lets out a sigh. "You're right. I was just helping out. This place is your problem now."

"Thank you," I say, turning to put the last few supplies away. I shut the cabinet and move down the hallway to the former director's office. I push open the unlocked door and step inside, flicking on the lights. The overhead bulbs buzz to life, but they barely cut through the stale, shadowed corners of the room. The air smells old and musty. No one has been in here for some time. Reid follows me in silence, leaning in the doorway, his broad frame filling the space like there's nowhere else to stand.

I glance at him before pulling out the desk chair to confirm what Kayla told me—sure enough, a two-drawer file cabinet sits beneath the desk. I tug on the handles to the drawers. Locked. I walk over to the windowsill and tug on the shades to let in some light. I fix my eyes on a sad looking rubber tree plant in a terracotta pot. Just as Kayla had said. I lift the pot and find a small gold key.

Bingo. I hold it up, pleased with myself, nearly forgetting I'm not alone.

"What are you doing?" he finally asks, letting out a breath of air.

"I'm looking for Dr. Young's notes on the turtles." I walk back over to the desk and crouch down to unlock the cabinet.

"Why do you want to know about the turtles so badly?" Reid asks, sounding annoyed with me.

"Because my sabbatical gives me a wide scope," I say, straightening and meeting his gaze. "I'm here to look at population decline across the marsh—patterns, pressures, what's changing and why. Dr. Young's work on the terrapins fits squarely into that. They're an indicator species—and plus, I've always had a soft spot for them."

Reid frowns. "Indicator species. What does that mean?"

I pause, then straighten, shifting into professor mode without meaning to. "It's a species that reflects the health of the whole ecosystem. If terrapins are declining, it usually means something deeper is wrong. It could be habitat loss, pollution, a disruption to their environment. They're sensitive in ways other species aren't." I slide the key into the lock beneath the desk. "So, when people tell me not to look there, it only tells me I should."

"Doc," Reid pleads.

"Stop calling me that." I narrow my eyes at him.

He doesn't reply so I busy myself pulling out file folders until I find it. A black notebook at the bottom of the cabinet. A label across the front reads: *Terrapin Turtle Population Notes – P. Young.* A rush of excitement surges through me. I pull the chair back and flip the notebook open.

"Well, I guess I'll get out of your hair." Reid's voice startles me, but he doesn't immediately move. He's waiting for my acknowledgment, and I'd already forgotten his presence.

I exhale slowly, looking up to meet his gaze. "Reid."

He raises his eyebrows at me in response.

"Will you show me the marshes? You were right. It was a

mistake going out there last night alone."

The corner of Reid's mouth twitches, but he doesn't smile. "I'll meet you at your dock at four o'clock."

I meet his eyes. "Thanks."

He gives me a nod, turning to go and just when I think we're done talking I hear him say, "Have fun with your turtles."

I intend to.

CHAPTER EIGHT
REID

CHRIST, SHE'S BEAUTIFUL. I keep telling myself to let her be, but I can't. I'm drawn to her in a way I can't explain. It's probably because I haven't been laid in a year. But I can't seem to stay away from her.

I work at the marina for the morning, fixing a couple of engines, replacing nozzles, and bringing in a few boats. I refuel a couple center consoles before popping over to the bait shop to check on Tate.

He's busy assisting some tourists with kayak rentals, making me wait. I walk out of the bait shop and find my gaze landing on the research center. I fight the urge to go inside and check on Emery. I want to invite her to lunch, but I know that's a bad idea. Why is this woman the first person I've come across in years that makes me want to let my walls down? I can't explain it. She's brilliant, that much I can see, but not particularly warm. Her boy band playlist showed me she has a playful side—one I find myself wanting to see more of.

Tate interrupts my lusting with a slap on the back. "Lunch?" He tugs on a shirt. This guy never has a fucking shirt on.

"Sure." We start for The Drift Net just in time to see Dale Langford making his way up the dock.

"Well, hell," Tate drawls moving to face him.

I square my shoulders and follow him.

Langford is the owner of the boatyard and a former classmate of ours. His father and Tate's late father didn't get along, and it carried over. It was never just a personality clash. Men like the Langfords don't feud—they erase obstacles. Penny was an obstacle.

What's worse, Dale does everything his daddy says. He has the power to change things, but he's just as dirty as the rest of them. I watch as this asshole marches his way up our dock like he belongs here. Aviators, a crisp white button down, pressed too neatly for this town. A cocky smile spreads across his face, but it doesn't reach his eyes—it never does.

"Afternoon, boys," he says, his voice smooth and practiced. "Fancy meeting you here."

"We own this place," Tate growls. "Where else would we be?"

Langford ignores him and flicks his gaze at me. "Just passing through. I heard you have some new faces around here. Thought I'd try to be neighborly."

New faces.

Emery. Fuck. Penny had been a new face once too. Right up until she wasn't.

"Neighborly," Tate repeats.

That's what he called it when he wanted to know who was asking questions—and how loudly.

I don't move but I narrow my eyes at him. "We're not running a welcome center."

"Damn, Morgan, you really are always a ray of fucking sunshine." Langford grins.

"You're at the wrong dock," I say, my voice edged with steel. "If you're looking for someone, use your fucking radio."

Langford takes a step closer to me, testing me. I've seen this play before. Pressure first. Next, politeness goes. Problems handled quietly after that. I move closer, prompting Tate to put a warning hand between us.

"Figured I'd come see for myself," Langford says. "Town's a-changing. Can't be too careful these days." He makes a clicking sound with his tongue.

"Yeah well, you've got your own dock. And we all know you

don't take detours unless you got a reason." I purse my lips. "You got a reason, Dale?"

Tate stays silent but I feel him bristle beside me.

"You two always this twitchy?" Dale counters. "It's a public dock."

"We're just wondering what the boatyard owner needs at a recreational marina," Tate finally says. "Unless you're ready to sell me that dry dock and move on."

Dale lets out a low chuckle, shaking his head. "You couldn't afford me." Then he holds up his hands. "All right, all right, no need to get your panties in a bunch, gentlemen." He fixes his gaze on Tate. "You run a tight ship, Maddox. I'll be on my way."

"Good idea," I growl.

Langford turns and marches back down the dock the way he came.

When he's out of ear shot, Tate says, "You think he's trying to get a look at the new girl?"

I don't answer immediately. My pulse is steadier, but the weight in my gut is lingering.

"They're still up to their same shit," I mutter.

"He's looking for something. And he's not going to stop," Tate agrees.

"Not if I can help it."

I MEET EMERY just like I promised at four p.m. on her little wooden dock, but the tension I feel from bumping into Langford hasn't ceased. I can't tell if it's from setting foot near Blackbird Cottage more times this week than I have since Penny...or from Langford sniffing around the new girl. Either way, I force it down and school my face into a neutral expression.

Emery's already in the skiff, the motor running when I walk up. I step in carefully, so my weight doesn't rock the tiny boat. She's wearing a long sleeve gray T-shirt and a blue ball cap that reads Cape Atlantic University. Her eyes are fixed on the horizon.

"Sup, Doc?" I say, unable to hide the twitch of my lips.

"For the love of God." Emery groans, but she's smiling.

"What? You don't like Bugs Bunny?" I quirk a brow.

"Oh, everyone likes Bugs Bunny, it's just...*you* don't look like you'd like him." She gives me a sideways glance.

"What do you mean?" I frown.

"Reid, don't take this the wrong way but...you're kind of cranky." She winces, biting her lower lip. The sight of it sends a jolt straight between my legs.

"I'm not cranky. I just keep to myself."

"Must be exhausting," Emery says lightly.

I glance at her. "What?"

"Carrying all that solitude around," she says. "Some people talk too much just to avoid it. Others disappear into it. And I think I know which one you are."

Something about her read on me lands too close. It's uncomfortable.

Suddenly I'm desperate to take the attention off me. "You speaking from experience?"

She shrugs but doesn't reply.

The ten years I spent as a SEAL forever altered the course of my life and the person I have become. I left after a terrible accident that haunts me every day when I look at the scar on my chest. Tate knew immediately upon my return home, to his couch, that I'd need help. He found some veteran support groups in Beaufort. My cousin Sophie in New Jersey found me a therapist I meet with virtually—now only as needed—but still. It will take a lot for me to let someone in. And somehow Emery clocked that in less than two days.

"Can I drive?" I ask, nodding toward her hand on the throttle.

She rises without a word, switching places with me. Once I'm settled, I guide us away from the dock. Neither of us speak as I guide us through the marsh, taking in the egrets stalking the shallows for fish, the reeds swaying in the breeze, the hum of insects filling the air like radio static.

Emery sits across from me, legs crossed at the ankles. Her eyes track my hands, my face, and the way I move the boat. She's watching me the way someone does when they're trying to figure you out rather than make conversation. "You always this quiet?" I finally ask.

"Only when I'm paying attention." She smiles lightly, but she still doesn't try to fill the silence.

I don't return her smile but something in my chest tugs. Dr. Emery Caldwell keeps surprising me. Most people get restless out here. She seems to settle, content to observe nature in all its solace.

I guide us further into the estuary, where the water narrows and the green rises up on either side. I point up to a clump of grass breaking the current.

"Terrapins nest up there," I say, pointing to the sandy area beyond the marsh. "You'll want to come back when the tide's lower. You'll see tracks on the banks, sometimes the nests if you know where to look."

She leans forward, eyes following where I point. "You sure know a lot about them. I thought you worked at the marina."

"I do. I just pay attention." I toss her a wink.

"But you know tide patterns, nesting seasons, where to find species others have missed for years."

I meet her gaze. "I grew up here in these marshes. You learn things."

She stares a beat longer, then shakes her head. "That's not exactly what I meant." She hesitates before speaking again. "Have you always worked at the marina?"

I stiffen, but the words come out before I can stop them.

"No," I say. "I was in the Navy. I was gone a long time."

Her eyes soften—not curious now, just aware. "That explains a few things."

"It explains why I don't talk much," I counter. "Did you find anything in Dr. Young's notebooks?"

"I found her notes," Emery says carefully. "But pages are

missing."

"Torn out?" I ask, frowning.

"Yeah. Like...someone didn't want them found." Emery's voice wavers.

I lick my lips and press them into a tight line. The skiff bobs lightly as we enter a narrow inlet. I kill the engine, letting us drift.

"You can come back on your own," I say, changing the subject. "Long as you don't get stuck. The choke is sticky sometimes, so bring oars. If you can't get it started, you'll be paddling out."

"I'll be fine." Emery says, her voice clipped.

"I wasn't asking."

She cocks her head at me, brow furrowed. "Are you always this charming?"

I huff a laugh. "I try not to be."

For a moment, the only sound is the water lapping against the hull. Our gazes lock and a shiver runs up my spine.

She looks away first. "We should head back."

I don't disagree, giving the choke a pull and turning us around. The whole way in, I feel her gaze lingering on me. Like she's trying to figure out what I'm hiding.

She won't find it. I buried it deep.

But something about her makes me want to tell her anyway.

CHAPTER NINE

EMERY

I SPEND THE next few days at the research center, reading over Dr. Young's research. Turns out, there were more notebooks than just the first one. I also found a thumb drive containing photos of the turtles and their tags and several pages of a report she was working on. Kayla takes me out in the research center skiff and shows me the eelgrass beds where she's been tracking juvenile fish and invertebrate populations for her AP Marine Bio class. It's clean and careful data, and Kayla's enthusiasm for her studies is infectious. But when I tell her I want to pick up Dr. Young's research, Kayla's easy chatter falters.

"She stopped bringing the tags back here near the end," she says, eyes fixed on the water. "Started logging everything somewhere else."

I frown, chewing on my lower lip. "Did she say why?"

Kayla shakes her head too quickly. "She just said some of the numbers didn't make sense. By the time she died, I didn't know much about it at all anymore."

The skiff drifts in silence.

"I'm sorry," I say, my voice soft.

Kayla shrugs and turns her attention back to her own notes, effectively ending the conversation.

I can't figure out why research on terrapins would make this sixteen-year-old so nervous—but it does.

I mostly avoid Reid. I see him each day, but I try to keep it to polite "hi and bye" conversation. He makes me nervous in all his sexy marsh man glory, and getting close to him would be a bad idea. But I keep things friendly, and each day that passes, I feel more of my stress melt away. Just the very idea of not teaching summer classes makes me excited. The next steps are right in front of me. I just have to figure out what they are. All in all, my time here so far has been slow and peaceful.

Lena wants to know everything about Tidehaven, and I have nothing to report, unfortunately. Tidehaven is peaceful and, dare I say, a bit boring?

Finally, after five days of working in the research center and learning the lay of the land, I feel confident enough to take the skiff out myself before dawn. The mist is thick as soup but I want to set some floating traps so I can start tagging turtles and monitoring their nesting patterns. I fill a travel mug with coffee and take it with me. The mornings in the marsh are chillier than I expected. I put on a windbreaker, waders, and a ball cap that I fix my headlamp to. Then I march down my rickety dock and climb in, pulling on the choke and starting the engine. It hums to life easily, but just before heading out, a nagging voice in my head gives me pause. It's Reid's. Remembering what he said about getting stuck, I climb back out of the boat and grab the oars at the shoreline. I can't be too careful, especially in the dark.

I move through the marsh slowly, the only light from my headlamp. I pass an old, abandoned dock that doesn't appear to have a house attached to it. I didn't notice it the other day with Reid. Probably because I was noticing *him*, broad shoulders tapering down to strong forearms, as he gripped the throttle and maneuvered the boat. Good to know it's there though.

I steer around the bend, until I find the place where Reid showed me a nest and get to work setting some floating traps. I stagger them and then take my night vision camera out of my bag. I adjust the lens and snap a few photos of the traps, the nesting area, and my surroundings so I know to come back to the same place.

I'm about to head for home when a center console boat moves into my frame, the whir of its engine startling me. It's not even six a.m. It seems odd for anyone besides me to be out in these back bays before dawn. Heat crawls up my neck, and I instinctively dim my light, ducking down.

I watch as two shadowy figures climb out of a boat larger than mine dragging someone to the dock I've just passed. A third man stands on the edge of the boat and gives an order I can't make out, but his voice is low and cold. There's some rustling, sounds of a struggle from the victim, muffled voices. I shift my weight, scanning for a quick way out, my pulse hammering as I brace for what comes next. Fear runs through me and with it a sharp wave of nausea. I can't see faces but from what I can tell, I've seen too much already.

A gunshot breaks the eerie silence, and a gasp escapes me. My stomach turns so violently that I nearly choke on the bile rising in my throat, fighting the urge to vomit off the side of my skiff. A rough, strangled grunt carries across the water as the figure crumples. The men kick him once before he disappears beneath the surface, then turn back toward their boat. I'm shaking so uncontrollably I can't process what I've just seen. A gunshot. A man collapsing. The sound of his body hitting the shallow water. The metallic scent of blood heavy in the air. And now the sickening sound of silence. My brain can't file it under real, but my fight or flight knows I have to get out. I stifle a gag, and the camera slips from my shaking hands, hitting the metal hull of my skiff. The sound might as well be another gunshot. *Fuck.*

One of the figures spins back around. "Did you hear that?"

Shit. Shit. Shit.

I fumble with the backup oars, silently thanking Reid for the suggestion but it's too late. Their boat roars to life, and they're coming for me. My eyes burn, and I realize they're filled with tears. This is it. This is going to be the day my life ends. I swallow the rising panic, determined not to let the fear paralyze me. I have to fight.

Then another loud crack from the opposite direction. Muffled voices, sounds of the men cursing, trying to figure out the source of the noise. A moment later, the engine whirs louder and they're moving—but it sounds like it's *away* from me. I use it as my chance to get the fuck out. I pull off to the closest clearing, collect my belongings as quickly as possible, and abandon my skiff. The sound of my pounding heart is deafening as I race through the woods, trying not to drop everything.

Branches brush against my arms as I push against the underbrush, breath tearing out of my lungs. My boots slip on damp leaves and catch on roots. I stumble, but I don't fall. My pulse is so loud, I've convinced myself footsteps are behind me, but I don't dare look back. I'm moving by instinct, guided by the first slivers of daylight and desperation. My fingers are numb. My lungs burn. My legs threaten to buckle.

Just keep moving, I tell myself.

I have to put distance between myself and what I saw. Between me and whoever that was. I push harder, tears blurring my vision. My foot snags on a root and I hit the ground. Hard. Pain shoots through my hip, but I scramble up again, clawing at vines and roots, willing myself to keep going. And then I see it. Blackbird Cottage. Safety. I run faster than I ever have before.

Bursting through the door, I drop my things on the armchair and run for the bathroom, retching into my palm before I make it to the toilet. I vomit until I can't anymore, and then I curl up on the tattered couch and give into the heaving sobs.

As daylight breaks, the low sound of a boat's motor stirs me from the light sleep I managed to fall into. I sit up, pressing my palms to my cheeks. Maybe it was a terrible dream. I stand, moving to my kitchen window to see Reid tying up my abandoned skiff and then making his way to my door. I meet him there.

I swing open the door and there he is, looking as if he hasn't slept at all, his shirt already damp from the humidity. "You dropped this." He holds out my camera bag. His gaze fixes on me, waiting for me to make a move. My eyes drop to the bag as I try to process what this means—why Reid has my camera bag.

I blink rapidly, and the truth comes into focus. It wasn't a dream. And Reid was there. Was he one of the men? I take the bag, backing away slowly, fear clouding my judgment. My eyes fill with tears.

"Emery," Reid rasps, stepping inside. He looks like he wants to reach for me, but he restrains himself.

"H-how?" I whisper.

Reid rakes a hand through his beard, stepping closer. He holds up his hands. "I'm *not* a stalker," he starts.

I let out a low bitter laugh. "That's a relief."

"Look, I know what you saw. I was there too." Reid steps closer, prompting me to back up again.

"Why? Why were you there?" My voice comes out brittle and strained.

Reid sighs and gestures to the wooden chair at the small dining table to his right. "May I sit?"

He doesn't move without permission, instead fixing his eyes on mine. Finally, I nod slowly, cautiously, staying where I am. Something in my gut tells me this man isn't dangerous.

He takes the chair furthest from me. "Our properties... They're close," he says quietly. "Not many people know that. And when I can't sleep—which is most nights—I walk the trails behind the marsh. It's always in the early mornings, before the sun comes up. That's the only time the world and my mind finally feel quiet."

My breath stutters. That might explain his uncanny appearance at my door.

"I always carry my weapon," he continues. "Old habits die hard. Training like mine doesn't just go away. Every sound registers." His jaw tics. "So, when I first heard the commotion, I was down by the tide flats. I knew it wasn't just the sounds of the marsh."

"And you just...walked right into danger?" I whisper.

Reid nods, eyes softening. "I saw your skiff was gone and worried you might be out there. I know I told you not to go out in the marsh alone, but you don't seem like the type to listen." Reid's lips twitch slightly.

Something in my chest shifts. *He wasn't following me. He was protecting me.*

"I wouldn't expect you to know this, but I wasn't just in the Navy. I was a SEAL," he says, voice low. "I don't sleep much, and I like my solitude. But my awareness is always heightened. I've suspected things go on in this sleepy little fishing village for some time now. Usually, I turn the other cheek because I came here to keep my head down."

"Okay..." I murmur, still processing.

"So, I was up because I'm always up at that hour." Reid's voice roughens. "I heard the gunshot and ran to investigate. And when I realized you might be out there..." He shakes his head once. "I wasn't about to let anything happen to you."

My pulse hammers. Reid was worried about me. *Focus, Em.*

I swallow hard. "I heard a bang... You threw something?"

Reid shakes his head. "No. I fired my gun into the air. I wanted to spook them...give you time to get away."

I nod, moving to sit in the chair next to him. "W-who are they?"

Reid shifts uncomfortably. "I have my suspicions. But it doesn't matter. Nothing will happen to them, but *you* shouldn't be out there alone."

At this, I bristle. "I'm fine. I have pepper spray."

"Emery." Reid looks at me very seriously. "Have you ever fired a gun?"

I recoil. "What? No."

"I have a handgun you should take. If you're going out there alone. I mean it. I can show you how to use it."

Reid's expression is so earnest, I almost agree, but then logic returns.

I rise and walk away from him, picking up my camera. I got a few photos before...my stomach churns and the sour heat creeps back up my throat. I shake my head. I can't even look at them.

"Okay, Reid. I can't." I meet his gaze that's burning straight into me. "I can't do this. I'm not taking a gun with me to research *turtles*."

"Enough with the fucking turtles." Reid's voice comes out sharp. "Leave the turtles alone. Stay out of the marsh. Find a new project."

I narrow my eyes at him. "No."

Reid stands, pacing, his breaths coming in angry and ragged. "Then I'm coming with you."

"Fuck no you are not." I cross my arms. "Don't be ridiculous."

"I am awake anyway, why not?" Reid argues. "Emery, it's not as safe as you think out there."

"I don't even know you. How do I know it wasn't you out there on that dock?" The question goes too far. I know it does, and I say it anyway. Who does this guy think he is coming here like this?

Reid flinches like I slapped him. "Excuse me?"

I drop my hands in defeat. "Fine. I'm sorry. But no. And shouldn't we just call the police?"

Reid shakes his head firmly. "No. Absolutely not."

"What?" I squeak. "Why wouldn't we report what we saw?"

Reid moves his chair closer to me, his body invading my personal space. He's large and masculine—burly even. A far cry from Jason. He smells like salt air and pine, and he's looking at me like I'm something precious to protect. "Listen to me, Emery. I will handle this. You do not say a fucking word." His voice is low and firm, sending a heat running through me that I'm not sure is from fear alone.

"But—"

Reid rubs the back of his neck, his jaw ticking. "Emery, you did *nothing* wrong. But you want to stay under the radar. Don't go poking around things you don't know about. If you're going to dig, you better know how to defend yourself when something bites back."

I suck in a shaky breath. "So...we witnessed a *murder*, and I'm just supposed to forget it? Pretend I saw nothing?" My voice is high and trembling, trying to outrun my fear.

"Yes." Reid's the opposite. Stoic and secure. Protective. Numb. "Promise me you'll keep quiet."

My cheeks heat and tears brim my eyes. I put my hands to my face and meet his gaze.

"Promise me, Emery," Reid repeats. "This isn't a fucking game."

"I—I promise." I sniffle. I move to the couch and sit, pulling my knees up to my chest.

"Are you going to the research center today?" Reid asks, his tone softer.

I shake my head, giving in to the rush of tears.

Reid stands for a moment, uncomfortable, before finding a pen and paper on the end table. He scribbles on it and hands it to me. "This is my number. Call me later, please. Let me know how you are."

I wipe my eyes and nod.

With one last long look, Reid turns and goes, locking the door behind him.

CHAPTER TEN

REID

SHIT. I DON'T feel good about this at all. This fucking woman has been looking for trouble since she arrived and now, she's found it. Those guys know someone saw them, and they probably won't give up looking until they find out who it is. I don't like that at all. Emery and I aren't exactly friends—colleagues at best—but I can't in good conscience leave her to figure this one out on her own. God dammit.

After leaving her cottage, I walk back along the trail to my cabin and hop in my truck. Tate's opening the marina today, but I'm due down there. I park at the marina but jog across to Poppy's for a coffee, already feeling like I've been awake for twelve hours. When I return, Tate's waiting for me on the dock.

"Yo," he says, doing a double take. "You don't look so hot, bro."

"I'm good," I say slowly, hesitating. Not because I don't trust Tate—but because once you say something like this out loud, it doesn't belong to you anymore. What happened this morning isn't the kind of thing you toss around lightly in a town like Tidehaven. People talk. Stories bend. And if the wrong ears catch wind of it before we know exactly *what* we're dealing with, someone innocent could end up paying the price.

Tate suspects as much as I do—I can see it in his eyes when Langford or one of the good old boys comes sniffing around—but suspicion isn't enough. Not yet. Not when there's no proof and too many people who know how to make problems disappear around here.

Up until now, I'd been able to live with that caution. Able to keep my distance and watch from the edges.

Until the beautiful, unsuspecting doctor walked straight into the middle of it.

"You sure?" Tate frowns.

"Yep." I keep it short, and Tate doesn't press. He's used to me.

"Morning, fellas." Colt comes up, putting his arms around both of us. "Beautiful day."

"Fuck off," I growl.

"Damn, Morgan, who pissed in your Cheerios?" Colt asks, adjusting the gun holster on his hip.

"Didn't sleep much last night." I shrug, hoping that will get these two off my back.

"Do you ever?" Colt asks, appearing genuinely curious.

I let out an exasperated sigh. "I was getting better until this damn professor showed up."

By the looks on their faces, I know already that I said the wrong thing. Now they will be relentless.

"Oh, man, Reid, are you coming out of solitary confinement to bone the new doctor?" Tate asks, looking mighty pleased with himself.

"I still need to get a look at her," Colt says, pursing his lips and looking in the direction of the research center. "She in? Maybe I ought to introduce myself."

"She's sick today," I say, my voice jagged.

"Well, damn." Tate's eyebrows shoot up. "Reid Morgan, I didn't think you had it in you."

"I don't," I snap. "I just saw her this morning."

"If you say so." Colt tips his head, studying me. "Bring her by the station and let me meet her."

"Fat chance." I smirk, moving down the dock. "I'm going to check the fuel bins."

My day moves at a snail's pace with nothing distracting enough to take my mind off Emery. I left her my number but stupidly, I didn't get hers. What if whoever was in the marsh this morning knew it was her and she's not okay right now? *Fuck*. Her face flashes in my mind, mud on her cheek, tears in her eyes. The way she trembled when I first got to her door.

"Come on, Reid, get it together," I mutter to myself, pacing.

Breathe.

I inhale through my nose for four counts, hold it in, then let it out slowly. Again. The rhythm settles my pulse, just like it had on ops when everything went sideways. I have to assess the situation. Emery is safe. For now. But she saw something she shouldn't have. That makes her a threat—to someone. I don't know who yet, but I will figure it out.

Around five, I can't take it anymore, I tell Tate I'm leaving and head out. But I don't go home. I stop at The Salty Spoon and grab take-out. Two burgers, fries, and two rice puddings for dessert. I stop at Mama T's and get a six pack of beer. Then I head straight for Blackbird Cottage. Emery and I are going to make a plan.

It's six o'clock by the time I knock on her door. She seems surprised to see me.

"Reid." Her voice is breathy and soft.

"You never called me," I grind out. "I was concerned."

"I never left here today," she admits with a shrug.

I take her in for a moment, blond hair disheveled into some kind of top knot, pieces falling loose around her ears. She's wearing loose pajama shorts and a hooded sweatshirt. And those fucking glasses—but behind them, red puffy eyes.

"Can I—can I come in? I brought food." I force a lighthearted smile which immediately catches her off guard. Probably because I don't give them out often enough.

"I guess." Emery steps back, holding the door open further. Once I'm inside, she pushes it closed and locks the dead bolt.

I set the food on the table and crack open two beers. Emery sits, picking one up and inspecting the label.

"Low Tide Lager," she reads. "Local beers are my favorite at home." She takes a long sip and finishes it with an "ahh" sound.

When she sets it down, I see she drank a third of it in that gulp.

"Are you okay?" I ask, peering at her from my seat across the table.

Emery lets out a laugh that sounds borderline manic. "Okay? Why wouldn't I be okay? I just witnessed a murder this morning, that's all. No big deal. A dead body is in the bay just behind my house. Over yonder. But it's okay. I'm totally cool." She picks up the beer and downs another third, slamming the bottle on the table.

I have seen so much death in my time as a SEAL that it stopped shocking me years ago. You see enough of it, you stop flinching. But that doesn't mean it doesn't get in your bones. You just file it away in the back of your mind like everything else. Emery's never seen anything like she saw this morning. Her reaction is normal. If she wasn't behaving this way, I'd think it was weird. But I'm not sure what to do for her.

She pauses, eyeing me. I can see it in her eyes she is trying to reconcile how we both saw the same thing this morning, and I barely flinched while she's over here falling apart. I busy myself unpacking the burgers. The fries have gone cold but it's okay. I put the food in front of us and watch as she takes a bite of her burger, chewing slowly. The look on her face says, *I need to understand you.* So, I swallow and give her something—a piece of me I'd long ago buried.

"The first time I ever saw someone die, I was twenty-two."

She puts her burger down, going still.

"We were sweeping a compound—intel said weapons, no hostiles. The villagers had cleared out. It should've been a ghost town." My jaw tics as the memory plays out like a movie I've seen one too many times.

"A kid—not more than fifteen—came out from behind a curtain holding an AK-47. He could barely hold the thing upright. It could've been fear, or a reflex maybe. I yelled and he flinched firing his weapon." I pause, my throat tightening. I work to steady my voice. "I didn't pull the trigger on him, my teammate did. But I saw it happen. Heard it." I sigh, pushing my plate away. "Immediately after, I threw up behind a wall, and no one said a word. We kept moving."

Emery bats at her eye behind her glasses and pushes her plate away too. "But Reid, that was war. What we saw today? That was murder." Her voice catches and I know she's right. There's a difference. I want to reach for her, pull her in close and keep her safe. The feeling overwhelms me.

"Yeah. It was murder. But you were never supposed to see it." I reach across the table and cover her hand with mine. The warmth sends a jolt of electricity straight up my arm, and I wonder how long it's been since I've had any human contact. Too long. But before I can comfort her any further, she pulls her hand back, picking up her beer and chugging the rest of it.

"So, we just do nothing?" she asks, clearly outraged.

"No," I say, firm but quiet. "*We* stay alive." I let that hang in the air for a moment.

"You think justice is found in a courtroom? Maybe in New Jersey but not in small towns like this in rural South Carolina. We don't even have our own chief, only a deputy chief. Here, you stir up the wrong hornet's nest, you don't get a fair trial. You disappear. And sometimes the good guys aren't really the good guys."

I know Colt is a good guy. I've known him my whole life. But there are people above him that make sure some secrets stay buried, and I know his hands are tied. Emery reaches for another beer, opening it and taking a long pull.

"You want to fight this? Fine. But you don't do it loudly by running to the cops. You do it smart—quiet. With your head, *not* your heart." I pause, letting that sink in.

"I don't want to fight this. I just want to study the fucking turtles," Emery growls.

"Here we go again with the turtles." I sigh. "Just promise me this, Doc," I say, eyeing her carefully. "Don't go out before first light again. Not yet. Give it some time."

"Why do you care so much what happens to me?" Emery frowns, picking at the label on her beer bottle.

The question catches me off guard, pulling at my chest. Why wouldn't I care? Why would I want something to happen to her when it could be prevented? I'd hate myself if something bad happened to her. But that still doesn't convey the feeling that has been curdling inside me for the past week as I've observed her working at the research center, her cute nose scrunched in concentration. I'm interested in her.

"Because. You matter to me." I let out a breath. "More than you think." *More than I'm ready for.*

Emery swallows, her eyes finding mine. She licks her lips and sucks in a breath. Silence hangs between us for a beat.

"I'm scared." Her voice is small, and the sadness behind it pulls at me in a way I'm not prepared for. "What if they know who I am?"

I hesitate before answering. It's possible, especially if they noticed the cottage is occupied now. But I don't say that to her. "Do you want me to bring you a gun? I have one."

Emery frowns, shaking her head. "No. I'd never be able to use it."

"Okay," I say, cautiously. "Then..."

Emery downs the last of her second beer. "Could you just... maybe stay here? Until I fall asleep."

Stay here. With her. While she falls asleep. I fight the twitch of my lips. For longer than I care to admit, I haven't wanted to stay with a woman when there's nothing in it for me. But I'll do it for Emery.

"Yeah. I'll stay."

CHAPTER ELEVEN

EMERY

Reid Morgan is a tough guy to crack. He's far different than any man I've ever met before. But it's more than the obvious—his muscular frame, broad shoulders built like he's fresh out of basic training, his unreadable, piercing emerald-green eyes, military grade crew cut, and a beard that I imagine would pinken my lips if I ever got the chance to feel it against my skin. No, it's the way he moves, sharp and calculated. He doesn't speak unless he has something to say, and even then, he's direct and to the point. There's no charm to him, no flattery. He's not trying to impress me. He's steady and intense, and yet, I feel incredibly safe with him here in my cottage. Safer than I've felt all day.

I crack open my third beer, in an attempt to dull the ache in my chest, and move over to the couch. Reid takes the one he's nursing and another and follows me, parking himself in the armchair adjacent to me. It's only seven o'clock. I can't imagine what we'll talk about until I fall asleep and yet, I don't want him to go. He reaches for the television remote on the end table, right next to the note he left his number on earlier today and flicks the TV on.

"I haven't figured out how to work it yet," I admit, gesturing to the TV.

"Well, let's get it going then." He stands, moving over to the TV mounted on wood paneling above the fireplace. He sets the remote down and pulls the TV off the mount just slightly, feeling for a cable box behind it. When he finds it, he pulls it out just enough for me to see. "Small cable box. You probably won't get many channels, but it's something." He presses a button and the TV turns on, first flashing a rainbow screen and then connecting to the local ABC station. Jeopardy is on.

Reid pushes the TV back onto the mount and returns to his chair. We sip our drinks silently, turning our focus to Ken Jennings and his three contestants.

Double Jeopardy appears on the screen and Ken introduces the next categories.

U.S. History
Marine Life
Environmental Science
American Literature
Tough Guys in History
Talk Like a Sailor

"The irony," Reid mutters as Jennings reads the categories. I settle in, game face on, and shoot him a look.

When the first contestant says she'll take Marine Life for four hundred dollars, I sit up a little straighter. Reid smirks, taking a swig of his beer.

"This process allows certain fish to glow in the dark ocean depths." Jennings says.

"What is Bioluminescence?" I answer at the same time as the contestant.

"Lucky guess," Reid chides.

"I'll take Marine Life for eight hundred, Ken," the same contestant says.

"The largest living structure on Earth, visible from space, is this reef system."

"Great Barrier Reef," Reid and I answer together. He shoots

me a satisfied look and warmth runs through me. It's been a while since I've felt anything remotely close to whatever this is. For the briefest of seconds, Jason crosses my mind. I always used to try to get him to watch Jeopardy with me. He always waved me off saying it was my thing, not his. These are different circumstances but still, Reid seems to be enjoying it.

I finish my drink in one long gulp and set the bottle on the coffee table.

Reid opens his next one at the commercial break, and I move back to the food, left untouched.

"Do you want me to try and warm up our food?"

He tips his head back, looking at me from behind, the smallest smile tugging at his lips. "I will eat it cold."

"Suit yourself," I say, bringing him his burger and some of the fries.

"You get used to eating at random times when you're out in the middle of nowhere," he says. "I'm just happy I get to eat whenever I want to now."

I try to picture Reid, not in jeans and a worn T-shirt, but his desert camo, gear strapped to his chest, a rifle slung across his back. Moving through chaos with calm precision. Just like he'd done for me this morning.

I warm my burger and snag a bottle of white wine from the fridge before making my way back over to Reid. He watches me carefully as I unscrew the top and take a swig from the bottle, but he doesn't say anything.

Jeopardy returns with the middle contestant asking for U.S. History for four hundred. Reid looks alert, fixing his eyes on the question.

"This document, adopted in 1787, begins with the words 'We the People.'" Ken asks.

"The Constitution!" I shout, pointing at the TV.

Reid rolls his eyes. "Come on, that's basically a freebie."

"Don't hate the player, hate the game, Morgan." I smirk, leaning back on the couch and taking a long pull of the wine.

Reid watches me before picking up the remote, muting the TV, and shifting his body to face mine. "Are you okay, Doc?" The question is soft—all his previous sharpness blurring at the edges.

My eyes water on instinct and I sniffle. "I told you to stop calling me that."

He gets out of his chair and sits on the other side of me. The ancient couch creaks with his weight and he's so close to me goosebumps rise on my bare legs. The proximity makes my heart hammer in my chest. He takes the bottle of wine from me and sets it on the coffee table before taking my hands in his.

"Emery. Are you okay?" His voice has a slight rasp to it making him sound gentler than he has before.

Then my tears are falling again. If I thought I was all cried out earlier today, I was wrong. Where Reid looked uncomfortable with my emotions this morning, he now opens his arms for me to fall into. I give into the big heaving sobs, hiccupping into his soft gray T-shirt. His strong arms fold around me and he shifts me into his lap, holding me in a way I've never been held before.

"I just can't unsee it, you know?" I say, through my cries. "How am I supposed to forget it happened?"

"You won't," Reid says simply. "But you'll learn to live with it to keep yourself safe. And in six months, you'll go home and move on with your life."

I nod, sniffling and relax into him, taking brief comfort in the image of celebrating Christmas with my parents and siblings. His hand finds the small of my back, and he strokes lightly, until my cries slow and drowsiness takes over. For having such a hard body, Reid sure is a soft place to land. And then, I feel it—his desire making itself known. Heat moves to my lower region before I can wrap my brain around what's happening between us. Do I want him? No. No way. It's the alcohol. It's the trauma bonding. It's... hot.

I stay like that, curled into him, his arms pulling tighter around me. We don't speak, simply watching one another for some kind of reaction. Beneath my sweatshirt, my nipples pull tight, and

I'm certain wetness is gathering between my thighs. Still, neither of us moves. I'm afraid if I do, the moment will pass, and we'll both remember all the reasons we shouldn't be here.

"Emery," Reid murmurs, dipping his chin toward me.

"Uh-huh." My voice hitches, only allowing a breathy sound to escape.

"This is a bad idea," Reid says carefully. "I'm not—you don't..." He lets his words fall away.

I sit up, feeling it then, his erection pressed tightly into his jeans. I press a palm to his cheek, feeling the prickle of his dark beard. Our eyes lock momentarily before Reid dips his forehead to mine and lets out a low growl.

"Not like this," he whispers, but he still doesn't move.

I lick my lips. "You make me feel safe."

At this, Reid's arms circle me tighter, pulling me close. "You are. You are safe with me." Then he presses a featherlight kiss on my neck, so soft I almost don't feel it. Tiny explosions of fireworks fill my belly, a feeling that fizzled out with Jason so long ago that I forgot what they felt like.

"I should go to bed," I finally say, pulling back from his embrace. "I feel like I've been awake for a thousand hours."

"Okay," Reid says, nodding. "What do you need from me?"

"I'll just...go get ready for bed and maybe you can come sit in there with me? Just till I fall asleep, I swear. Then you can leave." I shift, feeling his bulge press into me, suddenly so desperately *not* wanting him to leave.

"Okay." His voice is husky, thick, and I'm relieved I'm not the only one that wants whatever this is.

I clamber out of his lap and walk down the short hallway, pausing in front of the dresser. Sexy pajamas would send one message. An old T-shirt would send another.

I hesitate, then choose something in between—boy shorts and an oversized tee.

I tug my hair free from the bun on the top of my head, combing my fingers through it. Once I'm in bed, I call for Reid.

In no time, he's standing in my doorway, forearm resting on the door frame. His eyes find mine. I pat the space next to me, silently beckoning him to come lay down too.

He does. Kicking off his boots at the foot of my bed, he climbs on next to me. I flick off the lamp on my bedside table.

"Thank you for staying," I whisper.

"You're welcome," Reid murmurs.

"You'll lock up when you leave?" I clarify.

Reid laces his fingers through mine, beneath the blanket. "Mm-hmm," he hums his agreement.

The last thing I remember before drifting off is Reid towering over me, brushing hair off my face and planting a soft kiss on my forehead.

I fully expect him to be gone when I wake up, but when I come out of my room in the morning, I find the food and bottles from last night cleaned up and Reid curled up on the couch under the hundred-year-old quilt.

He stayed.

CHAPTER TWELVE

REID

I HEAR EMERY moving around before I see her, but I pretend to be asleep. I didn't mean to fall asleep on the couch. I meant to clean up and lock the door behind me. But just as I was about to leave, I heard her cry out in her sleep. I hesitated, my hand on the doorknob the way a parent might before going into their crying child's room. Her cries were muffled for a few more moments before they stopped, but it was too late. I was already kicking off my boots again, making myself comfortable. I couldn't bear the thought of her waking up in the night, terrified and alone. *Shit.* I'm so fucked.

"Reid," Emery whispers, leaning over me. Her blond hair tickles my face, and her warm palm finds my bare chest. My eyelids flutter open at the contact, and suddenly I'm desperate to see what she looks like fresh out of bed. "I thought you left last night," she says, a smile curving the corners of her mouth.

"I tried to," I say, sitting up. The truth is, I sat on the couch and watched an episode of Dateline after I heard her cries, telling myself I'd go home when it was over, but I was never really going home. Emery sits next to me, her hand mere centimeters from mine. I want to hold it, but without the alcohol haze from last night, I'm not sure if my touch would be welcome. "You were crying in your sleep. I didn't want to leave you."

Emery's face shifts into something I can't read. She bites her lower lip. "Thank you." She nods. "Really." Then she puts her warm palm on mine, and the sizzle between us makes me immediately react. I turn to her, startling her, and I can see that she feels it too. That there's something between us here—something I haven't felt in years. Desperate to keep people, women especially, at arm's length, I haven't allowed myself to feel anything for anyone. Everything is compartmentalized with clear boundaries. If it doesn't serve a purpose, it doesn't belong. I keep my walls high and my trust scarce because I can't afford to be vulnerable. It never bothered me before now. Now, I suddenly, desperately, feel like something is missing from my life. A void I didn't know I had.

I fight the urge to pull her to me. Instead, I clear my throat and stand. "What time is it? I was supposed to open the marina."

"It's seven," Emery says. "Or a little after."

"Shit," I mutter. "I'm late."

"Sorry." Emery winces.

I slip into my boots and move back toward her, cradling her face. "No. Do not for a second be sorry. We're in this together, okay?" I lick my lips at the same time Emery's breath hitches, and I drop my hands.

"Okay." Her voice comes out as a whisper.

I straighten, taking a step back. "What are you going to do today?"

"I don't know..." Emery's voice wavers. "I'm a little nervous to go back to the research center."

"It's worse if you don't go." I meet her eyes. "Don't go back into the marsh until I can go with you."

"I really don't want to," she admits. "But I have to check my traps. I can't leave the turtles in there."

I push my lips together. "Let me make a call."

I open Emery's front door and go out onto the porch, dialing Tate as I pull it closed behind me.

"Reid, everything okay?" Tate answers on the first ring. Probably because I'm supposed to be at the marina and he thinks something is wrong.

"Yeah. I'm late. I just wanted to give you a heads up."

"You? Late?" Tate barks out a laugh. "Are you seriously getting laid, dude?"

"No. Shut up. I overslept. Can you get over there?" My voice comes out as a growl.

"I guess," Tate drags out the word, trying to elicit guilt from me. "What's really going on with you?"

I let out a long, disgruntled sigh, debating how much to share with my oldest friend. "I have to help Emery with something. With the turtles."

"Turtles..." Tate repeats. "She's studying turtles? In the marsh?"

A knot forms in my throat. "She wants to pick up where Penny left off."

"She needs to be careful." Tate's voice is firm, edged with warning.

That's the understatement of the fucking year.

"She's fine." I brush him off. "I'll be in when we're done."

"Later." Tate hangs up.

When I get back inside, Emery hands me a cup of coffee and sits across from me at the table. She wraps both hands around her mug, gaze fixed on the surface, waiting. "Listen. I'm going to go in late so we can check your traps together." Really, I'm worried about her moving through the marsh and coming face to face with the man whose life was so easily discarded yesterday. I don't want that for her.

"Oh, Reid," Emery begins, like she wants to resist, but then thinks better of it. "Thank you."

We finish our coffee and slip into waders before making for the dock. Emery doesn't stop me when I climb into the driver's seat, taking the lead. We slowly maneuver the curve of the marsh, neither of us saying much. I don't know about Emery, but I can't stop thinking about last night and the way her body fit against mine. I wanted nothing more than to carry her to bed, kiss her, taste her, make us both forget what we saw. But the moment wasn't right, and I don't make promises I can't keep. There's no denying that something is brewing between us, but the more I get to know Emery, the more I care for her, which makes this all the more dangerous.

"We're approaching the dock," I warn, wanting Emery to prepare herself for whatever we might find. But as we slowly creep by, there is nothing. No body. No blood. No sign there was a struggle just over twenty-four hours ago. Either the tide came in high today, or someone came and moved it. I'm betting the latter.

"There's nothing here," Emery says slowly, shaking her head in disbelief. "Did we dream it?"

I huff a low laugh, shaking my head. "No, we definitely didn't dream it."

"Then where did he go?" Emery's voice wavers. "Maybe he wasn't dead?"

I press my lips together, shaking my head. "No. More than likely someone moved him. They knew they were seen, and they're covering their tracks."

Emery pales, and I kill the engine, reaching for her hands. "Listen to me. This is good. It's not in your backyard anymore. You don't have to worry about seeing it. I will figure this out for us. Okay? Take a breath with me." I demonstrate a slow cleansing breath, and she mimics me. "Okay? Let's find these traps."

"Okay," Emery says, nodding. "You're right. This is good." She meets my gaze. "Now I don't need my bodyguard coming out here with me every day." She bites back a smile.

"Yeah. You do." I fix my eyes on her, first her mouth, then her blue eyes.

I give the choke a hard pull and start us up again, but we move slowly through the turtle's nesting zone. While I steer, Emery pulls on a pair of latex gloves. As we reach the area, she leans out, gripping the edge of a floating trap.

"Need help?" I ask, eyeing her.

She ignores me, hauling it up with both hands and sloshing water over the hull.

"There you are," she says to the turtles inside. One lifts its head, blinking slowly, its shell no bigger than her palm. Their shells are smooth and dark, etched with pale rings and streaked with marsh mud.

"Can you hand me my bag?" she asks.

I toss it to her, and she pulls a notebook out. Pushing her sleeves to her elbows, she picks up each turtle one-by-one, speaking aloud everything she jots down. "Three juveniles, 1-2 years old. A male and two females. Just little babies."

I watch her note shell texture, weight, the faint abrasions along the edges—details I'd never think to look for.

"Shells in good condition, smooth and glossy. Some scuff marks. No lesions or scarring present. A bit light for their size," she says, writing it all down before looking up at me. "Still think I needed help?" she teases.

"I didn't say you couldn't do it. I was being nice," I say defensively.

She grins, quick and sharp. She's not shy or sweet when it comes to her work, just confident.

Emery turns back to the turtles, humming softly as she scans the individual shells for markings and jots down more notes. She reaches in her bag and removes three tags, fastening one to each shell before setting the turtles free. I watch her longer than I probably should, her every move pulling me in deeper as she checks the numbers twice before writing them down.

"The tags will tell me where they go," she says quietly. "And where they stop."

I marvel at her, hoping I'm not too obvious.

This gorgeous woman doesn't need a damn thing from me. She's smart, strong, resilient. And for reasons I can't yet name, that makes me want to give her everything.

CHAPTER THIRTEEN

EMERY

A FEW DAYS have passed since the *incident*—that's what I'm calling it. I don't know how else to refer to it that won't make me spiral. Each day, I've woken up before dawn. Reid meets me at my dock and steers the skiff into the marsh so I can check my traps and tag my turtles. Things have been eerily quiet, but instead of letting that freak me out, I'm choosing to let it make me feel safe. I may be delusional.

Reid has been a source of comfort for me—I think we're actually becoming friends. He still doesn't tell me anything personal but occasionally, he'll drop a tidbit about his time as a SEAL, and I see glimpses of the gentle man beneath his gruff exterior. Afterward, he takes me to the research center and goes to work at the marina. It's like we're a pair, only not. Reid has made it his personal mission to see that I'm safe and that much I can appreciate.

This morning, I decide not to go right to the research center. It's taken me a couple of days, but with how quiet it's been, I feel safe to go alone a little later. What I don't tell Reid is, I think I'm ready to look at the photos on my camera from that night. I kick off my waders at the door, leaving them on the screened porch and powering up my laptop on the kitchen table. While it comes alive, I make myself another cup of coffee. If it weren't for the *incident,* Tidehaven would feel peaceful. I hadn't realized how much I needed to step back from the rat race. Now that I'm here, I appreciate the quiet. And yet, the calm feels conditional—the quiet soothes me, but it also makes room for thoughts I can't quite rationalize. I can't reconcile the stillness with what I *know* I saw, only that both exist here at once. Beauty and something broken. Peace layered thin over something I don't yet understand.

My phone buzzes loudly from the table, startling me. Lena.

"Hey, Leen," I say, cradling the phone to pour creamer in my cup.

"Just making sure you're still alive," Lena jokes. The irony is not lost on me.

I huff a laugh. "I'm alive and kicking. What's up?"

"Not much. Same old. The department is quiet since classes let out. I'm only teaching a couple of summer classes. Alan has the other two. I think that's it. It's boring around here. I miss my beach buddy." Lena sounds dejected.

"You know," I say, pulling out my chair. "I'm starting to like boring."

"Well, you have no choice out there in the middle of nowhere," Lena retorts.

I cradle the phone and plug in the camera's cord to the side of my laptop. A bunch of thumbnails fill the screen. I hit import without looking. It usually takes a few minutes.

"How's your research coming along?" Lena asks.

I let out an audible breath, debating how much to tell her. "Good, I think. There is definitely a population decline. But I've started tagging the turtles and tracking their locations and their habits. It feels like undergrad again."

"That's good," Lena says, her voice a bit too bright.

I click on the first thumbnail and begin absentmindedly flipping through my photos—first of the traps, and the locations, then the nesting areas.

"So, I saw Jason at the grocery store, ironically," Lena starts slowly. "He...doesn't look good."

I'm about to reply when my eyes catch on the last photo—a

blurry picture of the dock, a sliver of a boat in the background. I don't remember taking it. Maybe when I dropped the camera, it went off. I zoom in on the lettering on the back of the boat. It's a bit hard to read, but I know I've seen it before. The only letters I can make out read, *ss Tidehaven.* My pulse picks up. I know I've seen this boat before.

"Em, are you there?" Lena asks. "Did you hear me about Jason?"

Panic rushes through me, my heart hammers in my chest. "Just...hold on a sec," I mutter, squinting at my screen.

ss Tidehaven. What is the rest of that word?

Then it hits me like a freight train. *Miss Tidehaven.* I can picture it clearly. The boat is a large center console fishing boat I've seen in the marina. What the hell would a boat of that size be doing in the marsh before dawn? I swallow the tightening in my throat.

"Did you hear me? I saw Jason. He doesn't look good." Lena repeats, enunciating her words, waiting for my reaction.

"I...heard you," I breathe, my voice barely above a whisper. "Can I call you back, Leen?"

"Uh, sure." Lena doesn't bother to hide her annoyance.

"I'm sorry, it's just something came up. I'll call you tonight." I slam my laptop closed and race to my room for my sneakers.

"Okay, Em. Talk to you later," Lena says, and then she's gone.

I don't have time to worry about it. I slip into my shoes without untying them, toss my hair up, and run out the door.

It takes me exactly seven minutes to run to the marina. I find Reid and standing with another man, who I presume to be Tate outside the bait shop. They appear to be talking closely.

I slow my pace as I approach. Reid looks up, concern immediately creasing his brow.

"Emery," he says, his voice gruff. "I thought you weren't coming in today. This is Tate."

I glance at Tate. "Nice to meet you, officially." A beat passes before I clear my throat and flick my gaze back to Reid. "Can I talk to you? In my office."

Tate lets out a snort, a glint of amusement in his eyes. "Have at it," he says with a smirk.

Reid gives him a shove and takes a step toward me, his palm finding my lower back. He hasn't touched me since the night when I found comfort in his embrace. I force myself to ignore the sizzle beneath his fingertips.

Reid unlocks the blue door, and we step into the lab. He drops his hand and pulls out a stool at the lab table, taking a seat. "What's up?"

My façade crumbles, and I begin involuntarily trembling before I'm even able to get words out. Reid hesitates, his lip tugged between his teeth, almost like he's fighting back the urge to reach out and steady me.

"I finally looked at my photos from...the *incident*." I swallow audibly.

"And?" Reid asks, tipping his chin toward me, a slight quirk of his eyebrow.

"And...who owns the *Miss Tidehaven*?" I begin nervously gnawing at my bottom lip.

Reid's jaw tics, his shoulders stiffening. A rapid and noticeable change from concern to defensiveness. "Why?"

"I can't say for sure, but I somehow got an accidental photo of the end of the dock—probably when I dropped my camera. And that boat is in the background of the photo. It's blurry, but I'm certain it's the one." I'm rambling now, fiddling with the hem of my T-shirt.

Reid studies me for a long beat before his head tips in denial. "No. It can't be. You're wrong." His jaw is set.

"I'm not, I'll show you," I say, my voice wavering. Panic prickles up my chest, heat pressing at the back of my eyes. "You have to believe me." *We're supposed to be a team*, I want to say. I bite it back.

Reid exhales hard, frustration etched in every line of his face. "Beau Rigsby is a lot of things, Emery, but a killer isn't one of them.

Trust me."

My pulse pounds so hard, I'm certain he hears it. "Maybe someone else used his boat. It's flimsy but not impossible."

Reid rakes a hand through his beard and steps in front of me, his hands settling firmly on my shoulders. His gaze locks with mine. "Emery, listen to me. Really listen."

I force myself to swallow and nod. "Okay."

"Leave this alone. You've got to leave it alone." His tone softens, almost pleading. "It's for your safety and mine. *Stop* digging."

"But why? Reid, I can't get the image out of my head." My voice cracks then and I know I'm going to cry.

Reid sees it coming. In the next breath, I'm folded against his chest, his arms cinched tight around me.

I give in, letting the tears fall as I sag into him, wondering for the first time since I got here if I should just go home. Leave all of this behind.

Reid's palm finds the back of my head, his fingers weaving gently through my ponytail. "Promise me," he murmurs in my ear. "Just track your turtles and move on."

I sniffle, pressing my face into his shirt, comforted by his familiar scent. "I'll try," I whisper.

Reid pulls back, brushing a tear from my cheek with his thumb. A small smile pulls at his normally frowny face. "Why don't I come by tonight? Let you beat me at Jeopardy."

A shaky laugh escapes through my tears and I nod. "I'd like that."

He steps back, and I immediately miss his warmth. I don't bother to scold myself for it this time.

"I'll see you at seven. I'll bring dinner." His eyes linger on mine before he finally turns for the door.

CHAPTER FOURTEEN

REID

I LEAVE EMERY alone in the lab because if I don't get out of there, I'm going to do something stupid. I've had to talk myself out of wanting her every day for the past three weeks. Tate would tell me to fuck her and get it out of my system, but it's much more complicated than that. I'm not sure I'll ever be able to get Emery out of my system.

And fuck if she didn't just accuse Beau Rigsby—or someone using his boat—of the murder in the marsh. I promised Beau we'd look into his concerns, doubting we'd find anything. Now I'm not so sure. But I've been wrong before, and it led to major mistakes. As a result of that, I've ignored my instincts and lost someone I cared about. My mind is a mess, but the fact remains—I don't trust my own judgment and I'm not sure what to do about it yet.

"Your shirt is wet," Tate says, eyeing me suspiciously. He's right where I left him, leaning against the bait shop's tattered cedar shake wall.

I pull down the hem of my shirt to look. There, in a perfect Emery-sized spot, are her tear stains, just below my peck, darkening my light gray T-shirt.

"Huh," I say. "Must've leaned on the sink."

Tate rolls his eyes. "Right. What sink comes up to your chest, bro?"

"I don't know, man. Why are you on me?" I walk past him,

down the dock to check the log, Emery's suspicions weighing on me.

Tate follows me though, falling in step beside me before I can get a good lead. "What's going on with you and the doctor?" His eyes glimmer with amusement, and I realize he thinks something *good* is going on.

"Nothing," I say with enough force that I hope it's convincing.

"Hey man, I'm just happy for you. You've been moping around this place for two years without so much as looking at a woman." Tate shrugs. "I'm not trying to be nosy."

At this I exhale, letting my guard down. Tate's not wrong, and if I'm suddenly spending time with Emery like this, he's bound to think something is up. Everyone will. "Nothing has even happened yet."

At this, Tate looks oddly pleased with himself. "Yet."

"I'm just helping her with the turtle stuff." I move to the booth and start flipping through the day's log. I don't even know what I'm looking for. Tate leans against the booth watching me.

"I'm just glad to see you getting back out there again." Tate lets out a low chuckle then glances my way.

I'm skimming the logs from this morning's arrivals and departures. Everything looks ordinary, nothing out of place. I flip back to yesterday, careful not to go too far—if I dig a week back, Tate will know I'm fishing for something. His gaze presses against my shoulders, making it harder to concentrate.

"Anyone keeping an eye on things at night?" I ask, forcing evenness into my tone. "Before we're open?"

Tate shifts, his easy grin faltering. "Not really. Griff used to, but he's old. I lock up and one of us comes back at dawn. Maybe a cop strolls through, but he's not counting boats."

I nod, turning a page, my finger trailing down a neat column of slips. "So, if somebody cast off at, say, three a.m., that wouldn't show here."

"Reid," he says, my name edged with a warning. "This is Tidehaven, not a naval base. Folks head out before sunrise all the time. Especially the crabbers. They're out before dawn most days. I don't write down every time they come and go or I'd never sleep." I recognize the defensiveness in Tate's voice but it's not sharp. More like, he thinks I'm accusing him of not running his side of things right.

"I was just curious," I say, closing the log. I don't look at him, instead casting my gaze across the still water of the back bay.

Tate studies me, his brow furrowed. "You're digging at something, Morgan. I've known you long enough to know when you're holding back."

I turn and meet his eyes but don't give him anything. "Old habits."

He studies me, and in that silence, I can feel the weight of our years. Two boys pulling crab traps up from this very dock, growing into men building lives in the same town. Then Tate lets out a breath and shakes his head. "You ever decide to trust me with what's really going on, I'll be here. Till then, quit looking at me like I'm blind."

I nod once, unable to answer. Because the truth is, I don't know yet if he's blind or just looking the other way.

I PULL UP to Emery's just before seven, a pizza in one hand and a half gallon of cookie dough ice cream in the other. The door swings open before I can knock. I lift them in offering. "Brought provisions."

Emery reaches out, taking the shopping bag with ice cream and peering inside. "Where's the beer?"

I smirk, peering down at her. "Sometimes we have to choose not to drink our feelings away, Doc."

Emery marches to the kitchen and shoves the ice cream in the freezer. When she spins back, her eyes flash. "In case you haven't noticed, numbing my feelings is the only way I'm getting by lately."

Guilt tugs in my chest. I should be doing more to help her

through this than showing up with food. "Well, I'm here now. Let me distract you."

As soon as I've said it, I realize how it sounds. Emery does too because a pink blush slowly creeps across her chest. "Whatever," she says, plopping in a chair. She flips open the pizza box and tears into a slice, devouring it in three bites.

I laugh, shaking my head. "What are you a caveman? Where are the plates?"

"Cabinet next to the stove. Help yourself." Emery juts a greasy thumb over her shoulder before grabbing another slice.

I grab the plates and drop them on the table before moving into the open living room and flicking on the TV. Jeopardy's theme song blares. I turn back to Emery, and she's watching me, a half-eaten piece of pizza dangling in her hand.

"You look good here—comfortable," she says quietly.

I clear my throat crossing back to her and taking a seat beside her. "Penny—Dr. Young—and I were friends."

Her eyebrows lift. "Friends? Or *friends*?"

I bark out a laugh. "The former. She was like sixty. But I helped her with things around here. We got to know each other."

Emery chews slower this time, thoughtful. "How did she die?"

A tight breath leaves me. "They ruled it a suicide, but..." I hesitate, reaching for a slice.

Her eyes sharpen. "But...you don't think it was?"

I shrug, biting into the crust. "I don't know. She never seemed depressed to me."

Emery's voice is soft. "Well, that's the thing about depression. It hides. You never know what people are going through."

Her phone buzzes against the table. A name flashes. *Jason.*

We both see it. She doesn't move.

"Boyfriend?" I ask too quickly. Of course she has a boyfriend.

"Ex." She exhales, shoulders slumping. "It's...recent." Her face contorts from confusion to something bordering sadness.

"Do you want to talk about it?" The words surprise me as

much as her. Talking about feelings isn't my style—she's only been here three weeks, and even she knows that.

She sets the half-eaten slice she's holding back in the box and tugs her knees up to her chest. "There's not much to say. We have different priorities. I never felt supported or..." She pauses, the words stuck in her throat. "Cherished. We were just going through the motions—stagnant. This opportunity came up, and I took it for what it is...a chance to reset and figure out what I want."

I pull my bottom lip between my teeth. Her gaze locks with mine. "So, why is he texting you now?"

She glances at the screen, then slides the phone toward me. Four words glow. *I made a mistake.*

"Damn right he did," I say, pushing the phone back.

The corners of her mouth lift and warmth flickers in my chest.

"Hey, Jeopardy is half over." I say, standing and heading for the couch. "I guess you're not beating me tonight."

"There's always tomorrow." A moment later, Emery drops beside me with the ice cream carton and two spoons. She curls her legs under, shoulder pressed warm against mine. The contact makes my skin hum with electricity.

"Now you want to eat straight from the carton?" I give her a mock frown. "Savage."

Her laugh bursts out, full and unguarded. She thrusts a spoon at me. "Take it or leave it."

I grin, accepting the spoon. "I'll definitely take it."

CHAPTER FIFTEEN

EMERY

"WANT TO WATCH a movie?" I ask. Jeopardy has been over for forty minutes, but Reid is still here. The ice cream has turned soupy, and our fingers are sticky. Each time our forearms brush together as we battle our spoons together for the piece of cookie dough, my heart races a little bit more. Jeopardy was our excuse to see each other, but I realize now, I don't want him to leave.

Reid shifts his body to face mine and suddenly our knees are touching. *That's* what strikes me as oddly intimate, even though we've been eating ice cream from the carton together, double dipping repeatedly.

He's quiet for a beat, making me nervous that he'll say no. I pick up the ice cream, place the lid on top and return it to the freezer. I come back with wet paper towels for our fingers and the old coffee table where the ice cream dripped.

"I should probably get going," he finally says.

My face betrays me then. It's not that I'm afraid to be alone anymore. I have felt better the past few days. It's that I'm enjoying his company so much.

"It's just that, I have to open tomorrow. I've dropped the ball on Tate this week too many times already." Reid scratches his jaw.

"Okay," I say, keeping my distance. "I want to get out to the marsh before first light anyway. I should probably get some sleep."

Reid doesn't move, his eyes finding mine. Instead, he relaxes into the couch and pats the spot I just got up from. "How about...I stay for another hour, and we just talk? Continue getting to know each other."

I smirk. "You hate talking."

Reid scoffs, shaking his head. "I do not hate talking."

I smirk, crossing my arms. "Reid, I've been here for three weeks, and I already know that about you." I grin.

Reid looks away, setting his gaze on a State Farm Insurance commercial before flicking his eyes back to mine. "For reasons I can't explain...I don't hate talking to *you*."

It's raw and honest, and it makes me want to climb in his lap. Instead, I walk back to the kitchen, grabbing two bottles of water from the fridge. I hand him one and settle myself on the other end of the couch, straightening my legs out so the tips of my heels just graze his thigh. His very large, rock-hard thigh.

Reid takes a swig of cold water, letting out an *ahh* sound before placing it on the end table. Then his large palms circle my right foot, kneading the arches and eliciting a moan out of me.

Reid looks my way, a flush creeping up his neck. "I was going to rub your feet but not if you make noises like that."

A laugh bubbles out of me. "Noises like what?"

"You know. That moan that just came out of you. I can't have that."

"Oh no?" I frown, attempting to pull my foot back but Reid tightens his grip. "And just why not?"

"Emery." Reid's voice comes out like a rasp, husky and filled with everything I'm feeling inside.

"Reid," I whisper.

"What's your favorite color?" His lips quirk and I appreciate the change of subject. There's an electric charge between us that it seems we're both desperately trying to fight. Suddenly, I can't remember why.

"Sea foam green. What's yours?"

"Black." His answer is automatic.

"Like your soul?" I tease.

"Very funny." He digs his thumb into my foot playfully and I let out a little yelp.

"Favorite band?" I purse my lips.

"Pearl Jam." Another auto answer. "You?"

"I like all music," I admit with a tip of my shoulder. "I don't really have a favorite."

"Song then." Reid waits, studying me.

I pretend to mull this over, but I don't even have to think about it. "Into the Mystic by Van Morrison."

A smile tugs at the corners of his mouth. "Figures you'd pick a song about the sea. It suits you, Doc."

"Thanks." A soft smile pulls at my lips.

Reid's thumbs work in slow circles over the arch of my left foot before he moves back to my right. He kneads, strong and careful at the same time, watching me, and I let my eyes flutter closed. The room is quiet except for the hum of the old fridge in the kitchen and my own uneven breathing.

"This is the first time in weeks I've felt human," I murmur.

"Guess I've still got some skills besides hauling in boats and fixing engines." His voice is low, almost teasing, but there's something real beneath it. Reid slides an index finger up the length of my foot, tracing a circle around my ankle before moving up my calf, tickling behind my knee.

I squeal, jerking my foot back.

"What?" Reid's brow pulls tight.

I bite down a laugh. "You tickled me."

The corner of his mouth twitches, like he knows. "Did not."

"You did." I wiggle my toes on his thigh, and he catches my foot before I can pull it back again. His hands wrap around my ankle, pulling me closer until I sit up, a jolt running straight through me.

The playful air shifts, now sharp and charged with longing. His grip softens but he doesn't let go and in one unthinking movement, I slide into his lap, my knees bent awkwardly and my breath caught in my throat.

Reid's hands find my hips, almost instinctively, steadying me. Then my legs are on either side, straddling him. I grip the collar of his worn T-shirt.

"Careful," he rasps, but he doesn't sound careful at all.

My pulse thrums. We're too close, our faces inches apart, his breath warm against my cheek. Every reason I should stay away from Reid dissolves under the weight of his touch.

"Emery." His voice is rough, jagged and sexy. "We shouldn't."

"I know...but I can't remember why."

For a long, suspended moment, neither of us moves. Reid's jaw tics as my fingers curl into his shirt, our breaths synchronized and desperate. And then his mouth is on mine.

The first brush of his lips steals the breath from my lungs. It's not tentative, it's urgent, restrained only by his desire to remain in control. I feel him harden beneath me, and I press myself into him, eliciting a throaty groan from him. He tastes like salt and the faintest hint of cookie dough ice cream, and when his hand slides higher up my waist, I let myself melt into him.

Every thought, every doubt about what this might be, scatters. All that exists is the press of his mouth, the rough scrape of his beard against my skin, and the ragged sound he makes when I kiss him back. It's reckless, but it was inevitable, like the tide pulling me under. Reid opens deeper for me, his mouth slanting over mine with a hunger that makes my thighs ache. I cling to him, running my fingers up the buzzed hair at the nape of his neck.

Reid nips at my lower lip and pulls back, resting his forehead on mine. His breath is still ragged, his chest rising hard beneath my hands.

"Emery," he says, my name on his lips is gravel and restraint, a warning and a plea all at once.

I swallow, my heart crashing against my ribs. The room tilts, the thick air filled with everything we've both been fighting since the day we met. I should move, I should say something intelligent, remind myself of all the reasons this is dangerous. But my body betrays me, and I lean into him instead of away.

"I—I..." My voice cracks, too soft. "I shouldn't want this."

"Yeah," Reid says, brushing a thumb against my waist. "Me neither."

But neither of us lets go.

I fold into him, my body still humming, my lips swollen. Reid's hands draw lazy circles on my lower back, like he can't seem to make himself stop touching me.

I open my mouth to speak but I can't find the words. All that comes out is a shaky exhale.

Reid draws back an inch, peering down at my face as if he's memorizing it. His jaw is tight, his eyes dark green with a fire that makes my stomach flip. For a moment, I think he might kiss me again, drown us both in the inevitability of it all. Instead, he presses a kiss to my forehead, his lips soft and warm.

"I should go," he murmurs. His hands linger at my waist for a moment longer before he gently lifts me off and stands. "I'll see you in the morning. Before first light." His voice is low, rough with want, and when his eyes lock with mine, I see the desperation to stay.

He turns for the door, bracing one hand against the frame, his knuckles white. He pauses, taking deep breaths for a moment before looking back at me. Our eyes lock and the heat in his gaze is enough to buckle my resolve—to make me run to him and pull him to my bed. But neither of us caves, and then he's gone, leaving me wondering what I could've done to make him want to stay.

CHAPTER SIXTEEN

REID

I DON'T SLEEP much after leaving Emery's cottage. It took everything in me not to turn around and go right back inside. I can't explain this hold she has on me. Maybe it's just that I've been alone for so long. Maybe I'm finally ready for a partner. Maybe we're bonding over the trauma of what we saw. But Emery? She's not in a place for this. She's here on borrowed time. If not for those early morning hours in the marsh two weeks ago, we probably wouldn't even be as close as we are.

I am usually good at compartmentalizing my thoughts and emotions. Clear cut, black and white boxes. I don't typically get attached to women I see—though admittedly, it's been a while—and I like to think I could keep my head in this game. But I still know it's a bad idea. I tell myself all of this as I head down the wooded path to her dock at five-thirty a.m. Not even twelve hours after I kissed her. If I don't keep repeating the reasons, I'll have my hands on her the second I see her.

My pulse jumps when I spot her. She's waiting at the edge of the dock, headlamp strapped to her battered university cap, an oversized hoodie swallowing her up. Somehow, she looks perfect.

When she sees me, she meets me halfway. "Hi," she murmurs.

"Hi."

"Listen—"

"About last night." We speak at the same time.

A quick smile curves on her lips, and she gestures toward me. "You first."

"No, you." I figure it's safer.

"I was just going to say I'm sorry I threw myself at you. You totally didn't ask for it, and I'm mortified. So, if we could just forget it happened, that would be great." She bites her lip, eyes darting up to mine.

I laugh softly, shaking my head. "Emery, you didn't throw yourself at me. That kiss was mutual. I haven't wanted someone like that in...a long time."

Her lips part, but only a small "oh" slips out.

I push past the tightness in my throat. "But if you're uncomfortable, if you want to keep things professional, I'll respect that." Even as I say it, the lie sits heavy in my chest. Professional is the last thing I want with her.

"M-maybe that's for the best," Emery stammers, but regret flickers across her face.

I nod, sucking in a breath and stepping around her toward the skiff. "Shall we?"

"Reid." Her voice stops me. I turn, meeting her gaze in the thin gray light of dawn.

"I'm sorry," she whispers.

A sad smile finds my lips. "You've got nothing to be sorry for."

"So, WHAT ARE we looking for today?" I ask, steering the skiff through the still half-dark marsh, mist curling at the surface. Dawn is slowly creeping in, turning the water shades of gray and rose.

"I'm losing signals on some of these turtles. One of my transmitters must be out. The battery life is short on these. It probably just needs to be reset." Emery stands as the skiff enters the turtle's nesting zone. "There," she points to a PVC pole jutting just above the grass line. "Kill the engine, will you?"

I follow her line of sight. To me, it looks like nothing more than a stick in the mud.

Emery is already pulling on thigh high waders and nitrile gloves.

"What are you doing? Can't you just check it from here?" I frown. "You really need to risk sinking out there?"

"I don't have X-ray vision," she says, quirking her eyebrows. "If it makes you feel better, you can get us a little closer." She tucks a small notebook and pencil into the pocket of her hoodie while I grab the oars and move us closer.

She pauses to snap a couple of photos of our surroundings. Then, clipping her waterproof camera to her chest, she swings a leg over the side of the boat.

Before I can argue, she's off, marsh water climbing to her knees, mud sucking her boots as she wades toward the pole.

"It'll just take a sec," she calls over her shoulder. But she falters. Movement near the reeds sends a jolt of alarm straight through me. I climb out of the boat before I can think better of it, wading straight to her.

When I reach her, she's crouched down, holding a turtle and closely examining its shell.

"It's one of mine," she says, shaking her head in confusion. "I tagged her three weeks ago, but..." She swallows audibly. "Someone cut it off."

"Cut it off?"

"See here, the epoxy scar is jagged, raw against the carapace, the transmitter is gone." Emery frowns, shaking her head. "And this chalky white stuff..."

"That's not mud," I state the obvious. "Look." I point to the reeds behind her. More of the chalky residue clings to the grass, forming cloudy patches where the mud meets the shore. I suck in a breath, realizing the air has a faint chemical tang.

I move closer, and a scrap of plastic between the reeds catches the light—thin, torn, half-buried in the muck. It looks like the corner of a vacuum-sealed bag, with jagged edges and a strip of silver tape hanging off like it was ripped open. The rest of the package is gone. Probably washed away, but the white residue remains, clinging to the marsh grass, swirling in milky clouds when the breeze stirs the water.

"Oh my God." Emery's hands tremble as she lifts her headlamp for a clearer look. The residue glows white in the light of her headlamp. She turns her attention back to the turtle. "I need photos before I move her."

She fumbles with her waterproof camera slung across her chest, snapping quick shots from every angle.

"There's a plastic carrier in the boat. Can you get it for me?" she asks, her voice laced with worry.

"Sure." I rise quickly, trudging back to the skiff just twenty feet away. I return a few moments later, passing her the ventilated plastic carrier lined with damp towels.

Emery opens it, carefully lowering the turtle inside and clicking the lid shut.

"Em, you know what that is, don't you? On her shell, in the reeds?" I ask, my voice low and sharp.

Emery swallows hard, hugging the carrier close. "I'll swab it to confirm. But yes."

The marsh is too quiet—the only sound is the faint cry of the gulls in the distance.

"Then we need to move," I say. "Because whoever left that for your turtle to find? They'll definitely be back to clean up their mess."

THE HUM OF refrigeration units fills the lab as Emery flicks on the lights, immediately shifting into action. I lock the door behind us while Emery pulls on a fresh pair of gloves and covers a metal tray with damp towels.

My eyes immediately dart to the windows, scanning for any danger that might have followed us here.

"First step is documenting," Emery says, snapping more

photos. "Tag scar here," she murmurs, angling the shell under the light.

I watch as she snaps photos from every angle, moving in closer with each shot.

"And residue."

I move to her side as she picks up a sterile swab and carefully drags it across a chalky streak. Sliding it into a vial, she adds a chemical to it in small drops. For a moment, nothing happens. Then the liquid blushes blue.

I let out a breath. "What does that mean?"

"Cocaine. Confirmed." Emery doesn't look at me, her gaze fixed on the little turtle as she cleans her up.

My shoulders tense. This is a truth that feels like it's been waiting for me. "Damn it. I knew this shit was going down," I mutter. "Didn't have proof till now."

Emery jerks her eyes to me before carefully setting the vial down. "Then we take this to the authorities. Someone has to know. If there is cocaine residue on one of my turtles and in the reeds then...it's got to be in the water, hurting the wildlife. Someone is using or running drugs through their habitat." She gives me a pleading look.

"No." My voice is sharp and final, and my whole body feels tight.

She turns on me, stunned. "What do you mean *no*? This is huge, Reid. Your friend, Dr. Young? She must've known this was happening even if she hadn't finished her research. This is not something we can ignore. We have evidence."

"And the second you show it, you paint a target on your back," I growl. "The council's in bed with the bastards running this, guaranteed. You think handing them a neat little sample fixes anything? It gets you silenced." I drag a hand down my face, pacing the room. Emery is right, Penny must have known. The revelation sends a shiver through me. If she knew, then that reinforces all my doubts about her death that I've buried deep inside. I can't face those fears—not yet.

Emery's face contorts from confusion to anger. "So, we just sit on this? Like we're sitting on the *murder* we witnessed?" she snaps.

"Lower your voice."

"Reid." Emery stares at me, all tenderness from last night gone from her eyes.

"We move quietly. Carefully. Let me talk to Colt. Just until I know who we can trust." I force my voice to remain steady.

The turtle shifts in its tray, claws tapping against steel—a reminder of the fragile, innocent life tangled up in something far bigger than the two of us. We both stare at it.

"Promise me, Em," I beg, my voice gentler. "I don't want anything to happen to you."

Emery doesn't meet my eyes. "I can't." Her voice wavers. "I can't promise that. And I wouldn't be doing the *job* I came here to do if I swept this under the rug."

I run my hand down my face, exasperated. "Have it your way, then. Don't say I didn't warn you."

I make for the door, refusing to look at her as she calls after me.

CHAPTER SEVENTEEN

EMERY

THE DOOR BARELY clicks shut behind Reid before silence sets in. I stand in the middle of the lab, arms wrapped around myself, watching the female juvenile turtle swim aimlessly around the tank.

I'm struggling to sort out the emotions surging through me. Last night, Reid kissed me like I am something precious to him. This morning, he is treating me like a liability. The swing between the two leaves a hollow ache in my chest. I want him here, steadying me, but he walked away. Because to him, keeping us safe means shutting this down.

My throat tightens. Maybe Reid can stay silent, but I can't. If I don't speak, the marsh stays poisoned—its wildlife pawns in someone else's careless game. The thought is unbearable.

I think about what Alan would do. I pick up my phone, scrolling to his name, my fingers hovering over the call button. Alan would understand both the science and the risk. I can hear his voice in my head. *Document everything. Collect the evidence. Don't jump until you know where to land.*

I sigh, dropping my phone back on the table. I won't bring Alan into it yet, but if it comes to it, I will. I will need back up. Someone to tell me I'm not crazy and it's worth the risk. For a brief instant, the image of the body in the marsh flashes in my mind, and I'm immediately nauseous. I shake my head to clear it. I have so many conflicting emotions.

I square my shoulders and pull my notebook closer, words just waiting to pour out of me.

Specimen T-1147. Transmitter forcibly removed. Residue tested presumptively positive for cocaine. Report to authorities.

I underline the last line.

Reid's warning echoes in my head—*You'll paint a target on your back.*

Maybe so, but what's the point of science if you bury the truth? I like science because it is cut and dry, indisputable. Data doesn't lie, and if I collect enough of it, no one can argue. In this case, it isn't just numbers in a spreadsheet—it's proof. Proof that might stop someone from hurting the marsh, from hurting the turtles and other wildlife.

I'll call Alan tomorrow. For now, I'll build my evidence, piece by piece, until no one can ignore it.

The turtle drifts in slow circles, its claws tapping faintly against the glass. I watch her move, my jaw tightening. "Don't worry," I murmur. "I'll figure this out."

I DON'T KNOW how long I've been compiling data. I haven't seen Reid since this morning. Save the sound of the filters and splashes from my turtle girl occasionally, the room has been silent for hours. It's two p.m. when the screen door slams shut, startling me. I'm instantly hopeful that it's him and annoyed at myself for being disappointed when it isn't.

"Hey, Doc!" Kayla calls, dropping her book bag on the counter. She immediately notices the turtle in the tank. "Aww, hey! A turtle." She ducks down, watching the reptile for a few moments.

I smile to myself, watching her, briefly forgetting the stress of the morning. I see so much of myself in Kayla. She's eager and enthusiastic, yes, but she really loves animals.

"Does she have a name?" Kayla spins around, grinning at me.

"A name? Specimen T-1147." I force a smile in return.

"No. She needs a *real* name." Kayla turns back, watching the turtle again closely. "How about Trixie?"

I huff a laugh. "Sure. Whatever you want." Turning back to my screen, I scroll through the data I've compiled on a chart that shows each turtle I've tagged.

"Hi Trixie," Kayla says softly. "So why is she here?" Her gaze is still fixed on the turtle.

"I brought her in for tests. She lost her tag." I try to keep the details vague.

"Lost it?" Kayla bends over the glass to get a closer look. "It looks like it was ripped off. And what's the white stuff on her shell?"

I sigh. "It's residue. I'm running tests."

Kayla looks up sharply. "That's so messed up. People are hurting the turtles and just get away with it?"

I blink at her. Kayla's anger burns hotter than I expected.

"I know what I said before," Kayla continues, folding her arms. "People don't like it when you start poking around the marsh. But if someone's actually hurting the animals..." She shakes her head. "You have to do something."

I swallow. "Like what?"

"Like...you could tell the town council. They have a meeting on Thursday night. My mom always goes. At the end, they let members of the community speak. You should go. Tell them about this. They might not care, but I know if anyone could make them, it's you." She crouches back down, watching Trixie again.

I force a smile. "Maybe."

Kayla's hands find her hips indignantly. "It's their job to protect this community. The marsh. Our waters. If they won't, then who will?"

LATE AFTERNOON LIGHT slants low over the marsh, turning the water coppery and bright. The heat has softened, cicadas humming like static as I step carefully through the eel grass, the transmitter heavy in my palm. Kayla's words echo in my mind the entire time I work. She's right. If I don't protect the environment, if I don't speak up, who will?

I crouch near the first trap, adjusting the tag and making a quick note on my waterproof clipboard. Everything looks normal. Reid was right—the packaging we saw earlier is gone. Someone cleaned up their mess, covered their tracks. I'm not sure if that's a good thing or a bad thing.

I'm reaching to tighten the strap on the transmitter when the prickling sense of awareness hits right between my shoulders. A feeling like I'm not alone out here.

I straighten slowly, memories of the darkness the marsh can carry sending a shiver up my spine. At first, I don't see anything. It's just grass swaying in the breeze, the marsh stretching quiet and wide around me. I spin in a circle, reassuring myself that I'm alone.

Then I spot him. A man, half-hidden by the tall grass maybe fifty yards out, standing still enough that I almost miss him. He's dressed plainly—dark shirt, boots muddy at the ankles—as if he's walked in from somewhere deeper in the marsh.

Watching me.

"Don't be ridiculous," I whisper to myself, even though my pulse is hammering so loud I can hear it. "No one is watching you."

This is Tidehaven. People fish, walk, wander. Maybe he's just curious as to what I'm doing out here alone.

I lift a hand and wave. "Nice day, isn't it?"

The sound carries farther than I expect, thin and exposed. The man doesn't respond. He doesn't wave back. He just looks at me—his gaze locking onto mine with an intensity that makes my smile falter. Maybe he didn't hear me.

For a beat too long, neither of us moves.

Then he turns to go. He doesn't hurry. He steps back into the grass and disappears on foot, swallowed by the green as if he was never there at all.

I stand frozen, listening for evidence that he's still here. Nothing but insects and the soft lap of water against mud. My heartrate settles with a few slow, deep breaths.

Probably a local, I tell myself. Someone checking crab pots. Surely no one is wondering what the new girl is up to.

I shake it off and crouch back down, finishing my adjustment and jotting another note. I don't have time to spook myself. Not now. I have real work to do if I'm going to build a presentation for the town council that will force *someone* to listen.

Still, as I sling my bag over my shoulder and head back toward the skiff, I glance once over my shoulder.

The marsh *looks* empty. And yet, the feeling lingers.

BY THE TIME Jeopardy comes on, Reid still hasn't called. He must be mad at me. I fight the urge to pick up the phone, beg him to come over, and let me beat him in our favorite game show. But I don't because somewhere deep down, I know he and I are not a good idea.

Meanwhile, Jason won't stop texting apologies. I've ignored him for days, but tonight I finally respond, needing to relieve some of the weight I'm carrying around. I tell him gently it's definitely over, that he should move on. His last reply—a simple "okay"—leaves me feeling guilty, my thoughts more tangled than before.

Jeopardy drones in the background as I curl under the grandma quilt, staring at the blank notebook in my lap. I'd come home from the lab, showered off the marsh muck, and pulled on my softest lounge set, determined to draft a letter to South Carolina Fish and Wildlife. But the page remains empty.

Reid's warning echoes in one ear. Kayla's insistence in the other.

Tell. Don't tell. Stay safe. Do the right thing.

A sudden knock rattles the door, making my pulse jump. I set the notebook aside, wishing for a peephole to see who's out there.

When I swing it open, Reid stares back, his hands shoved in his pockets and his expression unreadable.

"I wasn't expecting to see you," I say cautiously.

"Mind if I come in?" His expression is filled with the same yearning I feel in my chest.

"Sure." I step back, pulling the door wider for him to enter.

"You're watching without me." He nods at Jeopardy on the TV.

"It's background noise tonight." I fold my arms over my chest protectively.

We stand side by side, the glow of the TV painting us in blue light. For a long stretch we don't speak, instead listening to the contestants answering questions about world capitals and Shakespeare. Finally, Reid exhales, rubbing a hand over his beard.

"Em, about this morning." His voice is low and rough. "I shouldn't have walked out on you like that. That was...shitty."

The knot in my chest loosens and the corner of my mouth upturns. "Yeah, it was." I nod. "Thank you."

The apology hangs in the air for a beat. Then he turns, and before I can blink, his hands are cupping my jaw, pulling me in. The kiss is hard, hungry, the control we'd both clung to this morning burned away. I gasp against him as he walks me back, my shoulders pressing into the wall with a dull thud. His body crowds mine, his thigh parting my legs as he presses his hips into me. Our mouths are desperate, and for a dizzy, reckless moment, I let myself sink into it.

My hands fist in his shirt, my whole body thrumming with need. This is what I want: him choosing me, the two of us standing together.

But the words rise from my throat like bile, breaking the spell. "Reid." I pull apart from him, breathless. "I talked to Kayla today. She agrees with me."

"Emery—" Reid warns, stepping backward, breaking contact. "Why won't you let this go?"

I reach for his hand, desperate not to lose our connection but determined to make him see this my way. "We *need* to bring attention to this. It's hurting our wildlife. Kayla suggested the council meeting Thursday night." I continue, ignoring his protest.

"Emery, no." Reid recoils, backing further away from me, the heat in his eyes flaring into something sharper.

I narrow my own. "Why not? It wouldn't be a report. Just sharing data and my suspicions. You can't keep telling me to stay quiet. This is evidence. It matters."

Reid looks away and begins to pace, jaw tight, hands flexing at his sides. "You don't get it. The council isn't who you think they are. Marching in there with your slides and samples—"

"I can't ignore it," I argue.

"Well, I can't watch you do it. You'll only draw negative attention to yourself," he barks back, hard and final.

"So, you're going to make me go alone?" I hear the desperation in my voice, but I don't care to steady it.

"I don't know yet," he growls, turning away from me and rubbing the back of his neck. The silence is brutal.

Then he whirls back, fixing his eyes on mine. "This was a mistake. I have to go." He moves quickly, yanking open the door. And then he's gone.

CHAPTER EIGHTEEN

REID

I'M BACK IN the Gulf—salt burning my nose, the taste of brine thick on my tongue. Gunfire rattles in quick bursts, each shot vibrating through the sea like a drumbeat against my bones. The strobe of muzzle flashes filters down in fractured bursts of light, turning the water around me into a flickering grave.

A voice cuts through the comm in my ear, sharp and urgent. "Move, move—*" Then static. Then nothing.*

I twist in the dark water, straining to hear, lungs burning. Where's my team? I can't see them. Just shadows, a flash of limbs, the churn of bubbles that vanish too fast. My chest seizes. The silence is absolute now, swallowing everything. I'm alone.

I jolt awake, lungs heaving, my legs tangled in the sheets. My heart slams against my ribs, sweat beading along my hairline. My cabin is dark and still, but my pulse still refuses to slow. The silence feels like an enemy I can't see. I swing my feet to the floor, press my palms into my eyes, trying to breathe past the pounding in my chest. Nights like these don't come as often now, but when they do, they leave me stripped raw. Always when I'm under stress. Always when I let myself care too much.

I pace the room, practicing the box breathing I have worked so hard to master. The trigger isn't usually so clear cut, but it's easy to pinpoint this time: Emery. The way she looked at me when I kissed her. The way her eyes hardened in defiance when we fought.

The taste of her still lingers—soft, sweet, and desperate. The way her body fit against the wall beneath me. I want her with a hunger I haven't felt in years. I know she feels it too, this pull between us. She's hard for me to resist, which is why my restraint has evaporated twice now.

I'm taking it to the council, she had said. And she will too. She's tenacious and unrelenting.

"Fuck," I mutter.

Once again, I stormed out like an ass. All I'm trying to do is protect her, and she won't let me. She's brilliant, stubborn, and walking straight into danger. I don't have proof Penny was in trouble either, but she's gone. And between what Emery found in the marsh and the way Penny's death was written off so quickly, every instinct I have is screaming at me now. I don't know how to make her see that this is a bad idea.

Instinct has kept me alive more times than I can count. It's also failed me once.

Once, I hesitated. Questioned myself. Talked myself into believing I was seeing ghosts instead of danger. My CO paid for that pause with his life.

After that, I stopped trusting my gut completely—started chalking every red flag up to PTSD, to shadows where there weren't any. It's why I didn't push harder with Penny. Why I told myself she was safe, the old boys were just giving her a hard time. I was projecting.

And now Emery's standing in the same place—unwilling to be afraid—and the thought of being wrong again makes my chest feel too tight to breathe.

This is why I've not been able to sustain a relationship since my return. I am always on high alert. It's become my nature. But it's hard for me to explain why to the women I date, and I end up pushing them away. I don't want to push Emery away.

I drop into the chair by the window and stare at the shadowed marsh. I can still see her flushed cheeks, the fire in her eyes. I want her. God help me, I want her. But wanting her and protecting her don't line up, and I don't know what to do.

I fiddle with my phone and debate calling Tate. I know he has suspicions too. Maybe he'll have some insight. Ultimately, I decide against it. If I know Tate, he'll guess something's up before I can say a word.

I lean forward, bracing my elbows on my knees, breaths coming heavy. I could walk away, let her fight her fight, pretend I don't care. But I already know I won't. I couldn't stop caring now if I wanted to. And the thought of her standing in that chamber alone, with no one watching her back makes my chest clench.

I close my eyes, my jaw tight. I don't know if I'll stand beside her up there. But I do know I won't let her fight alone.

BY THE TIME I make it down to the marina, I know I look like hell. Coffee and a cold shower did nothing to hide the circles under my eyes. My boots drag a little on the weathered planks, gulls wheeling overhead and squawking ominously.

Tate's in the booth, the day's log open in front of him, flipping through columns of neat handwriting. He glances up, then does a double take and squints. "Jesus, Morgan, you look like shit."

"Didn't sleep," I mutter.

"Yeah, no kidding. You want to tell me what's got you wound so tight?"

I hesitate, leaning against the doorframe. "Emery found one of her turtles yesterday, the tag ripped clean off."

Tate's eyebrows shoot up, and he lets out a low whistle. "Shit. That's not good."

I push my lips together, shaking my head. "Nope. And what's worse, she wants to take it to the council. Tell them someone's messing with our wildlife."

That gets his full attention. Tate sets down his pen and fixes me with a look. "That's a terrible idea. You've got to stop her. You know how they are—she won't make it five minutes before they shut her down. Or worse."

My jaw tics, but before I can answer a deep-throated engine rumbles across the water. I glance toward the channel just as a familiar Hatteras Yacht noses toward the dock. Dale Langford stands at the bow, cocky grin on his stupid face, tossing a lazy wave, while his father, Warren, guides the wheel with the calm precision of a man who thinks he owns the whole damn town.

"Fuck," I growl.

"Let me handle this," Tate says, pressing the logbook to my chest. He slips past me, plastering on his easy smile as the boat edges into a visitor slip.

"Morning, boys," Dale drawls as he hops onto the dock, line in hand. He ties off with practiced ease, then turns with a smirk, his eyes finding me immediately like a hound scenting blood. "Workin' hard or hardly workin'?"

Tate straightens, smile thinning. "Something we can help you with, Dale?"

"Just checking in," he says, too casually. His gaze flicks to me, sharp and curious, sniffing at the edges of something he can't quite see but knows is there. "Always good to know who's coming and going."

That's what they always say. Like it's friendly. Like it isn't a warning.

It's then that I realize I'm still holding the damn logbook. My grip tightens before I toss it back into the booth and step out, squaring my shoulders.

"Good morning, gentlemen." Warren Langford steps down from the yacht, moving to stand beside his son. He wears the kind of polite smile that never touches his eyes.

"Mr. Langford." Tate nods. "What can I do for you?"

"We just wanted to introduce ourselves to the new director." Dale nods in the direction of the research center.

Tate glances at me, and I wonder if he's thinking what I'm thinking—how do they even know she's arrived? My teeth clench. I keep my expression flat, my body tight as a wire. Same old story just with a new face. They never cared about the science—only who occupied the land it sat on. If Dale suspects that Emery is poking around, if he even *sniffs* it, we're in deeper than I thought.

"Too bad," I say, my voice edged with warning. "She's not in today. Sick with the flu or something."

Dale lets out a chuckle, low and mocking, like he doesn't quite believe me. "Awe, ain't that a shame?" He looks at Warren. "Maybe we ought to pay her a visit at the 'ol Blackbird Cottage."

My fists ball at my sides, my pulse spiking. I've seen what happens when they decide to insert themselves. It never stays polite for long.

"We're busy, gentlemen," Tate cuts in smoothly, crossing his arms. "So why don't you tell us what you came for, and we'll all move on with our day."

"That was all," Dale says innocently. "We just wanted to give *Dr. Caldwell* a warm Tidehaven welcome."

"You're four weeks late," I snarl.

Dale laughs, shaking his head. "You're always so uptight, Morgan. Dad, let's get a bite to eat, shall we?" He pats me on the shoulder as he passes, smug and deliberate, and it takes everything in me not to put my fist in his face.

"Good day, boys." Warren tips his hat as he passes, as if we're all neighbors and not players on opposite sides of a game they pretend doesn't exist. Father and son stroll off down the dock, their shadows long in the morning sun.

Tate exhales, slow and heavy. "That guy's always sniffing around. I don't like it."

"Yeah," I say, my voice low. "Me either."

"I'll catch you in a bit," Tate says, starting for the bait shop.

"Later," I mutter.

I duck back in the booth, pulling out my phone and thumb out a text to Emery.

Don't come down here today. You're sick.

Her reply is almost instant.

Emery

What?

Just trust me. For once.

I drop my phone on the counter and suck in a breath, chest tight, heart hammering like I'm still under fire. A buzz breaks the silence.

Emery

I trust you.

The words loosen something in my chest, but the weight settles right back in. All I can think about is how badly I want to keep her safe and how easily I could fail.

CHAPTER NINETEEN

EMERY

I'M ALREADY HALFWAY out the door when Reid's text comes through telling me not to go down there today. It startles me, sending a wave of panic straight through to my bones. I don't think I've done anything to attract negative attention yet. I want so badly to ask him why, but our last exchange was hot and then contentious and now I don't know where we stand.

I hop in my skiff, deciding that checking on my traps and tagged turtles is better than sitting around worrying about things I can't control. I didn't sleep much last night after Reid left. I can't remember a time when I've wanted someone as badly as I wanted him in that moment. He's grouchy and bossy and annoying as hell, and for some reason, I find that appealing. But I'm frustrated.

The first day he took me out in the marsh, he knew all about the turtles. He even seemed to *care* about them. So why doesn't he see the importance of it now? If their habitat is compromised, if they're being hurt or killed, that should matter to him. He is the one who grew up in these marshes, learning the back bays and estuaries. Watching wildlife. I thought he was as invested as I am, but maybe I'm wrong.

That leads me to wonder, if he's not invested in these animals, why *is* he spending so much time with me out here? I want to believe it's because he likes me, but when he keeps storming out, I think I'm kidding myself. This is nothing more than physical attraction and a rebound for me.

I kill the engine when I reach the nesting area and paddle to my traps. I hurl the first one over the side of the skiff, but I quickly see that it's empty. I row to the next one, coming up empty there too. Nothing but a few crabs and a couple of bait fish. This is odd, as I usually have at least one juvenile in the traps. I frown, resetting it.

When I reach the third trap, I know something is amiss. It's completely untouched, no turtles, no bycatch, not even the usual marsh crabs. It's like the area's been purposely cleared out. A gnawing feeling fills my gut. Something isn't right here.

I pull the receiver out of my canvas backpack, stained with marsh water, and sweep the antenna around in a slow circle. A few turtles ping back faintly, but several that have been tagged in the last week, aren't moving. In fact, it looks like they're in exactly the same cluster they were in 48 hours ago.

"That's weird," I murmur to myself, chewing on my lip. Terrapins are very active feeders and almost never stay that still. Unless something is wrong. My throat tightens and suddenly, my whole body *knows* something is wrong.

I put the receiver away, pull out my camera, and stand in the small boat to take in my surroundings. There's an oil sheen on the surface near the mouth of an adjoining creek, too far inshore to be from commercial traffic. I snap a photo. The mud along the bank shows deep ruts, like something heavy was dragged over it or a boat got stuck at low tide. Snap. Perhaps the most alarming thing is the reed bed that looks flattened, trampled, like a boat pushed through where it shouldn't fit.

I plop down in my seat and dig through my notes from each of my marsh visits. My heart sinks. The missing pings line up with the discreet back routes that still lead out to the main channel. The ones I take nearly every morning before dawn. And almost exactly where Trixie was found yesterday. It's not proof of anything specific, but now I know, *something* is disturbing my turtles.

My mind is spinning as I tug on the choke, restarting my

engine. I race my little skiff through the marsh faster than I ever have back to my cottage. After kicking off my waders on the screened porch, I take the fastest shower of my life, powering up my laptop while I'm still in my towel. A knock on the front door startles me. I'm not dressed, so I duck out of eyesight, peering out the back kitchen window. There are no vehicles. Whoever it is, they must have come here on foot. Reid wouldn't wait this long. He'd be calling for me by now, or he'd probably just walk in.

"Maybe she really is sick in bed," one of the voices says from beyond the door. Male for sure. Maybe older.

"I guess so," the other voice agrees. This one is also male, but a higher pitch.

"Let's go. We don't want to disturb her." I hear footsteps retreating and the slam of the screen door.

My breath catches as I peer out the window. Two men, identical builds, about thirty years apart, trek back through the trees. Who the hell are they, and what do they want with me?

I hurry, throwing on clothes, before racing for my phone, quickly tapping out a text to Reid.

Two men just knocked on my door. I didn't answer.

Reid

Good. Stay put.

Nerves run through me, but I do as he says. Except I refuse to forget about the turtles. They feel like they're mine now.

Moving back to the table, I sync my receiver with my laptop and plot the turtle pings onto my digital map. That's when I really see it—the gaps are glaring. There are clusters where turtles should be spread out and blank spaces where I should be getting signals.

I don't even hesitate this time. I need someone who

understands evidence—how to separate noise from pattern, coincidence from cause. Someone who won't tell me I'm overreacting just because the conclusion is uncomfortable. I pick up my phone and dial Alan. We haven't spoken since I arrived, and I sure have a lot to tell him.

"Emery!" he says when he answers, his voice bright. "I was wondering when I might hear from you."

I let out a low laugh. "Yeah, sorry. I kind of went off the grid."

"You're allowed to. How are things? How are you liking Tidehaven?" Alan peppers me with questions, his excitement palpable.

"Well, I found something...concerning. And I need your take." I suck in a breath.

"Start at the beginning," he says, his tone turning serious.

I pace across the cottage, the floor creaking beneath me. "Yesterday, I recovered a turtle with a cut tag. Not shed. *Cut.* There was residue on the shell. I ran it at the lab." I swallow. "It came back positive for cocaine."

Alan is silent for a beat. Then, "Cocaine?"

"Yes. Presumptively, of course." My voice cracks on it. I push on. "And this morning my traps were empty. Not unusual, except...my tagged turtles aren't moving. Three of them have been clustered in one location for two days. Another hasn't pinged since last night. And the spots line up with side creeks that could easily be used for—"

"Drug routes," he finishes, his tone grave.

"Maybe. I don't know." I drop onto the edge of the couch, gripping the phone tighter. "I've got data. Patterns that don't make sense otherwise. This isn't natural behavior. Something is harming my turtles."

I hear his heavy sigh through the line. I picture him leaning back in his chair, pinching the bridge of his nose. "Emery, if what you're telling me is accurate, this isn't just a research problem. It's a law enforcement problem."

"I know." My voice comes out quieter. "That's why I'm calling.

What should I do?"

"Keep gathering data. Document everything—photos, logs, metadata. Don't make accusations without proof. And Emery—" His voice dips lower, like he's trying to anchor me. "*Please* be careful."

I let out a sigh. "I'm trying to be, but—"

Alan cuts me off. "If your evidence is strong enough, we can push it to Fish & Wildlife or the DEA. But not yet. Right now, you're a scientist. Do what you do best—collect the truth."

I nod, even though he can't see me. "Okay. Yeah. I can do that."

"Good." His voice softens. "And Emery? Call me anytime. I'm here for whatever you need."

I let out a grateful laugh. "Tell me something I don't know."

When the call ends, I stare down at my phone, heart pounding. His advice was measured, rational, safe. But my chest is tight, my throat hot, because waiting feels the same as enabling.

I sit at the edge of the bed, the glow from my laptop still painting maps and notes across the screen. My notebook lies open, pages filled with clusters and red circles, arrows that only I understand. Tomorrow the council will hear me, whether they want to or not. Like it or not, I'll be ready for them.

I get to work, preparing a presentation that will hopefully make every citizen of Tidehaven care about the marsh like I do. I work for hours organizing my data and notes in layman's terms, missing lunch and only stopping for a bowl of cereal for dinner. Before I know it, it's nine p.m. I close the laptop, the silence of my cottage suddenly overpowering. I glance at my phone one more time, thumb hovering over Reid's name. Nothing. Not a text, not a call. Just silence.

I tell myself I don't need him to stand beside me. But as I turn out the light, the lie hangs heavy in the dark.

CHAPTER TWENTY

REID

I SKIP MY usual marsh run with Emery Thursday morning, and by the time I make it to the marina, the air is already thick with humidity. I find Tate, shirtless as usual, in the bait shop. He's leaning on the counter like he was expecting me.

"Well?" he asks, raising his eyebrows. "Did you talk her out of it?"

"I haven't talked to her much at all," I mutter. "I'm not going to change her mind."

"You two lovebirds have a fight?" Tate smirks, amused with himself.

I ignore that. "I thought if I gave her some space to think about it, she would come to her senses, but I don't think she's going to."

Tate shakes his head. "She's going to the meeting tonight? Going in front of the council?"

"Yeah." My voice comes out sharper than I mean it. "I practically begged her not to. She's convinced showing them her charts is going to change something."

He blows out a slow breath. "And you think she's going to make herself a target like this." It's a statement more than a question.

"She's digging into things they want to stay buried."

Tate takes a sip of his coffee. "What are you going to do?"

"I'm not sure yet," I admit, crossing my arms. "I don't know if I can go there and watch her throw herself to the wolves. But how can I not?"

Tate leans back, eyes on me. "You can't cage her, Morgan. Sounds like she's going to do what she's going to do."

"I'm not trying to cage her. I'm trying to keep her breathing."

Tate narrows his eyes, pushing his lips together. "You still think they did something to Penny, don't you?"

Before I can answer, my phone buzzes with a text.

Emery

Will you be there tonight?

My stomach knots and I type out the only thing I know right now.

I'm not sure.

I AVOID THE research center all day, and for the most part, things are quiet. Boats come in, I tie them up and log them. I refill fuel bins. Work the bait shop for a couple of hours. Anything to keep my mind off Emery. I'm calling it a day by mid-afternoon when Kayla comes bounding out of the lab, backpack bouncing as she moves past me toward the gravel lot.

She waves. "Hey, Reid!"

I stop, wary. "Shouldn't you still be in school?"

"Half-day." She grins and I see how young she really is. "I came to help Emery. She says I'm getting good at checking tags and recording data. Isn't it awesome what she's doing?"

I stare at her. "Awesome's not the word I'd use."

Her smile falters. "She's trying to save the turtles."

"She's risking her life for some reptiles, and there are people who won't think twice about shutting her up," I mutter. "And you cheering her on like it's a pep rally isn't helping."

Kayla blinks at me, stung, but her chin lifts. "You sound like you're scared."

"I'm not scared." The words rip out before I can stop them. "But she doesn't know when to stop. And neither do you."

"I guess you won't be there tonight then..." Kayla lets her voice drop, disappointment written all over her face.

I meet her eyes and shake my head, feeling her glare burn into me as I turn my back and head for home.

I CIRCLE THE courthouse square twice before I finally pull into a spot in the back. Emery's navy-blue Toyota Prius sits in the front row. I'm sure she was here early. Guilt twists in my chest at the thought of her waiting there alone, watching for my arrival.

I glance at the clock on the dash. Seven-thirty seven. The town business bullshit should be wrapped up by now, which means they'll open the floor to community members to speak. I should just drive away. I told her I wasn't sure if I was coming. I have no obligation here. It's probably better to let her have the floor, let her get shut down, let her see for herself how pointless this is. I'm not fit to protect anyone—I've proven that time and again with my failed mission. I missed all the signs with Penny. I couldn't protect her. I don't know what makes me think I can protect Emery now. But the thought of her standing up there alone—face to face with the good old boys of Tidehaven—turns my stomach.

For a long beat I just sit there, forehead against the steering wheel, fighting myself.

"Fuck," I mutter. Then I shove the door open and step out.

By the time I push through the doors, her voice is already carrying over the microphone, steady and confident.

My throat tightens, because she's doing it without me, just like she said she would.

I head for the back row, sliding into a seat in the shadows. Her eyes catch on mine, but she keeps talking.

The projector hums behind her, maps, charts and graphs that probably don't mean much to the average resident. Mayor Wynn nods politely, but I can see the irritation in the tight line of his mouth. Councilman Roy Beck leans back in his chair, arms folded, eyes narrowed like he's already decided she is a nuisance.

Then a picture of the turtle we found yesterday fills the screen. A close up of its damaged shell, the white chalky residue obvious to even the untrained eye. When she mentions the cut tag and the residue test, a murmur ripples through the room.

Roy Beck leans forward, cutting her off. "Dr. Caldwell, are you accusing your *neighbors* of criminal activity based on a blurry photograph and a field test you can't verify?"

Emery doesn't falter. "I'm presenting facts. Data. Science doesn't lie, Mr. Beck. Ignoring this isn't going to make it go away."

Beck smiles without warmth. "Sometimes what you *think* you see in the marsh isn't your business to explain."

That does it. I'm on my feet before I know it, fists clenched at my sides. Heads turn; eyes dart. Emery's gaze flicks to me, a look of surprise flashing on her face, but I can't sit still while they dismiss her like that. While they subtly threaten her in front of everyone.

I stay silent, but the message is clear: I'm with her.

"Miss Cald—" the mayor interrupts.

"Doctor," Emery corrects and pride flares in my chest. That quickly turns to fear when I think about how dangerous it is to poke these men in public.

"*Doctor* Caldwell," he repeats. "We're done here." He bangs his gavel sending the message that she's been dismissed.

Emery keeps her chin held high as she gathers her things. My pulse is hammering in my ears, and the crowd is chattering, watching us as I meet her at the doorway.

"Let's go," I grind out, guiding her out before she can argue.

We're barely in the hall when we come face to face with Dale

Langford, leaning against the wall like he was waiting for us, a smug grin on his face. He straightens, stepping close enough to her that I prepare to take a swing at him.

"Dr. Caldwell," Dale drawls, too friendly. His palm finds her lower back, and she shifts uncomfortably. "Brave speech tonight. This town cares a lot about its reputation." He pulls a business card out of his pocket. "If you want to see the boatyard sometime, I'd be happy to give you a tour."

I step between them so fast that Dale drops the card, sending it fluttering to the floor. "She's good, Langford," I say, my voice gravel. "She's not interested."

Dale shoots me a wide smile, his eyes sharp and glittering. "I'm just being neighborly, Morgan."

"You don't know the meaning of the word," I growl.

Behind him, his father tips his hat, silent and watching.

Emery lets out a breath beside me, shoulders tense but head still high. I take her arm, peppered with goosebumps, and steer her toward the exit. My hand burns with the need to hit something, but I keep it steady on her instead.

Once we're outside, she jerks free, glaring. "I could've handled that."

"Like hell you could," I snap. I look at her, at the fire in her eyes, and I know this fight isn't over. Not between us, not between her and the town.

"I don't need a fucking bodyguard." Emery narrows her eyes at me.

"Langford put his hands on you. You did." My voice is rougher than I mean it.

"Jealous?" she scoffs, turning away.

"Emery. Fuck!" I shout in frustration, following her to her Prius. She ignores me, climbing in.

"I'll see you around," she mutters, slamming the door. She throws the car in reverse, and a second later her taillights bleed red across the blacktop as she pulls away, leaving me standing in the lot.

I stay there in the dark, fists in my pockets, watching her go. Every instinct in me shouts to follow, to make her understand what she just stirred up in that room. But chasing her down in the moment will only make her dig her heels in deeper.

So I let her go. For now.

CHAPTER TWENTY-ONE
EMERY

I AM SO fuming mad at Reid that I am barely out of the lot before I have to pull over and calm my nerves. He showed up—of course he did—but not until I was halfway through. He didn't stand there with me. In fact, the only time he stood was when they shut me down, and he still didn't say anything. All of that shouldn't make me mad. He told me not to do this; he told me it would fall on deaf ears. I guess I'm mad because the only time he really spoke up for me was when that slimeball hit on me on the way out. He was so jealous he couldn't see straight. Like some scum bag matters more than what I came here to say tonight.

I tap the CarPlay button on my car's center screen and call Lena. She answers immediately.

"Hey there, my long-lost best friend," she coos, her voice dripping with sarcasm.

Just hearing her voice soothes my nervous system.

"I'm sorry," I whine. "I know I've been a terrible friend."

"Not terrible..." Lena drags out the word. "I just haven't heard from you in way too long. I'm codependent."

A laugh slips out of me, and it gives me the calm I need to start driving again. "Things here have just been kind of crazy."

"Crazy?" Lena sounds disbelieving. "I thought you said things were boringly quiet."

"Ordinarily, I suppose they are but..."

"Okay, sis, start at the beginning. I'm getting comfortable," Lena says.

I turn the Prius onto my little driveway. Much as I want to unload on her, I don't have time to explain because there, parked in front of my little cottage, is a familiar navy-blue pickup truck. I pull up alongside him and put the car in park.

"Ugh," I groan, hitting the steering wheel with my palm. "How did he beat me here?"

"Uh...Em?" Lena asks uncertainly. "Did you forget I'm here?"

"No," I grumble, pressing my head back on the seat and closing my eyes. "I just...have to have it out with someone now. That I wasn't planning on dealing with tonight."

"Oooh, a fight? Leave me on speaker." Lena sounds downright gleeful.

"Um...no. It's either going to be a knock down drag out or it's going to be super-fast when I show him the door." I instinctively reach for my lip gloss. The kind that makes my lips tingle and plump up. I don't know why I do it. I'm annoyed at myself for it.

"Oooh...*him*? Is he hot?" Lena asks excitedly. I imagine her curled up in the recliner, feet tucked under her with her glass of wine and smutty romance novel, and suddenly I miss her so much it aches. "I feel like you could use a hot fisherman rebound."

I let out a laugh, and it loosens the aggravation weighing heavy in my chest. "You're insane, you know that? I'll call you back."

We hang up, and I move toward my screened porch. Reid is already out of his truck, leaning against the front bumper.

"What are you doing here?" I ask, crossing my arms with a glare.

"You don't have to be so hostile, Doc." Reid meets my eyes and steps closer to me, the corners of his mouth twitching like my anger at him is funny. "Trust me, you don't want Dale showing you around his docks."

I shove his hard chest, so he stumbles back up against his bumper. "That's *not* why I'm mad at you."

"Then why are you mad?" He frowns, as if the reason is really lost on him.

I bound up the steps and unlock the door, pushing it open. He follows me inside, shutting the door more forcefully than I'd expect. I whirl on him, ready to give him a piece of my mind.

"I'm the one who should be mad at you." He beats me to it, crossing his arms. "What the fuck were you thinking?"

I hold my chin higher and meet his angry gaze. "I was thinking that they need to *know* what's happening out there. That if they saw the data—"

"Trust me. They know and they don't give a shit about your data, Emery," Reid growls. "All you did was paint a target on your back that says, 'Look at me, catching you in a crime!' Guess what? Now they're looking." His tone stings.

I swallow, refusing to flinch. "You don't get it. They were already looking. They were already targeting me. Probably Dr. Young, too."

He jerks his head like he doesn't believe me. "What are you talking about? No one pays any attention to the marsh. Except that it gets them where they need to go. No one knew about you and your turtles until you brought it to their attention tonight. So yeah, you called attention to yourself. Now if they're really running drugs through there, and you get in their way..." He doesn't finish his sentence.

I grab my notebook off the counter and shove it open between us, showing him the pages filled with maps and pings. "Look at my data, clusters of turtles in one place for too long, pings that have just dropped off. And then Trixie and her missing tag." My voice catches. I have to make him see why this matters.

"Trixie?" Reid's brows knit together.

"The turtle we found. Kayla named her." I sigh, plopping into a dining chair. "They know what they're doing and I'm a threat to them."

Reid shakes his head. "Why would they even bother messing with the turtles? It's not like they're smuggling them."

"They don't care about the turtles," I snap. "They care about the tags."

He freezes, eyes narrowing.

"Every transmitter logs movement," I press on, voice sharp with adrenaline. "Locations, times, routes. The turtles are living GPS markers, Reid. They can't lie. They swim the same channels every night. When an obscure boat starts cutting through at two a.m., their paths shift. They dive. They scatter. Sometimes they're dead the next morning. When I plot it out, it shows a heat map of abnormal activity."

Reid looks skeptical, and it's taking every ounce of resolve I have not to shout in his face.

The words come faster now, all the fury and fear boiling over. "Sure, ordinarily they'd pay no mind to the wildlife. But if they see a tag, they care. They don't need to know why they're tagged. All they see is a device glued to a shell and it looks like surveillance. For all they know, they could think the DEA put them on the shells. So, they rip them off. Erase the evidence." My throat tightens. "They think of the turtles as spies."

The cottage goes silent, Reid's jaw ticks. He drags a hand down his face, and for the first time since I've known him, he looks shaken.

"Jesus, Doc," he says, softer now. "You just made this a hell of a lot more dangerous."

Silence hangs in the air between us, both of us lost in our own thoughts. It's me who speaks first.

"What do I do then?" My voice is quiet.

"Lay low," Reid mutters, with a shrug. "You don't have to quit. Just...change how visible you are. No more obvious traps. No more routines they can track. Stay out of their way."

I scowl at him. "And just let these innocent animals be trampled on?"

"Emery. This is your *life*. You are worried about the turtles now, but what's going to happen when they figure out that it was you who saw the murder in the marsh?" Reid paces, angrily running his palm over his buzzed head. "This is serious."

His tone startles me, and I curl my legs up to my chest. "Okay. I'll pull my traps. For now. Just until things quiet down."

"Give it a day or two," Reid suggests. "Let them think they scared you off."

"Okay." I nod, sucking in a breath. "I'll do that."

"Thank you." Relief washes over his face. "I'm just trying to protect you."

"I know," I say with a sigh. "I was just trying to protect them."

CHAPTER TWENTY-TWO

REID

MY PHONE'S ALREADY ringing when I slide behind the wheel. Tate's name lights the screen. "Yeah?" I mutter, jabbing the speaker button and dropping it onto the console.

"I thought you were going to talk to her out of it?" Tate's voice filters through, roughened by static and the clatter of other voices in the background. The Drift Net, maybe.

"What did you expect me to do?" I bark in frustration. "I don't control her. You said so yourself."

Tate lets out a low whistle. "I know, I know. It's just...she caused quite a stir after you guys left."

My chest tightens, anxiety creeping in the way it used to when I first became a SEAL. Fear of the unknown. Only this time, it's not fear for myself—it's fear for Emery.

"What do you mean she caused a stir?" It comes out harsher than I intend. Tate's just the messenger.

"Just that half the town started talking about the cocaine thing. Barb Maynard was shouting that someone was dealing drugs. Griff laughed and said it was worse than that. They went back and forth till the mayor slammed the gavel and sent everyone home. I hung around a bit, talked to Griff. When the old boys came out, they looked...tense." Tate pauses, waiting for some kind of reaction from me.

"Old boys?" I know damn well who he means, but I ask

anyway.

"You know...the old boys. Beck, Judge Ware, Langford Senior. Dale, too. Mayor Wynn trailed behind like a lost dog. I don't know, man. She better be careful." Tate's voice is edged with warning.

The leather seat creaks beneath my weight. "Yeah well, I think I knocked some sense into her just now. But she won't give this up without a fight." I lean my head back before starting my truck.

"These men... They won't hesitate to make someone disappear, Reid," Tate says, his voice low. "And they'll get someone else to do it, so their hands stay clean."

"Tate. Don't," I snap, my voice tight. "I know how it all works. Trust me, I'm paying attention."

I take the turn onto my drive too fast, gravel spitting under the tires, and slam the brakes at the porch steps. The sudden silence afterward is loud enough to hurt.

"Okay, sorry. I just... If you're seeing her, I thought you should know *they're* paying attention too." Tate pauses and I can picture him, perched at the corner of the bar, beer in hand, talking low so as not to call attention to himself. He's just trying to be the friend he's always been to me.

"I appreciate it," I manage, my throat suddenly dry. "She just frustrates the hell out of me."

Tate laughs low. "That just means you love her."

"I don't *love* her," I bark, then let out a breath, catching my reflection in the rearview mirror. The porch light casting a spotlight on the exhaustion under my eyes, the days of worry carved into lines across my forehead. "I don't even know her."

"Sure you don't," Tate says, and I can picture his knowing smirk. "See you tomorrow, man. Take it easy tonight."

"Yeah. Later."

The call ends. I grab the phone, shove it in my pocket, and climb the steps. Each one feels heavier than the last. By the time I reach the door, I'm not sure if it's fatigue or dread pressing down harder but either way, Friday can't come soon enough.

I FIGHT THE urge to stay away from Emery, and I lose. By the time I trudge through her yard the next morning, the sun is just burning through the fog, and the air smells like pine and sap. Relief floods through me when I see her skiff tied up where it normally is. Her car is still parked on the dirt drive, dew coating the windshield.

The dock creaks under my boots, boards soft from years of neglect. Once again, I make a mental note to fix it for her. The screen door bangs open behind me, and I turn just in time to see her stride out, squinting against the light.

"I didn't expect to see you today," she says, shielding her eyes. "Thought you were mad at me."

"I am," I growl, but I can't fight the twitch of my lip. "I can't leave you for dead though."

She swats my chest. "Too soon, Reid."

"Probably." I huff a laugh. "Tate opened today so I have a little extra time. Thought I'd drive you, if you're ready."

Emery's hands find her hips, and she narrows her eyes at me. "I thought I told you I don't need a bodyguard."

"If that were true," I say, meeting her stare, "I'd listen."

A quiet beat stretches between us, heavy and charged. Finally, she drops her arms. "Can I ask you something?"

"Sure."

She hesitates, her eyes flicking to the creek. "Do you—do you think the man in the marsh was involved in the..." She trails off, lowering her voice to a whisper. "Cocaine?"

"Probably." I shrug, though it's not casual. "If they're running product through those channels, they've got bodies tied to it—one way or another."

"People, Reid. He was a person," she says sharply. "I don't know if I've been dissociating or what, but I pushed all thoughts of him aside until last night."

"Dissociating is normal in these circumstances," I say,

watching her carefully. "It's just important that you make calculated moves now. Be smart. Watch your back."

Her throat works as she swallows, and for the first time in days, she looks genuinely rattled. "Do you think I'm safe?"

"For now," I say, gruffly. "Just lay low."

Emery sucks in a shaky breath. "Okay. I can do that."

"Come on, let me buy you a coffee." I turn toward my truck, gravel crunching underfoot. When she doesn't follow, I glance back.

"Do you think it's smart for me to go into town?" she asks, worry edging her voice.

"I think it's smart for people to *see* you," I say. "Let them think you've moved on to something else."

"Okay. Let me just get my things."

Before I can reply, she's jogging back toward the house. I climb into my truck, start the air conditioning, and wait. The air is still thick from last night's rain, cicadas droning somewhere in the trees. My stomach knots itself tighter the longer she's gone. My feelings for this woman are so complicated. It could be because I haven't wanted to pursue anything with anyone for a long time. And deep down, I don't think I'm deserving of the privilege to love and protect someone. It could also be that while I find her irresistible, I also find her tenacity irritating. Dangerous.

She pulls open her door and climbs in, startling me from my thoughts. "Hey," she says, as if we weren't just talking moments ago.

"Hi." I look in her direction, her cheeks flushed, blond hair piled on top of her head. My chest squeezes tight. All I want is to pull her into my chest and reassure her that I'm here and I won't let anything happen to her. That suddenly feels ridiculous though and I push away the urge. "I'll take you to Poppy's," I say, shifting into drive. "You been yet?"

In my peripheral, I see her shake her head. "I have just been making Nespresso."

"Probably tastes better." I chuckle, trying to cut the tension.

"Maybe I'll hang around the docks today. Do some non-confrontational public research at the marina."

When I glance over at Emery, she's chewing on her lip again. A nervous tic maybe.

"What kind of research?"

"I don't know. Oysters. Water quality. Seagrass surveys. Something that looks nonthreatening." Emery shrugs, looking at me, hopefulness etched across her features.

"Sounds perfect. I'll be around today too."

We climb out of the truck and head toward Poppy's, sunlight glinting off the bay windows. Inside, the place smells like cinnamon rolls. We order, exchange polite smiles with Poppy himself, then drift apart—me toward the marina, her toward the research center.

She hesitates at the corner.

"Hey, Em," I call after her.

She turns, blond hair catching the light.

"You're okay," I assure her. "Call me if you need something."

She gives me a small smile. "Thanks. I'll be fine."

And then she's walking again—away from me.

By four o'clock, I haven't heard from Emery at all. I head for the research center and spot Kayla just as she's leaving.

"Kayla, is Emery in there?" I call, hoping to catch her.

"She left about an hour ago," Kayla says, intercepting my path.

"What? Did she say where she was going?" I bark, running a hand through my beard.

"Calm down, Hulk." Kayla laughs. "I think she just went home. She seemed pretty tired. Said she didn't get much sleep last night."

"Thanks." I say, my tone clipped. I move for my truck.

"Okay, *bye*," Kayla calls. "Nice talking to you, you grouchy giant."

I give her a wave before throwing the truck in reverse and flying toward Blackbird Cottage. I don't know why, but Emery leaving without a word when things seemed okay between us this morning doesn't sit well with me.

I gun it up the narrow strip of Main, sand and grit kicking up dust beneath my tires. The town blurs past—weathered storefronts, the bay flashing silver between them—and I take the turn onto Emery's drive too hard. The truck fishtails once before catching, throwing up a cloud of dust. She's at the end of the dock, feet dangling over the water. The sound must startle her, because she jerks around, hand flying to her chest. When she realizes it's me, she shakes her head and turns back toward the bay.

That's when everything comes into focus. The yard doesn't look right. There are deep tire tracks gouged into grass, looping like someone spun out on purpose. Big donuts like we used to make for fun when we were teens. Except these ones look angry, like someone marking their territory.

I kill the engine and jump out, my boots crunching over disturbed ground. I crouch, running my hand along one of the ruts. Deep tread, wide spacing. Jeep, maybe. Something heavy.

I look up and my stomach drops. Across the white siding of her cottage, scrawled in brown spray paint, one word: *LEAVE*. My heart slams against my ribs. I move closer, dragging my fingers through the tacky paint. Whoever did this wanted to send a message, loud and clear.

I glance down at the sand beneath the wall. Footprints—big ones, likely made by a pair of boots.

Rage floods my chest, hot and sharp. "Who the fuck did this?" I mutter, voice shaking more than I want it to.

The gulls scatter overhead at the sound, but no one answers. I can't get to her fast enough.

She hears me coming and shifts over just enough for me to drop down next to her.

I crouch close, knees brushing hers and she rests her head on my shoulder like it's the most natural thing in the world. My palm finds the side of her head, fingers slipping into her hair, my thumb tracing circles on her temple.

"Who would do something like this?" Her voice is so low, I almost don't hear her.

I swallow hard, forcing my voice to stay steady. "I don't know. Are you okay?"

Emery straightens, eyes snapping to mine—bright and angry. "I'm fucking pissed."

"Okay," I say quietly. "Pissed is better than scared."

She exhales through her nose. "Who do they think they are telling me to leave? I'm not going anywhere." Her gaze drifts to the water. "All they did is ruin my cute little house."

A bitter laugh slips from me. "Emery, *this* is the *warning*. It'll be worse next time."

"Then let it be worse." Her arms cross over her chest, defiant and trembling all at once.

I drag my hand down my face. "How about you let me take you to get something to eat? Maybe a drink."

This woman isn't going to give this up, and now I know I'm going to stick by her through it all. That's the hold she has on me already.

She studies me, lips pressed together like she's weighing whether she's conceding or just tired. Finally, she nods. "Sure. I'd like that."

I stand then, reaching for her hand to help her up. Her fingers slide into mine, warm, steady. Neither of us lets go as we head up the dock. The sun glints off the bay, scattering gold over the water, and for a second, the world feels deceptively calm.

Her hand tightens once, like she knows what I'm thinking.

I shouldn't want her like this. Not when things are getting dangerous.

But I do.

And every step away from that vandalized cottage makes it harder to pretend otherwise.

THE DRIFT NET sits on the edge of the marina, its wood planked siding weathered by salt and sun. By the time we walk up, the parking lot is full. The place is alive with regulars and tourists alike. Music drifts out through the open walls, and laughter and conversation spill across the lot. Ceiling fans whirl lazily over the porch, stirring the smell of beer, fried shrimp, and low tide.

It should feel easy. Safe. We don't get too many tourists here in Tidehaven, but on summer Fridays, the locals turn out. The restaurant area is filled with dockhands fresh off their shifts and couples clinking their bottles together in cheers for the weekend. Kids with sunburned cheeks chase each other around the outdoor tables while a bluesy guitar hums through the speakers.

But something feels off. It's too loud, too cheerful. Too forced, almost—like I'm watching the set of a movie play out. Emery walks beside me, her fingers still laced in mine. She's trying to look relaxed, but her shoulders are tense. She scans the faces while we wait for a table. A few people look up with the kind of idle curiosity that small towns thrive on, but one pair of eyes sticks. And it sends a shiver down my spine.

Willie waves from behind the bar, and I catch sight of Tate, Colt, and Griffin Monroe sitting in the corner.

I lean toward Emery, my voice low. "Want to just eat at the bar?"

"Sure," she murmurs, gripping my hand tighter as I lead her through.

The place is crowded and close, thick with chatter and salty air. When we reach the corner, my friends fall silent—beer bottles halfway to their mouths, eyes flicking between me and Emery.

"Evening, boys," I say, pulling out a chair for her.

"Reid." Colt nods at me before flicking his gaze to Emery. "I don't believe we've met. I'm Deputy Chief Colt Riggs." He holds out a hand to her, and she has to let go of mine to take it. I immediately miss it, a foreign feeling for me.

"Emery Caldwell," she says, her voice quiet, as if she doesn't want to draw attention to herself.

"Well, Emery, if you need anything, you be sure to let me know. I run these parts." Colt grins and lifts his beer in salute. I look at him, still in uniform, completely at ease. He's probably this town's most eligible bachelor and he's totally oblivious to it.

"There's...no *actual* chief?" Unease crosses her face. "Just a deputy?"

"We share a chief with Hollow Creek," I answer for Colt. "Small towns like this, we get by with a deputy chief and a small department."

Emery nods slowly. "I'm not sure if that makes me feel better or worse."

The comment hangs in the air briefly before Colt speaks. "Don't worry. We know what we're doing." He chuckles but the air feels taut again.

I clear my throat, ready for a subject change. "Em, you've already met Tate. This here is Griff Monroe." I gesture to the older gentleman on the end with gray hair and kind blue eyes. "Griff was the harbormaster here for many years. He's since retired."

"Hello," Emery says, a polite smile on her lips. Then her brow furrows curiously. "Who is the harbormaster now?"

Tate lets out a low chuckle. "Griff was irreplaceable. 'Fraid the job will be open indefinitely."

Willie comes over, a teasing glint in his eye. "Well look what the tide dragged in. Haven't seen much of you lately, Morgan." He plants a cold Miller Lite in front of me. "The old lady keeping you locked up?"

Emery and I exchange confused glances before Willie laughs and slaps the bar. "Kidding, man. Just kidding. And who's this pretty thing?"

"I'm Emery," she says, as Willie places a menu in front of her. "Could I have a white wine please?"

"White wine, huh? Classing up the joint. Coming right up."

Willie disappears and I take the seat next to Emery.

The group quiets again. "So, what's going on?" I ask, sensing the weight hanging between them. "Guys..."

Tate's the first to speak. "Langford was around here earlier. Poking around like he owns the place."

Emery stiffens beside me, and my hand finds her thigh under the bar, a reassuring anchor.

"I hate that guy," Colt growls. "I wish I could charge him with something."

"You'll never touch him," Griff says, voice rough. "Not as long as his daddy is still around here pulling strings."

Tate nods. "Best to just steer clear. Play nice."

My jaw tightens. "Is there something else?"

The three of them glance at each other, but no one answers. The silence says enough. Whatever it is, they don't want Emery hearing it.

Before I can push, a voice cuts through the din behind me.

"Well, I'll be damned if it isn't Reid Morgan in the flesh." A hand claps me on the back so hard I jolt forward.

I know who it is before I see him. I spotted him across the bar when we first arrived. Atlas Rourke, an old SEAL buddy—though I use the word loosely—who I haven't seen in years. We were in some Veterans groups together before he seemingly dropped off the face of the earth.

I don't flinch. "The world is full of surprises."

He barks a laugh, sharper than the easy smile he wears. "I thought you lived around here. Still got that dry sense of humor, I see. Some things never change."

"That's one way to put it," I say, taking a sip of my beer.

Atlas glances around the bar, taking stock of the place. He nods at a few strangers who clearly don't know him. "Tidehaven's a nice town. Quiet. Maybe a little *too* quiet if you catch my drift."

"It's perfect," I say, casting my eyes toward my friends who are watching the scene with great interest.

"Don't think we've met," Atlas says, directing his attention to Emery.

She offers a thin, polite smile. "I'm Emery."

"Emery, what a pretty name," Atlas says easily. "Must be new in town."

I bristle, cutting in before she can answer. "She is. And she's busy."

Atlas's grin doesn't fade, but something sharp flickers behind it. "Anyway, I didn't mean to interrupt. Just wanted to say hey."

"Hey," I echo flatly.

Atlas gives a short laugh like I've told a joke only he gets, then taps the bar twice with his knuckles. "Good seeing you, brother."

He turns and strolls off toward the door, all easy swagger and superficial smiles. The second he's gone, the noise in the bar feels thinner, like the air's been sucked from the room.

Emery's still watching the door when she speaks. "Old friend?"

"Something like that." I keep my eyes on my beer. "He wasn't discharged the way the rest of us were. Lost his clearance. That doesn't happen for nothing." What I don't add is he's the kind of guy who finds work where rules don't apply and the fact that he's here can't be good. My gaze lands on the muddy boot prints fading toward the door. Familiar. A cold weight settles in my gut, and suddenly I'm not hungry anymore.

CHAPTER TWENTY-THREE

EMERY

WE'RE QUIET ON the ride back to the cottage, no sound except for the hum of Reid's truck and the quiet rush of summer air through his cracked window.

"You can stay at my place, you know," Reid tells me, throwing a glance my way.

The last streaks of sunset have bled out over the marsh, turning the starry sky into indigo. Everything looks softer, but it feels more dangerous somehow.

I don't answer as he pulls in, the motion light flickering with the movement of his truck. It casts an ugly yellow glow on the words defacing the side of the house: *LEAVE*. My chest tightens.

The night is quiet and still, the kind of silence that hums with something underneath. The marsh is awake with the sounds of frogs, cicadas and other insects in the air, the occasional sound of moving water. But beneath it, there's a heavier sort of quiet—the kind that waits for you.

Reid cuts the engine, and the silence overwhelms me. My pulse thrums in my ears.

"Emery, did you hear me? I said you're welcome to stay at my place," Reid says quietly. I look over at him.

"That's okay," I say quickly. "I'll be fine."

Neither of us moves. The truck ticks as it cools down, the smell of salt air and pine thick between us. I should thank him.

Tell him good night. *Oh, how I don't want to tell him good night.* Instead, I reach for the door handle but hesitate.

"Hey," I say softly. "Can I ask you something?"

Reid turns toward me, his shoulders tense. "Yeah."

"The other day I was in the marsh, adjusting my transmitter." I pause, eyes flicking toward the marsh. "I saw a man watching me. Near my traps."

Reid stills, his jaw tight. "Watching how?"

I shrug, trying not to make a big deal out of it. "Just standing there. Half-hidden in the grass. I waved, said hello. He didn't say anything. Just looked at me for a second and walked off."

Silence stretches for a brief moment.

"What did he look like?" he finally asks.

"Dark shirt. Boots. Mid-thirties maybe? It was hard for me to tell." She gives a small, self-conscious laugh. "I know it's probably nothing but now with this." I gesture to the word on the side of my house, then shake my head. "I'm probably just imagining it."

His gaze stays locked on mine, intense enough that my smile fades.

"And he didn't approach you?" he asks.

"No. That's the weird part." I shake my head. "He just...left." I study his face now, searching for some kind of reaction.

"How long ago?" he asks, and I catch the edge beneath his calm.

"It was the same day we argued. Before the meeting." A flicker of concern passes through me. "I should have told you."

"It's okay," he says, but his tone is careful and controlled.

I smile, trying to ease whatever tension I've stirred. "I figured it was just a local."

"Probably," he agrees.

Silence falls over us again, and Reid starts the engine. I decide that's my cue to go and reach for the door handle.

"Emery," he says, his voice raw.

I glance back.

"Lock up." Reid's hands tighten on the steering wheel, his

knuckles turning white.

"I will," I promise.

I slide out of his truck, and the night wraps around me like a sauna. I trudge up the front steps, the planks creaking, feeling Reid's eyes on me the whole way.

The porch light flickers, swarms of tiny insects floating around it. I glance back just before opening the door. Reid's still watching, one arm draped across the passenger seat. I give him a tiny wave and he nods.

Inside, the cottage is just how I left it. It smells like lemon soap and the chemical scent of cool air from the window unit. Safe. For now, anyway. But as I turn and lock the door, my eyes catch on the marsh, the water black in the night.

And as the quiet presses in, I can't shake the feeling that someone is out there, waiting for me to turn off the light.

I MAKE IT through the night, but not without anxiety. Sleep comes in shallow bursts, every sound jolting me awake, convincing me someone's outside my window. By dawn, I've given up pretending to rest. For the first time since I got here, I really consider leaving. Maybe this isn't worth it—my safety, my sanity. But then I think about my work. How maybe Kayla and I are the only ones who care enough to notice what's happening. And the alternative—going back to academia, to the sterile halls, and a relationship that barely had a pulse—feels worse. Whatever this thing is between Reid and me, real or imagined, the idea of walking away before I find out terrifies me more than staying.

I throw the covers back just after seven before digging through my drawers for a pair of cut-offs and a dingy university tee. Throwing my hair in a messy knot on top of my head, I fill a bucket with hot soapy water. I find a large, stained sponge under the kitchen sink and briefly wonder what Dr. Young was scrubbing before she passed. Grabbing my air pods, I queue up some angry rap and set off to scrub the side of my house.

My arms ache by the time the last of the brown letters fade into streaky white two hours later. The siding still bears a faint shadow where the paint sank in, visible only when the sun hits it just right. I swipe at it with the sponge one last time, my breath coming hard, my wrists raw from angry scrubbing.

It's cleaner but not gone. The word still lingers, just quieter now. But I'm not leaving.

Inside, I grab a yogurt and a bottle of water before collapsing onto the couch to call Lena. It's Saturday. My only plan is to pull my turtle traps this afternoon and strip the remaining tags from any I find. Maybe it'll prove that I'm not a threat. Maybe if they see I've backed off, they'll leave me alone. I can't lose sight of why I came here—to figure out what's next. To finish a paper that might earn me a grant. To decide if I even belong in academia anymore.

I dial Lena and she answers on the first ring.

"Girl! You left me hanging the other night. What the hell is going on there?"

I sigh, sinking into the lumpy cushion. "If you knew, you'd flip out."

Silence for a beat, then, "Try me."

I hesitate, debating whether or not to mention the murder in the marsh. Deciding against it, I tread lightly. "I'm surprised Alan didn't fill you in."

Lena snorts. "Alan barely tells me when the coffee is out in the break room. Spill it."

"It seems my research has potentially uncovered a cocaine running route." I wait for her reaction.

"Shit," Lena breathes. "Did you tell anyone?"

I swallow the sudden tightness in my throat. "That's the thing. Alan told me not to yet."

"But you did, didn't you?" I can hear the smirk in her voice.

"I couldn't help it. I love the turtles," I admit, my voice wavering.

"But?" Lena presses.

I exhale. "But now I've made myself a target. Someone spray painted the word *leave* on the side of my house."

"Geez, Emery." Her voice goes quiet. "What are you going to do?"

"I'm pulling my traps this afternoon. Then I'll lay low."

Lena pauses and I imagine her curled up on her couch with her Saturday morning cup of coffee, her toddlers playing on the floor. "Em, have you thought about coming home? If you're in real danger, maybe you should."

"I can't. Jason and I are done. I need the space to figure out what's next." I rub my temples. "I just need time."

"You can figure it out here. Stay with us," Lena insists gently. Her offer is kind, but something tells me staying in a house with her, her husband, and their small children, would not offer the kind of quiet I came here for.

"I'll keep it in mind, Leen. Thank you," I say, knowing her offer is genuine.

"So, who was the guy you were fighting with?" Lena's voice turns sultry, like she's fishing for the juicy gossip.

"Ha!" I bark out a laugh. "Reid. A grumpy, ex-Navy SEAL who needs to mind his own damn business," I mutter. Then I immediately feel guilty. I don't want Reid to mind his own business and the truth is, I've done nothing but depend on him since I got here.

Lena giggles. "Is he hot?"

"That's beside the point."

"Ahhh, so he *is* hot," Lena teases.

"You must've missed the part where I said he's grumpy too."

"Maybe you need a grumpy rebound," Lena suggests, and I can hear her smile.

"Okay, no. Enough about me. Talk to me about what's going on with you."

As Lena starts rambling about how the baby walked this week and the three-year-old dropped an F-bomb, my mind drifts. Maybe I *do* need a grumpy rebound.

But what if I don't want it to be a rebound at all?

I'M CLIMBING INTO my skiff in the late afternoon when my phone rings. Reid.

I settle myself on the tiny bench seat and tap the screen. "Hey," I say, cautiously, knowing he's going to insist on coming out here with me.

"What are you doing? I haven't heard from you all day." His tone is sharp, edged with irritation.

"I was busy. I scrubbed the side of the house, called my best friend, watched a little Netflix." I push a loose strand of hair off my sweaty forehead.

"You should share your location with me," Reid suggests, his tone lower now with the kind of calm that's worse than anger.

"Respectfully, hell fucking no." I laugh in an attempt to diffuse him. "Are you insane?"

"Emery, this is serious."

"I *know*, Reid. I'm going to pull my traps now and remove the tags from whatever turtles I can find, okay?" My patience with him is thinning.

"Good. Glad you're giving up on this."

"I'm not *giving up*. I am just lying low for a while." I cradle the phone between my shoulder and ear and give the choke a good tug.

Reid must hear it. "You're already out there?"

"Yes. I waited for later in the day. Less chance of anyone watching."

"Wait for me. I'm coming with you," Reid orders.

"Again, respectfully, no. I'm going to be a while, and I need to get started." I tap the speaker button and steer toward the marsh that is as familiar to me now as the back of my hand. The afternoon sun hangs low, a burnt orange sinking behind the reeds. Shadows stretch across the water.

"Keep me on speaker, at least," he urges.

I imagine him pacing his porch, jaw tight, probably in a T-shirt that hugs his shoulders too well. The thought makes my stomach flutter—until a ripple of unease cuts through it.

"No. I'll call you when I'm done." I tap the screen to end the call before I lose my nerve.

Reid calls me back a moment later, but I ignore it. The familiar hum of the motor and the sounds of nature should calm me, but the air feels heavy—thick and still, like the marsh is holding its breath. I suck in a breath of my own, willing myself to be calm. The sooner I get this over with, the sooner I'll be back in the cottage with a glass of wine and a rom-com.

I find my first trap easily, right where I left it. I hurl it out of the water to find it's empty, the bait missing. Easy enough. I move onto the second trap and find it has three juveniles inside. My heart flutters, a mix of relief and sadness curdling in my chest. As much as I want to take them out and examine them, I don't. I pull on a pair of gloves, carefully lifting each turtle and then gently setting them free. I toss the empty trap at the other end of my skiff. I'm on my way to the third trap when I hear the low hum of another engine. Probably Reid checking on me. Overprotective and relentless, he is taking the whole bodyguard thing way too seriously.

But the engine grows louder, it's coming fast, now in my line of sight.

"Hey! Slow down!" I shout, waving at the driver.

The boat doesn't slow down—it accelerates, barreling toward me aggressively, far too fast for comfort. I duck as it slices across my bow, the wake slamming into my skiff. The world tilts. Water splashes over the sides, soaking my shorts. My phone slides off the seat.

I remain crouched low but peer up at the other boat that has slowed. A man dressed in all black with a neck gaiter covering his face stands at the helm. There is something familiar about his eyes. I've seen them before. He shouts something, the wind carrying only fragments of his angry words. Before I can react, something heavy whistles past my head, thudding against the hull with a sharp metallic crack.

My foot slips on the wet boat floor and I go down hard, catching myself on the edge of the trap. Pain explodes through my palm. I jerk my hand back, hissing. But I don't bother to nurse my wound. I grab the throttle and slam it forward, gunning the engine toward the cottage.

The skiff bucks over the chop, wind tearing at my face. My heart doesn't slow until my dock comes into view. And then it spikes again.

The door to my cottage is wide open.

"No, no, no—"

I leap from the skiff, my boots skidding on the deck planks and thunder up the rickety steps. The place has been ransacked. My notes and papers are strewn about the cottage, scattered all over the floor. What would they have done if I were home? The thought terrifies me.

I scan the room, and then I see it. The terrapin tank is empty. My heart sinks.

"Trixie," I whisper, a knot forming in my throat.

I back away, fumbling for my phone in my pocket before realizing I left it in the skiff. Panic claws at me. I stumble back outside, nearly tripping down the stairs. I race back to the dock, reaching for it, pain searing up my arm from the wound on my hand. I look down to find a crimson stain on my shoulder seeping through my T-shirt sleeve. My hand throbs, blood slicking the wheel as I reach the skiff and grab my phone.

"Shit," I mutter. I scroll to recent calls, tapping Reid's name.

It rings three times before he answers.

"Emery?" he says, his voice sharp and alert.

"Reid." My voice trembles. "I need you."

CHAPTER TWENTY-FOUR
REID

"HOLY SHIT, EMERY."

I'm out of my truck before the engine cuts, gravel crunching under my boots. Stunned, she stands in the middle of the yard, still torn up with tire tracks, arms wrapped around herself.

Blood. Down her arm.

"What happened? Who did this to you? Where are you hurt?" I reach her in two long strides, my hands cupping her cheeks before she can answer. Her skin is cold and clammy.

"M-my hand," she stammers. "I cut it on the wire of a trap, but my shoulder is bleeding too. I don't know how. Maybe I was hit. I tried to look but then I got dizzy." Emery's words are choppy, coming out between erratic pants.

"Hey, hey." I pull her to me, gently so as not to jostle her wounds and cradle her head. "You're okay, baby, I got you." The word falls from my lips so naturally. *Baby.* "Let's get you inside."

My hand finds the small of her back, warm and trembling beneath my palm, and I guide her up the steps. The cottage looks like a bomb went off.

"Holy shit," I mutter for the second time, scanning the wreckage. "What the fuck happened?"

"Someone raided my house. They tore up my notes, tossed everything everywhere. They took Trixie." Emery's voice cracks.

"Your laptop?" I ask, scrubbing a hand down my face.

"I had it with me, thank goodness." Emery's face grows pale. "I don't feel so good."

"Sit," I say, helping her into a chair. "Don't move."

I trek down the hall to her bathroom and rummage around in a tall cabinet, relieved when I find a rusted first aid kit. I pop it open and find it mercifully stocked. When I return, she's white as chalk.

"Here." I lift her hand, resting it on a towel. The cut runs jagged and raw across her palm. I flush it with saline.

Emery hisses, her shoulders jerking. "Ouch."

"Easy. I know it burns." My voice drops low, softer than I mean it to. "When's the last time you had a tetanus shot?"

"I'm not sure." She winces.

I press my lips together. "From the marsh water alone and the rusty traps...you probably need a booster."

"I'm fine. Just bandage it already," Emery growls.

"This may sting." I open the antiseptic and wipe what's left of the active bleeding. My hands work, steady and practiced, but the sight of her shaking wrecks me.

She sucks in a sharp breath. "Oh my God."

"Sorry," I say with a grimace. I grab a couple of pieces of gauze and cover the wound with some medical wrap. "We have to get a look at that shoulder."

"Okay," Emery says, moving to pull back her sleeve. It's stuck to the now drying blood. "Ouch." Her voice trembles. "Help me take my shirt off, please." Her eyes find mine, trusting and vulnerable. Something in my chest twists.

"Okay," I say, reaching in the first aid kit for a pair of scissors. "I hope you don't care about this shirt."

"I don't." She shakes her head. "*Please.*"

My breath catches as my fingers grip the hem of her T-shirt. Her fingers link through mine for a split second before she pulls her uninjured arm out. I slowly help her lift it over her head, trying not to touch more skin than I have to. When my knuckles graze her ribs, a shiver runs through her. Surely, just a chill, but I feel it too.

The sight of her in her pale pink bra, blood caking her ivory skin causes a swirl of heat and rage pulsing through me. My fingers hover, then trace a path from her collarbone to her neck, my thumb brushing her pulse. "You're safe now," I say quietly, though my voice sounds rough.

When I lean in to check the wound, my lips instinctively graze her shoulder. She exhales a tiny sound that cuts through me. Her hand lifts, trembling, resting at the back of my head.

It's not lust, not really. It's need. Connection. And I can't help but feel that we both desperately want it.

"I should've been there," I rasp. "Should've protected you."

"I was stubborn," she says, her voice cracking. "You tried."

I sit up, my eyes searching hers. "I will not let them get near you again." It's a vow and Emery knows it because she nods.

"Ready?" I ask, casting my eyes toward the part of the wound that's still covered.

"As I'll ever be."

Bracing her bicep with one hand, I gently peel off the T-shirt sleeve, glued to her skin with blood. Emery winces and I catch her gaze just in time to see a tear roll down her cheek.

"Scissors," I grit out.

She passes them to me, and I cut the bulk of the shirt away, leaving just a four-inch patch of fabric.

"It'll be easier this way," I say quietly.

She nods, sniffling. "Okay."

I gently pull the fabric around each side until only a small piece is stuck on. When I free it, the bleeding stars again. I reach for the hand towel and apply pressure. Another tear slips down her cheek, and I thumb it away without thinking, my hand lingering at her jaw.

When it's finally clean and dressed, she breaks, quiet sobs shaking her body. I pull her in, feeling the tremor of every breath. Her bare skin is warm against my shirt, as her tears dampen my collar.

"Are you scared or in pain?" I murmur in her ear.

"Both." She hiccups.

My lips brush her temple, barely there. "I've got you. You're safe."

She nods into my chest, and I keep tracing small circles at the nape of her neck until her breathing slows.

"Baby, I think we better get Dr. Michaels to come look at this. You need the shot."

She sits up, eyes searching mine, but she nods.

"And—" I pause, licking my lips. "I want you to come stay with me for a while."

To my surprise, she doesn't argue. Instead, she directs me to her closet to find a few weeks' worth of clothes and a fresh tank top that I help her into.

"Dr. Michaels makes house calls?" Emery asks faintly, watching from her chair as I move around her space.

"Not usually," I say, offering my hand. "But he owes me a favor. And it's best if we're discreet. Be right back." I'm already dialing him as I step onto her porch.

Doc Michaels is surprisingly quick to agree, and when I step back inside, Emery looks even more exhausted than when I left her two minutes ago. I sling her duffel over my shoulder and pick up the research backpack that she takes everywhere. "Doc's on his way. Let's go home."

I help her into the truck, throwing her bags in the backseat before sliding in myself. It's only now I realize I never shut my truck off.

I back out of the dirt drive and set off for the main road that links our two places. "I have to make a quick call," I say quietly, glancing at Emery.

Her head rests against the window, her eyelids slit with exhaustion. They flick to me. "To the police?"

"Not exactly," I say, tapping Colt's name on my truck's center screen.

He answers on the second ring, his voice thick with fatigue.

"Morgan. You good? You never call me."

"Yeah. We need to talk. Off the books, okay? You alone?"

"Yeah. What's going on?" Colt sounds awake now.

"Someone broke into Blackbird Cottage. Ransacked the joint. They ran Emery down in the marsh too. She's hurt." I let out a defeated sigh, guilt nagging at me as I say the words. *She's hurt.*

"Well, did you call it in?" Colt asks.

"No. You know why." I glance toward Emery, watching me, arms wrapped around herself again. "Just swing by my place when you can. I don't need any of the old boys catching wind of this."

"You're saying you don't trust your own department?" Colt's voice is edged with irritation.

"No. I trust you. I don't trust the guys who pay you."

Colt is silent for a moment, then, "I'll come by. But if this is a crime scene, I can't promise I will ignore it, Reid."

"I appreciate it." I hang up before he can argue.

By the time we pull up to my cabin, the last light is gone from the sky. The air smells briny, the way it does when a storm is hitting just offshore, headed for us.

"This is it." I murmur.

"This is where you live?" Emery blinks, disoriented. "So close to me."

"Yeah," I say, killing the engine. "But you'll be safe here."

I help her inside. I keep the place tidy, old military habits die hard. Emery sits gingerly on the edge of the couch while I lock up and bring her some water. By the time I get back to her, she's trembling again, shock setting in. I crouch in front of her, steadying her shaking knees with my palms.

"You're okay. You're with me now," I say softly.

Headlights sweep across my front window, two quick flashes before going dark again.

"That'd be the doc." I move to answer the door before he has a chance to knock.

"Evening, Reid." Dr. Michaels says, stepping inside.

"Hey, Doc. Appreciate you coming out." I clap him on the

shoulder.

"Where's the patient?" He looks over my shoulder, and I step aside. "Let's have a look Dr. Caldwell," he says with a smile.

I hover long enough to make sure she's okay, but when the headlights flash across the window again, I know it's Colt. I step out onto the porch before he's out of his truck.

He's in jeans—no uniform—a deliberate choice, I'm sure. Even his cruiser's dark. He doesn't need to say it, but the fact that he came like this tells me he knows we're in some kind of trouble.

He takes one look at me and nods toward the house. "She all right?"

"Banged up. Doc Michaels is patching her up now."

Colt nods once. "So, tell me what happened."

"Someone spray painted the word *leave* on the side of the cottage yesterday," I start. "Tire tracks all over her yard. Today, they ransacked her place, trashed her notes and her research materials. Stole a turtle from the tank."

Colt's jaw tics. "How did she get hurt?"

"I haven't gotten that out of her yet. She was in the marsh, someone tried to run her down. That much I know." I lean against the railing, looking out over the black marsh.

Colt lets out a low whistle. "And you think this is related to her...*suspicions*?"

I debate telling him about the body in the marsh, but I don't think he would keep it off the record if I do, so I swallow it down.

"Hard to say," I say cautiously. "I think it ties to every shady run between here and the Sound."

"And you really don't want to call it in?"

I shake my head adamantly. "No. I don't want to give them another reason to look at her. If the chief gets wind of this, Roy Beck and Judge Ware will squash it before he can even look into it."

"He's about to retire too. He won't want to touch this," Colt agrees.

"If he does, Judge Ware will pull all your funding."

"Circle of Hell, Tidehaven Edition," Colt mutters. Lightning strikes across the marsh, lighting Colt's hard face in blue. For a second, he looks older than I remember. "So, you play this close to the chest," he says quietly. "But you know who you're up against, don't you? Those boys won't blink if it means protecting their operation."

"Neither will I," I say, my voice stoney.

Inside, the low murmur of Dr. Michaels' voice carries through an open window, calm and professional. It's followed by a soft, tired laugh from Emery. The sound does something to my chest I can't quite name.

"All right, I'll drive by a couple of times tonight. Keep it quiet. Is she staying with you?" Colt says finally.

"She has no choice."

"Figured as much." The ghost of a grin crosses his face before he gives my shoulder a clap. "Watch your six, brother."

"Always do."

He turns to go. "And Reid? Don't wait so long to call me next time."

He disappears into the dark, and I watch the road until his taillights disappear.

I step back inside, and Emery is sitting up, her shoulder neatly bandaged, a band aid on the other arm where I assume she got a tetanus shot.

Dr. Michaels picks up his bag. "Keep the wound covered, make sure she rests. I'll stop back by tomorrow evening to change the dressing."

"Thanks, Doc."

When the door clicks shut, silence falls over us again, the only sound is the wind picking up over the marsh and thunder in the distance.

Emery looks up at me, weary and yet still so beautiful.

I move to sit next to her and drape my arm over the back of the couch, prompting her to curl into it.

"Thank you," she whispers.

I lean down, planting a kiss on the crown of her blond head. "Of course."

"You didn't tell him everything, did you?"

I pause, looking down at her. "No, not yet."

She sucks in a shuddering breath. "And you really think I'll be safer here with you?"

"No," I admit. "But at least I'll know where you are."

Emery sighs, nuzzling into me, and I encircle her waist with my free hand, tugging her closer.

"Let's get you something to eat," I murmur.

I force myself to let her go, even though every muscle in my body screams against it. For a split second, I feel her heartbeat against mine—proof that she's here, alive, and for the first time in a long time, the only thing I can't afford to lose.

CHAPTER TWENTY-FIVE

EMERY

ONE WEEK. THAT'S how long I've been lying low around Reid's cabin. The last weeks of June are upon us and I'm starting to go a little stir crazy. My wounds have healed nicely. I've spent plenty of time on his couch reading, binge-watching shows while he works at the marina, and falling asleep each night in his guest room. Things have been eerily quiet—no unfamiliar boats, no voices carrying over the water, no sense that anyone is watching. The kind of quiet that doesn't reassure so much as make you listen harder. I tell Reid I feel safer now, that maybe it's time I moved back to my cottage. I know he's been there. He cleaned up the mess they left and brought back some of my belongings. But when I suggest going with him, his expression shutters. He turns cold.

What's worse is we seem to have plummeted right back into the friend zone. We haven't kissed in weeks, both of us seem to be tiptoeing around the inevitable. I'm starting to wonder if he's already decided we're a bad idea. But then I'll be washing dishes, and he'll come up behind me, his hand curling around my waist as he reaches for a dishtowel to help me dry, and my heart starts racing again. Part of me thinks he's wound so tightly, he wouldn't give in even if I threw myself at him. He just won't let his guard down around me, and it's slowly killing me.

I haven't been back to the research center. Kayla is taking care of the other two turtles in the tanks there, and we're just about ready to set them free again. There are still no signs of Trixie, and my heart hurts thinking about what could have happened to her. I need to convince Reid to let us go into the marsh to release the others and to get the third trap, but he has been so quiet and contemplative.

Each morning, when I wake up, he's got breakfast ready, eggs one day, oatmeal the next. He always has a cup of coffee waiting for me and a tight smile, but he's distant. It's getting to me today, so I'm making dinner for us and I'm finally going to confront him. Ask him what the hell is going on in his head.

I venture into town around noon. I have the strange feeling that everyone is looking at me, but when I clock my surroundings, everyone seems to be minding their own business. I park my Prius right outside Mama T's and duck inside.

"Oh, hello, Emery!" Rosie chirps from behind the register. "I haven't seen you in a while."

My cheeks heat. I haven't been here in some time, choosing instead to thrive on take-out and whatever Reid stocks the fridge with.

"Hi, Rosie," I say quietly. "I'm sorry, I've been recovering." I stupidly gesture to my still wrapped shoulder.

"What ever happened, dear?" Rosie soothes, her voice etched with concern.

I realize almost immediately that I shouldn't have called attention to it. In a town of this size, all Rosie has to do is mention to someone that the research center director is injured and everyone will be looking my way again.

"Oh, uh, I slipped and fell in my boat. Got a little banged up. I'm okay though." I turn, fixing my gaze toward the butcher at the back of the store. "I'll see you in a few minutes," I say without turning back around.

I wander to the back of the store and ask the butcher for two strip steaks. I don't cook often, but I know how to make this. Once I grab my meat, I get some potatoes and salad ingredients before making my way back to the register.

"This looks like a fancy meal you're cooking up," Rosie muses, a twinkle in her eye. "For you and Reid?"

The question catches me off guard. How would she possibly know I'm staying with Reid? I have hardly left his house this week.

"I see you two venturing downtown together sometimes," Rosie offers. "I'm just so glad to see that boy moving on."

"Moving on?" I squeak, casting my gaze to the scanner as she swipes my items.

"It's just, he's always been sort of a loner, but especially so after the military messed him up." Rosie shrugs. "I knew his mama. She'd be happy if she could see him now, settling down with a purty girl like you."

I open my mouth to speak and then close it again, offering her an uneasy smile.

"That will be forty-seven fifty-three." Rosie grins. "Cash or card?"

"Uh, card," I say, fishing my Visa out of my purse.

Rosie swipes it on the reader and hands it back to me. "You take good care of that boy, now, okay?" Her southern drawl makes the remark sound vaguely threatening.

I swallow. "I will."

"Bye, now," she calls as I turn to go.

I can't get back to the cabin fast enough.

REID COMES HOME just after four, the same time he has for the past week. I've already got dinner underway, but I'm feeling jittery trying to work up the nerve to talk to him. We've been tiptoeing around this thing between us for weeks, and I need to know where we stand.

"Smells good in here," he calls, closing the front door. "I guess you're feeling better."

I smile from my place at the counter. He walks into the kitchen, that easy strength radiating from him. He leans against the counter across from me, and I hand him the cold beer I've already cracked open.

He takes a long pull. "What's all this?"

"I'm going a little stir crazy," I admit, wiping my hands on a dish towel.

He watches me closely for a beat. "Huh," he says, like he's reading between the lines I haven't yet spoken.

"I was thinking," I start, forcing air into my lungs. "It's time for me to go back to the cottage..."

"No." His reply is instant, his eyes lit with frustration.

The words feel like a slap.

"It's been quiet," I press.

"It hasn't been long enough." He puts his bottle down with enough force that the noise startles me.

"Then...maybe I can go back to work, at least. Kayla has been taking care of the turtles, and it's time to release them." My voice trembles on *release them*. It's not just about turtles, and we both know it.

He exhales hard, raking a hand over his hair. "I don't feel right about any of it yet."

"What *do* you feel right about then?" I snap before I can stop myself. "You want me to hide here forever? Because if that's the plan, I might as well go the hell home to New Jersey."

Something shifts in his expression, a flicker of panic, maybe, before it softens. He works his jaw. Then he steps forward, close enough that I feel the heat radiating off of him.

"I feel right about you being here. With me." His voice is low, rough around the edges.

"But why?"

"Isn't it obvious? To keep you safe." Reid huffs.

"That's the *only* reason?"

He folds his arms, shuts down. Classic Reid. "Emery."

"No, Reid. Don't fucking *Emery* me. What is this?" I gesture between the two of us. "We go from kissing like we're about to burn down the house to you acting like I'm your roommate. No, worse, your ward. So, which one is it?"

He sighs, dragging a hand down his face. "You're still healing."

"I'm fine." My voice cracks on the word. I bite my lip to keep it from trembling. "You just...got me out of your system. Right? You scratched the itch, and now you're done." I force out a laugh that sounds nothing like me. "Just say it so I can stop waiting for you to reach for me."

His head snaps up, eyes blazing. "Is that what you think? That I got you out of my system?"

"What other explanation is there?" My voice drops low, laced with disappointment.

He takes a step closer. "Did you ever think that maybe I'm trying not to hurt you? That every time you walk past me in those little gym shorts and those sexy fucking glasses, I'm not this close to losing my mind?" He pinches two fingers together. "Or, that I want you so badly I can't see straight, but the only thing worse than losing you to the monsters in this town would be losing you because I didn't know how to *do this*? Because I don't. I've been alone for years, Emery, by choice. I've made my peace with it. And then you show up and ruin all of it." He's pacing now, agitated, running a hand over the back of his neck.

The air between us crackles.

I turn away so he can't see the sting of rejection on my face. I open the oven just to have something to do with my hands. The heat burns my cheeks. There is so much I don't know about Reid—I can't just demand that he let me in.

"I don't know what you want from me, Reid."

"God," he mutters from behind me.

When I turn, he's already moving, his eyes dark with hunger. My pulse picks up, and I instinctively take a step toward him.

"Fuck it," he growls and then he's on me.

His mouth crashes into mine with a force that steals my breath. It's not gentle, it's hungry and aching, weeks of restraint snapping all at once. The sound that escapes me is half surprise, half need. His hand cups the back of my head, as his lips claim me again and again, deeper, harder, like he's trying to memorize me from the inside out. His other hand finds my thigh, gripping my ass as he lifts me easily. My legs move instinctively around his waist, and he backs me against the wall. He tastes like salt and beer and a hunger he has kept buried for too long.

I cling to him, my fingers fisting the back of his shirt, tugging him closer because I can't get enough. Because I've wanted this just as badly, and the relief of his mouth on mine is all consuming. The air between us sizzles, every brush of his lips against mine a promise and a warning.

When he finally pulls back, his forehead rests against mine, both of us breathing hard, our lips still brushing. His voice comes out rough, almost broken.

"Tell me to stop," he rasps.

"Don't stop," I breathe, kissing him again.

It's slower this time, tender where the first one was aching and urgent. And this time, it feels less like a collision and more like surrender.

Reid lifts me and carries me into his room, softly laying me on the mattress, his eyes searching mine. "You have no idea what you do to me."

"Then show me," I whisper.

Reid brushes hair off my forehead, his eyes darkening, torn between caution and surrender. "I want to take this slow." The words are ragged, like they're costing him something.

"I don't." I run my hands over his chest to the back of his head. "I'm tired of being afraid. Of everything. I want you."

For a second he stares at me and then his control breaks. He kisses me again, deeper this time, a low growl vibrating in his chest. His hand slips beneath the hem of my T-shirt, his palm warm against my skin as it trails up the length of my ribcage. He lingers just over the band of my bra, hesitating.

I clutch at his shoulders, the world tilting around us. "Reid."

He pulls back just enough to look at me, his breaths coming rapidly, his eyes wild. "You need to tell me to stop."

"I won't."

A muscle tics in his jaw, his thumb tracing tiny circles around my ribs before his fingers slip beneath my bra. Finding a nipple, he lightly brushes his fingertips over it before his mouth finds my neck. I gasp at the feeling of his hands and his mouth on me at the same time.

"You don't know what you're asking for," he rasps, planting a trail of kisses along my jaw.

"Yes, I do."

That's all it takes for his mouth to find mine again. "You undo me," he murmurs, breaking our kiss. "You have since the first damn day."

"Then stop fighting it." My heart thunders in my chest as I sit up, tugging my shirt over my head and unclasping my bra in one fluid motion.

Reid's breath catches, and he presses his forehead into mine. "If I don't slow down right now, that's it."

I nod, dizzy and trembling as I reach for the hem of his shirt, pulling it off to reveal ripples of lean muscle.

He gives in then, pushing me back gently on the sheets, slowly working the button on my shorts, his desire tight against his own.

I run a hand over his zipper where his erection is begging to be let out. "I've been dreaming about this since Jeopardy."

A laugh bursts out of him. "Me too."

CHAPTER TWENTY-SIX

REID

I LOWER MYSELF next to her, taking in every inch of her. The soft rise of her chest, the faint flush along her skin, the way her eyes search mine like she's still trying to convince herself this is real. I trail my fingertips up her ribcage, lingering on a pert pink nipple. Dipping my head, I take it in my mouth, sucking gently. She lets out a breathy moan, and I move to the other side, desperate to hear it again.

"Reid," her breath comes out like a whisper, a plea and a question all at once.

I meet her eyes, brushing blond hair off her forehead. "It's been...a long time for me." I say, my voice low and unsteady. "Just... tell me what you like, okay?"

I run a palm up her side and a shiver runs through her.

"I like...you. All of it," she breathes, closing her eyes.

That's all I need. I move slowly, giving her time to feel, to breathe. The tension between us hums, thick and electric. Every sigh, every touch saying the things we've both been too afraid to speak aloud.

I slide a finger through her center and feel just how much she wants this. My name falls from her lips again as I hover over her, kissing down her sides until she's trembling. I lick across her hipbones, and she hisses.

"Is this okay?" I pause, looking up at her.

"Y-yes. Please." Her words are barely audible.

It's been years since I've been intimate with someone I care about. When I first returned from active duty, I took women out, but it never lasted more than a couple of weeks. They asked too much of me. I don't know what Emery wants, but I want to give her everything.

I move lower, planting kisses on her inner thighs before parting her folds and sinking my mouth into her. She cries out with pleasure, and I take it as a sign to keep going.

I flick my tongue over the bud of nerves, alternating between biting and sucking. When her legs begin to tremble, I slide in a finger, then another, feeling her walls swell against my hand.

"Reid," she moans. "This is..."

"Don't hold back," I growl.

"It's too much," she cries, and I sink my tongue further into her, dragging my teeth over her swollen nub.

That does it, she comes undone around me. When I look at her again, her cheeks are flushed, lips parted. Her eyes are glassy with emotion, but a content smile spreads across her face.

"That was incredible," she whispers.

I move over her again, my eyes meeting hers. She traces a hand along my jaw, our gazes locked.

"Do you...want more?" she asks, pulling her bottom lip between her teeth.

"I do if you do," I say, my voice husky.

She brings her arms up around my neck then, a teasing smile playing on her lips. "Oh, I do."

She tugs at the waistband of my boxers, pushing them down and freeing my rock hard dick.

Her breath hitches but her hand wraps around my length, gently stroking. A growl rumbles through me.

"Baby," I murmur.

"I'm on the pill," Emery offers. "I haven't been with anyone new in five years."

I swallow, pushing the thought of her with anyone but me

from my mind.

I haven't been with *anyone* in years, but I don't say that. She feels like she's always been mine.

I clear my throat. "I'm good too."

Emery pulls me to her, kissing me deeply. This kiss is different than our earlier ones. They were urgent, hungry. This is tender, like she's been yearning for it in the same way I have. I kiss her back, my hands finding her hair, my dick hovering over her slick heat.

She reaches down and rubs the tip between her folds, and I let out a groan.

"I'm ready for you," she whispers, kissing me again. Her hands find my hips, and she pulls me to her. It's tight at first, I am only halfway in, but Emery shimmies her hips and opens wider and I sink into her. The rush of emotion overwhelms me. I've been without it so long, I've forgotten what it feels like to be this close to someone, not just the touch but the trust beneath it.

I move with fervor, driven by the ache, the longing I've felt for connection—for *her*. My hands find hers above her head and it's like we're anchored together. Her gasp hits my neck, and the sound goes right through me. My hands tremble where they rest on her skin and my mouth finds hers again. I could live inside her forever.

The years between now and the last time I let myself get this close to someone come rushing back to me. The walls I built to keep people out, the guilt I carried, the belief that I'm better off numb. All that comes crashing down with every quiet sigh, with every look she gives me that says she sees me and all my scars.

Emery arches her back, meeting me thrust for thrust. The pressure inside me coils tighter, at the feel of her bare, burning through every nerve until it breaks. My whole body shudders with it—relief and ache all tangled together. For a heartbeat, there's nothing but white noise in my head and the sound of her name on my lips as she finds her release with me.

I collapse on top of her and roll to my side, the whole world fading away except the two of us breathing the same air. For the first time in weeks, I'm not thinking about danger, or guilt, or keeping her safe. I'm just here, with her heartbeat against mine, our hands clasped together, the steady rise and fall of her chest under my palm.

It feels like coming home to a place I didn't know existed.

And suddenly, I'm terrified. Because if anything ever happens to her, I don't know what would be left of me after that.

I press a kiss to her temple and whisper her name, just to hear it on my tongue.

Then—*beep-beep-beep!*

We both jolt upright, startled by the piercing sound of the smoke detector. The smell of something burnt hits my nose.

Emery bursts out laughing. "Shit! The potatoes."

I drop my head to her shoulder, laughing too, the tension dissolving into something warm. "I distracted you."

"It was worth it." She sighs.

I swing my legs out of bed, ready to grab the fire extinguisher, then I turn back, kissing her softly. "Definitely worth it."

SUNLIGHT CUTS THROUGH the blinds, thin gold lines across her skin. Emery is asleep in my arms, her breathing is soft and peaceful, like the last few weeks never happened. Her blond hair spills over my bare chest, tickling me, but I don't dare move. I let myself feel it. The weight of her leg draped over mine, the sweet scent of her hair, the softness of her bare breasts on my skin. It feels like home.

After some take out, we fell back into bed, exploring each other all night long. It's the most connected I've ever been to anyone. Emery can read me like a book, and it scares the fuck out of me.

And yet, last night was a mistake I'd make a thousand times over. It was her hands on my back, her voice in my ear, the way she says my name like a promise and a prayer. Every wall I've worked so hard to build, gone in an instant.

All this time I told myself I was protecting her. Getting tangled up with her puts her at risk. This is about safety. But I was lying to both of us. I was protecting myself. Now that I've let her in, she's the only thing I'm terrified to lose.

She stirs, a soft sound escaping her throat as her palm moves over my chest, finding the scar there. My hand finds hers and my heart twists.

"You okay?" she murmurs, half-asleep.

"Yeah." I clear my throat. "I didn't mean to wake you."

She smiles against my skin, her eyes still closed. "It's okay."

"Go back to sleep. It's early." I brush a strand of hair off her face and press a kiss on her forehead.

"Mmm," she hums, curling in the crook of my arm. I pull her in closer, savoring the feel of her against me.

But I can't ignore the familiar feeling of dread, like something is coming. My gut is tight with the old familiar instinct. It never stays quiet for long.

I'll let her sleep a little while longer, let her think everything's okay.

Then I'll get Tate to help me pull the traps she left in the marsh. We'll check the docks, scope out the cottage. Keep our guards up, see if anything is out of place.

For now though, I let myself breathe her in. Let the world stay still.

Just for a little while longer.

CHAPTER TWENTY-SEVEN

EMERY

Waking up in Reid's arms is nothing short of amazing. The warmth of his skin against mine, the way our legs stayed tangled all through the night, the steady rhythm of our synchronized breathing. It's almost too much to process. I'm sure everything is heightened by the recent events, but we slept through the night clinging to each other as if sleep itself might tear us apart. I've never felt anything like it.

"What do you say I go pick us up some breakfast?" he murmurs in my ear, tugging me closer. His voice is rough with sleep, and the sound vibrates down my spine.

I've drifted in and out of dreams for the past hour, half-awake, half-floating in that space where reality blurs with all your deepest desires. The sunlight creeping through the blinds finally forces me to open my eyes.

I roll over to face him, blinking against the golden light. For a moment the world narrows to nothing more than this bed and this man.

"Hi," I whisper.

"Hey," he rasps, brushing hair off my cheek. His thumb lingers for a heartbeat too long and my pulse picks up.

"So, this is new." A nervous laugh escapes me, and I feel like a teenager again, completely undone by her first crush.

"Yeah. Yeah, it is." He studies me with that quiet intensity of his. "Are you...good with this? No regrets?"

"No regrets," I echo. The truth of my words catches me by surprise. "Are you?"

He pulls me into his chest, wrapping his strong arms around me and planting a kiss on the crown of my head. "Emery, you're the first person I've let break down my walls in years. Now I see how much I have needed connection. So, yeah, I'm *so* good with this."

"Great," I breathe, snuggling into him.

He lies with me for a moment longer before rolling out of bed and stretching.

I watch as he pulls on some gym shorts and a T-shirt, slipping his feet into a pair of sandals. It's the most relaxed I've ever seen him and something in my chest twists. I *get* to see him like this.

"I'll get us some food. Be back in a bit." And then he's gone.

Once I hear the door shut, the silence washes over me. I nestle back under the down comforter, my skin still tingling from his touch. And I marvel at how for the first time in a long time, I feel wanted, cared for, *seen*. Not as a distraction or a problem to be managed as Jason so often treated me—but as myself. Exactly as I am. And yet, beneath the glow of it all, I'm left wondering why the hell he has been alone for so long. What ghosts keep him company when the lights go out? I stare at the empty doorway, wondering if he'll ever trust me enough to let me see the parts of himself that even he is afraid to face.

By Monday, I've managed to convince Reid to let me go back to work. He's protective but surprisingly agreeable. I can't hang around his cabin all day. No matter what dangers lurk around this sleepy little town, I'm still being paid my annual salary to conduct my research and it's time to do my job. We move through the morning in an easy rhythm, with the kind of quiet familiarity that feels like we've done this a hundred times before. We stop by

Poppy's for coffee and pastries, before going our separate ways for the day.

There's something about the ritual of normalcy: caffeine, sunshine, purpose.

Kayla is on summer break and keeps me company most of the day. We start by compiling all of Dr. Young's notes on the turtles with my own. Something about her final entries feels... unfinished. The notes don't taper off or resolve—they just *stop* mid-thought. One page is dense with questions and margin notes, hypotheses circled and underlined, arrows pointing toward next steps. And then suddenly, nothing. Maybe, it's because she passed away, but it almost reads like she was on the verge of some kind of breakthrough—as if she knew what I know—and then suddenly, nothing.

Kayla thinks someone found out about what Dr. Young had discovered and silenced her. I don't indulge her theory, at least not fully. She's a teenager, and the last thing I want is for her to feel afraid of the place she's called home for her entire life. But I can't shake the feeling that she's not entirely wrong.

Nevertheless, she's inspired and is encouraging me to finish this research. So, we spend the morning sketching out the next phase of the study. Our new hypothesis builds on Dr. Young's work: the terrapin population isn't just declining, it's being *displaced*. Nesting grounds are being disrupted by increased boat traffic, chemical runoff, and possible illegal activity in the surrounding marshes. My working theory is that the routes used for smuggling are the same channels vital to the terrapins' migration and nesting cycles.

If we can document changes in the turtles' GPS-tag patterns and correlate them with unusual boat traffic, we might be able to prove it. Whether or not I actually want to risk my life by publishing these findings is another thing.

Regardless, it feels good to have my mind occupied again. When I walk the docks to meet Reid for lunch at The Drift Net, I even feel happy. The sun is shining off the still bay, gulls are crying, circling overhead in search of their next meal, and people are milling about. It almost feels normal.

"Hey, baby." Reid sneaks up behind me, his breath tickling my ear.

I turn my head to catch a smile on his face that stops me in my tracks.

"I didn't know you *actually could* smile this big," I tease, planting a kiss on his lips. "You must be in a good mood."

Things between us feel so right, so *normal.* Almost like it was always this way. Reid today isn't even a little bit like the man I met six weeks ago.

"It's because you're here." His voice catches and for a moment, I wonder if he's letting himself relax into this, if his guard is coming down. His hands linger at my waist, and he pulls my back into his chest, sucking in a breath.

"Will you two get a room?" calls a shirtless Tate, brushing past us in the direction of the bait shop.

"We have one, thanks," Reid calls after him, laughing in a carefree way I've never seen. He lets his arms fall and links my hand with his. "Come on, let's eat."

THE DRIFT NET is casual, like everything else around here, so it's seat yourself. Reid leads me to a table at the far side of the restaurant, overlooking the bay. There's a salty breeze blowing through, and the only noise is the soundtrack of summer, sounds of flapping water and sea birds flying overhead. Tidehaven, in many ways, is like the Jersey Shore, where I'm from, but much quieter. The town is so small, it almost doesn't feel like a community. While I came here for solitude to clear my head, that may be the part I miss most.

At home, in mid-June, there are plenty of summer festivals and farmer's markets. There are beach days with friends and nights out having drinks by the water. Perhaps it's because I've only made friends with Reid, but I am missing a sense of belonging.

Reid hands me a menu and we're quiet as we both look it over. I don't even know why I'm looking. I know I'm going to eat fish and chips. Anything besides fresh seafood isn't an option.

Willie treks across the restaurant to take our order. The look on his face says we're putting him out.

"You couldn't sit at the bar today?" he grumbles. "Making this old man walk all the way over here."

I let out a gasp before biting back a grin.

"Oh, come on, Willie, you've already got a table across the way." Reid gestures to a table of four women in their thirties. A small toddler sits in a highchair, and another woman slowly pushes a stroller back and forth, presumably to soothe a baby inside.

"Yeah, yeah. What'll it be?" Willie asks, flipping open his notebook.

"Fish and chips, please," I say, and as an afterthought, "And a Coke."

"Great. Morgan?"

"I'll have the same, Willie. Wouldn't want you to work too hard." Reid smirks.

"Why are you so happy?" Willie mumbles.

"Isn't it obvious?" Reid gestures at me and my neck heats.

"Stop," I say, feeling the flush creep to my cheeks.

"Whatever, love birds." Willie stomps away.

"So," Reid says, holding his hand out across the table.

I take it, the warmth of it sending goosebumps up my arm, despite the warm day.

"So," I repeat. "How come no one expects you to be happy around here?"

Reid brings his eyes up to mine, studying me for a beat. "I was pretty messed up when I got out of the SEALs," he admits, his voice edged with sadness. "Everyone knew it, and people I've known since I was a kid kept trying to help me. Make me feel better. But I kept snapping at them. I didn't know how to transition back to civilian life, and I was in a dark place."

A quiet "Oh" falls from my lips.

"Before long, I'd earned the reputation of being cranky, mean even. Eventually, most of them stopped trying. They said I'd never be the same." He scratches his jaw, looking out over the water.

"And? Are you the same?"

He turns back to me, a small smile at the corner of his mouth. "I'm...seeing glimpses of my old self the last couple of months. More so lately." He squeezes my hand.

"Oh," I whisper again.

"I was just walking around numb—to everything. Tate is the one who pushed me to get help. Found some Veteran's groups I could join. He's the brother I've never had." Reid's voice trails off. His eyes drop to our joined hands and then flick back to mine. "But you...Emery, you've made me *feel* again."

Before I can reply, my phone buzzes next to me on the table. We glance down at the same time, and Jason's name lights up the screen.

"What does he want?" Reid asks, his tender tone shifting toward irritation.

"I don't know. I haven't talked to him in weeks," I say, freeing my hand to pick up the phone.

"Tell him you're with someone else now."

My jaw falls slack, and I look at him before opening the text. "Is...that what this is?"

"I thought it was obvious." Reid's tone softens and he grabs my hand again. "What I just told you...I usually don't let anyone see those parts of me."

I lick my lips, letting out a slow breath.

He's quiet then, watching me open Jason's text message. A simple "How are you?" and nothing more. I lock my phone with a sigh and set it down without replying.

Reid turns his gaze back toward the water, silence weighing heavy between us. It's not like there's anyone else. I don't remember ever feeling the things I feel for him in past relationships. But how much of that is us seeking solace in each other in a time of uncertainty and how much of it is real feelings?

"Reid," I start.

I'm interrupted by Willie bringing our sodas. As if he can sense the shift in Reid's mood, Willie sets them down and wanders away without a word.

"Reid." This time my voice is firmer.

He flicks his eyes toward mine in response.

"If this is going to be a thing...a *real* thing between us... you have to trust me. I feel like despite all we've shared together already, we don't know each other that well. My feelings for you are strong, they are. But how much of it is because I'm afraid and you make me feel safe and how much is because I actually *know* you?" I sigh, then quieter. "I want to know you."

"I want you to know me too. I want us to know *each other*." He reaches for me then, his thumb tracing small circles on the back of my hand. The motion is simple, tender, and it undoes me a little. Neither of us moves right away when Willie drops our food.

"I'll try," he finally says, like the words cost him something.

"I'd like that," I whisper.

We eat in a comfortable silence, the kind that settles when something unspoken has shifted. Outside, the midday heat shimmers across the water, and the chatter of passing dockhands filters in through the open walls. Ceiling fans whir overhead, stirring the smell of salt and fried fish. For the first time in a while, it feels possible to breathe again.

"The Fourth of July Festival is going to be huge this year." A woman's voice cuts across the restaurant, breaking our silence.

The women at the next table burst into excited chatter.

"Fourth of July Festival?" I glance at Reid, with a small smile. "You mean this town actually has community events?"

Reid scoffs in mock offense. "Of course they do."

"It's just been so quiet around here, I didn't expect anything would go on for the Fourth of July." I shrug, plucking a fry off my plate and popping it in my mouth.

He leans back in his chair, a smirk playing on his lips. "As you can imagine, it's not really my thing. It draws a large crowd though, so I usually work extra security for Colt." He pauses, pointing to the small boardwalk that starts beyond the research center and goes along the bay. "It's a big block party sort of thing on the boardwalk. Lots of vendors, crafters, food trucks, a boat parade. Fireworks over the bay at night. People get really jazzed about it."

"Huh," I say, chewing slowly. "Maybe I could have a turtle booth."

Reid arches a brow. "Do you really think that's wise?"

"It could be a sea turtle *awareness* booth. Or marine life in general." I shrug, a surge of excitement running through me. "I bet Kayla would help me."

"Oh boy, here we go," he mutters with a shake of his head, but there's a trace of a smile there.

"What? I bet a lot of people would like to learn about marine life conservation," I say with mock defensiveness. "You're just being a stick in the mud."

"I'm just picturing you causing a scene on the boardwalk."

"Aww, come on. It's exciting!" I give him my most convincing grin.

He doesn't say it, but I see it in his eyes—a mix of amusement and underlying worry. Like he already knows, excitement here rarely comes without a cost.

CHAPTER TWENTY-EIGHT
REID

THE REST OF the week passes quietly. So quietly that Emery and Kayla somehow convince me on Friday to let them go into the marsh to release the rehabilitated turtles. I'm not dumb enough to let them go alone though, so first thing Saturday morning, I borrow a larger boat from Tate at the marina so the three of us can fit and head for Blackbird Cottage.

When I pull up to Emery's dock, they're in the yard with carriers and research gear, sunlight catching in their hair, both of them laughing about something that makes me feel like I've walked in on an inside joke.

"You girls ready?" I call, my hand braced on the edge of the dock.

Emery looks lighter and something tugs at me deep inside. I like to think I'm the reason. The yard's leveled now—thanks to my buddy's landscaping crew—and next week another old friend will start rebuilding the dock. I'd do it myself, but leaving Emery alone after work doesn't sit well. Not yet.

Emery and Kayla haul their gear over, their chatter like birds chirping in the breeze. When I help them both inside, Emery's fingers brush mine, and it's nothing, but it's everything.

"This boat is so nice," Kayla says, running her hands along the side.

"Yeah, it's Tate's, so don't mess anything up." I turn, giving them a teasing look as I back the boat away from the dock.

A laugh bubbles out of Kayla. "I'm not scared of Tate. He's way nicer than you."

"Hey!" I shoot back.

"Okay, okay," Kayla teases. "I'll admit, you've been way better since you two have started doing it."

"Excuse me?" I turn briefly, frowning at her, before returning my attention to the marsh, desperate not to let my embarrassment show.

"Oh...uh—we're not..." Emery stammers from her seat behind me.

"Oh, puh-lease." Kayla exaggerates the word. "I'm seventeen, guys, I'm not blind."

"Reid's just keeping me safe. It's been a little dicey lately." Emery's voice falters.

"Yeah, keeping you safe *in his bed*." Kayla cackles.

I briefly catch Emery's eye and smirk. "You caught us. We're dating. Way more than just *doing it*."

"Reid," Emery hisses.

A smile twitches on my lips, but I keep my eyes on the marsh in front of me.

"Aww, you guys." Kayla claps her hands dramatically. "I'm like your kid."

"No," I whirl around, laughing. "No, you're not."

Both girls burst into laughter, and I can't help but join in. This is the lightest I've felt in a long time. It feels easy. Normal. Like this—sun on our faces, laughing out on the water—is what life's supposed to feel like.

"So, where are we setting these babies free?" I ask, scouring the shoreline. "Same place as before?"

Emery stands, moving to my side. She shields her eyes from the sun's glare as she scopes out the shoreline and the reeds. Her bare arm brushes mine, sending a spark down my skin. "Let's try over there," she says, pointing to a patch of reeds. Then she freezes. "Wait. I don't like the look of that."

"What?" I follow her gaze. The reeds are matted down, streaked with mud where something—or *someone*—has driven through.

"Let me get closer," I say, steering the boat carefully so as not to get stuck in the muck.

"Tire tracks," Emery says, her voice catching. "Why are there tire tracks out here?"

Kayla leans forward, her voice trembling. "Is your transmitter broken?" She's pointing toward a bent pole half-submerged in the muck, its top sheared off.

"Sure looks that way." Emery sighs, chewing on her lip. "We can't leave them here."

"Oh man. I thought this was over." Kayla moans nervously. "What do you think it means?"

I scan the marsh, my SEAL instincts kicking in. The rippling grass, the sluggish water, everything feels too still.

"It means," I say carefully. "That someone's been here. Recently."

The girls fall silent. Even the cicadas seem to hush.

Emery moves closer, her voice barely above a whisper. "What if someone saw us come out here?"

I feel for the weapon concealed in the back of my waistband—a habit I've grown used to since Emery's been here.

My gut tightens. "Then we're getting out of here. Now."

I start the engine, my eyes sweeping the reeds one last time before turning us back in the other direction. The earlier laughter feels like it happened days ago.

As the boat picks up speed, I glance back at Emery. She's cradling one of the carriers to her chest, her hair whipping in the wind, her jaw set with stubborn determination. I feel that tug again—desire, fear, something deeper I don't have a name for.

"So, new spot?" I ask over my shoulder, trying to lighten the mood.

Emery points. "There. That stretch there by the cypress grove. The current's mild there and it's quiet."

I guide us that way, the air heavy with brine and the buzz of the marsh. When we reach water shallow enough for wading, Emery and Kayla hop out of the skiff, each holding a carrier and wading into the shallow murky water. The tension bleeds off her little by little as Emery kneels by the waterline, coaxing each turtle into the shallows.

"Go on," she whispers. "You're free."

They slip beneath the surface one by one, the ripples widening and fading. Watching her there, hair tousled by wind, soft smile on her face, I feel that old ache in my chest again. A sense that maybe there's something worth fighting for in this godforsaken town after all.

When she looks back at me, eyes shining, it hits like a punch to the gut. I clear my throat and start the motor.

"Let's head back before the tide turns."

The girls trek back to the skiff, and I hold out a hand, helping each of them out of the muck and over the side.

Kayla flops back on the bench, sun-drunk and grinning. "That was actually kind of perfect."

"Yeah," I murmur, eyes scanning the horizon. "Almost."

We reach the marina just after lunch and the easy feeling fades immediately. Docked two slips down is Dale Langford's yacht, gleaming obnoxiously in the sun. He's leaning against the rail, a cigar hanging from his lips, talking to two men I don't recognize and Atlas fucking Roarke. Their heads are bent together, like old friends catching up. Dale laughs at something Atlas says, clapping him on the shoulder.

The pieces click into place with a sickening certainty.

I don't hear a word they're saying. I don't need to. The second Dale's eyes land on us, the familiar smirk spreads across his face, the one that never means anything good. He dismisses the men, jogs down the steps of the yacht, and walks toward us at the end of the dock.

"Stay in the boat," I tell the girls, my voice edged with irritation.

Emery bristles but stays put. Kayla's chatter drops off.

"Well, well, well, if it isn't the marine biologist and her bodyguard," Dale taunts, sauntering closer.

"Don't," I warn Emery quietly. "Let me handle it."

I kill the motor and step out, looping the rope to the cleat. And then Dale is in front of me.

"Busy morning, Morgan?" He sucks in a puff of his cigar and flicks the ash in the water.

"Just work," I say flatly.

"Always nice to see people...getting their hands dirty." He flicks his gaze to Emery, lingering too long for my liking.

I square my shoulders, without taking my eyes off Langford. "Go inside, girls."

Emery hesitates, defiance briefly flashing in her eyes, but one glimpse of my face and she relents, nodding. She gives Kayla a gentle shove, and the two of them hurry toward the research center, disappearing inside.

Dale chuckles, low and knowing. "Protective, huh? Cute."

I step closer so I'm in his space. "I'm done playing nice, Langford. You stay the fuck away from her. From *both* of them."

Dale takes another puff of his cigar, inhaling long and slow. "I don't make promises."

"Yeah? Well, I do. And I can promise you this. If anything happens to either one of them, it's not going to turn out well for you," I grit out, my jaw clenched.

"That sounds like a threat, Morgan. I don't respond well to threats." Dale's lips twitch, like this is all a fucking game to him.

"That's too bad." I step around him, bumping his shoulder as I pass. "See you around, Dale."

THE WATER IS everywhere. Black and endless. And deep. It closes over my head before I can take a full breath.

The comm in my ear is dead, static burning my ear drums. The only sound I hear is the thump of my own heart. Erratic and ragged. Salt burns my throat. I blink through the murky water, the glow of my dive light illuminating my surroundings just enough to show the wreckage beneath me.

But I'm not in the Gulf. I'm in the marsh. The water is deep, thick and cloudy with sediment. The eel grass looks like hands reaching for me. Something flashes and then I see her. Her blond hair drifting like seaweed, eyes wide and unseeing. Emery.

"Em!" I shout, kicking down hard, my chest seizing. I reach for her, swimming as hard as I can, but the reeds twist around me, weighing me down. I can't get to her. Panic engulfs me—the same panic I had in my last failed mission. When I swam toward the voice that never made it back.

Only this time, it's her voice calling me.

"Reid!"

I reach for her fingertips, but I can't quite grasp them. And then she's gone.

Then, a light. The water brightens and a hull rises through the depths. Langford's yacht. On fire. It's burning under the water, glowing. The smoke curls, turning the surface red.

"Reid!" she calls again.

Then I see her, trapped in a dive cage, pounding on the glass. I push upward, pressure in my chest crushing me, desperate to get to her, to save her. Every kick is heavier than the last until I almost have her. Almost—

I bolt upright, lunging forward, an animalistic sound escaping me.

And then her arms are around my neck, hugging me from behind.

"Shh, shh. You're okay. I'm here," she soothes, whispering in my ear. She plants a soft kiss on my neck, and I feel my heartrate start to slow.

"Emery," I rasp.

"Shh. You had a nightmare."

It takes me a full second to come to—to realize I'm in my bed, in my cabin, with Emery naked, arms wrapped around me. The heat of her skin sizzles against my back. The fan hums overhead, the windows cracked just enough to let in a bay breeze.

I drag a hand down my face, and turn, planting my feet on the floor. Emery scoots next to me, clinging to my arm. My pulse is still pounding, a tremor I can't shake.

"You're sweating," she murmurs, brushing a hand over my forehead.

I let out a grunt and move to open my nightstand drawer, checking for my pistol. I pick it up, feeling its heaviness in my hand for a moment before putting it back, momentarily soothed by its presence.

It was just a dream. But in that dream, my worst fear.

I couldn't protect her.

CHAPTER TWENTY-NINE

EMERY

REID HAS BEEN skulking around the cabin all morning. He hasn't spoken two words to me since his nightmare. Frustration surges through me, and I find myself catering to him the way I have in past relationships. Offering to do things for him, rubbing his shoulders to soothe his nerves.

It's when I set a piping hot cup of coffee in front of him, and he doesn't look up that I decide I have to say something.

"Reid," I say slowly, perching on the chair next to his. He's sitting in his favorite armchair that faces a large glass door overlooking the marsh. It's taken me a few weeks to notice but this seems to be the place he comes to think.

He flicks his eyes up to me and then back at the marsh.

"Do you want to talk about it?" I ask, reaching for his hand. When he doesn't react, I let my hand fall away.

"Not particularly," he snaps.

I sigh, sinking further into the chair. I let the silence hang between us for a few minutes before I speak. He doesn't move and he doesn't look at me, and even though I know this is about his dream, I can't help but feel like I did something wrong.

"Reid, do you remember the other day at the Net when you said you wanted us to be together?" I ask gently.

He looks at me then before planting his elbows to his knees and burying his face in his hands.

"And I told you if it is going to work, you have to let me in? Not shut me out. You have to show me who you are." I move from the chair and kneel in front of him.

Reid lets out a sigh before bringing his eyes up to meet mine. "I remember."

"I'm here right now, baby. But I can't stay if you won't talk to me." I put a hand on his knee, and he covers it with his own, keeping his gaze focused on the floor.

"I have nightmares. Since I've been back. They're brought on by stress, and they're horrific. I have a hard time bouncing back from them."

"That much I got," I say, letting out a slow breath and waiting for him to continue.

Reid lets out a groan and rubs the back of his neck. "This one was awful."

"Okay," I say, squeezing his knee.

"I was a SEAL again. And you were there...and I couldn't save you." His voice cracks, prompting me to climb into his lap.

He opens his arms and when I nuzzle into him, he holds me tight. "They've been coming back a lot lately. And it scares me."

"Can you identify the triggers?"

He doesn't answer immediately, his hand tracing the length of my spine in gentle strokes. "No," he finally says, but I get the sense that's not true.

"And in the past, what have you done to work through this?"

He lets out a deep, relenting breath. "There are groups. Support groups, therapy meetings. In Beaufort."

"You need to go." I pull back from his grip, studying his face. "Take the day and go, Reid."

"I—I can't. I don't want to leave you alone." His voice is thick with something I don't recognize before I realize it's fear. He said he couldn't save me in his dream, and he won't leave me now.

"Reid, this is important. I'll be okay. I'll stay close to the house, and I'll be fine." I tip his chin upward, so his eyes meet mine. "Go."

He leans in, kissing me softly, and little fireworks go off in my belly. This is a breakthrough.

Reid leaves shortly after breakfast, hoping to catch a midday meeting in Beaufort. He tells me he might meet up with some old unit buddies too and to call him if anything comes up.

My plan for today is to do some laundry, putter around his house, and start my paper on the turtle findings so far. It should keep me occupied while he's gone. I pop some headphones in and get started, first with the laundry. I feel a sweet tug in my chest at the idea of our dirty clothes mixing in the washer. Something tells me that would be new for Reid. I think I like it. The idea of us being together—as long as he keeps letting me in.

I make myself a packet of ramen noodles, and I'm just sitting down to start my paper when a knock at the heavy front door startles me. I glance down at my phone—only one o'clock. The knock sounds again and my pulse hammers in my ears.

Fuck.

Reid does have a peephole, unlike the door at Blackbird Cottage, but if I approach, there's a chance that whoever is on the other side will see me from the windows.

My phone buzzes once with a text. I flick my eyes to it.

Lena.

I tap the text.

Lena

Surprise!

Another text.

Alan

Let us in!

It takes me a minute to realize that's who's knocking on the door. I hop off the counter stool I'm sitting on and dart through the living room, my socks skidding on the hardwood floors.

"Em! We know you're in there!" Lena's voice calls from the other side.

I swing open the door.

"Oh my God! What are you two doing here?" I shriek, holding my arms open to them.

"We thought it would be fun to come and check out your sleepy little town. You know, since you *never* call us," Lena exaggerates, leaning her head on my shoulder. "Summer sessions are on a one-week break, so I left Dave with the kids and we hopped a flight."

"Hold on, you two flew on a plane together and didn't kill each other?" I laugh, pulling back so I can look at them. "I don't believe it."

"It wasn't easy," Alan mutters, stepping inside. "Is this where Coastal Carolina put you up?"

I shake my head, squinting. "Oh yeah, how did you find me?"

"I tracked your location, duh." Lena rolls her eyes. She steps further inside, looking around. "Nice digs."

"This isn't where I'm supposed to be staying... This is Reid's house."

Alan and Lena exchange curious looks before turning their eyes back to me—Lena's full of amusement, Alan's wariness. I watch Lena rake her eyes up the length of my body, the sleep shorts and oversized hoodie belonging to the oversized man that lives here. Her wheels are turning already, trying to figure it out.

"You're getting laid," she finally says, a hint of mischief in her voice.

"Maybe I better start at the beginning."

AN HOUR LATER, we're perched at a high-top table in the far corner of The Rusty Anchor, the bar I noticed when I arrived in town but haven't been to until now. I thought it might be safer, filling them in without the listening ears around The Drift Net.

"How long are you guys staying?" I ask, as we get settled.

"Well since Tidehaven has two hotel choices and neither of them are five-star, we're staying the night here and then going up to Charleston to meet some old colleagues of Alan's," Lena says. "Now stop deflecting."

"I'm not deflecting." I hold up my hands. "I'm allowed to ask how long you're staying."

"Lena just wants the juicy gossip," Alan says, shooting her a sideways look. "I want to know if you're doing okay."

I suck in a breath to speak but before I can, a server comes over with three glasses of water and some menus.

"I'm Georgia," she says with a smile. "I'll give y'all a few minutes."

When she disappears, I sigh. "I'm doing okay."

"Well, that's a relief!" Lena says dramatically. "Are you going to tell Alan how you didn't listen to him *at all*?"

I kick her hard under the table.

"Ouch!" she chirps.

I ignore her.

Alan eyes me curiously. "Emery...what is she talking about?"

I glare at Lena before turning my attention back to Alan.

"Uh...I sort of took my suspicions to the town council," I say, instinctively lowering my voice.

Alan's eyes go wide. "Emery."

I wince. "I know, trust me. It wasn't a good choice."

"What happened?" Alan's voice rises, coming out like a demand.

"It's fine," I say, holding up my hands. "I just...made the mayor and the council a little mad. Defensive, maybe." I don't bother telling them about my injuries or the threats made against me. He'd insist I leave. He'd report it to the university, or worse, get law enforcement involved. Reid would be so angry.

Reid.

The man I'm trusting to take care of me.

I don't know, maybe I *am* crazy. Maybe it's crazy to trust him over my friends and colleagues who have known me for seven years. But I have never felt safer than I do with Reid.

"Are you in danger, Emery?" Alan looks at me very seriously. "Because if you are..."

"No. I don't think so. I mean, I'm staying with Reid for a while. Backing off the turtles. I removed all my traps. I'm going to write the paper, but I don't know what I'll do with it."

They're both quiet for a moment, digesting my words. If they only knew the half of it—they'd be demanding I fly back with them immediately. I won't do that though.

I feel so different from the person I was when I came down here. Six weeks ago, I was lost and looking for purpose. I've found that here. And I've found something else too. A strong, sexy, loving man who makes me feel safe—among other things. I can't possibly walk away without knowing what will come of both things.

"Em, I'm saying this as your boss and your friend. If you need to get out and come home, all you have to do is call." Alan covers my hand with his. "It's not worth putting yourself at risk."

I sigh, leaning my cheek on my hand. "I know. But you know, these past six weeks have made me realize something. Being in the field, exploring habitats, getting to know the animals again—it makes me feel alive. I hadn't realized how much I missed being out there."

"In the slimy marsh muck?" Lena grimaces. "No thanks."

I bark out a laugh. "Well, I didn't ask you."

"I'm glad, Emery. I really am. But just please be safe out there," Alan says.

"I will, I promise."

"Okay, enough of this. Can we please order some margaritas and *relax*?" Lena begs. "I haven't been kid-free in ages."

"Sucks to be you," Alan retorts, nudging me so I'll agree with him.

I roll my eyes, but I'm smiling, feeling lighter than I have in days. I hadn't realized just how much I missed my people.

"Margaritas it is."

CHAPTER THIRTY

REID

THE DRIVE INTO Beaufort takes just under an hour if the boat traffic cooperates and the drawbridge doesn't get stuck. The Spanish moss hangs low over the two-lane causeway, forming a tunnel of green that holds the briny scent of the coast. I turn off onto a quiet side street, past pastel cottages and boats bobbing against the docks.

The parking lot to the VFW hall is half empty—it figures, I'm early. I hate being early. It gives me too much time to think about turning back. Every step I take into one of these meetings feels like walking through marsh muck, heavy and challenging, no matter how good I feel when I leave. I kill the engine and sit for a minute, watching the gulls circle above the water tower across the street. The VFW is a squat brick building with faded military flags flapping in the breeze and a sign that reads *Veterans Always Welcome—Coffee's Always Hot*. There was a time when this place felt like home to me, despite the demons it forced me to face. It's been far too long since I've set foot inside.

I make my way up the concrete ramp leading to the front door and push it open. The air smells like burnt coffee. I pause in the foyer, scanning a corkboard displaying photos of soldiers, their arms around each other. Job postings, fishing tournaments, and an old, tattered flyer about PTSD in vets. I peer inside and see only my unit buddy, former U.S. corpsman Sean McMillan, unstacking and lining up chairs for the meeting. Sean has always been my lifeline—steady, compassionate, but still delivering tough love. He's now working at a VA clinic and dedicating his life's work to helping others like us.

Sean glances up, a look of surprise spreading across his face. "Well, if it isn't Reid freaking Morgan. Aren't you a sight for sore eyes?"

"What's going on, brother?" I ask, moving into the room and wrapping him in a hug.

Sean pulls back, giving me the once over. Then he grins, his eyes crinkling in the corners. "I was beginning to wonder if you'd forgotten about us."

"Naw." I wave my hand. "I know where my home is."

I start lining up chairs and we work in silent unison for a few minutes before Sean breaks the silence.

"You still running?" he asks.

"Most days," I mutter. "My knee is bothering me though. It's hell getting old."

"That's not exactly what I meant." He gives me a look that tells me his memories haven't faded. He too remembers everything I wish I didn't. He's checking on me because I haven't shown up to one of these meetings in months.

I shrug, staring at the empty room. "Depends who you ask."

The door creaks open, interrupting us, and the thick Beaufort heat rushes in behind Mike "Bama" Travers, a gregarious and foul-mouthed marine.

"I brought the good stuff," he bellows, setting a box of donuts on the table next to the coffee. "Yo, Morgan. What's up?" He claps me on the back.

"Bama." I nod. "How you doing?"

Bama laughs in that easy way he always does, and I wonder how he manages to push aside so much of the darkness and only give off light. "I'm good, man. I'm real good."

Luis Vega strolls in, swiping a donut from the box and shoving it in his mouth before looking around.

"Yo-o-o, Morgan!" he says with his mouth full. "How goes

it?"

I laugh, shaking my head. "It's good Luis, how about yourself?"

"Great, man. Good to see you."

Sean tears into a bear claw, and the three of them trade easy jabs while I pour myself a coffee. More vets trickle in slowly, some guys I know, some I don't. Small talk fills the room of VA appointments, boats, the upcoming Fourth of July, and a new barbeque place opening on the water. I plop down in a chair, picking up on bits and pieces of conversation.

Before long, Sean plops next to me.

"You look better," he says quietly. "You got someone keeping you busy?"

I lift an eyebrow. "Define busy."

Sean smirks. "Well, you're not snarling at everyone so either you found Jesus or you got someone keeping your bed warm."

I take a sip of coffee, letting it burn my throat before I answer. "You always were a nosy son of a bitch."

Sean chuckles, nodding. "Okay, okay. I can take a hint. Just don't screw it up. The good stuff doesn't come around too often for guys like us."

The words hit me like a punch to the gut, and I know he's right. When was the last time I let myself feel things for someone else? It's been so long, I can't even remember. Before I can answer, Bama claps his hands.

"Okay, okay, gentlemen, let's get started." He takes a seat in the chair at the front of the room.

Chairs scrape as we form a circle. I settle in, relief filling my chest. The last time I was here, I was feeling hopeless. Like I'd never see my way through the fog of guilt and grief. Today, I'm here because I knew I needed help. Emery helped me see that. And even though the nightmares are back, this time, I know I'll be okay.

It's late by the time I cross the causeway back into Tidehaven. After the meeting, Sean, Bama, Luis, and I grabbed a meal and a couple of drinks. Minutes turned into hours of catching up, easy laughter, and the kind of conversation that doesn't need explaining. I didn't realize how much I needed to talk to the guys who understand what it's like to walk around with ghosts.

Somewhere between appetizers and dinner, I ended up telling them about Emery—not everything, not the danger. But about our connection and how she went from driving me crazy to being someone I can't imagine my life without. The words coming out of my mouth surprised me just as much as they did them. After the trauma I've faced, I'm not sure anyone expected me to ever let another person in.

I asked them about nightmares and what they do when they come back. Sean said exercise. Bama said whiskey. Luis said both. All of them agreed they're brought on by stress. I've had a lot of stress in my life since Emery showed up, but all of it revolves around keeping her safe. And the nightmares *are* less with her by my side. By the time I left the guys, I couldn't wait to get back to her and tell her about today.

We haven't talked much since I left this morning, a few text messages in the early afternoon, but the drive into town feels like an eternity. I'm desperate to see her, to touch her. To feel the calm her presence brings washing over me. I race up the gravel drive to my cabin, my heart already thundering in my chest when I see her navy Prius reflecting the last glints of sun.

I take the front steps two at a time and turn the knob on the front door. Locked. Good. I told her to keep the door locked when I'm not here. I'm glad she listened. I fish out my key and turn the knob.

"Honey, I'm home," I call, giving my best Ricky Ricardo impression.

Silence.

"Em? You here?" I shout again, scanning the kitchen, the living room. No sign of her.

It's not a big house—surely she'd hear me. Her car is here.

I push open the bedroom door, spotless. The bed is made, no sign of Emery. I move to the bathroom, maybe she is in the deep soaker tub, unwinding from a day's worth of writing.

Not there either.

"Em!" My voice comes out sharper now. I push through the hallway, each room emptier than the last. A cold knot forms in my stomach. "Where the hell is she?"

I move room to room, checking and then double checking. The house is empty. Emery is gone. I move back out to the porch, calling her name only to be answered by the sound of cicadas and tree frogs—not Emery.

"Fuck," I mutter, patting my pocket for my phone. Only, it's not there. In my rush to see her, I left it in the truck. I jog back down the steps, bolting for the driver's side and sliding in.

I hammer out a text to her.

Where are you?

But I don't bother waiting. If she's in trouble, I need to get to her. I start the truck and hit call.

"Helloooo," comes a singsong voice after the first ring. "How's my sexy sssseal?"

Her words are slurred. Laughter and music pulse in the background. Relief hits so hard I'm dizzy.

"Where are you?" I try my best to ease my racing pulse—to keep the bite out of my voice.

"The Rusty Anchor," she purrs. "With Lena and Alan."

Lena and Alan? I rack my brain trying to figure out who they are. Colleagues maybe? But down here?

"Do you need a ride?" I ask, already backing the truck out of my drive.

"Alan's got us—don't you, Alan?" she calls away from the phone.

"I'm coming."

I hang up before she can argue. I can't get to her fast enough.

THE RUSTY ANCHOR is lit up like a ship at sea when I pull in. Glowing white lights strung across the deck, the scents of fried shrimp and beer heavy in the air, and a packed house. The place hums with laughter and live music. I spot her instantly, sitting under the glow of the string lights and giggling hysterically with a woman I assume is Lena. Alan looks bored, staring into a half-drunk coke. He perks up when I approach.

Emery's cheeks are rosy, her glassy blue eyes bright and a little unfocused.

"Emery," I say when I reach the table.

She turns and her face lights up.

"You came!" she hops off the stool, crashing into my chest.

"I said I was coming."

She loops her arms around my neck. "I know, but I thought you were mad," she says, her words running together. She rests her cheek against my chest.

"I am a little," I murmur, keeping my voice low. "I didn't know you were going out."

"I'm safe," Emery says in an exaggerated whisper, meant for her friends to hear. Then she whirls out of my arms. "Lena, Alan, *this* is Reid. My boyfriend and bodyguard."

"Hot," Lena whispers, not quietly enough.

"Excuse me?" I quirk an eyebrow.

"Oh, sorry." She laughs, a little flustered. "I'm Lena. Emery's best friend."

"Lena." I nod, then turn to Alan.

"I'm Alan, Emery's...erm, supervisor." Alan's face reddens.

"We just dropped in on her this afternoon. Sorry if she worried you."

"She didn't worry me," I lie easily.

"Reid doesn't worry about *anything*," Emery coos, planting a sloppy kiss on my cheek.

If she only knew.

"How much have you had to drink?" I ask.

"Oh, they're both about four margaritas deep," Alan says, chuckling. "Lena, I think it's time we call it a night or you're going to be arguing with me about heading up to Charleston at eight a.m."

Lena's lower lip juts out in a pout before she says, "Yeah, you're right."

Alan settles the check while Lena and Emery hug goodbye. I watch as Lena squeezes her tight, brushing her hair off her face. "I miss you so much, Em," she murmurs.

"I miss youuuu," Emery replies.

"Reid is hot," Lena adds, her tone conspiratorial. "In that whole touch her and die way, yeah?"

"*So* fucking hot," Emery agrees as if I'm not here.

"Okay, you two. Let's keep it moving," I say, fighting a grin.

"Bye Alan," Emery says, squeezing him in a way that shouldn't make me jealous but does.

"Call me if you need anything," he says, giving Emery one last once over. Then holds out his hand to me. "Take care of our girl here. We'd like her back in once piece."

"Will do." I shake his hand, trying to ignore the sinking feeling that fills my gut when I think of giving her back.

A few minutes later, we're in my truck, Emery's head resting on the seat. Her eyes are slits, and she has a goofy, sleepy grin on her face.

"You came in there like a bat outta hell," she murmurs, drowsy.

"You scared me."

"I'm sorry." Her voice is soft now, fading.

"You can't do that," I say, quieter this time. "I thought someone took you."

Her lashes flutter closed. "Okay, I promise."

I glance over at her—the way her hair spills across her shoulders, her lips still curved in that sleepy smile. The fear that gripped me only minutes ago melts into something deeper. Something that up until now, I've been too afraid to name.

I was terrified something happened to her. That fear was immediately forgotten at the sight of her talking and laughing with her friends, replaced with a warmth that settled in my chest that hasn't dissipated since I got here.

And then it hits me.

The ache in my chest. The heat in my throat.

I love this woman.

Emery.

I love her.

And for the first time in my life, I'm terrified—not of dying—but of losing the one thing I've ever had worth living for.

CHAPTER THIRTY-ONE

EMERY

I WAKE UP in Reid's bed, sweating, the sheets twisted in my legs, and a crushing headache. It's been a long time since I've drank four margaritas, and now I know that was a mistake. My stomach rumbles with nausea—did I even eat last night? I must have.

"Good morning, sunshine."

Reid's voice startles me, and my eyes fly open. I hadn't realized they were still closed.

I cover my face and groan. "It's so bright in here."

Reid chuckles, setting something down on his nightstand. "That's because it's nearly eleven a.m."

I jolt upright. "What? I haven't slept this late in...years." I rub my eyes, spinning to put my feet on the floor, but I'm halted by a wave of dizziness. A garbled groan escapes me before I can stop it.

"Whoa girl, settle down," Reid says, helping me back into bed. "It's Sunday. We've got nowhere to be."

"This feels wrong," I mutter, tugging the blankets up to my chin. "But I don't want to be right."

Reid smiles and gently plants a kiss on my forehead. "I brought you coffee, electrolytes, and Advil. Because you were definitely drunk last night."

"I was," I agree. "It was good to see them though. It's been a long time since I've felt like my old self."

Reid swallows, Adam's apple bobbing. "What do you mean?"

"Just that, they're *my* people, you know? I saw them every day for seven years and now I'm here in a new place and I don't know anyone..." I let the words drop off.

"You know me."

"Besides you. It took a while for us to like each other." I giggle.

"Naw, I liked you from day one." He inches closer to me, gripping my hand.

"Did you now?" I ask, nuzzling into him. He drapes his other arm over me, pulling me closer.

"Emery," he starts, his voice low.

I look up and study him. He seems to be wrestling with something he can't get out.

"What's up?" I ask, shifting to look at him. I wince.

"Are you okay?" Reid asks, concern clouding his eyes.

"Headache."

He reaches for the Advil and water on the table and passes them to me.

I toss the pills back and the electrolyte water soothes my dry throat. "Thank you."

"Of course." Reid tugs me close, pressing a kiss to the crown of my head.

"What were you going to say?" I ask.

"What?"

"You said my name, like you wanted to tell me something. What was it?" I bite back a smile, running my fingertips along his tight jaw.

"Oh, nothing." He gives me a soft smile. "How about I make you some breakfast?"

He's out of the room before I can reply.

THE NEXT WEEK slips by in a blur. Mornings with Reid always start the same way, him humming to himself in the kitchen while he fixes us coffee and breakfast before we part ways for the day. Nights end with his arm slung across my hip, tugging me close as we drift off to sleep to the sounds of the marsh. We fall into an effortless rhythm, cooking together, laundry, watching movies on the couch until we can't keep our eyes open. Blackbird Cottage feels like a distant memory. Every day I tell myself it's time to pack up and go back. It's too soon to cohabitate with a new partner. But every night I find another reason to stay.

I think I'm falling in love with Reid.

It's the kind of love that sneaks up on you—crashes into you like an ocean wave and knocks the wind out of you when you least expect it.

But I don't dare say it. He's just starting to let me in. Something tells me this would send him running in the other direction. So, I keep my mouth shut and enjoy every piece of him he'll give me.

By the time the week comes to an end, the town is abuzz with Fourth of July Festival preparations. For the first time in a long time, things feel almost normal. Almost.

THE FESTIVAL IS in full swing by the time Reid and I get to the boardwalk. He's carrying a folding table under one arm and a folding chair under the other. I've got a backpack full of supplies and box full of turtle pamphlets to hand out.

The air smells of funnel cake and corn dogs, and a band is set up on a small stage near the pier. Red, white, and blue streamers flutter from every post, kids dart between vendors with dripping ice cream cones—the boardwalk is alive in a way I've never seen.

"You sure this is the best spot?" Reid asks, nodding to the tent Kayla set up with a banner that reads: *Keep Tidehaven Wild: Save Our Marine Life!*

"Close enough to the action to get foot traffic," I say, spreading a tablecloth on the table he's just popped open. "But not so close that we call a lot of attention to ourselves."

"Strategic. Got it." Reid grins faintly. "I approve."

He watches while I spread out pamphlets, refrigerator magnets, coloring pages for kids, and a few laminated photos of turtles we've rehabilitated. The sight of my display makes pride bloom in my chest—I feel like myself. Like I'm just a scientist again, not some girl running from her own shadow. So much of that has to do with Reid and how safe he makes me feel.

"Is Kayla coming?" he asks, as the radio clipped to his belt crackles.

"After lunch. She's doing some raffle with her friends first."

"Good." Reid's hand finds the small of my back, and I know it's not just affection, it's protective. "You've got a good view from here. I'll keep close."

I know he means it, but when Colt calls over the radio for all security to report to the Police Department booth, I feel a pang of unease. This is the first time I've been in such a large crowd since I arrived. I brush my nerves away just as fast. I'm here to do my thing and he'll be close by. I'm safe.

"I'll be fine," I assure him, forcing a smile when he hesitates. "Go do your security thing. Colt needs you."

He lingers for another beat, his eyes searching mine. "You text me if anything feels off."

"I will," I promise, shooing him away with a laugh.

"Bye," he says, ducking out of the tent.

He's back not a moment later, striding toward me with purpose. His hand finds the back of my neck, the other tipping my chin up to his. His lips are warm, with the faint taste of salt on his tongue. It's not a deep kiss—after all, this is a family festival—but it sends a shiver through my insides.

"I couldn't leave without a proper goodbye." He smiles against my mouth.

"Much appreciated," I whisper.

Reid pulls back, and with one last long look, he turns to go. "I'll check on you in a bit."

And then he disappears into the crowd.

For a while, everything is perfect. The hum of conversation, the rhythm of the band warming up, the sea breeze rustling my hair as people stop to ask about the turtles and the future of the research center. I've forgotten how much I love teaching about marine life. Kids giggle as they color their pictures, parents nodding politely as I explain turtle nesting patterns. I lose track of time until the same prickling sensation I had that day in the marsh washes over me.

Two men stand near the end of the boardwalk. Dale Langford and Atlas Rourke. Dale is dressed impeccably in a pair of navy-blue trousers, his white linen button down rolled to his elbows. He wears aviators and Sperry's, and a cigar hangs out of his mouth. Atlas is sporting a pair of tan cargo shorts and tight-fitting black T-shirt. Neither of them looks as if they belong with the other and yet, they're talking, laughing, and looking my way. Dale says something low in Atlas's ear. He laughs before tossing me a wink.

My stomach twists.

I force a smile for the couple browsing my booth, but my hand trembles as I tuck a stray pamphlet into place. My eyes land on the men again. They don't appear to be watching me, yet I can't shake the feeling of unease. I pick up my phone and tap on Reid's name.

Hey. You close?

Reid

Always. Why?

Langford's here. And your friend from the bar. Atlas?

Reid

Stay put. Don't talk to them. I'll be right there.

When I glance up again, they're gone. It's as if they just vanished into the crowd. Still the back of my neck prickles as I scan my surroundings. Suddenly everything feels off—the music is too loud, the sun too bright.

I lock my phone and place it face down on the table, trying to steady my breath.

"I'm here, I'm here." Reid's voice cuts through the noise, and before I can speak, his arms are around me—solid and grounding. "What happened?"

"Nothing, they left," I murmur against his chest.

"Then why are you shaking?" He pulls back to look at me, brushing hair from my face until I meet his steady gaze. "You're safe, baby. I've got you."

And for the rest of the afternoon, he doesn't leave my side.

CHAPTER THIRTY-TWO

REID

I TOLD COLT I had to go—Emery needs me.

He gave me a look that said *you're so whipped* but didn't argue, and I've never moved so fast in my life.

When I find her—right where I left her—she's pale as a ghost and trembling. Guilt hits me square in the gut. I never should have left her to fend for herself.

By the time Kayla shows up an hour later, I've convinced Em to take a break. I tell Kayla to man the booth while Emery and I hunt down a funnel cake. She deserves to experience something good today.

The air smells like sugar, grease, and sunscreen as we step out into the crowd. Emery laces her fingers through mine, and leans into my arm, clinging to me with both hands like she needs the contact. I look down at her as we walk. She's perfect in a pair of cut-offs and a bright red tank top. Her blond hair is French braided, and a pair of black over-sized sunglasses cover half her face. She's way too beautiful for me and yet, somehow, she's mine.

I swallow the urge once again to tell her I love her. It's not because I'm second guessing it. I knew the truth the night she went out with her friends and my world went dark for the ten minutes I didn't know where she was.

I just don't know if she's ready to hear it. She's not a Tidehaven lifer. She deserves the freedom to choose where she belongs. She's never expressed interest in staying here, and I would never want to tie her down. So instead of telling her how I feel, I take what I can get—time with her until she leaves. And then maybe I'll go with her or maybe I'll say goodbye. But either way, I've been alone before, and I'll be okay because Emery's happiness means more to me than my own.

"Do you think I'm okay?" she asks suddenly, as we approach a booth selling fresh funnel cakes.

"What do you mean?"

"I don't know. Maybe this was a bad idea. I just can't shake the feeling that something is off." She bites her lip, and it sends a jolt right to my core.

I tug her close. "You're okay, baby. I'm not letting you out of my sight."

That earns a quiet exhale, and she slumps against me.

"You deserve to enjoy your holiday too," she says, her voice lighter now.

"I am." I grin at her before scanning the menu. "We'll take one original funnel cake and two ice cold lemonades, please."

The teenage girl behind the counter smiles and the boy working next to her perks up.

"Oh hey, you're the turtle lady, aren't you?" he asks, handing us our drinks.

"That's me," Emery says, but her voice is quiet.

"I think it's so cool what you're doing." The kid grins.

"You do?" Emery doesn't bother to hide her surprise.

"Yeah, I mean, let's face it, Tidehaven is small. Most people here only care about fishing and shrimping. Nobody talks about what happens when the sea life starts disappearing." He hands us some napkins as the girl brings over a piping hot funnel cake.

Emery blinks, caught off guard. "You think other people actually care?"

"Sure," he says. "It's just—some folks here like to look the other way."

"Or stay quiet," the girl adds softly. "Because they're scared."

"Why would they be scared?" I ask, tilting my head curiously.

"You know, if they aren't marine scientists, they couldn't possibly have proof." She shrugs. "Just scared no one would believe them maybe?"

"Part of me wonders if that old director had proof..." The boy trails off, his eyes darting to me, gauging my reaction.

Emery stiffens beside me, her fingers tightening around mine. "Thanks for the treats," she says, backing away.

"Happy fourth!" they call after us with a wave.

Heat pricks at the back of my neck as we walk down the boardwalk, that kid's words nagging at me. I force myself to let it go for now and focus on the day ahead and the beautiful girl next to me that I am hopelessly, madly in love with. If only she knew.

BY NIGHTFALL, THE festival has turned golden under strings of white twinkle lights. Revelers are camped out on the small beach and along the boardwalk, waiting for the fireworks to begin. Emery and I staked out a perfect spot, just at the end of the boardwalk. I stand behind her, boxing her in against the rails. The warmth of her body sends a shiver up my spine.

When the fireworks start, I'm not looking at them—I'm looking at Emery, each blast painting her face in strobes of color. I wrap my arms around her waist and pull her closer. She settles into my chest and sighs. I lean down, planting a soft kiss on her neck and debate telling her I love her for the fiftieth time today.

"This feels like a happy ending," she murmurs, looking up at me with a smile.

"God, I hope so."

The next bursts move slowly upward, making a whistling sound, their flashes of white lighting up the water. But the boom that follows doesn't match these fireworks. It isn't part of the show. It's deeper—like an explosion of some kind. The ground shakes beneath our feet, and the roar that follows is enough to vibrate through my chest. My instincts flare and I know immediately something's wrong.

For a second, no one moves. Fireworks continue overhead, their beauty masking chaos. Then everything happens in slow motion—someone screams, then another voice joins in. The crowd erupts and suddenly people are scattering, shouting, clutching small children.

"Reid." Emery's voice cracks as she reaches behind her and grips the hem of my shirt. "What was that?"

"Not fireworks," I grit out, the words tasting like metal. I grab her hand, pulling her behind me as I walk, scanning the horizon. A column of thick smoke curls up from the marina, turning the purple sky black. A second later, a thick orange glow crackles at its base.

"Shit," I mutter, my training kicking in before fear has the chance. "It's the docks."

Emery's face pales and her breathing goes shallow. "Kayla. She was stopping by the research center to lock up."

I catch her chin gently, but firmly, forcing her eyes to mine. "Hey. Stay calm. We don't know anything yet. We're going to stay together."

She doesn't have a chance to respond before the crowd presses in on us as more people realize what's happening. Sirens wail in the distance, and I tuck Emery under my arm, keeping her close as I push us toward the street. I choke on the thick smell of smoke permeating the air.

When we reach the street, Colt's cruiser skids to a stop and he's out of the vehicle before it's even stopped rolling. His radio crackles—backup is enroute.

"Are you guys okay?" he asks, frantic.

"We're fine. What the hell happened?" I ask him.

"Fire on the docks. Explosion. I called for more back up, but we need some help down there now." Colt is breathless, wiping sweat from his brow.

"I'm coming."

Emery grips my wrist. "Reid. Don't. Please."

My chest constricts. "I have to baby. This is my marina." I kiss her forehead. "I'll be careful."

I dig in my pocket for my keys and toss them to her. "Wait in the truck. Lock the doors. I'll come find you as soon as I can."

"Reid." Her voice is a whimper.

But I'm already moving through the crowd toward the blaze. The acrid stench of burning fiberglass fills my lungs, the hiss and crackle of fire growing louder. My boots hit the docks hard, but my heart is hammering harder.

By the time I reach the action, chaos has taken over. Men with hoses are trying to keep the flames from jumping to the next line of boats, their faces slick with sweat. Colt's backup arrives, shouting orders, pushing people back. The Drift Net sign flickers weakly overhead, glass popping in the heat.

I see Tate immediately, standing with Colt, and I instinctively move beside him.

He's somber, staring at the flames.

"Fuck," he mutters. Then again, louder and angrier. "FUCK!"

I clap an arm around his back, holding him firmly, supporting him the way he's done for me so many times. He looks at me, eyes ablaze, and sucks in a breath, steadier now.

Together we watch in silence as Tate's father's legacy burns into the bay.

I glance over Colt's shoulder, trying to catch a glimpse of what caught fire. Then I see it and my stomach sinks. Several boats in this row of slips are caught in the blaze but two of them catch my eye. First, the small skiff with Tidehaven Research Center emblazoned on the side, the letters melting off from the scorching heat. To its right, the *Miss Tidehaven*, half-engulfed, the name barely visible on its stern. Fuck. Beau has been away for work. He's going to be so pissed. A knot forms in my throat, and I have to look away.

Then, I spot him. Atlas Rourke. Leaning against the side of the research center, watching the fire destroy everything in its wake, like he doesn't have a care in the world. His gaze flicks to me, and the corner of his mouth tips up. He gives me a subtle nod—like a dare I won't take.

And suddenly everything feels far too quiet. The fireworks stopped. The crowds have dispersed. Only the fire speaks now.

Emery's boat *and* the boat she saw in the marsh all those weeks ago—gone. Destroyed.

And then I know.

This wasn't an accident.

CHAPTER THIRTY-THREE

EMERY

THE SIRENS FADE long before my panic does. Reid's truck rocks as people run by outside, frantic. One person shouts a name I don't recognize; another is yelling for water. A dog barks incessantly in the distance. All the while, I clutch my phone, my knuckles white and my fingers hovering over Reid's name.

He told me to stay in the truck, but it's been over thirty minutes since he ran toward the marina and every minute feels like an hour. Through the windshield, I can see the fire's reflection off the water in the night sky. And even inside the truck, I can smell it—salt, gasoline, and something sharp, like burning rubber or plastic. I turn on the truck enough to roll the window down but all I can hear is the distant hum of chaos. Most of the crowd is gone, but I hear far away shouts from emergency responders.

The celebration is over and now Tidehaven feels...hollow. I decide I'd rather have the silence and roll the window back up.

A moment later, a knock on the window startles me.

"Emery!" Kayla shouts from outside. "Are you okay?"

I unlock the door and fling it open. "Oh my God, where were you?" I pull her into a hug.

"At the research center. I was there when the explosion happened. I heard the blast and ran outside and saw the smoke. It's bad, Em." She pulls back, shaking her head, her breaths coming fast. "The marina."

I glance toward the marina, the orange glow brighter now. My eyes blur with tears. "Reid's down there."

Kayla grabs my hand and squeezes. "He'll be fine. He always is."

I nod, swallowing the lump in my throat.

"I have to go home. My mom is probably worried sick. Are you going to be okay?" Kayla's brow furrows.

"I'll be fine." I give her another swift hug and climb back in the truck.

Ten minutes later, Reid's sliding into the driver's seat, his hair damp with sweat, the smell of smoke permeating the space. I almost sob in relief.

"Hey," he rasps, brushing my cheek. "You okay?"

I nod, but it's a lie. My throat burns and I can't stop shaking. "You smell awful."

"Yeah." He nods sadly. "Half the marina's gone. Colt and Tate are still there, but the fire's contained."

"What happened?"

"Might've been a fuel leak. Maybe not. It's a little early to know." His voice is tight, like there's something he's not saying.

I study him, the glow of the streetlamp catching in his eyes. He looks exhausted. Haunted.

"I was so scared," I murmur.

He pulls me to him then, his hand drawing light circles on the back of my neck.

"Me too," he whispers. He dips his forehead to mine. "I shouldn't have left you here. I'm sorry."

"It's okay." I sniffle. "You're here now."

I curl into him, breathing in his scent of sea air, smoke, and sweat. His hand slides up my back, grounding me, and soon our breaths sync together.

"Take me home," I whisper.

"There's nothing else I'd rather do." He starts the truck and backs out slowly, careful to avoid any lingering onlookers.

The drive home is quiet except for the rumble of the truck

and the sporadic crackle of Reid's radio with updates from Colt. The smell of smoke clings to everything, filling the cab until it's all I can breathe in.

He pulls in his dirt drive and kills the engine. For a moment, neither of us moves, we only stare at each other. The world outside is chaos but in here, everything narrows to this moment—his eyes on mine, our mingled breaths, all the words we want to say out loud but haven't yet.

Reid sucks in a breath before finally saying, "Let's go in and get cleaned up."

Inside, we kick off our shoes and Reid moves down the hall to the bathroom. I peel off my tank top when I hear the shower turn on and he meets me in the hallway. He's shirtless and barefoot, soot streaked across his jaw that I hadn't seen until now. His shoulders are taut with tension, but he pulls me to him anyway, his hands finding the button on my denim shorts. He undoes it and the shorts slip to the floor. I step out of them and follow him down the hall.

Steam fills the bathroom as the shower warms and Reid slowly takes off the rest of our clothes. He pulls open the glass door, and I step under first, the hot water stinging my skin, washing the day away. His arms encircle me from behind, pulling me to him. The water runs over us, but neither of us speaks. Reid's hands skim down my arms, to my waist, slow and reverent. Every touch sends a spark of electricity straight between my thighs.

His lips find my neck, and I feel him harden from behind. A soft gasp escapes me as Reid's fingers dig into my hip bones, backing my ass into his length. Then he drags an index finger up my center, letting out a grunt when he finds the swollen nub that sends a wave of pleasure through my insides. I tip my head back, and his mouth finds mine in a kiss that's deep and aching and real.

I whirl around to look at him, searching his face for something but I don't know what. My hand drifts across his chest, finding the raised pink scar that begins under his collarbone and moves down toward his ribs.

"How did you get this?" I whisper, tracing the scar with my fingertip.

Reid exhales hard, pulling me closer so our bodies are flushed together, but his eyes stay focused on me. He looks as if he's having an internal struggle, and for a moment, I think he won't answer. Then, quietly, his voice husky, he says, "Afghanistan. We were sent to clear a building. Intel told us there were no hostiles... I had a bad feeling about it, but I listened to them instead of my gut. They were wrong."

He pulls back, letting the water run into his eyes. I think he might be done talking but then he steps closer again. "We walked right into an ambush. The first two shots hit my CO. The third one hit me." His hand finds the scar. "It went under my vest, caught a rib, and got stuck. I remember the pop sound before the pain—before everything went black. I needed emergency surgery."

"Reid..." My heart pounds heavy in my chest.

"I dragged my CO out, but I have no idea how. No recollection of it. I was released with honorable discharge. Got a Purple Heart too." He shakes his head. "I remember being air lifted to safety thinking this is it—I'm not making it out alive." He lets out a long slow breath, his hand tracing over the scar.

"But you *did* make it out." I press my hand to his.

"I was the only one." He looks away. "Sometimes I wish I didn't. You don't survive something like that and come out okay. It haunts you forever. You're breathing but you aren't really living."

"And now? Do you still feel that way?" I hold my breath, afraid to hear the answer.

He looks down at me, his green eyes dark and searching. "When you showed up...all the noise in my head, the guilt, the anger—it quieted." He steps closer to me again, pushing me up against the wall and when his lips find mine, the kiss is deep and tender—filled with yearning and hope. He pulls back, his thumb tracing my jaw. "You made me feel like there is something worth living for again. You make me want *more*."

I don't even realize I'm crying until he kisses the tears from my face, his lips soft and unhurried. I stand on my toes, cupping his face and kissing him again, slow and deep. He responds with a hunger that feels like a release. He pulls my hips toward his, his hardness pressing into me again. Reid's hands slide down my back, anchoring me to him. My fingers trace the lines of muscle and scar tissue, the map of where he's been and how far he's come. Every touch feels like a promise.

His hand dips back between my thighs and he slips in a finger—one, then two. When a third slips in, I let out a low groan.

His name falls from my lips in a desperate plea.

"I know, baby, it feels so good. You're so wet for me." His voice is rough in my ear, and I know he's trying to numb himself to the pain of the night and the memories we've stirred up.

Reid stops kissing me for the briefest of moments, brushing water out of my eyes. He watches my face as his fingers explore my body. The look on his face is filled with such tenderness that words get caught in my throat.

"Thank you for telling me that," I murmur, the words I really want to say on the tip of my tongue.

He responds with another kiss, deep and urgent. I pull back, stroking his cheek.

"Reid," I say softly.

"Yeah?" he murmurs through kisses.

"I love you."

He stills, water streaming down his face, and his eyes find mine. "Say it again."

"I *love* you, Reid."

A small, broken sound escapes him—a sigh of relief—and then he's kissing me again, as if those words are the only thing keeping him upright.

Reid's hands find my ass and he picks me up, guiding himself to my entrance. "Is this okay?"

A breathless agreement and a nod from me, and he slips in easily. I let out a whimper at the feel of him. We move together like two people trying to memorize the shape of the other. His movements are slow and purposeful, and each thrust sends a shudder through me.

"You're so beautiful, Emery," Reid says, slowing his movements. "I don't deserve you."

He shifts ever so slightly, allowing himself to thrust deeper. A moan that sounds borderline inhuman escapes me. How can this man know my body so well after only a few weeks? He holds me up with one hand, finding my clit with his other, circling it with gentle pressure until my legs tremble and my walls go tight.

"Reid," I whisper. "I'm going to..."

"Come, baby. Come for me." His voice is thick with emotion as he plows into me.

I cry out as my release finds me, my legs quivering around his waist. He plows into me, each thrust harder than the last as he searches for his own release. When he finds it, my name falls from his lips. He sets me down, burying his face in my neck.

"I love you, too, baby," he murmurs. "More than I ever thought possible."

We stay wrapped in each other, beneath the cooling spray, my head against his chest, his hands tracing lines up my back. Our hearts pound in sync with one another. Outside, the world is chaos, but in here, it's only us. Warm, steady, alive.

CHAPTER THIRTY-FOUR

REID

THE RINGING OF my phone jars me awake before dawn on Sunday morning.

"What *is* that?" Emery grumbles, rolling off me and pulling the blanket over her head.

I reach behind me for my phone on the nightstand.

Tate.

"Go back to sleep," I whisper, patting her shoulder. Slipping out of bed and closing the door behind me, I move to the living room.

"What's going on?" I answer. "It's Sunday." Tate never bothers me on a weekend, but after last night, I know it must be serious.

"You'd better get down here, man. Fuck." Tate growls.

"Tate, is that Reid?" I hear Colt's voice in the background.

"What happened?" I bark.

"A body. In the bay. Right by our boat ramp." Tate's voice is tired and shaky. He sounds far away. Maybe he's in shock.

"I'll be right there." I hang up, rushing to the kitchen for a piece of paper. Rather than wake Emery, I leave her a note. I'd rather she stays put then comes down there with me right now. I scribble quickly: *Tate needs me at the marina. Be back ASAP. I love you.* And I'm out the door.

By the time I pull into the lot, the overcast sky is heavy, a hazy wall of gray pressing down into the water. Police cruisers are parked crookedly near the docks, their lights flashing silently, reflecting off the bait shop windows.

The crowd parts as I approach, thick with the hushed murmurs that always follow when death shows up uninvited.

Tate stands near the end of the dock, arms crossed, jaw tight. Colt is crouched down, radio pressed to his ear. The minute I catch sight of what's in the water, my stomach turns.

A man I recognize, half submerged, tangled in sea grass and fishing line, with tattered clothes and gray, bloated skin and a hole through his back, bobs up and down. Beau Rigsby.

Fuck.

"Crabbers spotted him just before dawn. Tide brought him right in," Colt says without looking up. "Probably been out there a while."

"How long?" I ask, fear blooming through my chest.

"Coroner thinks four to eight weeks. It's hard to say with the summer heat." Colt says, confirming my suspicions.

I count backwards in my head, trying to discern how far back that terrifying morning in the marsh was. Six weeks? At least. Bile rises in my throat, and I stifle a cough.

"First the docks, now this. Fuck, Beau." Tate growls, turning his baseball cap backward. "The bastard probably tried to stop them himself."

But I'm not hearing them anymore, my mind flashing back to the pre-dawn morning in the marsh. The sound of the muzzle echoing in my head and the racing motor of their boat hunting Emery down. And her face when I finally saw her.

"Morgan, you good? You're white as a ghost." Tate squints at me.

I don't answer right away. The lie I've been carrying for six weeks burns in the back of my throat. I've spent weeks convincing myself that keeping it a secret was the right thing to do—it would keep her safe after all. But that's been proven wrong and now the truth's right here, floating in the bay.

I let out a sigh, scratching my jaw. "Ah, fuck. There's something I need to tell you both."

At this, Colt straightens, his eyes narrowing. "What?"

I glance over my shoulder to make sure no one else is within earshot, then I lower my voice.

"About six weeks ago, Emery was in the marsh near Cedar Creek. Before dawn. She saw someone get shot. I was out for a walk—you know I don't sleep." I pause, rubbing the back of my neck. "They heard her, came for her. We didn't know who it was, just that they were armed, they were chasing her, so I fired my gun in the air. Spooked them so she could get away."

"What the fuck, Reid?" Tate snaps. "This is what you've been keeping from me? Why you've been asking all those weird questions."

"I can't believe you fucking sat on this, Morgan," Colt growls.

"You think I wanted to?" I snap, dragging my hand down my face. "She was scared. Hell, *I* was scared and that's saying something. And then things started happening to her. I didn't know what to do except lay low and keep her safe."

"You come to me, that's what you do. Goddammit." Colt paces, his hand resting on the holster of his weapon.

"You kept it quiet and now it's right here." Tate shoots me with a long cold stare.

"If this is the same guy," Colt starts.

"It is," I say flatly. "I'd bet my life on it."

Colt finally brings his gaze up to me, his jaw locked. "Then you just made this a hell of a lot bigger than a harassment complaint against your girlfriend. I'm going to need every fucking detail—when, where, what you saw. Emery needs to give a statement too."

I nod, swallowing hard. "Yeah, I figured."

As the crew pulls the body up on the dock a sickly smell rolls through the air—rancid, like hot garbage in the summer sun. I have to turn away to keep from vomiting.

Tate inhales sharply beside me. "You know what they say."

"What's that?" I mutter.

"The marsh keeps no secrets."

I glance toward the horizon, where thunderheads are building dark and fast. "It sure doesn't."

BY THE TIME the coroner's van pulls away, the onlookers have mostly dispersed. The only ones left are a few dock hands, sweeping away salt where there is none and murmuring to themselves. Colt's giving orders to his deputies while Tate leans against a piling, staring out at the flat water where the body had been.

None of us are saying it aloud, but the tide just washed up proof that someone wanted gone.

I'm halfway to the bait shop for a bottle of water and a break from the tension when I hear it—footsteps on the dock behind me.

"Morning, gentlemen."

I turn to find Tate and Colt face to face with Councilman Roy Beck, Judge Everett Ware, and Warren Langford. I turn back to stand with them—three on three, old versus young. Roy Beck steps forward, his khakis too pressed for the setting, like he's on his way to Sunday service. His smile is tight and practiced.

Judge Ware looks every bit as smug and still. Warren, by contrast, looks casual, wearing his usual navy windbreaker, despite it being eighty-five degrees at seven a.m., an amused smile curving the corners of his lips.

"Councilman. Judge. Mr. Langford." Colt nods in greeting. "We've got this handled."

"We have no doubt about that, Captain," Beck says smoothly, his hands clasped behind his back. "We just came down to check things out. Awful business this...discovery. We're all shocked."

"Shocked," Ware repeats, though his tone carries more

warning than remorse.

Langford strolls a few feet away, pretending to examine the dock lines. “Any idea who the poor fellow is?” he asks, casting his gaze over the water.

“Beau Rigsby.” Colt’s jaw tics.

“Beau Rigsby,” Beck repeats with a surprised gasp that sounds artificial. “Foul play?”

“We’ll know more when we get the coroner’s report.” Colt doesn’t give him any more than that.

“Good, that’s good.” Beck nods. “Wouldn’t want anyone getting the wrong idea about our little town.” His gaze slides to me, casual but cutting. “Especially outsiders.”

I meet his eyes. “Outsiders aren’t dumping bodies in our bays.”

Judge Ware’s lips twitch, amusement ghosting on them. “Now, son, let’s not jump to conclusions. After last night’s fire, we’ve got enough rumors in the mill. Don’t need you adding to them.”

Tate shifts beside me. “You saying this doesn’t concern you, Judge?”

“Course it concerns us,” Beck answers for him, his voice oozing politeness. “That’s why we’re here—making sure everything stays...contained.”

Langford wanders back to us, his hands clasped behind his back, his eyes scanning the three of us. “We wouldn’t want anyone coming in here and stirring up trouble is all.” His eyes rest on mine.

“Trouble is already here,” I bite.

Beck barks out a laugh. “Morgan, you’ve been gone too long. Surely you haven’t forgotten the way we take care of our own.”

“Keep it in the family,” Langford agrees, snickering.

Judge Ware steps forward then, his voice low enough for only the three of us to hear. “If I were you boys, I’d stay focused on your boats, repairing this beautiful marina.” He holds a hand out, gesturing to our ash-dusted surroundings. “Let the right people handle this."

Colt steps toward him, arms folded. "With all due respect, Judge, the right people *are* handling it."

"See that you do." Beck winks, turning to go.

Ware follows behind, leaving the scent of expensive cologne in his wake.

Langford pauses, his gaze lingering on me, lips pressed together. "Terrible thing, bodies in the water. Isn't it?"

It's not a direct threat but his words send a chill to my bones.

He claps Tate on the shoulder—a gesture too familiar, too firm—before following the others to the parking lot.

When they're gone, I realize my hands are bunched into fists.

"You okay?" Colt asks, moving beside me.

I blow out a slow breath. "No. But I'm about to be."

"Morgan," Colt says warily. "What does that mean?"

"It just means I'm tired of waiting for the tides to turn," I say, watching the men duck into The Salty Spoon. "It's time we start digging."

Colt claps me on the back. "We will. Starting with statements. I'll see you and Emery down at the station. One p.m. sharp. Don't make me come for you."

I watch as he starts for his cruiser. "Fuck."

CHAPTER THIRTY-FIVE

EMERY

I'M PACING THE living room when Reid finally walks through the front door at nine o'clock. His shoulders are slumped, his face pale. He looks defeated and I rush to him.

"Are you okay? What the hell happened?" I put my arms around him, and he absently pats my back before pulling away.

"We need to talk."

His eyes meet mine and I'm instantly afraid. Is he about to break up with me? Of course, my mind shouldn't go there. It should go to the docks, the marina, last night's fire, the danger lurking around Tidehaven. But it goes there because I've fallen in love with him and I'm terrified of losing him.

"What's wrong?" I ask, my voice catching.

He gestures toward the couch. "Let's sit."

He doesn't wait for me to answer, instead moving to the sofa and kicking off his boots. His elbows find his knees, and he puts his head in his hands.

I sit next to him, keeping some distance between us and curling my legs up to my chest, guarding myself from the hurt I fear is coming.

"Are you breaking up with me?" I ask, my nose stinging as my emotions get the better of me.

Reid's head darts up, and he meets my eyes, his expression softening. "God, no." He inches closer, clasping my hand in his.

"Baby, you're *it* for me."

I let out a breath, releasing the tension I'd been holding. "Okay. Then what is it?"

"They found a body in the bay." Reid exhales sharply.

"Oh. Oh my God." My hand covers my mouth. "Who?" Panic surges through me as I run through the possibilities of who it might be, fearing the worst, that it's someone I know.

"Beau Rigsby..." His voice drops. "The owner of the *Miss Tidehaven*." He swallows. "And they think he's been in the water for four to eight weeks." Reid's eyes meet mine, as he waits for me to connect the dots.

It hits me like a ton of bricks. Four to eight weeks fits the timeline of the murder in the marsh. That body disappeared the next morning. Reid suspected it was moved. If this is the same person, then clearly it was dumped further out and it's just washing up now.

I swallow the tightness forming in my throat. "Oh."

"I had to tell Colt everything. Well, and Tate. He was there." Reid rubs the back of his neck.

Panic rises in my throat like bile. "What did you say?"

Reid shakes his head. "Just the truth. Exactly what happened." He turns to me. "We need to meet Colt at the station at one o'clock. He wants a statement from both of us."

"A statement?" My words come out like a whisper. "Are we in some kind of trouble?"

Reid moves closer then, wrapping his arms around me. "No. No, we're not. We're going to go in there and tell the truth. We don't know who it was. We didn't see faces and we ran to protect ourselves. When we went back the next day, the body was gone. We assumed they were okay."

I suck in a shuddering breath and nod. "Okay. I mean. Most of that is true."

Reid looks sharply at me. "It's all true. And then someone started harassing you and it became even harder to report it. You feared for your life."

"That's definitely true." I nod, feeling a little less anxious. "Okay, I can do that. What about the picture? Of the boat."

Reid drags his hand down his face, quiet for a beat. "The boat burned yesterday. That and the research center skiff."

I gasp. "What?"

"They're both gone, Em. They were docked next to each other. Maybe we leave that part out." Reid looks away, fixing his gaze on the black screen of the television.

"No. I won't do that. Don't you think there's a reason the fire started on that end of the docks?" A wave of nausea washes over me. "Someone knows they were seen. That fire...I don't think it was an accident."

"Me neither," he mutters.

"Then we have no choice. We have to tell the whole truth."

COLT MEETS US at the door to the station at one p.m. sharp. His shoulders are tense as he leads us down a narrow hall to an interrogation room.

"Colt," Reid says, his eyebrows pinching together. "You can't be serious. Putting us in here."

Colt is silent, mulling it over for a minute before he sighs. "Fine. We can go in my office."

He continues down the hall, and we follow him. Colt pauses at the door, gesturing for us to enter before closing it behind him.

All business, he moves behind his desk and pulls out two carbon paper witness statement forms. He sits, pulling his chair in. Reid and I remain standing until Colt looks up.

"Sit, please." He gestures at the two chairs in front of his desk. "Actually, Emery you can go first. Reid, you can wait outside."

Outside? My neck heats as anxiety surges through my bloodstream.

"No. Please, can he stay?" My voice wavers. "Please."

Colt sighs and points at Reid. "Only because I've known you

my whole life."

Reid lets out a low chuckle and sits down.

"Okay, Emery," Colt begins, meeting my eyes. "What can you tell me about what you witnessed in the marsh?"

I suck in a breath. "Well, it was about a week after I arrived. Maybe...the second or third week of May. I finally got the courage to go out in the skiff alone before dawn. I only had a headlamp on because harsh light disturbs the marine life. So just enough to see." I pause, watching him write down every detail and then it all comes pouring out. I tell him about the murder, the way the man grunted and slumped over before falling into the water. I tell him how I tried to be quiet, but I must've made enough noise to call attention to myself. I tell him how I dropped my camera and it went off, and later finding the photo of the *Miss Tidehaven*. I recall the sharp sound of Reid's weapon scaring them off and how I ran through the woods trying to escape. Lastly, I describe the relief I felt the next morning when Reid took me to check the traps, and the body was gone. Not even twenty-four hours later.

"We assumed that maybe he wasn't dead. That he got away. Reid said the less we know the better so...I kept quiet. But I've been sick over it since."

"And," Reid interjects, "someone is after her now."

"You'll get your turn, Morgan," Colt snaps before turning his attention back to me. "What is he talking about?"

I remind him about the words painted on the cottage, the ransacking of the inside, and the chase down in the marsh. I give him a description of the masked man on the boat and the injuries I sustained.

"Dr. Michaels cleaned me up," I say softly. "But we just told him I had a bad fall. I mean, that's true. But only because someone was hunting me."

"Right. I remember." Colt jots down a few more notes. "Has anything happened since?"

I shake my head and look over at Reid. "Not really. Because I've been staying with Reid. I'm never alone."

"Good." Colt nods. "Morgan. Your turn."

By the time Reid gives his statement, we're both exhausted. It feels like we've been sitting in his small, stale office for hours. Every detail we shared, every question we answer, peeled back another layer of the past six weeks until I felt raw and exposed.

And yet, somehow lighter.

Like I've been holding my breath since that day in the marsh and now I can finally exhale. I hadn't realized what carrying all this around has done to me—to my sense of safety, to the way I walk into a room, to how often I look over my shoulder. To my self-worth.

When we step outside, the world feels too bright. The sun hits us full in the face, blinding, the heat bouncing off the asphalt. The air smells like tar and salt and distant rain. Reid squints against it, jaw tight, shoulders tense like he's still ready to fight someone.

"That sucked," he says, opening the passenger door of his truck for me.

"Yeah," I say quietly, sliding in. "But at least...no more secrets."

For the first time all day, the corner of his mouth quirks up. "You would say that."

He huffs a soft laugh, then shuts my door and rounds the truck. When he climbs in, the leather creaks beneath his weight. The air conditioning kicks on, blasting away the heat and the last of the nerves from Colt's interrogation.

Reid glances over at me, eyes softened now. "Let's go home."

The way he says it—*home*—makes something loosen in my chest.

I watch the station fade in the side mirror as we pull onto the main road, sunlight flickering through the trees like a heartbeat. For the first time in weeks, I let myself believe it: maybe we're finally past the worst of it.

CHAPTER THIRTY-SIX

REID

By Wednesday, the South Carolina heat is brutal. It's the kind that makes tempers short and metal too hot to touch. Things are mighty quiet around here with half our docks now a pile of ash at the bottom of the bay. I've spent the morning replacing boards on the dry dock just to keep busy. By the time I wander into Tate's office, sweat has soaked through my T-shirt. The box fan in the corner does nothing to cool off the space.

I find Tate, behind his desk, making notes in a ledger. When he sees me, he snaps it closed.

"Thought you went home hours ago," he mutters without looking up.

I drop into the chair across from him. "Figured I'd check in on you. Make sure you filed the insurance claim before the adjuster comes by on Friday."

"Already taken care of." Tate leans back in his chair, arms behind his head.

"Good," I say carefully. "Because the damage from the fire wasn't minor. We have enough coverage to handle it?"

"We're fine." Tate shrugs, evasive.

"Fine doesn't mean shit to me, Tate." I nod toward the ledger. "You hiding bad news in there?"

He exhales hard through his nose. "You're wound tighter than barbed wire, you know that? Everything's under control."

"Yeah, I've heard you say that before," I mutter, shaking my head.

He looks up then, something flashing in his eyes. It's not guilt exactly but maybe exhaustion. For the first time since all of this came about, I wonder if he's lying to me.

He rubs a hand over his face. "Look, you've got enough on your plate with that girl of yours. Let me handle this."

"*That girl of mine* is part of the reason we're in this mess," I shoot back, ignoring the guilt that prickles at the base of my neck. "You think I'm just going to sit back and watch as everything we've built goes under?"

Tate's jaw tics. "*You* didn't build anything. You bought thirty percent."

The words hit like a punch to the gut. "I've worked these docks every damn day since I got out. You fucking know that."

Tate softens a bit, but not enough. "I do know that. And I appreciate it. But right now, I need you to trust me."

"That would be a hell of a lot easier if you'd tell me what the fuck is going on," I grit.

"It's not what you think." He shakes his head, pushing back in his chair.

"Then what is it?"

He doesn't answer. Instead, he stands, grabs his keys, and heads for the door. "Just drop it," he says over his shoulder. "I've got to make a few calls."

I watch him go, the office door swinging shut behind him. For a moment, I just sit there, staring at that closed ledger on the desk. Something isn't right. I can feel it in my bones.

"Fuck it," I mutter, grabbing the ledger.

The spine creaks when I open it, flipping to the most recent pages. I skim the line items, tracing each with my finger. Then I see it.

`Dock Repairs - $4800 - Paid Cash.`

No contractor. No vendor. Just a check mark next to a blank box.

A few pages back, I see another alarming note scribbled in the margin.

```
Fuel Delivery - Langford Marine - Cash
paid in advance.
```

I feel my stomach twist. Tate would never pay cash up front for anything, not unless he didn't want it traced. Even then—he's always been on the straight and narrow. I feel ill.

The fan hums, paper rustles, and I sit there with that sick, quiet certainty that something's gone sideways.

Maybe he's being squeezed. Maybe he's covering something up. Either way, the books don't balance. And I have the sinking feeling that I can no longer trust my business partner.

By the time I leave the marina, the sun is low and gold over the water, catching every ripple like glass.

I've got the windows down, the briny scent of the marsh flowing through the cab of my truck. But it does nothing to soothe the weight in my chest.

Tate's words echo in my head on loop:

You bought thirty percent.

You built nothing.

I need you to trust me.

It's not what you think.

I want to believe him. More than anything. I've known him since we were kids. But there is something about the way he slammed that ledger shut, refusing to answer my questions. Then what he didn't want me to see, the cash payments, the Langford note. None of it feels right.

I can't shake the thought that everything around me—this

town, the marina, the girl I'm in love with—is about to get swept up in a storm we can't stop.

I pull in the driveway just as the last of day turns into night. The porch light glows and through the window I can see Emery, dancing around the kitchen, blond hair piled in a sloppy knot on her head. She's wearing one of my T-shirts and it's falling off her shoulder, revealing her clavicle, a part of her body that has very quickly become irresistible to me. Warmth blooms across my chest and I watch for a moment, letting the tension bleed out of me before going inside.

She doesn't notice me immediately when I step through the door. She's too busy rocking out to nineties pop, and I'm enjoying the show. In the air, the scent of something soft and buttery fills the air. When she finally spins around, she startles, eyes widening for a split second before her mouth curves into a crooked smile. She taps her phone screen and the music stops.

"You're late," she says, stepping closer.

"Got caught up at the marina," I murmur, kicking off my boots.

"Everything okay?"

Emery moves around the peninsula to a casserole dish covered in foil.

I taste the lie on my lips before I can stop myself. "Just paperwork."

She eyes me for a second, like she knows there's more to it, but she doesn't press. "I made cornbread." She holds up the casserole dish with a smile.

"Cornbread, huh?" I move around behind her, my hands finding her hips while she cuts a buttery square.

"I needed a break from this paper. And carbs fix everything." She spins around, shoving the square in my mouth.

"Damn, this is good." I say, licking my lips.

Emery feigns offense. "Don't sound so shocked."

"I'm not shocked." I chuckle. "I'm impressed. With all you've been through these last few weeks, here you are being domestic."

"Just trying to make something good out of this mess." She sighs.

I brush a crumb off her cheek. "Hey. *You're* something good."

Her breath catches. "Reid..."

"I mean it."

She curls into me, my arms encircle her, and I tug her close. We stand like that in the kitchen, the light low and golden. I rest my chin on top of her head, syncing my breath to hers. All it takes to forget the stresses of the day is coming home to this woman wearing my clothes and dancing around my kitchen.

"You ever think this..." she pauses, looking up at me, "us, here together...wasn't an accident? Like maybe I was meant to find you?"

I dip my chin, pressing a kiss to her mouth. "Every damn day."

CHAPTER THIRTY-SEVEN

EMERY

THE NEXT WEEK passes by in a blur. Reid has seemed tense each morning as we part ways for work. When I ask if he's grabbing a beer with the guys for happy hour, he always says no, and comes home at his regular time. There's been no further talk of me going back to the cottage and right now, I'm okay with that. Both of us seem resigned to the fact that we're where we're meant to be—no matter how fast things are moving.

I've finished the outline for my paper and sent it off to Alan. It includes all of my research so far, my new hypothesis, and proposed solutions. He hasn't said anything yet, but I know he'll have advice. Given the mysterious circumstances of this sleepy little fishing village, I am thinking about holding off on writing my paper until things quiet down.

Colt took our statements and I'll admit, getting everything off my chest has allowed me to relax a bit more. I spend most days in the lab, or down on the small beach, researching other types of marine life. Turtles aren't off the table, but they're on the back burner for now. Just until I know I'm safe.

And most of the time I feel safe, but every so often I have the uneasy sensation that someone is following me—watching my every move. I don't tell Reid or anyone else. I've already earned myself the reputation of the woman who stirs the pot. So, I just keep my head down, get my work done, and spend a lot of time at home. Despite the troubles I've had, I think I needed to come here. I needed time in Tidehaven to reevaluate my path. Now, I've fallen in love, and I know this is where I'm meant to be no matter who wants me gone.

Reid has turned into an amazing partner—attentive, affectionate, determined to satisfy. He says he loves me but neither of us have talked about what comes next. That's what's on my mind as I leave the research center on this gloomy Wednesday in July. Reid needed to stay late today, something about Tate having to go to Beaufort, so we drove separately this morning.

I'm about to drop my things in my car and head over to say goodbye to him when I see it. It takes a heartbeat too long to register what I'm seeing.

The driver's side window of my Prius is shattered, jagged edges still clinging to the frame. Glass is scattered across the asphalt, glittering like diamonds.

A rush of panic punches through me. I freeze, my breath catching in my throat.

"Okay," I whisper to myself. "Stay calm."

I inch closer, crunching over broken glass, and open the door. Nothing inside the car looks disturbed. My bag's still on the passenger seat, charger cord dangling from the console. But then I spot it—something white tucked under the wiper. My pulse races as I open it slowly. One look at the words written in thick, slanted Sharpie and my blood goes cold.

Thought I told you to leave, it reads.

"Aww, hell," a voice comes from behind me. "Looks like someone wanted to get your attention."

I spin around slowly.

Atlas Rourke stands a few feet away, a cigarette pinched between his fingers. He looks too casual, amused even. Like a man who enjoys being where he's not supposed to be.

My stomach churns so tightly I think I might be sick.

He crouches next to me, close enough that I can smell the smoke on his clothes as he reaches inside the car to brush glass fragments from the front seat. "Shame," he murmurs. "Pretty thing like you ought to be careful."

His tone isn't gentle. It's a warning dressed up as advice.

My jaw falls slack and words escape me. I close my mouth, swallowing hard.

Atlas straightens, flicking the ash off his cigarette before tipping his head in my direction. "Bye, now." He walks off whistling off-key, his putrid scent lingering long after he's gone.

My hands are shaking as I pull out my phone to text Reid.

Car window is smashed. Atlas was here.

And then, as I tuck my phone in my pocket, I swear I hear it again. His whistling. Faint. Somewhere down by the docks.

"WHAT THE FUCK?" Reid barks, jogging toward me. "You just found it like this?"

I nod, fighting back the tears threatening to fall. "I was going to throw my stuff in the car and come say goodbye to you..." My words drop off as I hand him the note I found stuck beneath my wiper blade.

"I thought I told you to leave," he reads aloud before angrily crumpling it in his fist. "This has gone too fucking far."

I can't fight it then—a strangled sob escapes me and Reid's face falls.

"Come here," he murmurs, pulling me to his chest. "We'll fix this."

"Maybe I *should* just leave. Clearly, that's what they want. Whoever this is. And Alan said if I'm in danger, I should just go home." I sniffle into his shirt.

He tenses but holds me tighter. "You *are* home."

"Then what do we do?" I whisper into his chest.

"We have to file a report. Document everything," he says, smoothing my hair.

"I don't want to deal with this." I pull back searching his face. Frustration clouds his features.

Before he can reply, we hear it. The sound of a low male voice, talking to Kayla as she locks up the research center.

Atlas.

"You sure are a motivated young woman," he purrs, his voice carrying toward us.

"Yep. I love marine life," Kayla chirps. "I'm so grateful that Dr. Caldwell lets me help her."

I stiffen in Reid's arms but don't pull away.

"What do you help her with?" Atlas asks, falling in step beside Kayla.

"Right now, we're conducting turtle research. I'm not sure what we'll study next." Kayla admits, moving toward the parking lot. Toward us.

"Maybe you could show me around the lab sometime," Atlas says. "You know, I used to be in the Navy."

Kayla stills and Reid drops his arms from around me, moving in.

"Oh...like Reid." Her voice drops, uncertain.

"Yeah, like Reid," Reid growls, stepping into Atlas's space. "Dude, she's a teenage girl. Get out of here."

"I was just asking about her research," Atlas says, holding up his hands. "Chill."

Kayla's eyes dart to me then to Reid. Her cheeks are pink. "It's fine, Reid. I'm okay."

"Yeah, that's good. Go home, Kayla." Reid nods toward her car. "Rourke, if I catch you sniffing around her again, we're going to have a problem."

Atlas barks out a laugh and nods, turning away from us. "Yeah, okay."

Reid's quiet and pensive on our short drive back to his cabin.

"I'll handle this," he says, glancing at me as he turns down the dirt drive. "I promise you."

We climb out of the car. My hands tremble as I fumble with the key in the front door. Reid moves past me, checking all the doors and windows. He's silent, moving through the house with that calm, methodical precision I've come to recognize—his version of control. Mine looks different.

I head straight for the kitchen, finding the bananas that are spotted with brown. I open the cabinet, pulling down the flour and sugar and a big mixing bowl that I had to buy last week when I wanted to make cornbread. Reid didn't have one. I remember how I felt hopeful, buying something for our shared space, knowing he never would have needed to. He didn't ask for any of this—me, here stirring up trouble. Now I wonder if I should just walk away from all of it.

"What are you doing?" His voice cuts through my thoughts.

"The bananas are going to go bad. I'm going to bake something," I mutter. "I always bake when I can't relax."

He leans against the counter, arms folded, watching me as I mash bananas into a bowl with more force than necessary. "You sure this is about bananas?"

"He knew my car," I say, my voice wobbly. Dropping the fork, I turn to him. "Whoever it was. He knew it was mine."

Reid crosses the room in two long strides. "Hey." His hand finds my cheek, steady and warm, lifting my gaze up to his. "Look at me."

I do, and the calm I've been clinging to splinters.

"What if it doesn't stop?" My voice cracks. "What if they just keep pushing until I—until we—"

"They won't," he cuts in gently. "I won't let them."

"You're just one man," I say, shuddering.

Reid lets out an exasperated breath and pulls me to him. "I know. But you're...everything to me. I'll do whatever I have to do to protect you."

I nod, pulling away and turning back to my bananas.

"I'm going to talk to Colt." He moves toward the front door. "I'll be back as soon as I can. Keep the doors locked."

And then he's gone.

CHAPTER THIRTY-EIGHT

REID

EMERY IS TOO shaken to file the police report herself, so I leave her at my cabin, stress-baking banana bread. It kills me that she's living in fear like this. It's unfair. And if she wants to go home to New Jersey, I should let her. I shouldn't hold her back. Maybe I could go with her.

All these things are topics we've yet to discuss. I don't even know where she stands with that ex-boyfriend of hers, her job, or her place back in New Jersey. It's like she's embedded in Tidehaven now, her past life forgotten.

I make a mental note to bring this up to her when things settle down. For now, we need surveillance on Atlas Rourke...like yesterday.

By the time I pull into the station lot, the sun is dipping beneath the trees, but it does nothing to cool things off. Inside, the station hums with the sound of the AC, working too hard for its age. The faint clicking of someone typing and voices comes from the bullpen, but I head straight for Colt's office. The door is ajar, and I hear them.

Colt and Tate.

I pause outside the door.

Tate said he was going to Beaufort.

"The shipment's not supposed to move until after the storm they're watching next week," Tate says.

"You sure about that?" Colt asks. "That's a hell of a delay for something that might not happen."

"Orders from higher up," Tate replies. "They're waiting for high tide. No one's supposed to be on the water till it's over."

My pulse hammers in my chest.

Shipment? What the hell are you mixed up in, Tate?

I push open the door before I can think better of it. "Tidehaven gossip hour, or am I interrupting something important?"

Both men jolt like I fired a gun. Colt straightens behind his desk, but his expression is unreadable. Tate's sitting sideways in a chair across from him, shoulders tense.

"Jesus, Reid," he says, forcing a laugh that doesn't match his posture. "You move like a damn ghost."

I ignore his remark, moving further into the room, crossing my arms and fixing my eyes on him. "What shipment are you talking about?"

Tate's eyes flick to Colt and then back to me. "Just marina logistics. Fuel deliveries. You know, since we're down a few docks."

"Huh. That's funny." I frown, challenging him. "Because last I checked, marina logistics didn't require secret meetings at the police station." My eyes dart to Colt, but his expression remains impassive.

"It's nothing you need to worry about, Morgan," Colt finally says with a sigh. "What brings you in?"

I toss the folded note onto his desk. "Someone smashed Emery's car window while she was at work. In broad fucking daylight. Left that behind."

Colt unfolds it. "Thought I told you to leave," he reads. His jaw tightens.

Tate lets out a low whistle. "You got any idea who did it?"

I let out a breath. "No. But Atlas Rourke was conveniently there when she found it. She said he gave her the creeps."

"That I believe," Colt says. "He's an asshole for sure. But vandalism?"

"Haven't you seen him with Langford? He's trying to send a

message," I growl.

"Why would he do that?" Colt asks, locking his gaze on mine. "Listen, don't get all wound up before we know anything. I'll send someone to take photos of the damage."

I clench my fists at my sides, watching Tate. He's fidgeting—tapping his thumb against his thigh, eyes darting toward the window like he can't sit still.

"You look nervous," I say. "Something you want to share with the class?"

He bristles. "You think I'd keep something from you?"

"I think you've been spending a lot of time whispering with *Deputy Chief Riggs* here and I'm starting to wonder why my two best friends are having marina logistics meetings without me when I'm part owner," I say, flicking my gaze between the two of them, wondering who will crack first.

"Damn it, Reid." Tate stands abruptly, running a hand through his hair and moving closer. "You want to do your job or interrogate me? Because I've got enough shit on my plate without you breathing down my neck."

Colt stands, stepping between the two of us. "Knock it off, both of you." He levels a look at me. "Tate is not your enemy here, and the last thing the two of you need is to draw attention to yourselves."

I step back, sizing them up. "Fine. But if this *shipment* you're hiding ties back to Langford in any way, I want to know about it before it bites us in the ass."

Tate lets out a low chuckle. "You really don't trust me anymore, do you?"

"I trust what I see," I say flatly. "And what I'm seeing doesn't look good."

"You're fucking paranoid. Wound too tight. We're *all* on edge, it doesn't mean everybody but you is involved in some conspiracy."

I huff a sardonic laugh, stepping closer. "Funny. I didn't say anything about a conspiracy."

Tate stiffens, the air taut.

Colt sighs, pinching the bridge of his nose. “You two done measuring dicks? This isn’t helping.”

Tate exhales sharply, turning away from me. “You know, Morgan,” he says, facing the wall. “You’ve been off since that body turned up.” He turns back. “Maybe you need to take a step back.”

“Fuck off,” I growl.

“Watch yourself,” Tate says quietly.

“That advice or a warning?”

Tate doesn’t reply. Colt and I watch him for a long moment before Colt turns to me. “He’s right about one thing, you know.”

“Which part?” I ask.

“The part about taking a step back.” Colt’s voice drops, quiet but firm. “You and Emery both could use some distance from all this. Go away for a few days. Let things cool off here.”

I suck in a breath, looking to my friend for an honest answer. “This your idea or his?” I jerk my eyes toward Tate.

“Mine. I don’t like the way things are moving,” he says carefully. “And I’d rather you not be standing in the middle when the tide turns.”

I look from him to Tate. Tate won’t meet my eyes.

“Yeah,” I say finally. “Maybe you’re right.”

Colt nods once, like that’s the answer he was hoping for. “Go tomorrow. I’ll keep an eye on things here.”

I turn for the door, but Tate stops me with a hand on my shoulder. His grip is too firm.

“Stop looking for trouble,” he warns.

I look at his hand, then at him. “If trouble’s tied up at our docks, I won’t have to look at all.”

His expression flickers—something like guilt, or anger, or both. “You don’t know what you’re talking about.”

“Then prove me wrong,” I say.

For a second, it’s quiet except for the faint sound of the ceiling fan whirring overhead. Then Colt clears his throat and mutters something about filing the report.

“That’s what I thought.” I leave without looking back.

Outside, the air feels thicker, the sky is darker now. But even as I start the truck, I can still feel Tate's stare on my back—and I can't tell if it's regret or suspicion.

When I walk through the door, the cabin smells of cinnamon and sugar—a comfort that feels right and wrong all at the same time.

Emery is curled up on the sofa, two plates of banana bread sitting on the coffee table in front of her, tabs of butter melting on top. She's got her laptop open but her expression is blank, and I get the sense that she is only pretending to work.

"Hey, baby," I say, closing the front door and locking the dead bolt. "Smells good in here."

Emery looks up, dazed, like she didn't hear me come in.

"You okay?" I ask, sitting beside her. I give her foot a gentle squeeze.

Emery sighs, setting the laptop aside. "How did it go?"

I push my lips together, debating whether to share my suspicions about Tate and the secrets he's keeping. I decide against it. "Colt says he'll send someone out to take pictures of it. I've got to go back to town and drive it home for you."

"Okay," she whispers. "What else?"

"He said he'll file the report." I pick up the plate and take a bite of banana bread. "This is amazing," I say, swallowing. "Did it make you feel better?"

Emery lets out a low laugh. "Sort of. Not really." She shrugs. "At home, baking brought me comfort when I was stressed. It's not really working here."

"Maybe you need a change of scenery," I suggest. "Just for a few days."

Emery blinks. "What do you mean?"

I put my plate down and scoot closer, pulling her to me. "I mean, let's you and I get out of here for a couple of days. We can drive inland or up to Charleston. Anywhere you want."

"You think running will fix this?"

"I think breathing will," I say carefully. "We need space to breathe. Figure out the next steps."

Next steps for us. Next steps for keeping her safe. The future and if we want to do it together. I don't say all this though—she's had enough stress for one day.

Besides, Tate and I already burned through our words earlier. I can't remember the last time I raised my voice at him. But it's time some hard lines be drawn. He thinks I'm letting this get personal. I think he's wrong—and for the first time in a long while, I let him know it.

Emery lets out a long slow breath and nods. "Okay."

"I'll call Tate and let him know I need a few days off," I say, squeezing her thigh.

"You think he'll be okay with it?"

I give her a half-smile. If she only knew. "He'll live."

CHAPTER THIRTY-NINE

EMERY

"WHERE SHOULD WE even go?" I ask Reid as I shove a few overnight essentials into a duffel bag. I have to admit, the excitement of getting away with him for a few days has my pulse racing. We haven't talked about what we're doing—other than surviving—but traveling together is already a good next step in a relationship.

"I have a text out to a Navy buddy, Brian. He's overseas now, but he has a cabin on the Magnolia River. It's quiet, off grid. No neighbors, no cell service. You'll like it—nobody can bother us out there."

I nod, letting out a breath. "Okay. Good."

Reid moves around the side of the bed, tugging me into him from behind, his fingers digging into my hips. "This will be good for us," he murmurs in my ear. His breath tickles my neck, and it sends a shiver up my spine.

Just when I think things are heating up, his phone dings.

Reid steps away, picking up the phone. "It's him." He holds the phone up to me, a single text glows from the screen.

Brian

Sure thing. Key's in the same place.

I smirk. "How very trusting of him."

"We go way back," he says, hammering out a reply before

tossing his phone on the bed. He steps toward me, and I turn to him as his arms encircle my waist. "This will be good for us," he says again and I know right then, there's no way I'm telling him no.

"I don't doubt it," I reply. Then I melt into him.

We leave at six a.m., thermoses full of coffee and a "Country Roads" playlist on the stereo. The further west we drive, the quieter it gets and the denser the forest becomes. The boats, the bait shacks, even the constant hum of the gulls are replaced with endless pine forests and dusty winding roads that seem to lead nowhere.

Reid keeps one steady hand on the wheel and the other on my thigh. I alternate between watching him drum his thumb on the steering wheel and the gorgeous scenery outside my window.

"Are you sure you aren't taking me out here to kidnap and murder me?" I arch a brow.

He chuckles. "If I were bringing you out here to kidnap you, I'd have brought more snacks."

I laugh, tension easing out of me for the first time since the window incident. The sound surprises me—like I've forgotten that laughter is normal.

The road narrows until the trees form a canopy overhead. Spanish moss dangles low enough to brush the windshield, sunlight flickering through it in patches. The air thickens with the scent of river water and earth.

The truck curves around a bend and I see it—my first glimpse of the Magnolia River. Its water is dark and still, like mirrored glass. Cypress trees jut up like ancient sentinels, and somewhere in the distance, I hear a bull frog.

"Wow," I breathe. "It's beautiful."

"Yeah, it is." Reid slows the truck and we coast, taking in the scenery.

The cabin appears just beyond a stand of wide oak trees,

small and weathered, but homey. A porch extending the length of the house holds two rocking chairs facing the water. It's not all that different from Tidehaven. More remote but still surrounded by nature. It's peaceful.

Reid parks and kills the engine, looking at me. His lips curve into a slow smile before he swings open his door.

I follow suit, climbing out and stretching. I tip my head back to take in the cloudless blue sky, and for the first time in weeks, I relax.

"This place is incredible. I feel so...at ease." I move toward him, wrapping him in a hug from behind. "Thank you for bringing me here." I plant a kiss between his shoulder blades.

"You're welcome," he murmurs, turning to face me. "I stayed here a few times when I first got back. It's the perfect place to clear your head." He hoists our bags from the bed of the truck.

"And you thought bringing your stressed-out, semi-traumatized girlfriend was a good way to ruin that peace?" I tease.

His mouth twitches into a grin. "You don't ruin anything, Emery."

The way he says it—quiet and certain—makes something tighten in my chest.

"I do like that you referred to yourself as my girlfriend though," he admits, lacing his fingers through mine.

My heart does a little flip-flop.

He leads me up the cedar plank steps, crouching to get the key from under a long-deceased potted plant.

"If I remember correctly, this door sticks a little." Reid leans his shoulder into it, bracing against it, and forces it open.

The door opens before us, revealing a single room with a stone fireplace, a small kitchen, and a king-sized bed that looks too inviting for two people who are falling in love.

Reid drops our bags by the door and turns to me, a grin spreading across his face. "A couple of days. No interruptions. Just you and me."

"Oh yeah?" I step closer, tugging his hard body into mine.

"Just what will we do with all our time?"

Reid tips my chin, bringing his lips to mine. "I've got a few ideas."

"SHOULD WE HIT the grocery store?" Reid asks. He's lying on the bed, watching me methodically unpack my duffel bag. I unpack wherever I go, no matter how long I'm staying. This seems to amuse him.

"Sure. How far is town?" I push the dresser drawer closed and sit on the end of the bed.

"About five miles. I figure we can make an afternoon of it. Get some lunch, explore the little shops, and then grab some groceries." Reid opens his arms, and I crawl into them. He plants a soft kiss on my head.

"That sounds nice," I murmur, nuzzling into the crook of his arm.

"Well, I'm a nice guy," he teases.

"Could've fooled me when I first got here." I tip my head to look at him.

He feigns offense. "What do you mean?"

I snort, unable to hold back my laughter. "Please. You were *so* unapproachable. I planned on staying out of your way."

"For like a week," he counters. "Then I warmed up."

"Only because you had to." I rest my head on his shoulder, and we sit in silence for a moment.

"I'm glad you didn't though." His voice cuts through the air, thick with emotion.

"Didn't what?" I ask.

"Stay out of my way," he murmurs, his eyes searching mine. "You've changed me."

"You've changed me, too."

WHEN WE REACH the downtown, I realize I haven't a clue where we are. "What's this place called?" I ask Reid as he expertly parallel parks his truck.

"Willowbend," he says, killing the engine.

"Willowbend," I repeat. "I like it."

He smiles softly and it turns my insides molten. "Me too."

"What should we do first?" I ask when we climb out of the truck.

"I don't know about you, but I'm starving." Reid laces his fingers through mine. "There's a great little diner on the corner."

"Sounds good to me."

We walk along the block, quietly taking in the sights. Reid points out a few places that he's been to before and I listen intently. The sound of his voice soothes me, and the way he talks about this place makes me wonder why he doesn't live here.

"You seem to love it up here," I comment, glancing at him.

"I do. But it's not home. Tidehaven is home. As much as he drives me crazy, Tate is home. Miss Rosie at the grocery store is home. Even Tess and Willie. I don't know where I'd be without that place." He looks my way, gauging my reaction.

"You'd figure it out. I had only ever thought of New Jersey as home because it's all I knew. But I think home is what you make of it." I shrug, dropping his hand when we reach the diner. He pulls open the door and gestures for me to walk in first.

A sign at the front of the restaurant reads, "Please Seat Yourself," so Reid leads us to a booth along the windows. We slide in and a moment later, a server drops some menus, telling us he'll be right back.

"So," Reid starts, "is Tidehaven starting to feel like home?"

I suck in a breath. "It's hard for me to say." I bite my lip. "But my job, my life in New Jersey...it all feels so far away. It feels like it belongs to someone else."

"And if you don't go back?" he asks, not bothering to hide the hope crossing his sharp features.

I shrug. "I'm scared to want something new when so much of

this feels temporary. The job is temporary. You..."

Reid's gaze snaps to mine, intense and unflinching. "I'm *not* temporary, Emery."

The way he is looking at me sends a ripple of warmth through my insides.

I swallow hard. "Okay...then what is this? What are we doing?"

He exhales slowly, reaching for my hand, our knees brush under the table. "I can't say for certain yet, but I know I've fallen for you. That's something I never expected to happen to me again. And I liked the way it sounded earlier, when you called yourself my girlfriend. I don't have a perfect answer, but I do know I want to build something with you that lasts."

His words are spoken with such sincerity, and I can't help but think that every time I expect his walls to go back up, he surprises me by breaking them down himself. There are just so many complications surrounding this thing between us. Could I really just resign from my tenured position and move to Tidehaven permanently? There are people who want to *kill* me there. What about my parents, my siblings, my friends? It feels like something I need to figure out and yet, I don't want to think about it. So, instead, I squeeze his hand and match his gaze.

"Let's just start there then."

He brushes a thumb over my knuckles. "That sounds good."

CHAPTER FORTY

REID

EMERY IS DELIGHTED by everything she sees in Willowbend. I'm struck by it—because it's the first time since she arrived in South Carolina that she seems truly relaxed. The sight makes me ache a little. I should've gotten her out of Tidehaven sooner. She deserved to feel this safe all along, and it kills me that I didn't give her that.

We finish breakfast and start back down the block on the main street, hand-in-hand. The humidity feels less than it does at home, and there's a light breeze blowing through. It's a weekday, so the streets aren't crowded, just a few families wandering around on summer break.

"Let's go in here," Emery suggests, nodding toward a gift shop with a weathered wooden sign.

"Sure," I say, tugging open the door.

For the next ten minutes, I follow Emery up and down the aisles as she picks up every trinket and handmade item she finds. She peruses a wall of local art, watercolor prints, photography, and hand-woven baskets before moving onto locally made soaps and candles. She pauses in front of a jewelry case, necklaces made of natural stone carved into shapes of local wildlife line the case. Her gaze lands on a small turtle pendant, the green of river stone. It hangs sideways on a fine silver chain, as if swimming through still water.

A small gasp escapes her.

"Look," she murmurs. "A turtle."

I skim the sign above the glass case. "Crafted by local artisans and made only from stones found in the Magnolia River," I read.

Emery peers further into the case, scanning the price tags. "Seventy-five dollars, yikes." She wrinkles her nose and then shrugs. "I'm going to see if they have a bathroom."

She disappears down the aisle, and before I can think better of it, I grab the nearest employee and ask them to take out the turtle necklace. I've just finished paying and tucking the bag neatly in the pocket of my cargo shorts when Emery comes out of the bathroom.

"What did you buy?" She arches a brow at me when she finds me at the counter.

I reach in my other pocket. "Gum," I say with a grin. "Want a piece?"

It's late afternoon by the time we make it back to Brian's cabin. We walked all around town, chatted with locals, found a park near the river and fed the ducks. Emery seems so much lighter here—like she can finally breathe.

"Why don't you get comfortable, and I'll cook us some dinner?" I suggest.

"Mmm...that sounds nice." She smiles, wrapping me in a hug before disappearing down the short hallway to the bathroom.

I suck in a nervous breath. *Easy, bro.* I bought the necklace for her on a whim. I couldn't pass up the chance to surprise her once I saw how much she loved it. Now, to get the nerve to give it to her. This thing with Emery is unlike anything else I've experienced. I've dated, sure, but then I went into the SEALs and when I came out, I wasn't the same. Most of the time, I scare women off before I even have a chance to show who I really am. I've always just assumed that I'm better off alone.

But something about Emery... She's magnetic. Not only

do I want to protect her, I want to build a life with her. That's not something I can admit easily—I've only known her for two months. Still, I can't stop the gravitational pull.

I move outside to Brian's worn brick patio. There's a cinderblock firepit with a cover over it and some Adirondack chairs. I pull the cover off and trek down the yard in search of wood. We don't need the heat, but I thought I'd cook our dinner over the fire tonight. It doesn't take me long to find some logs piled on the side of the cabin. I start the fire with the wood and a few coals to pre-heat, before heading inside to prep dinner.

Emery and I picked up some chicken thighs, potatoes, and asparagus. I season all of it equally before rolling it up in foil and grabbing some metal skewers and a grill grate. I'm just getting the fire going when she comes outside, freshly showered, her long locks pulled off her face in a braid. She glows in the late afternoon light.

"Wow, you're a real survivalist," she teases, sitting in a chair.

"Oh, yeah, me and my grocery store chicken." I smirk. "I just thought it would be fun to sit by the fire. Then I thought, why not cook out here too? But Brian has no propane in his grill."

Emery laughs and her whole face lights up. My chest pulls tight. She is so fucking beautiful—her loose cotton shorts and snug fitting tank top leave nothing to the imagination.

"So, show me how." She scoots to the end of her chair and watches closely as I set the grill grate over the small flame.

I let out a low laugh. For some reason, I feel nervous.

"There's not much to it. I seasoned everything together and wrapped them in these packets." I gesture to the two foil packs resting on the small table. "We just put them on the grates and rotate them every few minutes."

"Cool," Emery says, leaning back in the chair. She tugs her knees up to her chest and watches as I situate the food over the flame.

"Tell me about New Jersey," I say softly, sitting next to her.

"What do you want to know?" Emery lets out a breath, her

eyes flicking to mine.

"Anything you want to tell me. Did you grow up there? Your family? All this time we've gotten to know each other but, not enough." I shift to face her.

"Yes, I grew up there in a small town in the woods, in an area called the Pine Barrens. It's just inland and has the best of both worlds. I can hike in the woods or be at the beach in fifteen minutes." She sighs dreamily, and I selfishly worry she misses it.

"Sounds a little like Tidehaven," I murmur.

"They're not so different. New Jersey is very populated though. More people crammed into less space. But...it's always been home."

She looks away and I worry I've upset her. I rise to turn our food and sit back down.

"Do you miss your family?" I ask, sincerely. I'm not close with any biological family and I've been on my own for years, so I forget that other people have normal relationships with theirs.

"Sometimes. My dad and I aren't super close. He's obsessed with his job, even at sixty-five. My mom is so overprotective and she's retired, so if she knew half of what was going on down here, she'd come down and drag me back herself." Emery lets out a low laugh. "But my dad is very much the type of parent who thinks you're totally on your own once you graduate college. So even though we've been close geographically, we aren't super tight, you know what I mean?" She grimaces, like the topic is uncomfortable for her.

"Do you have siblings?" I ask.

"I have a sister, Kate, who has young children. She's close to our parents. She lives nearby and sees them often. She's a stay-at-home mom and definitely the favorite. And I have a brother, Ben. He's the youngest and he jets all over the world. I honestly couldn't even tell you what his job is or the last time I've seen him." Emery doesn't seem sad exactly, but something in her tone tells me she wishes things were different.

"Family is funny," I say, because I can't think of anything else.

"Tell me about yours." Emery reaches for my hand. I clasp it but let it drop when I realize I'm probably burning our dinner.

I grab the tongs and pull apart one of the packets, revealing crispy potatoes and golden chicken. "Looks done," I say.

Emery passes me the plates, and I put a foil packet on each one.

"Forgot silverware," I mutter. I jog back up the steps and inside, buying myself a minute to think about how to answer her question. I return a moment later with forks, knives, and two crisp beers.

Once we're settled, I speak again. "My family was only ever myself and my two parents who argued more than anything. One day, my dad just left without a word. Well, actually, I think he said he was going fishing with his buddy, but he never came back. I remember I was in the front yard, getting my crab traps ready for the day. Tate and I used to fill them with white bread from our parents' kitchen drawers. My dad hated that. I remember thinking it was weird that he didn't scold me—he just ruffled my hair, mumbled a simple 'See ya, kid,' and passed by and that was it. I never saw him again." I take a sip of beer in effort to force the uncomfortable emotions back down.

"Oh, Reid," Emery whispers, pausing mid-bite. "I'm so sorry."

I shrug. "It's okay. My mom did the best she could, but the light in her eyes went out for good that day. I was so young I didn't understand it, but suddenly our friends and neighbors were around a lot more often. Rosie kept me after school for years. I thought it was so my mom could work extra shifts but thinking back, I think she was just so depressed." I pause, taking a bite. "I think about leaving Tidehaven sometimes, finding my mom, or just starting over somewhere new. But then I think about all the friends and neighbors who helped raise me and it's like...I can't. I owe them so much."

Emery puts her plate on the table and reaches for my hand, giving it a comforting squeeze. I shift, pushing my plate aside too and tugging her gently into my lap. She nestles into my arms, and

I hold her close. The sun is beginning to set now, reflecting off the still water of the river, and the cicadas and crickets are chirping through the dense forest.

"Thank you for sharing that with me," she whispers in my ear before pressing a soft kiss on my temple.

"I want to share everything with you, Em. And that's a foreign as hell feeling to me." My voice is thick, and I get the sense she knows how rare a connection like this is for me.

"I want to share everything with you too, Reid."

I shift, lifting my hips and reaching my left hand to the pocket of my cargo shorts, undoing the button and pulling out the small mound of tissue paper.

"I bought this earlier—when you went to the bathroom. I wasn't sure if it was too soon to give it to you, but how could I wait? I hope it's not too much."

A small gasp falls from her parted lips as she takes the package from me. "Reid," she whispers.

"Open it."

She does as I ask, carefully unfolding the tissue to reveal the pale green turtle carved from river stone on a dainty silver chain. She sniffles.

"You bought the necklace," she murmurs, running her fingers over the shape of the turtle. "You didn't have to do that. It's too much."

I shake my head. "You loved it, and I wanted you to have it. This way, you'll always remember your time here in Tidehaven. You'll always remember me." I bring her close, planting a kiss on the crown of her head.

She rests against me, holding the necklace close to her heart. "I was always going to remember you anyway."

CHAPTER FORTY-ONE

EMERY

THE EARLY MORNING glow filters through the thin curtains, waking me. I hear the movement of the river lapping against the shore, the cry of a heron somewhere distant. Reid's arm is heavy around my waist, his breath warm against the back of my neck. I lie there for a while, peaceful and content, tracing lazy circles on the rough skin of his forearm, not wanting to break whatever spell this is.

When I finally shift, he groans. "Where do you think you're going?"

A smile curves my lips, and I peek at him over my shoulder. "Just to make some coffee."

"Will you bring me some?" he murmurs, his eyes still closed.

"Of course." I tug on his T-shirt from last night that I find on the floor, that skims halfway down my thighs, and pad into the tiny kitchen. The coffee pot grumbles to life, and I lean against the counter, watching it drip for a few minutes before pouring two mugs—black for him, cream for me.

When I get back to bed, Reid is sitting up, his hair mussed, the sheet resting low across his hips. The sight of him—bare chested, broad shouldered, faint scar slicing diagonally down his chest—makes my heart skip a beat.

"Morning," I say softly, passing his mug to him.

His fingers brush mine and he studies me for a beat. "Morning. You sleep okay?"

"Better than I have in a while," I admit with a sigh. "It's so peaceful here."

"That's kind of the point," Reid says, taking a sip from his mug. He's quiet for a moment, then, "You ever think about what that peace might look like for you? Long term?"

I tilt my head. "You mean, when this is all over?"

"Yeah," he says, his tone careful. "What happens then? You go back to Jersey?"

The question lands hard, pulling the air from my lungs, as I realize what he's asking. Reid's all in and he wants to know if I am too. My throat burns at the thought of his walls going back up.

I look down at my mug and swallow hard. "I'm not sure. My relationship with Jason is over. I have to move out of our townhouse." I pause. "If nothing else, being with you has made me realize I deserve so much better than what he gave me. But I'm not sure where I'll go. New Jersey probably won't feel like home anymore."

Reid's expression softens but he doesn't let me off the hook. "What *would* feel like home?"

"I don't know yet exactly. It's hard to say without knowing what comes next." I bite my lip, meeting his eyes.

Reid sets his mug down on the end table and shifts to face me. "If I asked you to stay in Tidehaven, would you consider it?"

My heart stutters. "You mean...with you?"

"I mean with me," he says, voice low and sure. "Or *near* me if this feels too fast. I don't care where we end up, as long as I don't have to wonder where you are and I can see you every day."

For a long moment, I just breathe, the sound of my thumping heart echoing in my ears.

"I think," I say slowly, "if I went back to New Jersey, on some level, I'd always be looking for you."

Reid exhales, the corner of his mouth twitching into a half smile. "That sounds like a yes."

"It's a maybe leaning heavily toward yes. Assuming we stop whoever is after me."

He lifts my mug from my hands and sets it aside so he can pull me close. "I'll take it. And I won't stop until we do."

When he leans in and kisses me, it's warm and steady, the kind that feels like a promise. Outside, the river shimmers under the morning sun, and for the first time, I think I have a glimpse of what my future could look like.

WE SPEND THE morning in bed until finally, around noon, Reid suggests we explore. I'm content to explore him—every sharp angle of his muscular body—but I relent when he says there is a two-person kayak in the shed.

"Come on, get dressed." He throws the sheet off his legs revealing his bare ass, and the jolt to my core startles me once again.

I push to my knees, catching him around the waist before he moves, my bare breasts pressing into his warm skin. He pauses then, clasping his hands over mine.

"You haven't had enough?" he rasps.

"I'm not sure I'll ever have enough of you," I whisper, sliding my hands down his ripped middle.

He turns then, a playful smile on his face.

"You're trouble, woman," he growls, pressing a kiss to my mouth. It's not enough though, he hurls me over his shoulder and down the hall. "Find your swimsuit."

A few minutes later, I find him in the back yard, dragging a two-seater bright yellow kayak out of the shed. It's a smidge dusty but he takes a minute to hose it off.

"I used to kayak in this thing all the time. Always alone." He leads me to the edge of the riverbank.

"Good thing you'll have someone else to pull the weight now," I tease.

He gives me a skeptical look, like he doesn't believe I'll be helping all that much. "I'll steer, which means you sit in the front."

He pushes the kayak so it's partially in the water and partially resting on the small beach. "Get in."

I do as I'm told and he hands me an oar. When he steps in the kayak and settles himself, he gives us a strong push off the shore and we're off.

Our paddles dip in uneven rhythm, doing more splashing than slicing, but Reid doesn't seem to mind. He steers behind me, his voice steady and low with words of encouragement.

"Nice and easy," he says. "You don't have to muscle it. Let the paddle do the work."

"I *am* letting it." I twist around to give him a smirk. "Maybe the paddle is lazy."

A laugh bursts out of him, genuine and unguarded, releasing a swarm of butterflies in my belly. "Then maybe you should show it who's boss."

We wobble when I overcompensate. "There you go. Twist from your core, you'll glide smoother that way."

"My *core* wasn't consulted about this trip," I joke.

"Well, tell it to get on board. We're turning left up here which means you have to paddle right. Just a little. Not too hard." His voice is low and steady.

We find our rhythm after that, our strokes evening out, and the kayak glides smoothly through the water. A peaceful silence settles over us as we take in the scenery.

The river is still as glass, a long ribbon of green-gold light stretching ahead of us. Cypress branches dip toward the water, their reflections so clear they could be the real thing. Reid's paddle makes soft, rhythmic swirls behind me, each stroke unhurried. The farther we paddle, the quieter the world becomes. The hum of insects replaces the noise in my head, and even the air feels softer here.

"This is my favorite part," he says quietly. "No boats. No cell service. Just us."

"Also, the perfect setting for a slasher film." I glance back at him with a smile.

He grins. "If I was going to kill you, I'd have done it already."

We slow our paddling and drift for a while. Then I spot a heron perched on a fallen tree, its feathers glowing silver in the light. I lean toward it without thinking. "Look at that—"

Reid reaches out to steady me, but the kayak wobbles under our combined shift. I burst out laughing, which doesn't help. And then we tilt sharply to the right.

"Reid!"

The world tips cold and bright as the river swallows my gasp. When I surface sputtering, he's already laughing, water dripping into his eyes.

"You okay?" he swims closer.

I nod, breathless from laughing and treading water. "You were supposed to keep us *in* the kayak!"

"I tried," he says, grinning, his arms encircling me. I wrap my legs around his waist, allowing him to support us. "But then you had to go and smile at me." His fingers trace the water from my cheek, lingering.

For a heartbeat, there's nothing but the sound of the river and the thud of my pulse. Then he kisses me—wet, warm, inevitable.

IT'S LATE AFTERNOON by the time we return to the cabin. The sun hangs low over the treetops, turning the river to liquid gold. My clothes cling to me, sticky and damp, but I can't bring myself to care.

I plant myself on the riverbank while Reid drags the kayak in. He sits next to me, our shoulders brushing.

"You handled that pretty well," he says, his lips twitching. "Most people panic when they go overboard."

I huff a laugh. "I've had enough panic the last eight weeks. Besides, cold water is good for you. And I had a Navy SEAL with me, serving and protecting." I jut my thumb his way.

He turns to me at that, the last of the sunlight making his

green eyes look hazel. "I'll always protect you, Emery," he rasps. Then his lips are on mine as he hovers over me, gently laying me back on the sandy riverbank.

The kiss is deep and sure, like everything we've worked up to hangs in this moment. Two unlikely people, caught in the midst of a dangerous feat, somehow managing to fall in love. Out here, it's easy to forget the threat that looms over us back in Tidehaven, but Reid's assurance makes me feel cherished and safe.

"There's an outdoor shower, by the shed," he murmurs into my mouth.

"Will you show me?" I breathe.

In one swift motion, Reid picks me up, fireman style, and treks up the bank, straight for to the outdoor shower. It's a simple wooden platform surrounded by slats of weathered cedar, open to the warm air and the dimming sky.

He sets me on my feet and turns the knob, the water sputtering before cascading between us in a rush, cool against our overheated skin.

Reid's fingers find the hem of my tank top, and he lifts it over my head, leaving me in my bikini. I do the same for him, tugging his shirt up to reveal the body I've come to know so well. His mouth crashes into mine, his hands gripping my loose ponytail, as he pushes my lips apart, his tongue dancing with mine. With his other hand, he fumbles with the button on my denim shorts, letting them drop to the ground. Then, without breaking our kiss, he pulls the string on my bikini top, and it falls away. Just as quickly his mouth finds each breast, hungrily sucking and flicking the nipple until they peak for him.

I let out a soft moan. "This is so freeing," I murmur between soft kisses. I reach for the tie on his board shorts, tugging them down and wrapping my fist around his hard length.

"There's no one around," he growls. "The things I want to do to you..." His fingers slip beneath the waistband of my bathing suit, dragging a finger up my center.

"Reid," I whimper.

"I know, baby."

"This is..." I sigh, my words failing me.

"I know. I feel it too." He reaches for a bar of soap, lathering it in his palms and rubbing them over my body, lingering over my nipples and gently pinching them.

I groan. *This man.*

We take turns washing each other, hands slipping over the soapy lather, gentle kisses turning fervent as our bodies tangle under the water.

The sun is dipping lower, and I shiver under Reid's touch as a light breeze blows through.

"You're cold," he says, his mouth on my neck.

"A little," I admit.

He reaches up and removes the shower nozzle, rinsing the remaining soap from my body.

"And we have no towels," he says, a hint of amusement on his lips. "Want to make a run for it?"

I bark out a laugh. "Okay. Let's do it."

Reid turns the water off. We collect our things from the wooden floor and dart toward the cabin, cackles bursting out of us. If anyone saw us right now, surely, they'd get a laugh, but as soon as we're inside, all traces of humor are gone.

Reid's gaze turns on me, dark and intense, hunger flashing behind his green eyes as he steps toward me. We're dripping water all over the oak floor. He reaches for the throw blanket draped over the armchair, wrapping me in it and pulling me close. Suddenly, the air is thicker, full of want, yes, but it's more than that. It's a need—a necessity—I fear I can't live without.

Reid takes my hand and leads me to the bathroom, reaching in the small cabinet for bath towels. We dry off in silence, watching each other. My heart pounds so hard it feels like it's chasing his, and I know this want for him will never quiet. Our towels drop to the floor, and he steps closer to me again, his hands finding the curve of my ass as he lifts me. My arms fall around his neck, and his length settles between my legs as he kicks the door open and leads us back to the unmade bed.

He lays me gently at the end of the bed, bending my knees and spreading me open.

"So fucking beautiful," he growls, dragging a finger through my wet slit. He drops to his knees, his mouth finding my inner thighs, peppering a line of gentle kisses straight to my heat. When his tongue sinks into my center, a low moan tumbles out of me. "You taste so sweet," he says, sliding a finger inside and swirling it until I cry out.

"Reid," I whimper, my breaths coming in rapid pants.

"Shh," he whispers. "Just relax. This is as much for you as it is for me."

And then he buries his face in my core, his teeth dragging over my clit as he flicks his tongue in slow, agonizing circles. He slides in another finger, then a third, his free hand reaching up to graze a nipple. The sensations are too much and I'm feral.

"Reid, holy shit."

"You going to explode for me?" he growls.

"Y-yes." I can barely get the word out as my moans grow louder by the second.

"Good girl. Come all over my face, baby."

And then it hits me, flashes of light behind my eyelids as I tip over the edge, my orgasm sending my body into convulsions as it rocks through me with the crash of a tidal wave. Reid pulls back, watching me as I come down before flipping me over and without a word, sliding into my soaking wet center.

"Oh my fucking God," I cry out as he begins to move.

"Yeah. You take me so well, baby. Your tight little pussy was made for me," he murmurs, his hands clasping my damp hair.

His thrusts start slow, pulling all the way out before plowing back in, each new entry eliciting a desperate cry from me. His hand finds my ass cheek, the sweet sting of the slap jolting me back. I force myself to my knees, allowing him to thrust deeper. His fingertips dig into my hips, and his movements become more urgent as his climax builds.

"Oh my God, Emery." His words come in jagged staccato.

"I was. I was made for you," I whimper, backing my ass into him, matching him thrust for thrust.

That does it—his release finds him quickly and a roar explodes from his chest as he fills me. My second climax follows like an explosion, and I'm writhing beneath him. He collapses on top of me, both of us a heap of tangled limbs and erratic breaths.

Reid presses a kiss to my shoulder, brushing hair off my forehead.

"That was...wow," I breathe.

Reid lets out a low laugh. "It was... Sorry for all the dirty talk." He covers his eyes, embarrassed maybe.

"Sorry?" I ask, my brow knitting together. "You never have to be sorry for calling me a good girl."

CHAPTER FORTY-TWO

REID

I'M PRETTY BUMMED when our two days away come to an end. It's been the first real breath of peace in two months, but reality's waiting for us back in Tidehaven.

Tate still hasn't checked in. Colt has, though. He said they got photos of the car—no fingerprints, no clear leads. Whoever did it knew what they were doing. They're canvassing for witnesses, checking surveillance footage, but all they found was a pair of gloves and a crowbar dumped behind the research center. I don't tell Emery that part. She deserves a few more hours without that weight on her shoulders.

I've texted Tate a few times, tried calling once. His responses have been short, clipped—like he's talking to a stranger. He mentioned the insurance adjuster came out. That's good, I guess. But the space between us feels heavier than I want to admit. My best friend and business partner is keeping something from me, and I'm starting to realize it might change everything.

I tug the comforter up over the bed, tucking the corners the way my mom used to when I was a kid. Emery grabs the opposite end, smiling softly.

"Towels are folded and put away," she says.

"Thanks." I cross the room to grab our bags, forcing my focus on small tasks.

"I don't want to go," she admits quietly. "I love hiding out here with you."

"I know." My voice comes out rougher than I mean it to. "We'll come back. Before..."

Before she leaves. Before any of this has a chance to fall apart. I don't finish the thought, and thankfully she doesn't press.

She swings her purse over her shoulder. "Shall we? Nothing left to clean up, right?"

"We're good."

I move to the sliding glass door, pull it closed, and flip the lock. The click echoes in the small room. I draw the shade, and the light drains out, leaving us in the kind of dim quiet that feels heavier than it should.

Emery slips her hand into mine. "You okay?"

"Yeah." It's a lie, but I squeeze her hand anyway. "Just not ready to go back."

Outside, the truck waits in the gravel drive. The forest hums with late-summer life, all easy rhythm and calm, as if it doesn't know what we're heading back into.

I toss our bags in the bed of the truck and climb in, starting the engine. Emery pushes her sunglasses to the top of her head and start's typing the directions into the GPS app. I don't bother telling her I know the way.

"What should we listen to?" she asks, settling her phone in the cup holder. "Anything you're in the mood for?"

"Let's find a local station—AM radio—I've been getting weather alerts on my phone, I want to know what's going on." I turn onto the main road. The weather service is calling for Tropical Storm Maeve, but the sky is clear blue and summer sun shines brightly. It sure doesn't feel like a storm's coming. I reach into the center console for a pair of shades just as Emery's phone rings.

She holds it up, watching the screen flash. "It's Alan," she says. "Do you mind if I get it?"

"Not at all," I say, focusing my gaze on the road ahead. A breeze rustles the Cypress trees, and it's the only sign I can see that maybe the weather is changing.

"Hey, Alan," Emery says, tapping the screen. "Things are good," she says into the phone. She cradles it while reaching over to stroke my thigh.

I smile at her. Things *are* good with us. I just wish things were good with Tate and the marina and the damn town that raised me that somehow feels sinister now. Maybe it's always been that way, or maybe growing up I just never wanted to see it for what it is.

"Wow, really?" Emery's voice prompts me to look her way. "That's generous. I mean, to be honest, I haven't thought about what comes next. They don't want to meet with me or anything? They just want to give me the job?"

She pauses and my heartrate picks up, suddenly desperate for her to hang up the phone and tell me what's going on.

"Well, shouldn't we see where things land once the sabbatical is up in three months?" Emery eyes me, listening intently to the voice on the other end. "Well, okay, yeah. I guess that makes sense. How long do I have?"

I suck in an audible breath, and her eyes meet mine for a brief second, a small smile playing on her lips.

"Okay. I'll touch base next week then, once this storm passes. Thanks, Alan."

She hangs up and stares silently out the window.

"Well?" I ask incredulously.

"Well, what?"

"Are you going to tell me what that was all about?" I frown at the road in front of me.

"I thought you'd never ask," she teases.

"Ha-ha." I glance at her. "Tell me."

"Coastal Carolina wants to know if I'll stay on long term as a university field scientist and run an internship program out of the research center. They're expanding their marine biology program, and they're impressed with my resume so they wanted to give me the opportunity before they listed the position externally." She bites back a smile.

"I sense a *but* coming," I murmur, reaching for her hand.

"But...it would be a big move. A permanent one. It would mean leaving my tenured position in New Jersey to work for a new university where I have no job security. I told Alan I need to think about it." She squeezes my hand.

"Okay," I say carefully, moving my hand away so I can turn the corner.

Emery pulls it back.

"But..."

My lips twitch. "But?"

"I'm leaning heavily toward yes..."

"You are, huh?" I lick my lips, turning to face her.

"There's this guy I've fallen in love with, and now I can't imagine my life without him." Her voice is soft, like a whisper, a question she's waiting for me to answer.

I grin, glancing quickly at her then back at the road. "I've fallen in love with you too, Doc."

A comfortable, earned, silence settles between us as Emery fiddles with the radio in search of a local station. She's turning the knob when an advisory cuts through the speakers.

"—tropical storm Maeve is now expected to strengthen as it moves up the coast. Residents of Tidehaven, Hollow Creek, and Calusa Harbor are urged to prepare for possible flooding and gusts exceeding sixty miles per hour. Evacuation advisories may be issued later today. Residents are urged to secure property and be prepared to leave within twenty-four hours if conditions worsen."

"Shit," she mutters. "That's us."

"Yep." I let out a low breath. "Within twenty-four hours too. We'll need to board the cabin *and* the cottage. And I'll probably need to help Tate at the marina."

"Okay, well, we got this. We can do it." She squeezes my thigh.

"Never a dull fucking moment."

Tate still hasn't called. I thought for sure he'd check in with all the storm warnings happening. I hate that the silence between us feels louder than the thunder waiting on the horizon.

As the miles roll by, the landscape flattens, trees giving way to marshes and open sky. The radio fades in and out with weather updates, local officials, reminders to move livestock and tie down outdoor furniture.

Emery pulls her knees up, chin resting on them. "You think it'll be bad?"

"Bad enough," I say. "Storm surge will tear through the docks if we aren't prepared."

We cross the causeway as the wind picks up, rippling across the water. Some storefronts are already tacked with sheets of plywood, but fishermen are still drinking coffee outside the diner like it's any other day. Seagulls swirl low and restless. Tate's truck is parked crookedly by the boathouse, and he's standing on the dock with his clipboard, barking orders at his teenage deckhands.

I cut the engine. "Stay here," I tell Emery, though I already know she won't.

She follows me across the gravel anyway, hair whipping in the breeze, the rain smell already heavy in the air.

Tate looks up as we approach. His expression is unreadable with the same closed-off look he's worn around me for days.

"Figured you'd head straight here," he says.

"Maeve's moving fast," I say. "We need to haul in what we can and board some windows."

"Already started," he says, his tone clipped. He's all business, no warmth, like we haven't known each other for thirty years. "Half the charter boats are coming in now. If the track holds, we'll get the northeast side of it. That's the ugly one."

I nod, glancing toward the water. The tide's higher than it should be, the blue sky from earlier already bruising gray. "So, what's your plan?" I ask, knowing he won't be forthcoming if I don't.

"I want everything under thirty feet hauled out by tonight. Big boats get extra lines. Windows here at the shop go up first thing tomorrow morning if the ten a.m. advisory doesn't change." Tate flips a page on his clipboard, studying the chicken scratch.

"Whatever you need," I say, my gaze focused on Emery a few yards back, her arms wrapped around herself, eyes tracking the horizon.

The calm from the cabin feels a million miles away. Any peace we found there is gone now, replaced by the threat of the coming storm.

"I'm going to go check the research center," she calls when she catches my eye.

"Be quick," I shout back.

Tate nods. "Good call. We'll need to board it up—those back windows are old."

We both watch her go, the silence between us stretching. I can feel everything we haven't said about what's been festering between us.

Finally, Tate exhales, glancing out at the flat, glassy water. "Look, man... I know things have been weird between us. I'm sorry I've been distant. Been dealing with some personal stuff, that's all."

He sounds so genuine, I almost believe him. But he won't meet my eye, and his evasiveness still doesn't sit right with me. Nevertheless, we don't have time to hash it out now. "We're good," I say. "Let's just get through this storm."

He claps me on the shoulder. "Tomorrow we'll board the rest, make the call on evacuating if Maeve stays on track."

Before I can answer, Emery jogs toward us. "Looks like everything's secured at the research center. We just need to do the windows," she says, slowing her pace as she reaches us.

Tate nods. "We can do those in the morning."

"All right. Let me know if anything changes," I tell him. "Em, let's go grab some groceries before Mama T's closes."

Just like that, everything feels almost normal again—Tate standing beside me like he always has, ready to take on whatever life throws our way. But as the breeze shifts inland, carrying that faint briny tang of the low tide, the unease comes creeping back.

And I can't escape the feeling that everything's about to change again.

CHAPTER FORTY-THREE

EMERY

THE BELL OVER the door jingles as we step into Mama T's General Store. The familiar blast of cold air is a relief from the thick pre-storm humidity outside.

"Hello, you two," Rosie calls from behind the counter. "Shop fast, this old girl is closing up soon."

"Hi, Rosie," I say, grinning at her.

"Hey, Rose." Reid steps around the counter and plants a kiss on Rosie's cheek. "We'll be quick, don't worry."

Rosie pats Reid's bicep and shoots me a wink.

"Good boy," she teases. "They're saying this storm is strengthening. It might become a category two hurricane."

Reid's brow tightens instantly, the line of his shoulders going rigid. "Where did you hear that?"

"Just a few minutes ago on the radio." Rosie turns behind her, turning the knob on an old boombox. The speaker hisses with static, and Reid and I share a glance. "It was working a second ago."

I take my phone out of my pocket and pull up my weather app. A bright red HURRICANE WARNING banner stretches across the top of my screen. "She's not wrong," I say, holding the phone up to Reid.

"Shit," he mutters. "Rosie, who is boarding up your windows?"

"Dale said he'd send one of his guys by," Rosie says with a

casual shrug.

Reid's whole body bristles, jaw going hard. I can practically *feel* the irritation rolling off him. "Yeah, no. Fuck Dale. I'll be by first thing in the morning."

"Watch your mouth around your lady," Rosie scolds, though her grin is all mischief.

"Yeah, yeah," he grumbles, placing a hand on the small of my back and steering me down the first aisle. The warmth of his palm sizzles through my shirt. "Bread, milk, eggs. What else do you need for a hurricane?"

"Beer," I offer.

"Beer. Right." His laugh is quick, distracted. We stop in front of the refrigerated cases and peer inside. "What kind?"

"How about that local lager we had before?"

Reid grabs a twelve-pack like it weighs nothing. We toss in snacks, some candles, maybe more comfort food than is strictly necessary, and head back up to Rosie. Dare I say, I'm kind of excited about hunkering down with him.

"You were fast," Rosie says with approval as she begins scanning our items.

"We don't want to keep you here any longer than you have to be, Rosie," Reid replies, bagging the groceries with practiced ease. "You going to be okay through this?"

"Oh yeah." She waves her hand like this storm is just like every other one she's seen before. "I'm going to my sister's on the mainland."

"Good. How's she doing?" Reid asks, bagging our groceries.

"She's great. Thinks I should give up this place and move out there with her though, naturally. But I can't let it go. It's the last of our legacy." Rosie's voice softens, the humor slipping a little. Her eyes turn glassy.

"Rosie, I had no idea you were Mama T," I say, digging in my purse for my wallet.

Reid is faster. He slides his card across the counter, and Rosie swipes it before I can protest.

"My mother was Mama T. Her name was Teresa," Rosie says, turning wistful. "She left me this place. I've worked here just about every day since I was fourteen years old. It's not just a store—it's a piece of her. I can't let it go yet."

"That's really special," I say, reaching out to give her hand a squeeze. "We'll make sure she's boarded up tight."

Rosie squeezes back, her eyes crinkling with gratitude. "I like her," she tells Reid with a pointed nod at me. Then to both of us, "You two be careful."

"We will," I promise, heading for the door.

Reid puts his arm around my waist, pulling me close as the wind whistles under the eaves.

"See you on the other side, Rosie," he calls.

She lifts a hand in farewell. "Y'all stay safe!"

The door swings shut behind us, and the air outside feels heavier than when we came in—charged and expectant, like the whole town is holding its breath.

Morning comes quickly, and Maeve is already making herself known by the sounds of the whipping wind outside our windows—its long, low moans, threading through the marsh. The trees rustle outside, and it's almost as if they're shivering.

I stumble out of bed and move to the bay window to see gulls crying out over the water, circling before moving inland. Marsh grass whips in frantic waves, hissing as the blades snap together. Somewhere out in the early light, an egret shrieks once. But there is silence too. The early morning chatter of marsh animals seems to be absent. It's as if they know what's coming. No frogs, no crickets, no birds. Just the whistle of the wind and the tick of the clock on the wall. The sky hasn't even darkened yet, but the storm is already here in every sound except rain.

"We'd better get a move on," Reid murmurs, stepping behind me and pressing a kiss to my temple.

"You're right. We need to get plywood?" I turn to look at him and for the first time see the concern etched on his features.

"I have a shed full of plywood sheets. I reuse them after every storm. There should be some at Blackbird Cottage too. Then we'll see what we need for Mama T's." Reid moves toward the kitchen. "I'm going to make some coffee."

"Good idea. We'll need it." My phone buzzes in my hand and I glance down to see a text from Kayla. "Kayla's going to meet us at the research center to help in a couple of hours."

"She doesn't need to help. She should stay home and help her mom with her younger siblings," Reid argues.

"Try telling her that. The girl loves that place. She'll be upset if you turn her away." I move to the kitchen, taking the mug of coffee he's offering me.

"Get dressed in clothes you don't care about. Some old sneakers. But throw your waders in the truck too, just in case the tide's high." Reid slurps his coffee. "The sooner we get this done, the better."

WE START WITH his cabin. I follow him out to the shed, and he tosses me a pair of work gloves.

"Put these on. I don't want you to get a splinter," he says. He spins the combination lock and the doors pop open. The shed is deep, filled to the brim with tools. There are several sheets of plywood leaning against the right-side wall. "These may feel a little heavy to you. I'll take one end, you take the other. We'll start with the sliding glass door." He steps inside and grabs a screw gun. "This will make things go faster."

We lean each piece of plywood against the front porch railing. Reid has them labeled with where they go on the house, making the process quick and relatively painless. We remove the porch furniture and shove it into the shed where we've made some room.

We finish just as the wind starts to pick up, the sky turning a bruised gray color.

"You'd better run in and get a jacket. I have a SEALS wind breaker in my front closet. Get that," Reid says, coming out of the shed with a few extra pieces of plywood and some bungee cords. "I'm going to load the truck and then we'll head over to Blackbird Cottage."

I nod, ducking through the front door. The cabin has shifted into an eerie half-night. Daylight doesn't enter so much as leak through the seams in thin stripes across the floor. The corners of the room go almost black, swallowing everything beyond the reach of the single lamp Reid remembered to switch on. Shadows stretch in strange shapes, long and crooked, turning familiar things—his boots by the door, a coat hung on a hook—into unsettling silhouettes. I make quick work of finding the wind breaker, not wanting to linger here too long.

I hear him slam the tailgate on the truck closed as soon as I find the jacket. I throw it on over my head and rush toward the door.

"Do you need anything else from inside?" I call to him.

"Grab us a couple of water bottles," he replies, sliding into the driver's seat.

I do as he asks and when I come out, I see Reid has driven my Prius under the carport on the back side of the cabin. The window is still broken but he sealed it up tightly with heavy plastic and duct tape.

"I thought your car would be safer over there," he says, pointing, when I slide in the passenger seat.

"Thank you," I say, sucking in a breath. "We have had hurricanes in New Jersey, but this feels intense. Maybe because we're right on the water." I glance out the window and see the marsh water has already risen higher since we started boarding the place up. Now it looks choppy and rough.

"We'll be okay," Reid murmurs, backing the truck out. "Let's keep going."

CHAPTER FORTY-FOUR

REID

I CAN TELL the storm prep is wearing on Emery. She follows every instruction without complaint, but tension is coiled in her shoulders, her eyes flicking to the horizon like she's expecting it to look different every time. We get Blackbird Cottage boarded up with the extra sheets of plywood I threw in the truck and some we found in the storage shed there. It's smaller than my place so it's fast work. I've pulled the small skiff from the water and slid it under the porch. It won't fit in the shed but at least it will be tucked away from the wind. While I nail the remainder of the plywood to the back windows, Emery drags the broken rocking chair from the screened porch inside. She meets me back at my truck with a few bottles of wine from inside.

"In case we need more provisions," she says, trying for humor, but her smile is stretched thin.

I hook an arm around her waist and pull her in, pressing a soft kiss to her mouth. "We're going to be just fine," I assure her. I say it because it's true, but I'm also trying to steady her, to pull her out of that tight, uneasy place she's been stuck in all morning.

"I hope you're right," she murmurs.

We climb in and she fixes her gaze outside the truck window to the marsh. Whitecaps slash across the water—sharp and violent. The whole landscape looks foreign.

My mind is already on our next stop. Mama T's. Rosie can't

board up her place alone, and I'm damn sure not leaving it to whoever Dale Langford claims he's sending.

I parallel park right outside. The second my boots hit the pavement, the hair on the back of my neck stands up.

Dale Langford is already here.

He's supervising his two mules drilling crooked sheets of plywood to the large grocery store windows. My gaze pans down the side of the building and my throat tightens. One of them is Atlas Rourke.

A familiar unease settles in my gut, sharp and insistent. Atlas Rourke is dangerous enough on his own. Tied to Langford, he's a warning sign I can't ignore.

A slow grin crawls across Dale's face when he notices Emery climbing out of the truck behind me. He drags his gaze over her like he's taking inventory. My stomach drops into something cold and sharp. Dale I can handle. I've known him since he was five. He doesn't scare me. It's the man hanging plywood that stops me in my tracks. I don't trust Atlas as far as I can throw him.

"What are you doing here, Dale?" I growl, stepping closer. "Rosie's place has always been my concern."

"Right, right. She's a second mother to you and all since your own wants nothing to do with you," Dale spits, trying to get a rise out of me. "Well, you weren't here early this morning, so I sent my guys to step up." He gestures to Atlas and the other man. Atlas wears a sly smirk, like he's enjoying this too much. "You know, a little community service."

Of course, Dale sent *his guys* in—like he'd do any real man's work himself.

I take a step forward, squaring myself between his men and the store. "Yeah. Well, we got it from here."

"Rosie sure is a lucky girl, having two groups fighting over who gets to help her. But my boys have it under control." Dale steps so close to me I can smell his breath mint. He tips his head toward the windows his men boarded. The panels are misaligned. Screws barely sunk. One corner is already lifting in the wind.

"Doesn't look that way." I narrow my eyes.

"And you and *her*—" he nods toward Emery, "are going to do it better?"

"Yes." I don't raise my voice—I don't need to. "Your guys can take a break before one of them loses a finger."

Atlas's jaw tics before he bends to pick up his drill. He moves slowly, deliberately, as if he's trying to drag out the moment—irritate me further. His eyes flick from me to Emery in a way that makes my blood run cold.

"You know, not everyone appreciates neighborly help." Dale licks his lips, his eyes fixed on us, taunting. He lets out an exaggerated sigh. "Just thought it was the right thing to do."

I stare him down. "We didn't ask for your help."

Dale chuckles, rubbing his chin. "Fine, Morgan. Have it your way. It'll take twice as long." He looks over my shoulder behind me to where his guys have paused, watching our standoff. "Okay, boys, pack it in."

The two men obey, packing the tools slowly, but Atlas's gaze remains fixed on Emery in a way that unsettles me.

Dale brushes past, his shoulder bumping mine as he heads for his truck. It takes everything in me not to take a swing at him and wipe that smug look off his ugly face.

"Storm's coming fast, Morgan." The thin smile that never reaches his eyes spreads slowly across his lips. "Hope you've got somewhere to hide."

Hide.

Not "stay."

Not "ride it out."

Hide.

Emery bristles beside me. I don't take my eyes off Dale as he climbs into the driver's seat, and they stay glued to him until his truck is out of sight. As soon as he's gone, the air feels lighter—but barely.

Emery lets out a shaky breath. "He gives me the ick. I don't like him."

"You're not supposed to," I say flatly. "Let's board this place up right."

As I walk her back toward the store, I catch Atlas, still lingering at the edge of the lot, watching.

A sickening feeling unfurls in my gut and I know now, this storm isn't the only thing brewing.

ABOUT HALFWAY THROUGH securing Mama T's, someone jogs up. "Reid." Tate's voice startles me from behind.

"Sorry. We're coming over there to help you. This is just taking longer than I thought it would." I take the screw gun off my tool belt and secure the final corner of the sheet we're working on.

"Don't worry about it," Tate says, grabbing the next sheet for me. "I'm just about done. Paid some deckhands overtime to pull in a few of the smaller boats that were left."

My jaw tightens. Paying overtime to employees is usually something we'd discuss, but chances are there wasn't time. We're trying to get it done so we can go home and hunker down.

Hide.

Langford's sneer pops into my head again. Fuck that guy.

"Sorry." I grab the other side of the sheet he's holding, and Emery takes a step back, letting us take the lead. "We had to do my cabin and then the cottage. When I got here, Langford was already here with Rourke and some other guy. Doing it all wrong."

"I wouldn't expect Dale to lift a finger," Tate says with a smirk.

"Oh, don't worry. He was watching," Emery pipes up. "Supervising."

"Figures." Tate takes the screw gun I'm offering him and drills into his two corners.

"What else do you have to do?" Emery asks. She sits on the bench just outside the store, massaging her biceps. A rush of guilt runs through me for her discomfort.

"Secure some windows on the bait shop, pack in the tables

and cover the furniture in the Net, and cover the windows at the research center," Tate answers, reaching for another piece of plywood as I drill in my side.

Relief runs through me at the normalcy of all this. For weeks I've had the sense that Tate is keeping things from me—and maybe he is—but right now, he's here, working alongside me the way he always has.

"How about I go check in on Rosie and then head over to the research center?" Emery suggests. "Kayla will be there soon. She and I can get everything out of the screened porch and move the turtle tanks inside. Then we'll be ready for you."

"Good idea. Be careful," I grunt, turning over my shoulder.

She jogs up to me and plants a kiss on my cheek. "I will. Let's finish up so we can go the hell home."

When she's gone, Tate and I collect the rest of the wood and my tools and make our way around the other side of Mama T's. Only about eight windows left. It won't take as long with his help. Emery isn't as strong and it's hard for her to hold the wood in place for long.

"Listen, man," Tate says, once we get set up again.

I hold up a hand. "Whatever it is, Tate, it can wait. Let's just get through this storm and see what's left of our livelihood."

Tate lets out a hiss, like my words sting, but he nods. "I was just going to say, I'm sorry. I've been out there lately—preoccupied—but when this is all over, we can sit down and go through all the books. I'll tell you everything." His words are sincere, but it's the last line that has me tense.

I'll tell you everything.

Which means there's something to tell. My instincts weren't wrong. They never are. It's like Spidey sense. I don't want to be angry at my best friend, but whatever he's mixed up in that he's been keeping from me can't be good.

"I don't know what to say to that, man," I admit, reaching in my toolbelt for another handful of screws. I pass him two of them. "It doesn't make me feel great."

Tate lets out a sigh, taking them from me. "I know. And you've been asking me a lot of questions lately that I haven't been able to answer. But you're part owner and you deserve to know what's going on. I promise I'll tell you."

I pop a screw in my mouth while I do the first one, forcing me to bite back what I really want to say. I'll hear him out. He at least deserves that. But in the meantime, we've got to get through the next twenty-four to forty-eight hours.

"Okay," I agree. "Let's finish this."

By the time Tate and I wrap up and say our goodbyes to Rosie, the rain is starting. It's light at first, but the sound of thunder reverberates in the distance. It won't be long now.

"We've got to move," Tate barks.

We hop in my truck and speed toward the research center, the windshield wipers already struggling against the sideways sheets of rain. By the time I pull into the gravel lot, the tires skid slightly on the slick stones. I park crooked, half over the faded white line—not like it matters. The place is deserted. Tidehaven never fully empties during a storm, but today it feels...abandoned.

Wind drives the rain in waves across the marsh, bending the tall grass low. A loose shutter somewhere slams in rapid, uneven bursts. The kind of sound that jolts you and prickles the back of your neck.

Kayla and Emery are on the screened porch, dragging the wicker chairs through the door one by one. Rain whips through the screen, spattering their faces and darkening their clothes. Kayla's braid has come loose, strands plastered against her cheeks; Emery's waves are damp and sticking to her neck.

"Oh, good, you're here." Kayla huffs as she pushes the last chair inside. "Finally."

"We had to finish Rosie's," I say, sharper than I intend. The wind is already stealing half my voice. "What else is left?"

Emery gestures toward the windows. "The shutters and whatever plywood we can find. It's going to be lightning soon." She can't hide the worry from her voice.

Tate and I don't waste time. We jog back down the steps, boots splashing through shallow puddles forming on the wooden docks. The air smells like wet earth, decaying marsh grass, and the metallic bite of ozone—a storm so close you can taste it.

"What's our supply look like?" I shout over the wind.

"Bare bones," Tate replies, eyeing the stack of warped boards leaning against the wall. "There are a few extra pieces in the bait shop. I'll grab them." He's already jogging across the lot, head ducked, shoulders hunched against the gusts.

I start securing the hurricane shutters on the side windows while I wait. My fingers slip on the cold metal, and the bolts screech as I drive them in. Emery and Kayla move through the building behind me, the faint sounds of boxes thudding and doors slamming traveling through the walls.

"Kayla, I mean it, stay away from him." Emery's voice carries through the thin walls. This building will be lucky if it survives this storm.

"I *will*," Kayla says, annoyance edging her tone. "He's only twenty-six though. Not that much older than me. I'm almost eighteen."

"Kayla." Emery's tone is impatient. "Atlas gives *me* the creeps. That alone should be enough to deter you."

I don't like what I'm hearing at all, and I almost abandon my task to go give Kayla a firmer warning, but a flicker of movement catches my eye—Tate pushing violently on the bait shop's door. It sticks, like it always does, but opens with a sharp crack. He disappears inside.

I don't know why, but unease ripples low in my gut.

A minute later, Emery appears at my shoulder. Her face is flushed from effort, rain dripping off her chin. "The screened porch is as good as it's going to get. How's it looking out here?"

"Almost done," I say. "I heard you talking to Kayla through

the window. What the hell is going on?"

Something in Emery's tight, worried expression makes me clench, but she doesn't have time to answer me before Kayla's at her side.

"My friend is swinging by here to give me a lift home," Kayla tells us, chewing on her lip. "The rain feels a little lighter now, so I feel like it's a good time to bounce." She hugs herself, shivering. "My mom is already freaking out about the power, and the kids are going crazy."

I suck in a breath. "Yeah. You'd better get home."

"Thank you so much for your help, Kayla." Emery pulls the teen girl into a hug. "Please think about what I said," she whispers.

Kayla pulls back, rolling her eyes. "I will. Promise. You guys be safe!" She stands on her tip toes to hug me and I let her.

"Let us know when you get home," I say, just as Tate jogs up with two smaller pieces of plywood tucked under each arm.

"This is all I've got," he says, "Let's make it work."

Thunder cracks so loud the metal shutters vibrate.

"That's my cue," Kayla says, backing away. "Bye guys." She gives us a weak wave and runs off.

We finish the last window as the sky flashes a white-blue streak, lightning spiderwebbing across the clouds. Thunder breaks closer by the second.

Tate wipes the rain from his brow. He glances at the marsh, jaw grinding. "We should split. Roads are going to get ugly."

"It already is ugly," Emery says, shifting closer to me.

Tate forces a quick smile, but it doesn't reach his eyes. "Let's meet back here when the worst of it passes. Check the boats."

Something in his tone scrapes against my Spidey sense again. He doesn't check his phone. Doesn't glance at the radar like he normally would. It's not how Tate normally does things.

Emery's gaze drifts toward the bait shop door—for just a second—brows knitting. I know she senses it too: a wrongness, subtle but sharp, like the moment before a trap snaps shut. Even the rain seems to pause between gusts, the air going strangely still.

"Yeah, okay." I nod, draping an arm around Emery. "Be safe out there."

Tate salutes me and jogs for his vehicle. I check the dead bolt on the research center before we make a run for my truck.

As I open Emery's door for her, she hesitates and glances back at the research center—windows sealed, porch dark, the whole place swallowed in shadows.

"Feels like we're leaving something behind," she murmurs.

"At this point we have to," I say. "Let's go before this gets worse."

When we pull out of the lot, I catch one last glimpse of Tate's truck idling near the bait shop, headlights cutting through the rain like a warning. He hasn't left yet.

And for reasons I can't yet name, dread settles deep—cold and certain—as the storm closes in.

CHAPTER FORTY-FIVE

EMERY

By the time we reach Reid's cabin, the water in the marsh has risen to the dock line. The wind has picked up, and Reid pulls his truck right up to the porch to limit our time in the elements. Still, in the time it takes to unlock his front door, the rain has begun to feel like thousands of needles pelting my skin.

Reid pushes the door open and we shove inside. He had the forethought to leave a lamp on and thank goodness he did because it's otherwise pitch black. Luckily, we set various candles out around the front rooms of the cabin. We won't be in the dark for long.

"Get changed. I'll find the lighter." He moves to the kitchen and begins rummaging through drawers.

I strip quickly, shivering hard. The storm has sucked the near August heat straight out of the air. By the time I return wearing joggers and a hoodie, the room is washed in warm candlelight, and the gas fireplace crackles to life. For one surreal moment, it looks like a scene from a movie—storm raging outside, golden light reflecting in Reid's eyes. "I thought we could warm up a bit," he says, handing me a steaming mug of coffee.

"I know the storm has potential to ruin everything," I say softly, a smile tugging at my lips. "But I wouldn't want to be anywhere else."

Reid's answering kiss is warm and coffee-flavored. "Me

neither."

We head for the couch with our mugs and Reid throws a plush blanket over us. I sink into the corner of the sofa, my legs draped across his lap, and the tension finally starts to drain from my shoulders.

"I'm so tired," I murmur. "That was more manual labor than I think I've ever done."

"You kept up," he says, giving my foot a gentle squeeze. The simple touch drags my memory back to that first night when he rubbed my feet and everything between us felt reckless and impossible. It's wild to think how far we've come in such a short time.

But clarity hits at the same time as unease.

"Tate was kind of weird today, right?" I ask, biting my lip uncertainly. "I mean...he didn't seem like himself."

Reid's jaw works. "Tate hasn't been himself for a while now."

A cold chill runs through me. I knew I was picking up on something weird today, but I thought it was the stress of the storm. "Do you think he's worried about the marina? The storm?"

"It's more than that." Reid exhales heavily. "He's keeping something from me."

I stare at him. "Why didn't you tell me?"

He shrugs helplessly. "Honestly, I don't know. You and I have been dealing with a lot too, and you're the only thing I'm *really sure* about. I was actually considering asking Tate to buy me out and following you wherever you go." He pauses and then huffs a laugh, looking away. "Is that weird?"

My heart swells and cracks at the same time. I set my mug down and reach for his hand. "Not weird. I want to take the permanent position here for the same reason. Among all the dangers and unknowns—you're the thing I'm sure about too. You love it here. And I love you."

The relief on his face softens everything between us. He drags me closer, kissing the top of my head. "So, we're in this together then, huh? Here?" he asks.

"I wouldn't want to be anywhere else." I pause, resting my head on his shoulder. "And hey, you and Tate will sort things out. He's your oldest friend."

"I hope you're right." He reaches for his mug and slurps his coffee. "Oh, what the hell was Kayla saying about Atlas Rourke?"

I scoff. "Just teenage infatuation stuff. She thinks he's cute. He's been flirting with her, I guess. What looks like flirting to her looks like paying too-close attention to me." I sigh.

"He's way too old for her," Reid growls.

"That and the fact that I'm not convinced it isn't him who is harassing me. I have a visceral reaction every time he's near me. I can't explain it. He just gives me the creeps."

"He wasn't like that in the SEALs," Reid says, pushing his lips together. "I only did one quick deployment with him, so I didn't know him that well. And I was his superior, so I definitely wasn't fraternizing with him. But I don't remember him being so creepy. He's got a weird look about him now."

"PTSD maybe?"

"Maybe. Or something else." He yawns, setting his mug down and opening his arms. "I don't want to talk about Atlas anymore. Come here."

I curl into them, resting my head on his strong chest. It takes a few beats but eventually my heart rate slows in the comfort of his arms. Before I know it, the exhaustion of the day settles in, and sleep takes us both.

We wake hours later to the sound of Reid's phone buzzing sharply against the coffee table.

"What time is it?" I grumble, wiping my eyes.

"Five," Reid says, reaching for his phone. "Tate's calling me."

The dread that hits my stomach is instant.

"Answer it," I urge.

Reid answers and Tate's voice bursts through, loud and frantic. "Have you or Emery seen Kayla? Her mom called me looking for her. She never came home."

"What do you mean she never came home?" Reid demands.

"When did you two last see her?" Tate asks.

"Right before we sealed the last couple of windows. She was getting a ride home." Reid leans his elbows on his knees and turns to me. "Do you know who picked her up?"

I shake my head, guilt clawing at my chest. Her excitement about Atlas flashes through my mind. Her sudden departure.

No. No, no, no.

"Shit," Tate begs. "Can you two come help look for her? Her mom is losing her mind, and she can't leave all her siblings alone."

"Of course," Reid says. "We'll be right there." He ends the call and flicks his gaze to mine. "I have the sinking feeling that something isn't right."

Panic courses through my veins as I try to recall my last few moments with Kayla. She was talking excitedly about Atlas until I shut her down. Then it seemed like she left abruptly—before the job was finished. I swallow the knot in my throat and grab my boots. "We better go."

Reid nods. "Bundle up."

THE DRIVE TO the marina is brutal. Sheets of rain slam the windshield so hard the wipers can't keep up. Thunder and lightning call to each other in the distance, white webs spreading across the dark gray sky. When Reid finally pulls into the lot, it's already half underwater.

Tate waits for us under the Bait Shop awning, drenched and waving his arms. Even from the truck, I can see the panic in him. My gaze flicks beyond him to the boats in the marina, tugging on their lines like wild animals. A metal sign smacks repeatedly against a piling, each slam ratcheting my pulse higher. The wind is relentless.

"Look!" Tate roars over the storm, pointing to a center-console boat that's broken free on one side and is swinging violently with every gust, slamming into another hull.

We dive from the truck and run toward Tate, taking shelter under the small awning.

"Fuck," Reid growls. "If she tears loose completely, she'll take half the dock with her."

He turns to me, his voice commander-level serious. "Emery, I need you to wait in The Drift Net. You'll be safe there."

I shake my head. "No. I can help—"

"You help by staying out of this mess. Please." He hands me his keys, holding up a small gold one. "Let yourself in. We'll be fast, then we find Kayla."

I glance toward The Drift Net—dark, locked up since the July Fourth fire, but still standing. The explosion scarred the docks, not the building. It's the safest place here. A crack of thunder sounds, punctuating his command. I swallow the tightness in my throat and nod.

Reid and Tate sprint toward the bucking boat, I run toward The Drift Net, its porch lights flickering in the gale. The wind howls across the marina like a coyote, tearing at my hood and sending stinging rain into my face. I'm fumbling with the key for the third time when a figure steps into view.

Atlas.

"Emery!" he calls, waving like we're friends on any normal stormy evening. It's forced and practiced, and it makes the coffee I just drank roil in my gut. "Tate sent me to get you. The boat is taking longer than they thought. He wants us to start looking for Kayla."

"He...what? Five minutes ago, Reid told me to wait here. Inside." My voice wavers, my heartrate stumbling.

Atlas steps closer, water dripping off his jacket in rivulets. "I just passed them. Storm's getting bad. They want to find Kayla as soon as possible."

Every instinct I have screams *no*. But then the guilt pricks at the back of my neck. I should have watched her get in the car earlier, or better yet, brought her home myself.

Lightning flashes overhead, blinding, and Atlas is already

turning to go, expecting me to follow him.

"Come on," he yells.

I glance back squinting in the distance—Reid and Tate are still fighting the loose boat, backs turned, completely consumed by the chaos. If I shout now, the storm will swallow my voice whole.

So, I ignore my instincts and force a breath. "Okay. Lead the way."

Atlas smiles, sharp and satisfied, and starts up the dock, his boots splashing in the puddles. I stay several feet behind him, plotting potential escape routes, looking for something to grab to defend myself should I need it.

He stops in front of a storage shed and thumbs the combination lock. "In here. We'll need more supplies."

A cold dread runs down my spine. "Supplies? This doesn't seem like—"

He shoves me hard and I stumble into the darkness, crashing into something hard. A work bench maybe? Pain blooms through my kneecap, stopping me in my tracks, and before I can react, the door slams shut. Metal scrapes and the padlock clicks back into place.

"What the fuck, Atlas? Let me out! What are you doing?" I pound both fists on the door.

His reply comes muffled. "Should've kept your nose out of things, sweetheart. Now you pay."

His footsteps retreat, leaving me panicking in deafening silence.

And then I hear it. Crying. Shuddering.

"Hello?" I whisper into the void. "Who's there?"

A small, broken voice wavers back. "Emery?"

I crash to my knees, fumbling under my windbreaker for the pocket to my hoodie and retrieve the small flashlight Reid thrust at me before taking off down the road.

I flick it on and a narrow beam of light shines in the darkness.

Kayla sits in the confined corner, her wrists joined with zip ties. Her face is blotchy and mascara streaked, and she's trembling—but she's alive.

"Oh my God, Kayla." I scramble across the concrete to her, wrapping her in my arms. "Are you hurt?"

Relief collapses her into me, and she sobs. "No. But I should have listened to you. Atlas is a monster."

"Shh," I whisper. "Hey, I've got you, okay? We're going to get out of here."

"How?" Kayla wails. "What if he comes back?"

I pull back enough to look in her eyes. "Reid is here. Tate too. It's only a matter of time before they realize we're missing."

The storm rips at the roof above us, a violent reminder that time is ticking. I push to my feet, the pain in my knees stopping me in my tracks. I shine the flashlight around the tight space. Coils of rope, old nets, rusted tools, crates, the scent of gasoline and damp wood.

"We're not waiting," I say, steadying my voice into something fierce. "We'll signal them. Or make enough noise to wake the dead. But we're not sitting around here waiting for Atlas fucking Rourke to come back."

A flash of lightning lights up the space, illuminating the fear of Kayla's face and strengthening my resolve. It's followed by a crack of thunder that seems to reverberate through the shed.

And then everything goes black.

CHAPTER FORTY-SIX

REID

THE STORM IS beating the hell out of us and the marina by the time Tate and I get the loose boat secured. Waves crash on the docks, thunder rumbles like artillery. Rain is coming down sideways, pelting us like knives.

I should feel relieved to have the boat secure, but something feels off. The lights in The Drift Net never turned on.

Emery.

"Where's Emery?" I say aloud, feeling panic surge through me.

"Wasn't she going to The Drift Net?" Tate asks, shaking the water out of his eyes.

"The lights are off. Why would she sit in the dark?" I'm already heading toward it, Tate following behind me.

"Did we lose power?" he calls.

Our gazes shift to the streetlamp on the corner. It's flickering but it's on.

"No. Maybe she's in the bait shop." My pulse spikes. I jog toward the bait shop desperate to find her and stop dead in my tracks.

A bait box reading DRIFTWOOD MARINA lies overturned in the mud, but it's not holding bait. Instead, a small mountain of cocaine. Neatly wrapped, dry and protected—banded together in small bricks.

We've got proof now. And then my heart sinks.

Proof that my own marina is being used in a drug running operation.

And I'm the only one who didn't know about it.

Lightning tears across the sky as I whip around, somehow knowing he's behind me. I shove the brick hard into Tate's chest. "What the fuck is this?"

His face goes pale. "Reid—listen."

"You fucking lied to me, man." Fury runs through me, hot and blinding. "You've been moving drugs through your own marina? *Our* marina?"

"It's not what it looks like," Tate stammers.

"The fuck it isn't. You've got crates of coke here, Tate."

His shoulders sag, defeated. "I didn't have a choice."

"There's always a choice," I growl. "God, you put Emery right in harm's way. You acted like you didn't know, and not only did you know, you had a fucking hand in it. And now Kayla's missing. Goddamn it."

"I thought I could handle it." His voice cracks. "It wasn't supposed to go this far."

"Yeah. Well, it did." I rake my hand through my hair and turn away from him. "God, where is she? She wouldn't wander off like this."

A beat of silence passes, the only sounds are the heavy rain and the roar of the bay.

"Did you hear that?" Tate asks, taking a step back in the direction we came.

I follow, listening for what he heard. Then the sound cuts me in half.

Someone calling for help. It's faint, maybe even muffled, but it's coming from a person who is terrified. There's no mistaking that.

Then I hear something else—a scream. Someone wailing.

The rain has lessened, thinning into heavy sheets instead of a wall of water. It gives me just enough visibility to see what's happening.

A thin coil of smoke rises near the storage sheds. Without thinking, I bolt in that direction, splashing through rising water. The acrid scent of gasoline punches me in the face and now I know. Gasoline in a hurricane? This was deliberate.

"Help!" their cries come, louder now that I'm closer.

"Reid!" Tate yells behind me. "I'll call it in."

I don't bother to answer. I'm desperate to find my girl.

The fire is in the third shed.

"No," I mutter. "No, no, no. Emery!"

"Reid," she croaks, her voice weak. "We're in here."

"Emery, I'm right here. Stand back." I slam my shoulder into the door—it rattles but doesn't budge. Then I see it's padlocked. Looking around for something to break it open, I see it. The rusty anchor leaning against a dock post. "Hang on, girls."

I heft the anchor and swing with every ounce of strength I have. The impact reverberates through my bones. Again. And again, until the frame cracks. A third hit splinters the wood enough for me to kick through the rest.

The door bursts inward.

Smoke billows out. Flames flicker under the wall, crawling along a trail of gasoline.

They're huddled in the corner. Emery shielding Kayla with her body, flashlight trembling in her hand, a mix of fear and relief flooding her features.

Relief hits me so hard it staggers me. "Come on, both of you! Let's go."

Emery pulls Kayla up by her arm and I haul them both out, several yards away from the smoke. They're coughing and Kayla sobs into my shirt. An ambulance pulls up just as the cutting sound of an engine roars to life, loud enough to cut straight through the storm.

A jet ski.

Atlas.

"Come on," I bark at Tate. "You're driving."

"Don't go," Emery cries. "Please. Don't leave me."

"Colt will be here any minute," I say. "We have to."

"Reid," Tate says, hesitating.

I glare at the man I once considered a brother. "You got us into this—you're going to get us out of it. This ends tonight."

Atlas's jet ski is disappearing into the dark by the time we reach the end of the dock. Tate hesitates, and I know why. It's dangerous out there. Rain needles my face, but the storm has eased enough to see across the channel.

"Reid," Tate tries again.

"Move," I grind out.

We jump into the boat and Tate fires the engine. We tear down the channel, the hull slapping hard against the choppy water. Atlas's red taillights gleam ahead, a single, jerking beacon toward Langford's boatyard.

I should have fucking known.

I should have known when he showed up here no good would come of it.

"He's heading to the inlet," Tate shouts. "That leads to the back of the boatyard."

"Punch it!"

He does as he's told, the engine screaming, and we close in fast—too fast. Atlas turns back, sees us gaining on him and guns the jet ski harder. But the channel narrows, there is debris in the water everywhere—driftwood, rope, a random cooler. Atlas struggles to dodge it all at a high speed. Tate nearly crashes into a floating log. Atlas zigzags sharply in and out avoiding wreckage in his way.

"Cut him off at those pilings," I shout, pointing to my right.

Tate turns violently, water spraying in a full arc. We forge ahead, intercepting Atlas's line just as he reaches the pilings.

"Box him in!" I bark.

Atlas tries to weave around us, but without enough room, his jet ski clips our stern. He fishtails sideways, and he yanks the handlebars too late. The jet ski slams into a piling at full speed. We hear a deafening crack as fiberglass explodes, and the jet ski vaults upward before flipping over and tossing Atlas into the rocky water.

My chest seizes.

"Kill the engine," I yell.

Tate does it instantly.

I kneel on the swimming platform, my eyes scanning the chop. "Atlas!" I shout.

Nothing.

I call for him again and a moment later, his head surfaces. He gasps, choking on rain and bay water, reaching for the piling.

"Take my hand," I shout, reaching for him.

He glares at me, his eyes wild and unfocused with a mix of rage and terror.

"You don't get it," he growls, his teeth pink with blood. "Langford will bury you. All of us."

"Shut up and take my damn hand," I yell.

Atlas doesn't take my hand though, instead he lunges for me, trying desperately to pull me into the water with him. His nails dig into my bicep, fingers twisting into the collar of my windbreaker.

"Reid," Tate grunts, grabbing the back of my jacket.

Then Atlas's grip slips and he slams into the piling again. This time he catches his head on the corner.

"Atlas!" I shout, my eyes searching the water. But it's dark and unforgiving and the only thing I see now is a swirl of red blood at the surface.

Atlas doesn't come up after a minute. Not after three. The storm takes him without ceremony.

"He's gone," Tate murmurs, clapping me on the shoulder.

I recoil out of his grasp. "We need to get back now."

Tate nods and moves toward the helm. I move to the back of the boat and collapse onto a seat, suddenly bone-tired and freezing. We turn toward the marina, the channel only lit by the soft blue of navigation lights as late afternoon turns to evening. But as we get closer, I see them. Tidehaven Police Department cruisers, lit up, surrounding my marina. The marina that has become a home to me.

Tate eases the boat into the slip, and I hop out before it's even tied off, my eyes scanning the crowd for Emery. When my eyes find her, she's sitting in the back of an ambulance, wrapped in a wool blanket, Kayla beside her talking to her mother and an EMT.

When Emery's gaze catches mine, she runs.

I meet her halfway and she crashes into me, knocking the wind out of me. Sobs wrack her small frame, and I wrap her in my arms, cradling the back of her head.

"You're okay," I murmur into her hair. "I've got you."

"You went after him," she chokes.

"I had to." My throat tightens. "But he won't hurt you anymore."

We turn at the sound of Tate's boots behind us. His shoulders are hunched, like there's no fight left in him.

Colt greets him at the end of the dock. His jaw is set, hard and focused. The look he gets when he's about to do something no one's going to like. In his hand is a clear evidence bag. I immediately recognize its contents—a block of cocaine.

"We need to talk," Colt says, pushing his lips together.

Tate avoids my eyes and instead meets Colt's.

My stomach drops.

"I found this near your bait shed, and plenty more inside. Crates of it. Want to tell me why you're hoarding hundreds of thousands of dollars in narcotics in your shed?" His voice isn't loud. It doesn't need to be.

Tate's gaze lifts to mine. I've been looking at this guy my whole life—across the table in the cafeteria, running through marsh muck as rambunctious boys, working side by side on our docks. This look is different. This one holds an apology in it. And maybe...relief?

"Tell me it's not what it looks like," I say quietly.

He swallows, his eyes tearing. "I can't."

"Fuck," I mutter. The words are a punch to the gut.

"I thought I could keep you out of it," he says, his voice rough.

"I'm sorry."

He lifts his hands slowly, wrists together, and holds them out to Colt.

Colt lets out a defeated sigh. "Jesus Christ." He nods once and pulls the cuffs from his belt. "Tate Maddox—you have the right to remain silent. Anything you say can and will be used against you in a court of law. You have the right to an attorney..."

I turn, unable to watch my best friend be escorted away by my other friend in handcuffs.

Dale Langford is standing a few feet away, hands in his pockets like he's just out for an evening walk in a hurricane instead of gleefully watching my best friend get hauled off.

"Hell of a day," he drawls. His gaze darts to Emery, then back to me. "I bet it rattles you, huh? Finding out your buddy's been aiming for your girl behind your back."

The words land sharp. Dale studies my reaction a little too closely—like he's cataloging it.

Emery moves behind me, wrapping her arms around my waist.

I cover her hand with mine. "Get the hell off my dock, Langford."

His smile doesn't reach his eyes. "Just saying, people aren't always who you think they are."

"I didn't ask you," I grit, taking a step closer to him. Emery clings to me.

He raises his palms like I'm overreacting. "Relax, Morgan. Cops got who they wanted. Case closed, right?"

I don't answer. I just stare at him until the smile falls from his mouth. He backs up a step, then two, before turning and disappearing down the dock.

I watch him go. Emery's arms circle my ribs, keeping me anchored while the grief hits—sharp, sudden, suffocating. Tate isn't dead, but it sure as hell feels like I just buried him.

The rain has lightened to a mist now, soft and steady. The storm is over, but the air still feels charged. I keep my eyes locked on the water. I don't know what to do with any of this yet.

"Reid?" Emery's voice jerks me back to the dock. "Are you okay?"

I look down and see her blue eyes are full of worry.

"No," I say, shaking my head. "But you and Kayla are safe and Atlas is gone. So, it's a start."

She nods and slips her arms around my waist, pressing her cheek to my chest. I pull her in against me, grounding myself in her warmth, her weight, the steady rhythm of her breathing.

This night took a lot from me. But it didn't take her.

I stare out at the boatyard across the water, the place Atlas was racing toward. Probably to tell Langford the deed was done. Then the storm and his own terrible choices caught up with him.

Langford is still out there.

And for the first time, I know—with cold, clear certainty—that this won't end with a few bricks of cocaine and one dead mule.

This is bigger. Deeper. Rotten all the way down.

He thinks he owns this town because he's protected by the ones who do.

But he has no idea the lengths I'll go to prove him wrong.

CHAPTER FORTY-SEVEN

EMERY

IT STAYS DARK in the cabin for a long time after the storm. I sleep until eleven o'clock the next morning, and Reid shows no signs of getting out of bed. It's just as well. Yesterday was traumatic—a total mindfuck. Reid didn't say much on the way home. We said our goodbyes to Kayla and left as soon as the EMTs cleared me. We took a silent shower when we got home—me to wash off the scent of smoke, and Reid to warm up. Then we slipped into bed without even so much as a bowl of cereal for dinner.

I lie awake for a long time imagining Tate, the man I've come to know as a brother to Reid, lying on a hard cot in a jail cell. It doesn't make sense to me. Tate might've been tough sometimes, but a drug runner? My stomach is in knots over the fact that I made this discovery in the marsh, and had I not, Reid would never have known what was going on. He'd never have guessed Tate was being dishonest and putting everyone in danger. I stirred the pot and look what happened. Sometimes I wonder if it's better to just let the bad guys get away with it. Let karma step in.

When I can't lie still anymore, I slip out to the kitchen and start the coffee pot. It's still pitch black in the house. I probably can't remove the plywood sheets on my own, but I can at least open the hurricane shutters. I slip on some sneakers and step outside while the coffee brews. When I return inside, he's awake, sitting on the couch and staring into space.

"Hey," I say softly, sitting next to him.

"Hi," he rasps, but he doesn't look at me.

"Want some coffee?"

Reid shakes his head. "No. I don't think so."

"Okay. Are you okay?" I shift closer, unsure if he wants the comfort of my touch or his space.

"Not really, Emery." His tone is clipped and it startles me.

I move away, standing. "Okay, sorry. I'll just...leave you alone."

I start to walk away and he catches my hand. "I'm sorry. It's not your fault. I shouldn't have snapped at you."

I sit back down and keep my distance. "Thank you. Yesterday was pretty terrible for me too, you know?"

At this, his face falls. "Of course it was. I'm so sorry." He pulls me to him. "Are you okay?"

"Knowing Atlas is gone...yes. But I don't know about staying here now. I doubt he was working alone. Maybe we should just start over somewhere new." I shrug.

Reid's gaze darts to mine. "I can't. I'll be here cleaning up Tate's mess for a long while." He sounds defeated and it pulls my chest tight.

I sigh and reach for his hand. "Then, I guess I'll be here too." I pause, debating how to bring up the next thing. Reid's on edge. He's not going to like it. I decide the best course of action is just to lay it out in the open. "I think... I need to go home for a while, though. To New Jersey."

He turns sharply, devastation etched on his features. "Why? Because of all this? I guess I can't blame you after last night."

"Because if I'm going to make a big move, I need to tie things up there. I need to pack up my townhouse and resign from my job. Talk to my family. Now seems like a good time."

Make sure this is really what I want.

I shrug helplessly.

"But your car isn't fixed." Reid moves closer to me.

"I was hoping you'd drive me to the airport," I say softly,

taking his hand in mine.

"You'll be back though, right? This isn't going to be one of those situations where you leave and change your mind?" His voice wavers, and I see how vulnerable he really is.

"I'll be back, I promise. I want to do this right."

Reid nods. "Okay. How long?"

I let out a puff of air. "I'm not sure. A few days? Maybe a week?"

"A week," he repeats, rolling his lips over his teeth in thought. "Okay."

"OH MY GOD, I missed you so much!" Lena shrieks when I slide into the passenger seat of her minivan. She throws her arms around me instead of pulling away from the curb, causing angry Philadelphia drivers to honk at her. She pulls away, holding a hand out her window. "I'm going, I'm going, okay?"

Once she successfully merges, I relax into my seat and sigh. "Home sweet home."

Lena glances over, grinning wickedly. "Did you miss us?"

"You? Always. Everyone else? Meh," I say, a smile tugging at my lips.

"So...what's the reason for this visit? Sabbatical isn't over yet. Are you done with South Carolina?" Lena merges onto I-95 with the practiced ease of a northerner in a metropolitan area, and I marvel. Just add that to the list of things I haven't done in months that would probably scare me now.

"Quite the opposite actually." I pause, dragging my lip between my teeth. "I guess Alan didn't tell you?"

"Tell me what?" Lena frowns. "Don't tell me you're leaving me for good."

"For now. Coastal Carolina offered me a full-time research position managing interns out of Tidehaven. It's an opportunity I can't pass up." I hold my breath, waiting for her to reply.

She glances quickly at me then back to the road, since you can't be too careful with Philly traffic, but she's smiling. "That's really great, Em. You've been so bored with academia. This is just what you need."

I smile, reaching for her hand and giving it a quick squeeze. "Thank you."

"I'm going to miss the hell out of you though," she grumbles. "Our department is like *all* men."

I laugh. "I'll miss you too. And hey, you have Tina!" I remind her of our sweet secretary in her late forties with grown kids.

"It's not the same," Lena pouts. "But I guess I can't blame you for leaving. I wouldn't want to leave that hot ass rock of a man either."

At the mention of Reid my stomach flutters. "There's just a few things I have left to do."

TELLING ALAN WAS the easy part—I knew it would be. But being the professional that he is, he wouldn't accept my formal resignation until I've had the opportunity to meet with Coastal Carolina. In the craziness with the hurricane, we haven't had a chance to get a meeting on the calendar yet. I know he's right—even though I've made the decision in my mind to stay, I need to make sure it makes professional sense for me. I'm pretty sure it will. And even if it doesn't, I am not leaving Reid.

I already miss him terribly and it's been twenty-four hours. I'm holding onto that as I knock on the front door to the townhouse I once shared with Jason. I don't feel right walking in on him on a Saturday morning without warning.

I knock softly, and as soon as I hear the pattern of footsteps, my heart jumps to my throat. Then I hear voices—two of them. Before I can turn away, the door swings open. There stands Jason, his hair disheveled from sleep, wearing a tight-fitting T-shirt and the pajama pants I got him last Christmas. He's not alone. A petite brunette stands at his side, her purse over her shoulder like she was just leaving.

"Emery." Jason's voice is hoarse but laced with surprise. "Hi."

"Hi," I say, waiting for him to say more.

"This is Brea." He gestures to the woman sizing me up. She's cute. Her brown hair is curly and wild, and she has large almond-shaped eyes and a dimple on her right cheek.

"Hi," I murmur, flicking my gaze back to Jason.

"It's nice to meet you, Emery." Brea smiles, then standing on her tiptoes, she pecks Jason on the mouth. "I'll see you tonight." She scoots around me and waves. Together we watch her go.

"Do you want to come in?" Jason asks even though it's obvious that's why I'm here.

"Sure." I step inside and I'm floored to see the place is spotless. Not so much as a beer bottle or a takeout container. A pair of women's shoes that aren't mine sit by the back door. I vaguely wonder what she must think—staying here with the man she's dating when his ex-girlfriend hasn't yet cleared out her things.

"Do you want some coffee?" Jason asks, moving into the kitchen. Before I can answer he takes two mugs down. He hands it to me with a splash of cream, the way I like it. I'm surprised he remembers.

"So, Brea seems nice," I say, sitting at the table.

"Yeah. She is. It's new..." He lets his voice drop. "I can end it if that's why you're here."

"What? No." I shake my head. "Don't do that."

"Okay..." Jason pulls the chair out next to me and sits down. "Listen, Em, I was terrible to you. I'm so sorry."

I nod, offering him a tight smile. "It's okay."

"It's really not though. I should have come after you. Stopped you from giving up on us." Jason tries to reach for my hand, but I pull it back, unwilling to give him false hope.

"Jason, you don't need to feel bad. We aren't right for each other. I came here to apologize to you about the way I left but also to tell you that I won't be back." I force air out of my lungs, giving him a chance to digest. The truth is, I didn't expect Jason to be here with a woman. In fact, at noon on a Saturday, I expected him to still be in bed, or at the very least, playing video games on the couch. I never expected him to have moved on and the truth is, I'm glad he did. I felt absolutely nothing when I saw Brea kiss him and leave. Not an ounce of jealousy. If anything, it made me anxious to get home to Reid.

"You won't be back..." Jason repeats. "Ever?"

I take a deep breath. "I was offered a full-time position down there and I love what I'm doing. I decided to take it."

"Wow. Okay." Jason runs a hand over his jaw. "So, this is it then?"

I nod, biting my lip. "I came to collect what's left of my things." I pause. "But hey, you look like you're doing great. This is good."

Jason nods, the corner of his mouth upturning slightly. "Yeah. You're right. This is good."

"The sad truth is, we outgrew each other a long time ago." For the first time since I arrived, I allow myself to meet his chocolate brown eyes.

"We did," he says softly. Silence passes for a beat before he says, "Want help packing?"

CHAPTER FORTY-EIGHT

REID

I SPEND TWENTY-FOUR hours in bed after driving Emery to Charleston International Airport. With Tate behind bars and the marina in shambles, I don't see the point of doing anything else. She texted me, letting me know that it's going okay. She's collected her things and had a good conversation with her ex. It annoys me that she went to see him at all, but I understand why. I don't own her and she's giving up her whole life to be here with me. But my throat burns hot with jealousy.

My phone buzzes again, her name lighting up the screen. I pick it up, squinting at it in the dim bedroom.

Emery

Now, I just have to spend a few days with my parents and then I'm all yours.

I don't have the energy to respond to that. I let out a loud groan and pull the covers over my head, inhaling the soft scent of her shampoo that clings to them. My phone buzzes again, ringing this time. I ignore it, covering my head with a pillow. When it rings a second time, I pick it up.

Colt's name glows on the screen.

I tap to answer.

"Colt."

"Reid. What are you doing?" Colt's voice is firm—all business. "Are you able to come down to Tate's office and talk to me?"

"Tate's office?" I ask, sitting up. "You got something?"

"Maybe. I have a couple of things to ask you." He pauses and I hear him clicking his tongue against his teeth. He moves the phone away from his mouth and I hear muffled words to someone else. Then he's back. "Are you able to come now?"

"I'll be right there," I growl, hanging up before he can reply.

I dress quickly, sliding into a pair of sandals—my boots are still soaked from the storm. Grabbing my keys and a banana, I lock the door behind me. I have to admit, with Atlas gone, I'm not looking over my shoulder as much. Authorities recovered his body. Ruled it a tragic accident.

Town is still quiet in the aftermath of the storm, so it only takes me a couple of minutes to get to the marina. Colt's cruiser is parked alongside an unmarked SUV, its license plate frame reads U.S. Government. *What the fuck is going on?*

I hop out of the truck and find Colt waiting for me in the doorway of Tate's office. Inside, it looks like someone flipped it upside down and shook it. Evidence teams comb the space, collecting pieces of evidence into little bags and dusting for fingerprints.

"Christ," I mutter, taking in my surroundings. "You've torn this place up."

"Tate told us where to look," Colt says assuredly. "Come on in."

Colt moves into the room, behind the desk. "Fellas," he says, directing his attention to the crew collecting evidence. "Can we have the room?"

They nod and exit swiftly. I sit in the chair in front of Tate's desk and wait.

"What's going on?" I ask, growing impatient.

When the office door clicks closed, Colt turns, sliding a few pieces of shiplap out from the wall, revealing a secret storage space with a gray tackle box inside, the kind with a tight rubber seal and metal clasps. He pulls on some rubber gloves and works it free.

"What the fuck is this?" I grumble, leaning forward.

Colt pops open the clasps and lifts the lid on the box. Inside, there's a thick folder, a sealed envelope, and a flash drive. A note in Tate's handwriting rests on top. It reads: *If I don't make it out, give this to DEA Agent Dani Sullivan.*

"DEA?" My brow furrows.

"That's right," a woman's voice comes from the doorway. I whirl around to see a woman in her mid-thirties, hair in a long braid, wearing a windbreaker standing in the doorway. She flashes her badge. "Special Agent Dani Sullivan."

I clear my throat, rising to shake her hand. "Reid Morgan."

"I know who you are." She smiles. "Your partner, Tate Maddox... He wasn't dirty. He was one of us."

My jaw falls slack. "One of you? What?"

"He's been an informant for us for two years. And he's not the only one. Your friend, Dr. Young? Her too." She waits for me to digest this information.

"Penny..." My voice falls away and I swallow hard. I think back to the federal agents outside Blackbird Cottage six months ago.

"She's alive. I can't tell you where she is, but she's safe." Dani crosses her arms, watching me.

"Alive?" There was a body in a bag, on a stretcher. I shake my head in confusion.

"Yes. She was too close—we had to get her out. We've been trying to crack Langford and Son for decades." It seems they went to great lengths to do that. Dani has an answer for every question I haven't asked yet.

And I have *so* many questions. Everything in me goes still.

Finally, I clear my throat. "So, where's Tate? Why did they arrest him?"

I think back to the night of the storm—how Tate went willingly, held his wrists up for Colt to cuff him. Walked away without meeting my eye.

"Atlas's death blew our case wide open. Forced our hand. We were supposed to catch them in the act during the storm but there was no way. We had to pull Tate before Langford figured out he'd flipped. Now Langford thinks Tate's going down alone." Dani steps further into the room, helping herself to the handle of whiskey Tate keeps on the side shelf, like she's been here a thousand times before. She pours a cup and hands it to me.

I shoot it down, letting out a hiss at the burn. "He didn't tell me."

She shakes her head. "He couldn't. He knew you'd try to get involved and then get yourself killed."

I drag a hand down my face, the world tilting. Tate—my friend—working a case alone. Carrying all of it. Letting me think he was sinking when he was really trying to plug a hole in a sinking ship.

"The whole damn town thinks he's a drug runner now," I growl, shaking my head. I look at Colt, watching the exchange with his arms folded. "You knew about this?"

"Only for a few days. He told me the day Emery's window got blown out." I think back to the private conversation I interrupted that day in his office. And how uncomfortable Tate seemed. Now I know why.

Colt steps around the desk. "Listen, Reid, Tate hated every second of keeping this from you. Especially knowing Emery was in danger." He puts a hand on my shoulder.

"And how do I know she's safe now? Langford still wants her dead." I rub the back of my neck, tension coiling there.

"We're watching Langford closely. He won't make any rash moves right now," Colt assures me. "He's going to let Atlas and Tate go down for this."

"Where is Tate now?" I ask. "Can I see him?"

Dani shakes her head. "I'm afraid not. We had to get him out of here for a couple of months. He's at a safehouse upstate."

"Fuck," I mutter. "And I'm just supposed to...what?"

"You rebuild," Colt says, meeting my gaze.

"Rebuild," I repeat. "Just like that?"

"Just like that."

THE PLANE FROM Philadelphia lands early, but I've been parked and pacing outside baggage claim for an hour already. I don't tear my eyes from the escalator until I finally see her, duffel bag slung over her shoulder, hair twisted in a loose braid, and those damn glasses that drive me wild.

She steps off the escalator and when her eyes lock with mine, she drops her bag, running straight into my arms. I wrap her up and hold her there—I can finally breathe again.

"I missed you," she croaks into my shirt.

"I missed you more," I whisper back.

I pull away just enough to look at her, and the tension in my shoulders that I've been carrying since the storm finally loosens.

"I have so much to tell you," I rasp. "Starting with this—Tate wasn't running product. He was working with the DEA behind the scenes, trying to shield me and the marina while they built their case. He let everyone think the worst of him to keep the heat off me."

Emery's breath catches. "Reid... Oh my God." Her fingers curl in my shirt, her eyes shining with something like heartbreak and relief tangled together. "He was protecting you."

"He was," I nod. "Thank God. I was ready to kill that motherfucker." I huff a laugh. I cup her cheek, pulling her gaze up to mine, and kiss her softly.

"Ready to go home?" I rasp.

Her eyes soften. "I am home."

We reach the cabin at sunset, the sun glowing peach, purple, and gold over the flat marsh water. You'd never know there was a horrific storm days before. I already cleaned up the worst of the storm damage. While she was away, I took the boards off the windows and cleared the debris. Now the place is standing strong like it always does. The flat water is a mirror for the blazing sky.

Emery stands on the dock for a long moment, just taking it in.

"God," she breathes. "This time of day is magical here. I'd almost forgotten."

I step behind her, pulling her into my chest. She leans into me.

"You didn't forget," I murmur. "You just needed to come home."

"New Jersey was...a lot. Saying goodbye to friends. Packing up my things. I spent a few days with my family but even that was exhausting—trying to explain everything without *actually* explaining it. You know?" She glances up at me. "I'm relieved to be here with you."

"You have no idea how happy I am to hear you say that," I whisper, pressing a kiss to her temple.

She turns in my arms, her blue eyes shining in the golden hour light. "The night of the storm, trapped in that shed with Kayla, all I could think about was that I might not ever see you again. Might not ever get this moment again..."

Her confession cracks me open.

"I was scared too," I admit. "Of losing you. Of losing Tate. Of losing everything I care about."

"But you didn't," Emery says, her fingers grazing my face.

"No, I didn't." I sniffle when I realize my eyes are stinging. God, I don't even know who I am anymore with this woman in my arms.

The marsh breeze slips around us, carrying the familiar scent of salt and low tide. The sun slips lower, setting fire to the water, and Emery nestles into me, wrapping her arms around my waist.

"Reid," she whispers.

"Yeah?"

"The university is going to want to use Blackbird Cottage for its incoming interns. So...I was wondering..."

I pull back so I can look at her, a smile curving at my lips. "If we could make this living situation a bit more permanent?" I ask.

She nods, her voice is barely above a whisper. "I want to stay. Here. With you. If you'll have me."

I don't even let her finish the breath between us. I cup her face in my hands and kiss her—slow and sure, and deep enough that I feel it in my bones.

When I pull back, I rest my forehead against hers. "I've never wanted anything more."

EPILOGUE
REID

TEN MONTHS LATER

The Drift Net is alive tonight.

It should be. We're celebrating.

Edison bulbs are strung across the beams in the ceiling, glowing gold against the summer sky. A country-music cover band plays on the rebuilt stage, and someone's grilling shrimp skewers that make the whole place smell like home. Kids dart between tables, snow cones dripping down their hands.

After everything this place endured with the fire and the storm, it's good to see it breathing again.

Roy Beck, Judge Ware, and Langford Senior and Junior sit around a round table in the center of the room sipping whiskey like the kings of this damn town. Like they'll do whatever it takes to protect their empire.

They look untouchable.

I lean against the bar with Colt and Griff, each of us holding a beer. Tate lingers nearby but gives Langford a wide berth. Lucky for him, Atlas died before he could say what he must have realized in those final moments. As far as Langford knows, Tate's still the loyal guy he always was. Tate's not taking any chances—staying invisible is easier than stirring up suspicion.

Tate spent eight months away, "doing time" for his alleged

crimes while I got this place up and running again. That seemed enough to satisfy the masses who all like to pretend that storm didn't expose the dirty depths of this town. I know he's happy to be back. He looks rested, softer around the edges, but he's tired too. There's a shadow behind his eyes that wasn't there before all this.

Rage burns inside me at the injustice of it all, but I swallow it down when I catch sight of Emery across the room. She is laughing with Kayla and her mom near the food tables, surrounded by a crowd of her interns and Kayla's younger siblings running circles around them. She's talking with her hands the way she always does when she's excited—animated, bright, full of life—and her brand new engagement ring catches the glow of the setting sun perfectly. Every time she glances my way, she gives me that soft smile that tells me she's exactly where she wants to be.

Colt clears his throat, bringing my attention back to my friends. He's wearing his new chief's badge—finally official after the ceremony this morning—and there's pride in his eyes, even if he pretends it's no big deal.

"So, what's the first order of business for the new chief?" I ask, not bothering to hide my happiness for my buddy.

Colt's eyes track across the room, and he sucks in a breath, setting his beer down on the counter behind him.

"Actually, there's something I need to show you guys," he says, reaching in his back pocket for a small yellow envelope.

The hair on my neck stands up.

Tate steps closer, watching Colt closely, his expression wary. "What's up?"

Colt thumbs the envelope at its creases for a minute before speaking. "This was...left on my desk this morning. I guess during the ceremony. It wasn't there before."

My gut tightens. "By who?"

"No idea," Colt says. "But whoever left it wanted me to see it."

He opens the flap and slides out an old glossy photograph, creased in the corners, the orange digital date emblazoned on the bottom right corner: September 1999.

He hands it to me first.

A stage. A banner. Three teenage girls, the one in the middle beaming in a sash and white dress.

And standing behind them—half their current age—are Roy Beck, Everett Ware, and Warren Langford. Arms around each other. Smiling wide.

But someone has marked this copy.

The girl in the center, a sash over her chest, is circled in red ink.

"This the Miss Tidehaven pageant?" I ask, furrowing my brow.

"Looks like it," Colt mutters.

I study it for another beat before passing it to Tate.

"Do we know who she is?" I ask.

"Not a clue. But someone wanted us to figure it out," Colt murmurs.

"Someone wanted us to know she mattered," Griff adds quietly.

"Us?" I repeat.

The breeze shifts, blowing laughter from the good old boys' table toward us. They raise their glasses in unison, proud and satisfied, as if the whole town bows to them.

I swallow hard.

Tate shakes his head, shoving the photo back at Colt like it burns his fingers. "No," he says. "No fucking way. I'm staying the fuck out of this. I'm done. I've had my fill of secrets and ambushes and goddamn undercover bullshit."

He turns and takes a few steps toward the parking lot, leaving us staring after him.

Then he stops—his shoulders rising and falling, like he's mulling it over.

He looks over his shoulder at the men in the center of the room. The ones from the photograph. And I watch as a sickly, satisfied smirk curls on the corner of his mouth.

He turns, his voice low and dangerous.

"Aww, who am I kidding?" he says. "Let's burn this shit down."

THE END

ACKNOWLEDGEMENTS

It's hard to believe I am writing acknowledgements for my fourth book in thirteen months. Two years ago, I wasn't even sure I could write one. When I started writing *Tidehaven*, I knew I was stepping into something new. Romantic Suspense has long been a genre I've read and enjoyed, but building this small coastal town and its secrets stretched me in ways I'd never imagined. It was a challenge to balance a romance and suspense plot that left my readers feeling satisfied, but the end result is a sense of pride and accomplishment.

As a way to bring my community of readers into the story, I decided to crowd source various details on my social media and so many of you answered the call. To the readers who answered my questions about boats, coastal life, and investigative details—you helped bring *Tidehaven* to life. Your enthusiasm and willingness to contribute made this story richer than I could have written alone. An extra special thanks to: K Septya, Jackie Russell, Alexandra Oddo, Abigail Chapman, Christen Nascimento, Alexa Escapita, and Stephanie Ritchie. I hope you found your suggestions as you read!

My deepest thanks to the marine biologists and coastal researchers who generously answered my endless questions, Scott, Lisa, and Jamie. Your expertise helped ensure the science woven into this story felt authentic.

To my incredible critique partner, Christine Drummond, thank you for the late-night brainstorming sessions, the honest feedback, and for always reminding me when the story needed one more twist. You were right about the prologue!

To the team at Page & Vine, thank you for championing these stories and bringing them into the world with such care. To my agent, Katie Monson, for always believing in me and supporting my career goals.

To my street team, the Mack Pack! I still can't believe that this team of incredible, supportive women exists for little old me. And you have shirts! I'm grateful for each and every one of you. To Bekah, Jess, Kate, Kelly, Jamie, Morgan, and Miranda, my beta readers! Thank you for reading and loving the earliest version of this story. You helped shape it into what it is.

To my family and friends, I'm so grateful for your endless support. I don't know what I'd do without you, and I hope I never have to find out.

To my Hype Husband, Kevin, you are a dream come true. I know I've said it with every book, but I got so lucky when I married you. You're the reason these stories can exist. You support me in every possible way, and you do it with a smile. You pick me up when I'm down, talk me off the ledge when I'm spiraling, and pour the champagne when we're celebrating. Your love is monumental and I am so grateful for you. You even got to sign a book this year! The readers love you and so do I—more than you'll ever know.

And lastly, to my readers, old and new, for loving my books and for celebrating with me. I wouldn't be where I am without you.

ABOUT THE AUTHOR

Linny Mack grew up a voracious reader and writer. She spent her days of adolescence up in her room writing her own stories and cutting her characters out of the Delia's catalog. Now, Linny is a debut author of contemporary romance. When she isn't writing your next book boyfriend, she is spending time with her real-life romantic hero and their three children in New Jersey.

To learn more, visit: www.linnymack.com

Coming Autumn 2026

Whispers in the Dunes

By Linny Mack

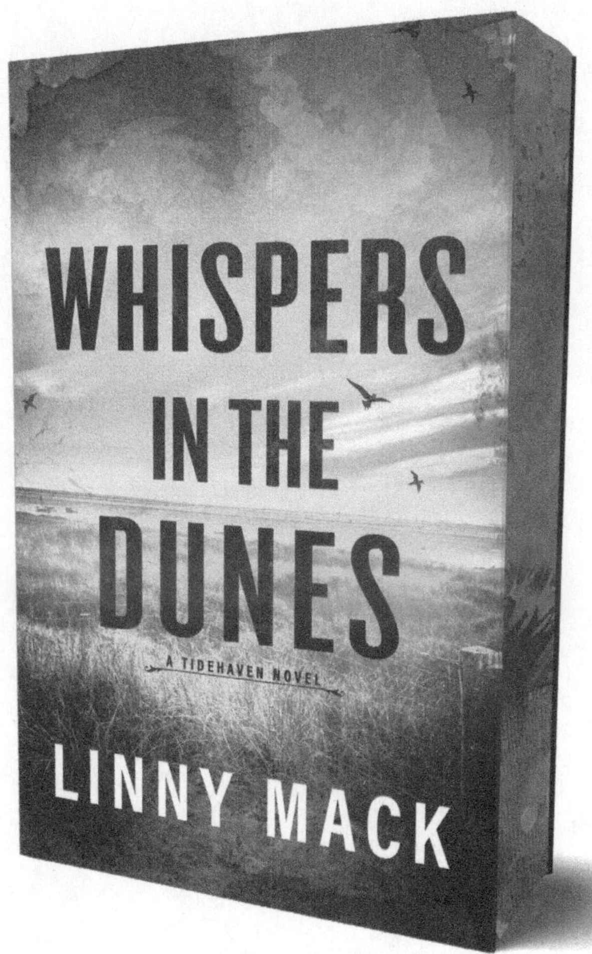

PAGE
&
VINE